Cover art by Elizabeth Best. See her art on Instagram

@artoferbest

Logo and Chapter Headings by Omni Jacala. See his art on Twitter

@artsyomni

This book was lovingly created by a human, not generated by A.I.

Content Warning. This book contains: Xenophobia, physical and mental abuse, dead

family, violent deaths, mild swearing, and violent injuries. Please take care of your

mental health if you find yourself struggling with the contents of this book.

Discover other titles by R. A. Meenan

Black Bound

Golden Guardian

Shadow Cast

White Assassin

Brothers at Arms

Umber Sky

Gray Matter

Mage

Angel

Facets of Color: Vol 1

The Drover's Tale: Academy

Outlander Sky: Summoner's Fellowship

Dedications

To Jess E. Owen, one of my Wingsisters, for helping me edit this monstrous thing, and for letting me borrow Rashard and Kjorn. By my wings, you will never fly alone.

As always, my writing group - Linda, Jill, Jim, Randy, Chris, Heather, and Victoria - for helping me see the problems in early drafts.

To my dad, Robert, who passed when I was twelve, for inspiring me to be an artist and writer, and instilling those values in me. I miss you, though I know my life would be very different if you were still here. Sometimes good things can come from tragedies.

To anyone who has ever been victimized by war, prejudice, xenophobia, transphobia, or homophobia, especially the victims of the Russian/Ukraine war and the victims of the concentrated attacks on the LGBTQ+ community, the disabled community, the BIPOC community, and those who can get pregnant, all of whom faced intense hate and specific attacks on their lives during the time I wrote this book. I can't promise it will get better, but I can promise you have people fighting for you. Fight when you can, rest when you need to.

Content Warning

War is a terrible game played by governments at the expense of their soldiers and citizens. It often brings out the worst in even the best of people in the name of survival. Sometimes victims must compromise their morals, beliefs, and ideologies to survive. Blame should be put on the governments and military officials who put their elite before their citizens - blaming soldiers and citizens as a whole is a xenophobic act, and individuals should be judged on their individual actions.

"Life is a repeated endless kick. And then when you think you got the hang of it, life is like, hey, I got these new boots I'd like to try out on your back." – Dan Avidan

Mage

Book Three

From the War of Eons Archives

By R. A. Meenan

Starcrest Fox Press

CHAPTER 01

HISTORIAN

Praeses Leah Nealia twitched her gray feline ears as she cross-referenced the runes from the Book of Summons, sitting in the Royal Library on Athánatos Island. Shelves upon shelves of books surrounded her, standing at least five meters tall, their towering presence overwhelming - all dust and age and secrets, like time itself, bottled up in something you could carry with you. Dozens of Defender historians had paired up with Athánatos historians, gathering books, translating runes, and digitally preserving the thousands of documents, as part of the Athánatos restoration efforts since Theron had been taken down.

Golden Guardians Azure and Gildspine had arranged this ambassador trip to Athánatos Island on Earth just a few months after their impromptu mission chasing Theron, the Cast, and the elusive Omnir. It felt great to be doing something normal again, after the Cast victims had been restored and the final scars from that battle were healed.

This two-year mission intended to help the Athánatos rebuild and establish a presence on Earth, since they had friends and allies there now. Guardians Azure and Gildspine had gathered a pack of about two hundred Defenders to come to Earth, bringing supplies, food, labor, and other services to help the Athánatos wherever they could. Only the best and most skilled Defenders had been brought along.

Leah glanced around, frowning. The best and most skilled. Definitely not her. Brand new, inexperienced, alone. And the fact that the other historians here had either ignored her or openly antagonized her since they first took off from Zyearth proved it.

And yet, somehow, she had been hand-picked by Guardian Azure himself.

Leah had only barely been inducted into the Defenders before this trip. She hadn't even finished settling into her office before Guardian Azure approached her. Physically. In person. Her heart raced with adrenaline thinking about it even now.

She had just settled into her chair at her brand-new desk in her own, tiny office. A literal office, not just a cubicle or a floating desk like most new historians. Her dissertation had landed her a job no new historians got – head of a department, created brand new for her. She was the newly named expert on the history of summons. She even had a little plaque on the door with her name and title.

What a title to live up to.

Uncle Garnet had been ecstatic when he learned the news, but Leah just felt… fake. She didn't deserve that honorific.

The office was all stark white walls, with an old desk, chair, bookshelf, and potted plant (fake of course). Boring, flat, and terrible for her wandering mind. She'd have to take care of that as soon as she could.

She had been about to contact the history department's A.I. to sign in for the first time, when someone had knocked on her doorframe. She turned.

And had nearly fallen out of her chair.

Guardian Azure. *Guardian Azure.* Wearing casual clothes, leaning coolly against the doorframe, his white, blue tipped quills rustling, ears perked, green eyes alert and focused.

He gave her a smile. "Sorry, was I interrupting something?"

"Uh, no, s-sorry," Leah said. "A-are you looking for Garnet Silverleaf? H-he heads the department."

Guardian Azure's smile faded slightly. Leah's thoughts – the Thought Factory as she called it – went wildly out of control, spiking her anxiety. *Why did you say that, of course he knows the head of the department, you should have saluted, you should have introduced yourself, you should have at least said hi, you absolute--*

"Ah, no," Guardian Azure said. "I'm looking for you, actually."

Leah flattened her ears, her fur standing on end. *"Me?"*

Guardian Azure nodded, his full smile returning. "Absolutely. Leah Nealia, right? I hope I pronounced your last name correctly."

He had, a miracle since most got it wrong and few bothered to correct it. "Y-yes... what can I do for you?"

His smile had evolved into a grin. "How'd you like to join the mission to Earth?"

It had taken Leah a solid minute to respond. And somehow, she had managed to get the Thought Factory under control enough to say "yes." It had been quiet and stuttery, but it was a "yes" nonetheless.

She really should have said no. She didn't belong here. Not after the way the senior historians had reacted.

Even now, one of the senior historians, Clint, glanced over at her, stared a moment, then flattened his leopard ears and frowned, gaze narrowed. The Athánatos historians gave him a wide berth.

Leah sunk down into her chair, burying her snout in the Book of Summons, her heart pounding. She glanced at him over her glasses. *Oh Draso, not now, no more drama, please.*

Clint took a step her direction, heightening her anxiety. She fought the Thought Factory, desperate to keep it running, rehearsing all the ways a conversation with Clint could go, trying to stop her brain from halting completely.

Nothing worked. *Thought Factory shutting down,* Leah thought. Dang it all.

But then Clint glanced up.

At the command of the royal Athánatos family, the six phoenix summons of the Order of Phonar had settled themselves in Leah's corner of the room since the moment she opened the Book of Summons, to protect the knowledge. All six perched on the shelves, chairs, and tables around her in their feral bird forms, little representations of their elemental magic floating about them. Excelsis himself had perched right next to her, orbs of violet fire wafting around, his shining blue gaze darting around the room.

That stopped Clint from saying anything. He shook his head and went back to talking with two other historians instead.

Leah heaved relief. She settled back in her chair and regulated her breathing. No confrontation. She was safe. Thank Draso.

She should *not* have taken that offer.

Excelsis cooed quietly. Leah adjusted her glasses, then reached over and stroked his head feathers. He purred at her. She had to admit, being surrounded by the most powerful and interesting summons she had ever known almost made the trip worth it. It helped that the Phonar stuck by her like old friends.

11

It was almost like having summons of her own.

"Prinkípissa Alexina is dead," Clint said suddenly. Leah looked up. "That's why Athánatos lost Kyrie and Archángeli. It's as simple as that. There's no great mystery to it."

One of the other Defender historians, a gray stoat named Holly, glared at him. "The Book of Summons says--"

"It says what?" Clint said. "No one even *knows* because the healer-S has been monopolizing it and no one wants to get near her."

Leah sunk into her chair. That was all she was to everyone. The novice historian. The healer-S. The magic user who could see all your ailments with a brush of her fingers against skin or fur – a terrible personal invasion. No one dared touch her. Hug her. Befriend her.

She might touch you and *know.*

Excelsis cooed again. Leah tried directing her thoughts to him. *At least I got to meet the Phonar. At least… At least Excelsis doesn't care if I touch him.* He moved closer to her, inviting more head scratches. She reached over and focused on the soft, warm feeling of his feathers.

Holly turned to her, a hesitant frown on her face. Then she flicked her tail and turned back to Clint. "Leah's the head of the Summon's History department--"

"An inflated title created just because she happened to write a dissertation on the subject," Clint said. "A dissertation is no substitute for experience. It doesn't *mean* anything."

Holly lashed her tail about, baring a fang. "She's the only one who--"

"I don't *care,"* Clint said. "The Book of Summons doesn't say--"

"You could just ask me," Leah said. Clint glanced over. Leah clapped her hand over her snout. Fire and *ice. Thought Factory back up and running, sort of.* Holly watched her, brow furrowed in worry.

Clint glared. "Fine. I'll ask you. Where in the Book of Summons does it say Alexina is alive?"

Leah reached over and picked at the tip of her tail. "W-well, if Alexina died, then one of the other royals would have Archángeli and Kyrie."

"Summons don't work like that," Clint spat.

"T-The Phonar are different," Leah said, *which you'd know if you'd let me speak.* "They only serve the Athánatos royal family," she said. "If a member dies, the Phonar redistribute to them. If Alexina was dead, Melaina, Ouranos, or Natassa would have her summons."

Clint flicked an uncertain ear back. He crossed his arms. "They're still *lost.* Even if Alexina is alive, it's not like it'd be easy to find them on a planet full of quilar. Without Alexina, Kyrie and Archángeli are as good as dead. A summon needs a summoner to be useful."

"We could go *find* her," Leah said. "It probably wouldn't even be that hard. Athánatos quilar stand out."

"They have differently-shaped ears, and are taller," Clint said. "That's it."

"That's *not* it," Leah said, her skin heating under her fur. "They're exceptionally tall, they have more animal-like feet and long tails, and their coloring is really unusual, especially for the royalty -- black with colored highlights. The royal family is *only* burnt orange or cream colored. Even among Athánatos they'd be easy to spot."

Clint narrowed his gaze. "I don't like your attitude," he said.

A splat of purple embers smacked into Clint's muzzle. He shook his head, wiping the cold embers and ash out of his fur.

Leah flicked an ear back. Excelsis stood next to her, head lowered, beak wide open, eyes glinting. He raised his wings to look bigger. A gentle purple ember landed on Leah's nose.

The healer speaks truth, Excelsis said.

13

Clint glared. He opened his mouth to speak, only to get a face full of water. He shook himself, raining water everywhere. Sémini sat on Leah's other side.

We have every reason to believe Alexina lives, Sémini said. She turned to Leah and nodded. *Have faith.*

Clint snarled, yowling angrily. He took one step toward Leah, teeth bared.

Leah tensed and stood, reaching for her staff for protection.

"Guardian present!" someone roared from the front of the library.

Everyone stood at attention. Clint glared a moment longer, then turned at attention.

Guardian Azure walked into the room. "As you were, everyone." The historians went back to normal, though Defenders and Athánatos alike stopped what they were doing as the Guardian walked through.

Clint relaxed a bit, though kept his ears pinned back, staring at Guardian Azure.

But Leah remained tense and rigid. Guardian Azure was walking *right towards her.*

"Hey, Leah," Guardian Azure said, as casually as he had been when he had first met her on Zyearth. "How's that report on the summons going?"

Leah flattened her ears, her fur heating up. "I-I... I'm um..."

"We'd have it faster if Leah wasn't dominating the Book of Summons, sir," Clint said, his voice bitter.

Guardian Azure turned to him. "I'm sorry?"

"She's had it for a majority of the time ever since we found it," Clint said, like he was tattling. Leah hung her head in shame.

Guardian Azure raised an eyebrow, frowning.

Clint lowered his gaze. "...Sir."

"Well, yes, I expected that," Guardian Azure said. Leah perked both ears. "She's the head of Summon's History."

14

"A brand new department created especially for her," Clint said, narrowing her gaze at her.

"But one more relevant than ever." Guardian Azure waved a hand to the Phonar. "I'm sure you read her dissertation. That's one of the reasons why I personally brought her here."

Clint twitched his whiskers, ears flat. Holly nudged him angrily and muttered *I told you so.* Clint glared at Holly, then turned to Guardian Azure. "Just one of the reasons? Sir, with all due respect, you know how dangerous a healer-S can be."

Leah furrowed her brow and glared. "I'm *not--*"

"As dangerous as a Black Bound?" Guardian Azure countered, his voice darkening. "Perhaps even a Black Bound with a social jewel bond?"

Clint frowned, tail drooping. "Apologies, Guardian Azure."

"I'd hope so," Guardian Azure said, arms crossed.

Leah stopped, frowning. This was her fight. She needed to say something. Anything. But the Thought Factory fought her at every turn. Nothing came out. Dang it all.

"Be better, Defender," Guardian Azure said. "Prejudice has no place here." He turned to Leah. "Honestly, the main reason I came here was to talk to you about the other reason I brought you along."

Leah perked an ear, despite her racing heart. "O-other reason, sir?"

"Our contact on the mainland," Guardian Azure said. "Trecheon Omnir. He's a healer, and he needs training. I was hoping you could help with that."

Leah twitched her whiskers, staring. *"Me?"*

"Her?" Clint said.

Guardian Azure eyed him. Clint backed down. A rush of guilt washed over Leah.

"I... I'm kind of with Clint on this one, sir," Leah said. "Why me?"

15

"Because you have a trait that almost no other healer in this military does," Guardian Azure said. "You actually *like* healing."

Clint rolled his eyes. Leah tried glaring at him, but it didn't feel right.

"So what do you think?" Guardian Azure said. "Feel up for it?"

Leah froze, thoughts spiraling out of control. If she said yes, what if she couldn't perform? What if Trecheon hated her? What if she had no idea how to teach him? What if Guardian Azure decided it was a mistake bringing her and sent her home? What if--

A hand gently gripped her shoulder. Her gaze focused on Guardian Azure's face, adrenaline rushing her system. An image of his body's recent health history flashed through her mind – little scars still healing, a mild cold he had fought off with ease, and… his status as a Black Bound. Why her magic marked that as an "ailment" she didn't know.

A final thing stuck out as well. His jewel bond. But it didn't feel bad. Scars were bad. Viruses were bad. Even the Black Bound thing didn't feel great. The jewel bond was just… present. Pleasant even. Homey. Comforting. Like it meant never being alone. Alone like she was.

It threatened to bring her to tears.

Guardian Azure frowned at her. He removed his hand. "Sorry, should have asked first. You okay?"

Clint eyed her and muttered. "See? Dangerous." But Guardian Azure didn't seem to hear him.

Leah fought the Thought Factory. *Forget about the bond. Forget the loneliness. Just work, dang it!* Took a moment, but she successfully prevented it from shutting down. "I'm… fine." She smiled as best she could. "I'd love to come to the mainland with you. Sir."

Guardian Azure smiled back. "Great. We leave tomorrow. You can talk to me about your report then, okay? No pressure to have it finished, just share what you have."

"S-sure," Leah said. "Thank you, sir."

"See you tomorrow." Guardian Azure left.

Clint shot one more glare at Leah, then stormed off. Holly glanced back at Leah, gave her a sad smile, and walked out as well.

Leaving Leah alone with the summons.

Guardian Azure's words bounced around in her mind. *Prejudice has no place here.* A shame that wasn't really true. Here or anywhere.

She really didn't belong here. Heck, she didn't even know if she belonged on Zyearth either. If only she had a way to prove she did. Her mind wandered, playing a daydream where she discovered Alexina through strange happenstance while on the mainland. Or maybe her offspring. Someone related to her. Someone who had the Phonar summons, proving she was right about the Book of Summons. Leah would be a hero. They'd restore all the Phonar. That'd prove she was worth something. That she belonged.

Assuming Alexina was alive. Or had offspring. Or that she actually *was* right about the Book of Summons.

But maybe that was only a pipe dream. Alexina was probably dead. She didn't have offspring. That was a fool's errand.

She buried herself back in the Book of Summons, looking for purpose, shoving Alexina and her fictional child out of her mind.

PRÍNKIPAS

Zeke Brightclaw, test pilot in the US Special Warfare Division, woke up sore, restless, and battered, cursing the corrupted, xenophobic commander of the Air Corps Academy for the umpteenth time for keeping him stuck as a test pilot and forever barring his way into a full battle-ready pilot. He slid his legs off the bottom bunk bed and gripped his stomach as he gingerly sat up.

Draso's horns, everything hurt. He'd sleep better if these damn things were large enough for zyfaunos of his height. Or with tails. He ran a hand down his orange muzzle, and shook his head, focusing on the sharp rustling sound of his black, white-tipped quills, trying to pull himself back to the present. He picked at the loose fur on his bent ears and worked the kinks out of his black, tufted tail. What he really needed was a shower. A nice, long, hot shower. A shame that'd never happen in the damn bunks with their limits on water use.

Yesterday had been brutal. He and Andre, his closest friend and test pilot partner, had tested the newest Raven troop transport, one of the few non-helicopter aircraft they had capable of hovering. The engineers were testing to see if they could get the same lift with smaller engines to save fuel.

Guess what? They couldn't, and both of them had barely escaped the planes before they crashed in colorful fireballs. Good Draso, Zeke was tired of fleeing fireballs. He had been lucky that Archángeli was there to blow their parachutes to safety.

It had been a damn stupid risk in the first place. After the crash, Zeke had read up on the old version of the plane. Developed during the War of Eons, it had been one of the most successful troop transports the military had ever known. Why mess with success?

Insurance, probably. Like it often was. Insure the new experimental plane, knowing it'll fail, and reap the money from to recoup lost investment.

At least he had the day off today. He and Andre had just been transferred to Owen Air Corps Base outside El Dorado, and neither of them had had much chance to check out the city. Might as well do that today.

The door to his bunk burst open and Andre walked in, grinning. His bald head shined in the overhead lights, and his dark skin contrasted with his plain white shirt and light blue jeans. "Yo, Zeke, you ready to die today?"

Zeke looked up through slitted eyes. Andre started every day with the same grim proclamation. "We're not flying today, Andre."

"Plenty of other ways to die," Andre said, winking.

Zeke flicked an ear back. "Funny."

"Oh, lightening up," Andre said. "Celebrate! Yesterday was hella brutal and we somehow survived."

"At least we got the data they wanted," Zeke said, stretching delicately considering all the bruising. *Because that's all we're good for. Data collection and insurance money for their damn planes.* "You know, you really didn't have to rip up your acceptance letter for flight school. You could be there now and actually doing something *useful.*"

19

"And leave you behind after everything we've been through?" Andre said. "I'd rather die."

"You might get your wish," Zeke said. "You know how damn dangerous this job is."

Andre just smirked. "You might as well just save your breath, Zeke. I'm not leaving. Not without you. You got that?"

Zeke sighed, but didn't respond.

"I'm just glad we're heading into the city today," Andre said. "Wanna have lunch before we explore? I'd like you to meet the boyfriend."

Zeke slipped on his glasses and raised an eyebrow. *"Boyfriend?* Last time you mentioned him, he was just a 'date.'"

"Yeah well… these things happen," Andre said, smiling sheepishly. "I think this move to El Dorado has done me a lot of good."

Zeke smiled. Finally some good news. "I guess that's why you've stopped flirting with me."

"Naw, dude, I stopped flirting with you because you're clearly more bothered by it than you let on," Andre said. "Hell, if you're not into *me,* you gotta be ace/aro. I respect that." His overly charming demeanor softened a bit and his face grew more serious. "I mean it, dude. You're my bud and I'm not gonna force you to put up with my bullshit. It ain't worth it."

Zeke took a deep breath, but his smile widened. "Thanks. I appreciate it."

"Yeah, well, don't credit my thick head for it," Andre said. "Archángeli had to point it out *several* times before I got the hint."

Zeke perked both ears. "Archángeli talked to you?"

"Yeah, they talk to me fairly frequently now, ever since that debacle with the Phoenix planes," he said. "Did you know they accompanied me on one of my flights? The one I took without you."

Zeke smiled. "Really, now."

"Really," Andre said. "Probably saved my ass too. They told me later 'I am only doing this for the sake of the Prínkipas.'"

"I'll have to thank them for that," Zeke said. "I've never gotten Archángeli to accompany anyone I care about before. Maybe I could get them to do that more."

"I'd honestly love the company," Andre said. He paused. "The hell is a Prínkipas?"

"Your guess is as good as mine," Zeke said with a shrug. "It means 'prince' in Greek, but Draso knows I'm not a prince. Archángeli has called me that since I was a baby."

"Huh. Odd." He held a hand out to Zeke. "Either way, wanna come with? I'll buy lunch."

Zeke took it. "Sure."

"Great," Andre said, grinning. "See you in five." He left the room.

Zeke got dressed in a gray shirt and black pants. Nice simple colors to contrast the burnt orange and black on his fur. Though he decided against boots. The fur on his feet had grown in extra thick after that catastrophic plane crash with the Phoenix dog fighters a year ago. The crash had burned several layers of skin off his foot soles, requiring skin grafts off his back, and it made wearing shoes uncomfortable.

At the last second, he slipped on his dog tags and his good luck charm, a series of six, oddly shaped, colored jewels on a woven bracelet.

Andre got them a driver through a ride share app and they took off. To Zeke's surprise, they headed to the auto district.

"The auto district?" Zeke asked. "Why here? Your boyfriend picking up his car from the shop or something?"

"No, he's an auto mechanic," Andre said. He winked. "Works exclusively with exotics and hydrogen cars. Don't get him started on it though, or he'll talk your ear off. And you'd look ridiculous with only one ear."

Zeke smirked. "Duly noted."

"Either way, he'll be joining us after work," Andre said. "Plus, there's apparently an *amazing* café here, called Suzy's. It's incredible the gems you find off the beaten path. Thought we could check it out."

The car stopped. Zeke thanked the driver and they started the walk to the café when Andre's phone beeped. He glanced at it. "Shit."

"Your boyfriend?" Zeke asked.

"Yeah. He's going to be late." He typed a moment, then laughed. "He wants to know if I can join him in the garage. Wants to show me off to his coworkers."

"Go then," Zeke said. "I'll get to the café and save a table for us."

"Thanks, Zeke." Andre patted his shoulder and headed into the shops.

Zeke walked along through the big warehouses and autoshops, counting the stares he got from humans as they walked by. Even a few quilar and other zyfaunos stared at him. He knew he wasn't really a "correct" quilar, what with his weird feet, his backward ears, and long tail. The skin on the inside of his ears was green, like his eyes, too, making him stand out more. Plus, he was way taller than most quilar.

He flattened his ears and stared at the ground instead. Social outcast, fighting xenophobia and corruption in a military no one liked.

He was stuck. Might as well get used to it. At least Andre had someone to live for now.

Zeke would just have to keep living for Andre then.

CHAPTER 03

PROVE IT

Leah leaned on the railing of the stark-white catamaran as Guardian Azure moored it against an old, rotting dock near a strip of abandoned casinos. He made sure everything was locked up tight, grabbed his bag, then waved to Leah. She picked up her own bag and saluted him.

Guardian Azure smiled gently. "Let's forget the saluting while we're on the mainland, okay? And call me Matt. This is a social visit, not a mission."

Leah sunk down. "I-I'll do my best, sir."

Matt lifted a brow. "And no 'sir,' please."

"Yes, sir," Leah said. "I-I mean… yes, Matt."

"Good." He sized her up. "One more thing. Take off the healer-S band. Trecheon won't care, and there's no reason to make you stand out."

Leah's eyes widened. "Really?"

"Really," Matt said. "I hate those things anyway."

Leah slowly pulled the green armband marking her as a healer-S off her arm and tossed it into her bag. She sighed. It was so freeing. Like a giant weight had been pulled off her.

Would Trecheon really not care? She doubted it. But still, hope remained. Maybe she'd be lucky with an Earthling.

Matt walked down the gangplank. Leah followed, ears flat and tail twitching.

Trecheon Omnir waited for them on the sand. His red, black-streaked quills stood out against white ruins of the casinos. He wore a simple black and white biker jacket with red accents, and a very distinguishable smirk.

"Hey, you space aliens remembered a boat this time!" he shouted.

Matt waved a hand with a scoff. "What, you think we were gonna try landing a *space plane* on this Draso-forsaken strip of beach? You're dreaming." He pointed to the Defender pendant around Trecheon's neck. "Nice swag, as the kits say."

Trecheon lifted a brow and smirked. "Naw, this thing's a piece of junk." He patted Matt's shoulder. "Great to see you, Matt. And without a sword at my throat this time."

Matt flicked an ear back. "I'm going to be paying for that for the rest of my life, aren't I?"

Trecheon winked. "Hey, you're *learning.*" He turned his vibrant blue eyes on Leah's green ones. "And who's this?"

Matt waved a hand. "DZ Nealia, newly-inducted Defender."

Leah flattened her ears. "J-just Leah is fine."

"She's a healer," Matt continued. "So I brought her along to help teach you. Izzy will join us later, but we wanted to start with a non-Black Bound healer first. Since Leah just finished her program, all her knowledge is fresh in her mind. Plus, she actually likes healing."

24

Trecheon perked his ears and turned to Leah. "Newly-inducted, huh? Does that mean I've finally met a Zyearthling who's younger than me?"

Matt chuckled. "Hardly. The Defender program is a twenty-year commitment, and Zyearthlings come of age at twenty."

Trecheon frowned. "Suddenly my three-year mechanics program seems like a breeze." He looked at Leah. "That'd make you at least forty."

"I, ah, I turned forty-two on the trip here from Zyearth, actually," Leah muttered.

"And like this asshole," Trecheon said, pointing to Matt. "You don't look a day over twenty-five." He tapped the cloth pocket holding his Gem. "These things are something else." He held a hand out to Leah. "Nice to meet you."

Leah held her hands up instinctively. "You, uh… you probably don't want to touch me."

Trecheon flicked an ear back. "Why not?"

"I'm um…" Leah muttered. "I'm a healer-S. I can see your body's ailments just by touching you. It's a breach of privacy."

Trecheon scoffed. He rolled up his sleeves, revealing two biomechanical arms. "My ailments are already public for the world to see. No biggie." He held his hand out again and smiled.

Leah flattened her ears, hesitant.

Matt leaned near Leah. "Come to think of it, have you ever touched someone with biomech before? Your powers might not have the same effect."

Leah's eyes widened and her ears perked. Wouldn't that be something? What would it be like to touch someone without fear?

Trecheon held his hand out further with an encouraging grin. Leah took it with vigor.

And her mind exploded with a wave of Trecheon's past trauma, blinding her. Tears spilled down her snout in rivers. Her thoughts swirled with his fear, his pain, his panic, his anger, every emotion possible, connected to the moment

25

he lost his arms, along with a hundred other scars and bullet wounds, all without context. Her own arms ached with his phantom pains and she stepped back, struggling to pull herself back to the here and now.

"Leah? Leah?" Matt's voice pulled at her and her vision returned. She stared at him through watery eyes, teetering slightly. He furrowed his brow and gripped her shoulder to steady her. His social bond floated through her mind again, drawing her fully back to reality.

Trecheon stood near him. "Hey, you okay? The hell happened?"

She stared at him, the tears coming back full force. "I... I felt it. When you lost your arms." She hugged herself.

Trecheon's eyes widened. "You felt all that?"

She nodded. "What... what happened?"

Trecheon flattened his ears. "...Sniper rounds," he said. "Chasing down a... well, technically chasing down my boss in the Battle of DC. He had a sniper protecting him." He rubbed his arm. "I really only remember the first shot. The second one blacked me out immediately. Next thing I knew I woke up with no arms, surrounded by doctors claiming my survival was a damned miracle."

"H-how did you survive?" Leah asked.

Trecheon shrugged. "Hell if I know. I always attributed it to Carter." He glanced at Matt and stared a moment, then shook his head. "But I guess my Gem had something to do with it too."

Leah's chest ached and her tail puffed. "Trecheon... I am so sorry..."

He held his hands up and offered a tiny smile. "It's okay, really. I'm alright. I survived. And it's all over." He wrinkled his snout. "Sorry you had to go through that... I'll make sure not to touch you again. No sense in reliving that over and over. I let it go a long time ago."

Leah pressed her lips together, but nodded. One more zyfaunos unable to touch her. Even though Trecheon had a good reason, it still stung.

26

Matt gripped Trecheon's shoulder, rubbing it gently. "I'm very glad you survived, Trecheon."

Leah stared. They touched so easily, without fear. Longing chewed away at her heart, making her chest ache.

Trecheon stared at Matt a moment and smiled. "Yeah, me too." He gripped Matt's hand but after a moment, the smile faded.

Matt's smile faded too. "Do I really look like him? Like Carter?"

Trecheon blinked, as if coming out a trance. His ears flattened and his jaw clenched. "Honestly… who knows. Even now when I picture him, I just get vague colors. White and blue and green, all swirled together on dirty fur and quills. Despite being on a team for eight months together, the trauma of losing my arms with Carter right there erased him from my memory."

Matt's expression darkened. "I'm sorry."

"Not your fault, but thanks." Trecheon patted Matt's hand, then shook his head. "Carter… he was dear to all of us. Really helped keep the team together. Stuck by me while I was slowly losing my mind, comforted Neil during his early PTSD moments." He took a shuttering breath. "Wasn't expecting to drudge up old memories today, but… better to do that in the company of friends, I guess. Wanna get a bite to eat? I need a sugary dessert after all that. There's a nice café in the auto district called Suzy's. My treat, since it's not like you space aliens can do an interplanetary money exchange."

Matt's smile returned. "Sure, sounds good."

It took several hours to cross town to the industrial district and Trecheon's garage. Trecheon and Matt chatted the whole trip over like they had been best friends their whole lives. Leah sunk into her seat listening to them.

"So what's Neil up to these days?" Matt asked. "I'm surprised he wasn't with you."

27

Trecheon waved a hand. "He runs an HVAC business and he's been on constant calls since the spring heat hit." He smirked. "Or he's running around with Natassa and Damianos, take your pick."

Matt laughed. "Natassa *and* Dami, huh?"

"Yeah," Trecheon said. "They're dating. Well, Neil's dating the two of them, but I don't think Dami's interested in women, so it's a vee." He made a V-motion with his fingers.

"I forget Earth has a thousand terms for defining attraction, romance, and gender," Matt said. "We'd just call it a 'relationship' on Zyearth."

"It's a blessing and a curse," Trecheon said.

"Any news on how they explained the battle at the docks?"

Trecheon pointed to a newspaper on the truck's dash. "See for yourself." Matt snatched it. A picture of a white wolf and several humans all in lab coats blazed the front page. "Basically blamed it on EMPs, solar flares, and mass hallucination. I'm just grateful Ryota's last bout of lightning fried phones and CCTV cameras, or Neil and I would have been targets for the FBI."

They parked in Trecheon's garage and walked to the café. As they neared it, Leah caught a group of locals staring at her. She flattened her ears. Two humans, feminine, both with light skin, one blonde, one a redhead. The redhead had long braids along the side of her head. A long-eared rabbit with black fur and a thick jaw walked beside her. A gray, white-spotted stag with dark brown antlers that looked sharpened, and a tight shirt accentuating his prominent muscles walked along too. All of them kept their gaze on her throughout the whole walk.

She was about to point them out to Matt when the whole group turned a corner and vanished into an autoshop. Leah stared at them.

They stared back. Lightning ran down her spine and she fought the Thought Factory for the words. "U-um... M-Matt..."

"Here it is," Trecheon said. "Hurry, let's see if they have a seat indoors."

28

"B-But…" Leah tried, but Matt and Trecheon were already double-timing it to the café. Leah shook herself and ran after them.

The inside of the cafe was already packed full of Earthlings, so Trecheon got them a table outside. Leah glanced back at the autoshop.

The group was gone.

"Get whatever you want," Trecheon said, handing them both menus and breaking Leah's thoughts. "The Cloak gave me more money than I know what to do with, so I'm glad to spend a little of it on friends."

Leah's ears grew hot.

"If you don't mind, Leah," Matt said. "I'd be happy to listen to your report so far. Now that Clint isn't stepping on your tail."

Leah took a deep breath and gripped her tail for comfort, tugging at the hairs. She recounted all she had learned over the last week, spending particular time on her theory about Alexina. "I really believe she's alive, sir--I-I mean, Matt. Though where she is, I haven't the slightest."

Trecheon leaned back in his chair, sipping his water. "I bet she got caught up in the War of Eons. Heaven knows that war affected *everything*. I'm sure Athánatos would have gotten more involved if it wasn't for the Cast bullshit."

"Hmm," Matt said. "Makes me wonder if Embrik got caught up in it too. He's the missing Archon. Melaina's husband, actually. To the best of Natassa's knowledge, he left the island with Alexina looking for help during the Cast debacle."

Trecheon flattened his ears. "Ouch."

Matt turned to Leah again. "Is there anything else that would explain why Archángeli and Kyrie haven't shown up? It's been years."

Leah twitched her tail, ears flat. "Well… she could have had kits. The Phonar would distribute to her kits before her siblings. T-though that's not likely."

Matt raised an eyebrow. "Why's that?"

"The Ei-Ei jewels," Leah said. "Like with Lexi Gems, the jewels really slow the reproductive process, though the Ei-Ei jewels halt it completely. As far as I know, Athánatos have a procedure they have to do before either partner is even physically able to have kits."

"Whoa, whoa, *whoa,*" Trecheon said. "The hell does that mean? Slows it how?"

Matt turned to him with a raised eyebrow and a sassy grin. "I'll explain later. That is not a topic for lunch."

"Good Draso, I should have asked a hell of a lot more questions before Izzy stuck me with this thing," Trecheon said, rolling his eyes.

"Unless you're planning on having kits any time soon, I promise you'll be fine," Matt said.

"Note to self," Trecheon said. "Don't find a partner desperate for kits any time soon."

A white wolf with striking, icy blue eyes walked up to them and took their lunch order, a smirk on his face. Leah's skin grew hot. Had their server heard them? She had to hope not.

Everyone ordered and Matt turned back to Leah. "Alexina's been missing for nearly a century. It's possible she moved on and found a mate. I'm sure she'd know what to do if she really wanted kits."

"Or someone assaulted her," Trecheon said bitterly. Matt eyed him. Trecheon took a swig of water and shrugged. "This is Earth, Matt. I don't know how Zyearth handles sexual assault, but here they get away with it a *lot*. Especially against someone with no official identity, like Alexina would have. She'd be a perfect target simply because she'd have no way to report it, much as I hate to admit it. I don't know what Athánatos have to do in order to have kits, but it may not be necessary if one of the partners has no focus jewel."

Leah sunk down, her stomach churning.

Matt wrinkled his nose in disgust. "I'll pretend she found a mate and chose to have kits instead."

Leah shifted in her seat. "I-If she *did* have kits, it'd be easy enough to find them, a-as long as they're like… in some database somewhere. They'll look really unusual compared to everyone else. And if Alexina got involved in the war like you theorize…"

"True," Matt said. He leaned on his hands. "I know very little about that war. Perhaps knowing a bit more might help us decide how Alexina and Embrik could have gotten involved." He turned to Trecheon. "Would you mind?"

Trecheon took a deep breath. "Sure. We already started, might as well finish."

The white wolf server brought their lunch and they spent the next hour listening to Trecheon talk about the War of Eons and his experiences with it. It was heartbreaking to listen to, if Leah was honest. A full world war between nearly every major nation, fighting for oil on a planet that still relied heavily on non-renewable energy sources.

It felt supernatural in nature sometimes, what with the mysterious and invisible Desert Wall keeping troops from entering the Middle East, and the shadowy way the various Japanese hydrogen scientists appeared and disappeared at random intervals throughout the war.

"My own part was… problematic," Trecheon said. "I was a part of a special ops group run by a man named Bob Ackerson. He's the one we were chasing down in the Battle of DC."

Matt twisted a sliver of fried potato between his fingers. "He must have done something hellish to get you to go chasing him in the middle of a big battle."

"You don't know the half of it," Trecheon. "Ackerson had a bunch of little troops, all under enigmatic names, and he used them to carry out tasks that the United States wanted done but didn't want to be attached to. But halfway through the war, he started using them for his own gains. We never proved it, but I theorized he was taking bribes, like literal hitmen."

"Yikes…" Leah said, leaning down in her chair.

"Disgusting," Matt spat. He picked up another potato. "I think Ryota mentioned some of those teams to me when we first met. Outlander and Guardian and Angel."

Trecheon shuddered with the last word. "Angel is probably the one group I know nothing about. From my understanding, they were assembled near the end of the war. But the rumors surrounding it aren't pleasant. There's a saying in the military - 'Fear the Angel' - but since I was honorably discharged after my arm injuries, I don't know much more beyond that. But yeah, Outlander, Guardian, Mage, Chaos, and Hunt were the ones I knew of. I ran Outlander and both Neil and Ryota were a part of it."

"And Carter," Matt said.

"And Carter," Trecheon agreed. "Regardless, turns out that when you use military for your own gains, someone is bound to notice. He started pitting his teams against each other to cover his tracks."

Leah hugged herself. "Ohhh, that's awful."

"It really is." Trecheon stared off a moment. "It got to the point where several teams turned themselves in when they realized what Ackerson was doing. Though others went after him themselves." Trecheon closed his eyes. "Outlander included." He shrugged. "See? Sketchy. And it wasn't a good decision. I was angry. By that point, half our team had either died or betrayed us. I blamed Ackerson for it, so we chased him down. Cost me my arms, cost Neil his sanity for a time. He had debilitating PTSD for over a year, and though he's better, he still fights it daily."

Matt furrowed his brow. "You couldn't have predicted that outcome, Trecheon. There's no reason to beat yourself up over it."

Trecheon sighed. "I suppose not. Perhaps it's just a conclusion I've come to after all these years. Regardless, the Battle of DC absolutely wrecked us, and forced me and Neil to sit out the rest of the war. Not long after the Battle, they pierced the Desert Wall and brought the whole thing to an end. Ackerson was eventually charged for his actions, but was ultimately acquitted, probably because he did do some good, at least in the eyes of the US. Typical war criminal."

Leah frowned. "W-why didn't you report Ackerson sooner? You might have escaped some of that."

Trecheon laughed darkly. "The man was acquitted for *several* major war crimes, including *murder,*" he said. "Nothing I would have said would have done anything. Hell, it probably would have put a target on my back."

Leah twitched her tail. "But that doesn't make sense. Wouldn't they want to get rid of corruption?"

Trecheon leaned on his hand. "Look. You're coming from Zyearth, which apparently equates to a utopia compared to this shithole planet. Maybe the Defenders would be quick to get rid of corruption, but here, our military *uses* it." He looked off. "Like it or not, Ackerson got shit done. It wasn't done right, and it sure as hell wasn't pretty, but it got done. That justifies it in the eyes of the powers that be."

"You know," Matt said with a smirk. "If you ever get sick of Earth, you could always move to Zyearth."

"Hell no," Trecheon said, pointing at Matt. "Keep that shit to yourself, space alien. I'm still not fully convinced you're an alien to begin with."

"Remind me to take you on a space walk one of these days," Matt said.

Leah watched the pair of them, envy building in her chest. She picked at her salad, ears flat, trying to make herself small. She turned her gaze elsewhere.

The door to the café opened and their server walked out carrying a whole tray of drinks. But his bare foot caught on the sidewalk and he dipped the entire tray all over Matt. Matt yelped, and Leah and Trecheon scooted back from the table in surprise.

The white wolf drew his hands to his snout. "Draso's horns, sir, I am *so sorry.*" He immediately pulled out a towel from his apron.

Matt waved it off. "It's fine, accidents happen." He stood, shaking himself. "I don't suppose you have a restroom?"

"Ours is out of order, unfortunately," the wolf said. "But Tam's Donuts around the corner is letting our customers use theirs." He started mopping up the table. "Let me see if I can get the meal for free for you. I am so *sorry.*"

"Seriously, it's fine," Matt said.

"We'll still pay," Trecheon said. "Though I'd love one of your ice cream brownies, if you don't mind."

The wolf flattened his ears, but he nodded. "Right away, sir." He cleaned off the table and hurried into the building.

"I'll take you over to Tam's, Matt," Trecheon said. "It's easy to get lost in these cookie cutter warehouses. Mind waiting, Leah?"

"N-no, I'll be fine," she said.

Matt thanked her and they walked around the corner, snickering about the whole event. Leah watched them as they vanished from sight. What she wouldn't do for a relationship like that. She turned.

A quilar walked up and took a table across from her.

An *Athánatos* quilar.

Leah's whole body buzzed and she stared. No way. Impossible. Far too much of a coincidence. She was imagining things.

She squinted.

No… he was an Athánatos. Bent back ears, long, tufted tail, short quills, big, pawlike feet, mostly black, with a burnt orange snout. The color wrapped around his face and came to a point between his eyes.

Burnt orange. *Burnt orange.*

Royal colors.

Leah's fur stood on end and her tail puffed up. He was *royalty.*

But he also had white streaks on the tips of his quills. With all the Athánatos she had seen, Leah had never seen one with color-tipped quills. Or with white, for that matter. Gray and silver, yes, but not white. He also didn't appear to have the Ei-Ei jewels on his face, though after scanning him a bit, she noticed he had a woven bracelet on, and it glinted. Likely that held the jewels.

He looked so off. Simple street clothes. Black glasses on his snout. Phone in his hand. As modern as modern could be, despite being an Athánatos.

There was only one explanation. He had to be Alexina's offspring.

Her face heated up. What should she do? Wait for Matt and Trecheon to come back? But the quilar bounced his leg frantically, glancing around like he was ready to take off at any moment. She could lose him. That would never do.

Besides. This was the chance to prove she belonged here. That Matt had made the right decision bringing her along.

She had no choice, anxiety or not.

She swallowed hard, playing through a thousand scenarios in her head, hoping to cover all her bases, then stood up and walked toward him.

TROUBLE

Zeke tapped the table impatiently, trying to avoid the looks from the odd gray and white feline staring at him. Her gaze burned through his fur. She wasn't exactly subtle while she looked him over.

Curse his unusual appearance. Somehow it always attracted unwanted attention. He hated dealing with random girls trying to get his number. The dichotomy was annoying – either he was stigmatized and ignored, or he was pursued by people of all genders looking for a good time, and both came out of the fact that he was so different. It was one of the reasons he was so reluctant to let people touch him. Always a romantic agenda there.

He stared back, glaring a little, hoping to make her stop. She was… strange. She wore some kind of off-military uniform. And what was that weird holster on her hip? It didn't look like it held a gun. Who knew what it was.

Glaring didn't work. Maybe if he just ignored her, she'd stop staring. He turned his head. *Hurry up, Andre.*

But nope, no such luck. She got up from her table and headed his way, ears flat against her head. Great. He'd just have to cut her off at the pass. He did not have the patience to put anyone down lightly today. As she approached the table, he met her eyes. "Look--"

"I-I don't want to bother you," the feline said, her voice shaking. "But are you an Athánatos?"

Zeke blinked at her. That wasn't the greeting he expected. "What?"

The feline frowned. "An Athánatos quilar."

"The hell is that?" Zeke asked.

The feline's tail bristled, her skin coloring under her white and gray fur. "Y-you don't know?"

Zeke lowered his gaze. "If I knew, I wouldn't be asking, would I?"

"But... your mom... Her name is Alexina, right?" the feline asked. "You're an Athánatos prince. You have the coloring for it." She furrowed her brow, sheepish. "I'm sorry, I'm being a huge bother... but..." her voice trailed.

Zeke's eyes widened. She said *prince*. "Wait. You mean Prínkipas?"

"Yes, that!" the feline said, speaking too fast. "So you do know. Did I get your mom's name right?"

Zeke's heart beat in his ears, drowning out her words. He had never met anyone who knew the term Prínkipas. He had only ever heard it from Archángeli. But this lady knew? He held up his bracelet, ignoring her question. "Do you know what these are too then?"

The feline's eyes widened and she sat at his table. "You mean you don't?"

"No!" Zeke said. "I've had them my whole life, but--"

"Hey, look what we found," a gravely voice said. "A pair of *mages.*"

Zeke looked up. A thick-jawed rabbit and a muscle-bound stag hovered over them. The rabbit grinned.

The stag eyed them and turned to the rabbit. "We did not pick up their trackers on the scanner." He spoke with a thick accent. Russian or Ukrainian maybe. "We sure this is them?"

"'Course," the rabbit said with a Brooklyn accent. "That long-tailed, bent-eared quilar? A gray and white feline? Who else would it be? Don't think I'd ever miss them after DC. Besides, she's got that weird hip holster."

The stag took a step back. "And a Gem. You did not tell me she had a Gem."

The rabbit waved a hand. "She's only a healer. What harm can she do?"

"A healer-S."

"Then don't let her touch you," the rabbit snapped. "God, you're sensitive."

The stag pointed at Zeke. "But the Prínkipas--"

"He's not wearing his jewels," the rabbit said. "He's harmless too."

The feline stood up and backed away, though she furrowed her brow and glared. "Who are you? How do you know about my Gem? And the Prínkipas?"

The rabbit sneered. "You don't remember me, huh? Forgot all about our encounter at the Bank of the State?"

"I don't know what the heck you're talking about," Leah said.

The rabbit waved a hand. "Not like it matters."

Zeke stood up now and walked next to the feline. He didn't know who the hell she was, but these two looked dangerous. There was no way this five-foot cat could take on these thugs alone.

The feline hovered a hand over her hip holster. "What do you want with me?"

The rabbit smirked. "Nothing personal, Miss Leah. Just following orders. You understand, I'm sure."

The gray cat – Leah, he supposed – stared at the rabbit. She unhooked something on her hip holster and pulled out a small rod.

Zeke almost rolled his eyes.

Leah furrowed her brow. "How did you know my name?"

"Oh, come off it," the rabbit said. He slipped out a large pocketknife and twirled it about. "Leah and Zeke, the dynamic duo of DC. After our fight at the bank, how could I not?"

Leah looked over at Zeke. Zeke shrugged, but kept one eye on the rabbit's spinning knife. They needed to get out of there, *now.*

Leah turned back to him. "You're speaking nonsense."

"Deny it all you want," the rabbit said. "It changes nothing." He gripped the knife and brought it down hard on the feline. A sharp whine stung Zeke's ears.

But the knife stuck fast in the air, like it had pierced some invisible wall. Before Zeke could even process what had happened, Leah shook the rod in her hand into a long, metal staff, and smashed the knife and rabbit away from her. The rabbit squeaked and slid along the ground away from them. Other café patrons screamed and ran inside the building.

"Get behind me," Leah told Zeke, turning her gaze on the stag. He easily had two feet and two hundred pounds on her, but she didn't back down. The stag bared his teeth and stepped toward her.

"What the hell do you think you're *doing?*" Zeke said. "He'll kill you!"

"You're welcome to help out," Leah said, brandishing the staff.

"I'm unarmed," Zeke said. "What the hell do you expect me to do against a knife?"

"You know how to use those jewels on your bracelet?"

"I don't even know what that *means,*" Zeke shouted. The stag lunged, throwing a punch at Leah's face. She ducked and smacked him hard with her staff. The stag skittered back, but not far. He steadied himself and charged again. Leah pushed Zeke out of the way. He rolled on the ground to his feet, shaking himself, just as the stag went for another blow.

No! *Archángeli!*

The golden eagle shot forward and zoomed between Leah and the stag, filling the area with his clean air scent, sending them both staggering backwards. Leah stared at the bird, slack-jawed.

"Archángeli!" she spat.

Zeke gawked. She knew their *name?* How the hell did she know *that?* Who *was* this feline?

Archángeli turned too, clearly confused, but then shrieked and fell, brushing an angry claw against their neck, shredding feathers. A knife stuck fast in their plumes.

Zeke's bone buzzed. *Shit!* Could Archángeli *die?* This *could not happen.* Zeke had somehow given Archángeli extra power before. If he did it again... But how? He didn't--

"Look out!" Leah shouted.

Zeke turned. The rabbit had a second knife. He snarled and threw it at Zeke's face. Zeke held up his hands.

And once again, the knife stuck fast in the air. What the *hell?*

Then he noticed his jeweled bracelet glowed. Archángeli's wind brushed his face. *Trust the feline!* He glanced at his bird. Archángeli pulled the knife out of their neck, unharmed, and rushed the stag. Zeke stared after them.

"Watch out!" Leah rushed in front of Zeke, holding her hand out.

Her fingers brushed his bracelet.

And everything exploded in his mind.

Light blinded him, shooting stars through his vision. An intense ringing threatened to burst his eardrums, drowning out all other sounds. Images, thoughts, feelings, experiences, memories, *everything* rushed through his mind like fifteen movies playing all at once, at ten, fifty, a hundred times the speed, and not all of them his own. He saw his moms, alive, then in their graves, then Andre, Commander Berrycloth, Major Garcia... but also black quilar that looked like him, with tufted tails and bent ears, a white, blue-tipped quilar, a red furred quilar, black, blobby, inky monsters with glowing blue eyes, torn flesh, ruined faces, an old white lioness attached to an IV, flashes upon flashes of birds like Archángeli, all accompanied by loud, genderless voices screaming words that he didn't know how to connect.

White hot pain ripped through his spine, then turned red, then turned black and everything stopped at once.

CHAPTER 05

BOND

Ugh… everything hurt. Again. Still. Did he have a bad flight yesterday? Why couldn't he get his eyes to open? And why was his bed so hard?

With enormous effort, Zeke forced his eyes open. Turned out, he wasn't in his bed at all. He was lying on a hard, wooden board hung from the wall with chains like some European dungeon. In fact, it looked like he might actually *be* in a dungeon – bare, concrete walls, a single, tiny window so high above his head even he couldn't hope to reach it, a sink with a bucket next to it… and a thick metal door, with a tiny window and a slot near the floor.

He forced himself to sit up, groaning. What the hell happened? Where was he?

Zeke?

He opened his eyes wide and shot through the pain to full alertness. A strong smell of something sour, maybe lemon, permeated the air. "Who's there?"

I'm… it's in your head, Zeke. I'm… I'm talking to you telepathically. A pause. *Your name is Zeke, right?*

Zeke blinked, trying to get his bearings. *Leah?*

Yeah, the voice said. Leah said. *Guess you picked up my name from those thugs.*

Zeke sat back against the wall. Leah was talking to him. In his head. What the hell. This… this wasn't real. He must have hit his head and knocked himself out. This was all a dream. Hell, did he even leave his bunk? For all he knew, *everything* from that morning was a dream. Leah probably wasn't even real.

Zeke?

Shit. She was still there. He smacked his head with the heel of his hand. Maybe she was real then. *Who were they?* Zeke asked.

Who?

Those thugs that attacked us.

Heck if I know, Leah said.

Another pause. *Then… who are you? And how are you talking to me in my head?*

Leah didn't respond. The lemon smell faded in favor of… baking bread, he realized. Subtle. Contemplative. Zeke chewed his lip and noticed his mouth was quite dry. How long had he been out? He hoped this would all be cleared up soon. The last thing he wanted was to be forced to drink from that dirty sink. *Leah?*

Sorry, Leah said. *I'm just… I'm not sure where to start if I'm honest. I mean… you don't…* Silence. *Y-you really don't know what those jewels on your bracelet are?*

No, Zeke said, irritation bubbling in his chest. *But somehow you do.*

He could smell her hesitation. *Kind of.*

Just kind of.

43

I-I mean, I only have secondhand knowledge, Leah said. *But…* she sighed. For whatever reason, the sigh smelt strongly of coffee. *Simply put, your jewels are magic.*

Zeke blinked, trying to process the word. *Magic.*

Yes, Leah said. *They're called Ei-Ei jewels.*

Eye-eye jewels. He shook his head. *Do you think I was born yesterday?*

A sharp smell of spices bit his nose. *We're literally talking to each other with our minds, and you have a magic bird summon.* He could almost see her disapproving look, though it faded quickly in favor of something like shame. *S-sorry, that was rude…*

A summon. That was a new word. *It's fine, you made your point. But that doesn't explain why you're speaking to me in my head.*

The baking bread smell came back. *I think… I think it might be best if I just explain what I think happened all at once and let you ask questions. Okay?*

Uh, sure, I guess.

The coffee smell returned now and he thought he heard Leah take a deep breath.

Your Ei-Ei jewels have magic, as I said, she said. *And I have a magic jewel too, called a Lexi Gem.* She paused briefly. *Which I don't have with me right now, actually. Do you have your bracelet?*

He glanced at his wrists. *No. Dammit.*

H-Hopefully they're safe. A pause. *Anyway… I think you were using your magic at the same time I was using mine. I was shielding.*

Shielding? Zeke said. His mind wandered back to that fight. *Is that why that rabbit's knife just stuck in the air like that? You had some kind of… magic shield?*

Yeah, Leah said. *I don't know what magic you were using, though, if the jewels aren't bound to you.*

44

Bound? What did that mean? *I... I guess I was trying to give Archángeli some extra power so they could get that knife out of their neck.*

You guess?

I've never really used... "magic" on purpose before.

Ah. W-well, either way, it seems like our magic combined when I touched your bracelet while shielding.

And that means you can talk to me in my head.

That means, Leah said slowly. *That we've formed a... social bond with our magic.* A bright smell of cookies and cakes filled the room. Like... joy, despite their situation. But hesitant. Almost fearful. The competing emotions gave Zeke a headache. *We can hear each other's thoughts and feel each other's emotions. I think... through smell. I've been getting weird smells ever since you woke up.*

A smell of blueberry muffins, warm and fresh, assailed his nose. Clarity. *Draso's horns, I think you're right. Does each smell have a different emotion then?*

I think so, Leah said. There was a smell of... of a too-hot pan, smelling like burning. Hesitation again. *I know this is going to sound unbelievable, but...this might have also caused us to time travel. Probably to the past.*

Zeke blinked. *What?*

Before Leah could answer, a loud scraping and metal creaking sounded outside his door, like a heavy metal door opening. He stood up.

The door to his cell opened and a tall, beefy man walked in, with two armed guards on either side of him. Human. Square jaw. He had well-trimmed, brown hair and a neatly cleaned beard and mustache. He wore a full military outfit, complete with campaign ribbons, and a variety of medals, though no identifying insignia for some reason. Despite Zeke's abnormal height, this man was actually an inch or so taller than him. He wouldn't look Zeke in the eye. Instead he kept his gaze trained on the clipboard in his hand.

Zeke narrowed his eyes.

"Ezekiel Joseph Brightclaw," the man said, his gravelly voice echoing on the stone walls, stinging Zeke's ears. "Welcome to El Dorado." He shook his head. "Quite a name you have. Your parents religious?"

Zeke didn't answer. He checked his neck. *Shit.* No dog tags. That was how this loser knew his name.

The man tapped his clipboard. "Well, Ezekiel--"

"Zeke."

The man looked up and raised an eyebrow. He smirked. "So you can speak."

Zeke glared at him.

"Well then, *Zeke,*" the man said. "According to this, you're AWOL."

Zeke's ears went cold. "What?"

"Camp Bennett reports you missing as of December 28th, 2028," the man said. "Today is April 3rd, 2029." He shook his head, making a *tsk tsk* sound. "Bad move for a new recruit. I can't imagine they'll let you see combat after that, except as a bullet sponge. I'd say you'd be lucky if they even take you back, except for the fact that we're desperate for soldiers right now, what with the damn draft dodgers."

Zeke sat down and stared at the floor. What. The. Hell. That wasn't right. He let his vision blur as he tried to remember the date. The day before, he had logged his flight – May 10th, 2039.

And this guy was citing his AWOL date. His real and actual AWOL date, the one major stain on his otherwise perfect military record. His boot camp buddy Robert had convinced him to take an extended vacation, maybe even leave the military completely, though that'd be impossible to do legally in the middle of war.

Robert vanished not long after they escaped. Zeke never saw the white wolf again.

But everyone in his squad wanted to leave – after all, they were on the losing side of a dangerous war. A time in his life when he was afraid – afraid of the war, afraid of being shipped out, afraid of losing his parents, a real concern, considering they both died in the War of Eons…

Holy shit, he was in the *War of Eons.* He had time traveled. Just like Leah said. Draso's holy *aura*, he had actually friggin' *time traveled.*

And the war… the war that took his parents.

Waves of fear, grief, desperation rolled over his body, taking him back to the day he learned about his moms' deaths in the Battle of DC. He couldn't remember anything about it – where he was, what his plans were, what he had been doing… All he could remember was simple letter in the mail, a guttural cry from his throat, and a sharp pain in his chest that he carried for days, or weeks, maybe even months.

The last of his family. The last thing to keep living for. Gone. And he never really knew how or why. Everything blurred together. Nothing felt real. Nothing separated the days. He still didn't know where he was.

Then he had gotten their ashes in plain urns with no explanation, no flags, no fanfare, shipped in tiny cardboard boxes that weren't even marked well. That shredded the last of his will to live. He had reenlisted, hoping they'd put him on the front lines and he could finally end the pain.

Then he met Andre while training. Only Andre's friendship had dulled the wound well enough to reconsider.

But now he was in the past.

He racked his mind over the date. April 3rd, 2029. His moms were killed in the Battle of DC, sometime in July of this same year.

So that meant… as of that moment… they were still alive. They were *alive.*

Could he save his parents from death?

The man snapped his fingers in front of Zeke's face. "Hello, Earth to Zeke. Get your head out of space, beastie."

Beastie! Zeke bared his teeth. *I could break your neck you sonova--*

But he stopped. That'd guarantee permanent residency in this cell. If he was going to save his moms, he needed out. He shot a quick glance at the two guards. Both held M4 rifles. Both had the safeties off. He'd never be able to fight them. Not even with Archángeli's help. And even if he could, he had no idea where he was. He'd never be able to get out. He checked the motion and forced himself to calm down. "Sorry."

The man's smirk returned. "That's better." He stood straight again. "Now. I could send you back to Camp Bennett. But given your long absence and our desperate need for soldiers on the field, I suspect they'd send you straight to the front lines as cannon fodder."

Zeke suppressed a shudder.

"Or… you could work for me."

Zeke perked his ears. "What would that entail?"

"Top level black ops," the man said. "You run some spy missions. Take out some important targets. Generally do whatever the hell I say without question until the war is over and you can go back to being a normal soldier instead of meat for the grinder."

Zeke wrinkled his snout. "I'm not even finished with boot. What qualifies me for black ops?"

The man grinned. "You're AWOL. For all intents and purposes, you're dead to the US Military, while still possessing the skills of a soldier."

Zeke flattened his ears, weighing his options. Getting sent back to Bennett would guarantee being shipped out. Unless he could escape again. But that was unlikely.

Sticking with this man… he'd have a bit more freedom. But he'd also be under his thumb.

Neither option was great.

"Can I think about it?"

"Sure," the man said with a sly grin. "One of my teams needs members, and their leader will be here in three days. You have until then." The man tapped his clipboard and walked out, slamming the heavy door behind him.

"Wait! Aren't you going to let me out of here?" But the man was gone. Maybe he had left to find a place for him. A bunk or something he could stay at. Hopefully he'd at least bring dinner.

He sat back on the hard bench, and stared at the ceiling. Well. He had some time to think anyway.

He poked his mind, hoping to find Leah. But there was nothing. No smells, no voices. Maybe that was all a dream and he had hit his head. Draso's mercy, he felt so drained, and everything ached. He laid on the bench, hoping to rest.

But after all that, he couldn't shut his brain off.

The War of Eons. The Battle of DC. He could get there.

He could save his parents.

CHAPTER 06

ACKERSON

Leah managed to keep a straight face and a quiet tail at this strange man's proposal to work for him. Quite a feat, considering she was shaking with anxiety on the inside, fighting to keep the Thought Factory up and running. How did this happen? How did she get here?

How was she supposed to respond?

The man tapped his clipboard. His armed companions shifted. "Well?"

Good Draso, he was smug. Reminded her of Holly before they had made nice. Holly though… she was using that to hide something. This man could be doing the same.

She took a deep breath. Keep the Thought Factory running. Keep going strong. She'd get out of here.

Besides. She wasn't alone.

"W-what reason would I have to join you?" she said. Dang it. It never came out as strong as she wanted.

The man's smile turned sly. "I'll give you two..." He pulled out her Defender pendant. "...Miss Defender."

Her eyes widened. "What?"

"Or," the man said, pulling her Gem out now. "Should I say Miss Zyearthling?"

Her jaw dropped. "I... what...?"

"You are an alien, military invader," he said. "Don't ask me how I know, because I'm not sharing. However." His smile disappeared completely and his face grew intensely serious. "No one is looking for you. No one can help you. You can't escape and if you don't work for me, you can sit here and rot and no one will miss you." He put her pendant in his pocket.

She stared, panic threatening to take her.

The man smirked at her.

She pinned her ears back. "Y-you said black ops."

"I did, yes."

She forced her ears back up. She had to stay in control of herself. "What kind of black ops?"

He threw her Gem up and down. "For you? With this? I'd stick you in Mage. They could use some new members."

She paused. Mage. *Mage.* Trecheon used that name. A group of military black ops working for... for... "You're Ackerson." She clapped her hands on her mouth. *Why the heck did I say that?*

The man lifted a brow. His two companions exchanged looks. But he smiled. "It seems my reputation precedes me. Yes, I'm Ackerson." He made a mock bow. "Well, Miss Zyearthling, I'll leave you here to think. Mage's leader will arrive in three days. Think hard." He pocketed her Gem and left, slamming the heavy door.

Leah sat down. Dang it all, why couldn't she keep her fat mouth shut? She just gave away her only edge.

But she wasn't alone. She had Zeke... whether he liked it or not.

Her mind buzzed. She had a social bond with him. A real, true social bond, like Matt and Ouranos. It was with a stranger but still... warmth filled her chest. Perhaps he could be a friend.

Though after everything they'd been through already, he'd probably hate her. She'd be stuck having a social bond with someone who didn't even want her. She shuddered. *Calm down, Thought Factory.*

But all that did was fuel every terrible scenario it could think of. Curse her anxiety. She hugged her knees.

Regardless... Zeke was stuck with her. At least for now. Perhaps more than he realized. After all, he was an Athánatos. And there was no mistaking it. He had to be Alexina's child. He had the right coloring. The jewels. And the biggest clue... Archángeli. One of Alexina's summons.

She thought back to her notes on Athánatos. The royal summons would redistribute to any children the royal family had.

But he only had one, at least that she saw. Not two. So either she had two children... or she was *alive.*

Zeke!

A smell of... fruitcake, Leah decided, wafted under her nose. Smelled... unwanted. Her stomach churned. *Oh, you're back. I was hoping you were a dream.*

Your mom, Leah said. *Was her name Alexina?*

A short pause. *Neither of my moms were named Alexina.*

Leah frowned. *You... you said 'were.' Past tense.*

Yeah, Zeke said. *They were both fighter pilots. They died in the Battle of DC during the War of Eons.*

Leah let out a little gasp and flattened her ears. *I'm... I'm sorry. I didn't know.*

Silence. Then just *yeah.*

Leah looked off, rubbing her arm. *My father was military, too. He was killed on what should have been a peaceful mission.* She took a deep breath. *My mom died last year. I don't want to cop out and say I know how you feel but... I can at least say you're not alone.*

Several minutes passed before Zeke responded. A smell of baking... yams, Leah thought, permeated the air. Thoughtfulness. *I'm sorry.*

Yeah, well, you can't change the past, Leah muttered.

Except... we're in the past.

Leah sat up. *You know that for certain then?*

A man came to my cell, Zeke said. *He said today was April 3rd, 2029. But my last flight was yesterday, on May 10th, 2039.*

You're a pilot?

Air Corps reserves, Special Warfare Division, Zeke said. *I'm a test pilot.*

She twitched her whiskers. He was military then. Good. Ackerson would want him. *So you believe me when I say we time traveled.*

I'm... I'm not sure what I believe, he said. *But if we are in the past...* His voice drifted away. *Did someone come talk to you too?*

Yeah, Leah said. *A man named Ackerson.*

The scent of hot, burned bread nearly blinded Leah's senses and she reeled back. *S-something wrong?*

You know for sure that was Ackerson, Zeke said, his voice dripping with anger. A hot spice, like fried habaneros, stung her nose.

Leah winced. *Y-yeah.*

He's the man who killed my moms. Or had them killed anyway.

Leah flattened her ears. *...I'm sorry.*

What did he say to you?

Leah frowned. *He... he asked me to join his black ops team. Mage, specifically... Since I have magic.*

He knows about your magic?

53

...I guess so.

Would he know about mine?

Leah twitched her whiskers. *I don't know,* she admitted. *But maybe.*

Zeke was silent for quite some time. Leah sniffed. Hmm... Smelled like... like herbs being cut up. Strong, but contemplative. *We need to do what he asks, then.*

I... I think so, Leah said. *I don't see any other way out of this. I don't know what we'll do after that though.* She chewed her lip. *Today's date... does that mean we're in the War of Eons?*

We are, yeah.

Leah furrowed her brow. That meant Trecheon was still here. *I assume the Battle of DC hasn't happened yet then.*

It'll happen this July, Zeke said. *On the 14th.*

Leah twitched her tail. If the battle hadn't happened yet, then Trecheon still had his natural arms. Carter was still alive. And... *You said your moms died in the Battle of DC.*

Yes.

Then we need to get to DC, Leah said. *So we can save them.* And so she could save Trecheon, Neil, and Carter. That was why she was here, she decided. Why Matt brought her here, even if he didn't know it. To be a Defender. To save people. She'd prove it.

A smell of some kind of fruit pastry - kiwi, if she was reading that right - drifted under her nose. Curiosity. *You're willing to help me with my moms?*

Of course, Leah said. *I'm a Defender. That's my job.*

A pause. *What's a Defender?*

It's... good Draso, that'll be a whole worldview revision, Leah said. *Let all the other stuff I've told you settle first.*

Uh… Okay then. A soft smell of cookies flew about the room. *I'm going to try and sleep then, and hope they bring dinner soon. I suggest you do the same. Save your energy.*

Good idea. Leah wanted to bring up the social bond. Ask if Zeke was okay with it. If… if he'd be her friend. But she couldn't find the words. The smells faded.

She sighed. Thought Factory shutting down. She settled in as best she could on the wooden plank. It was only after she settled down that she realized she never got a straight answer about Zeke's possible connection to the Athánatos royalty. But… she did get some clues. He had two moms, and neither of them had Alexina's name. So either Alexina was using an alias, or he was adopted. Which meant Alexina might be dead after all.

Either way, she had already challenged his worldview enough. Best not to break him further. No point in worrying about it. They had bigger problems at the moment.

Trecheon had said that no one would do anything about Ackerson's corruption because Ackerson got stuff done. He used that to justify not turning him in because he hadn't believed there was a point.

But Leah would prove him wrong. No one wanted corruption in their military. The moment she could get to the right people, she'd turn Ackerson in. They'd take him down. All his black ops teams could be disbanded before they did horrible things… or before horrible things happened to them. That was the point of being a Defender.

And she'd prove Trecheon wrong. Prove them all wrong.

She was right. He'd see.

Leah fell asleep dreaming of all the ways Ackerson's rule of terror would end.

CHAPTER 07

MAGE

Leah curled up on bench, gripping her aching stomach and trying not to moan.

Three days. She had been here three days. At least as far as she could tell. But they hadn't brought her food, not even once, and everything seemed to blur together while she fought back intense hunger. She barely managed to convince herself to drink from the rusting sink – the water had a slight red tint to it – but if she was going to get through this, she did what she had to.

Now she wondered if it was even worth it. *Oh, just end this already…*

Zeke had stopped responding to her a day ago, taking the comfort of his voice and the gentle emotional smells with him. He had been her only solace. She had intended to use the time to explain what she knew about his heritage, but they ended up just talking about their lives instead. Bits and pieces. Nothing big. All of it hesitant. But it had been a reason to keep going.

Now she had none. Were they starving him too? Was he okay? What in Draso's name was with this military?

Good Draso, please just end this…

A metal scrapping indicated a distant door opening, but Leah couldn't muster the strength to stand. Even when her own door opened, she stayed where she was.

Ackerson walked in with two new guards, each carrying a rifle. Not that they needed to. Leah couldn't fight if she wanted. And that was the point.

"Up and at 'em," Ackerson said. "We have to talk."

Leah wanted to tell him to get stuffed. She wanted to just sit here and die and forget about it. But that would mean giving in, and she would not give Ackerson that satisfaction.

He. Would. Not. Win.

She forced herself to her feet, shoved aside the agony of starvation, and stared him right in the eye. But that was all she could muster.

He smirked. "More fight in you than I expected. Excellent. This way." He led her out of the cell.

They brought her to a room with white walls, a single window showing a blank hallway, and a simple table with chairs. Zeke was already there with armed guards on either side of him. He sat on one of the chairs, staring blankly at the table.

Leah twitched her whiskers. Just like she suspected. They had been starving him too. She tried reaching out to him. *Zeke?*

He glanced up, but didn't respond. No smells either. She frowned, but he managed to offer her a tiny smile.

She frowned, relief and joy at his smile warring with worry for his state of being. *Draso's mercy, you look how I feel.*

Tell me about it, he managed.

Ackerson forced her to sit in a chair next to Zeke, then he took a chair opposite them. Another human walked in carrying a tray full of food – hot, creamy soup, a loaded salad with egg, bacon, chicken, and a myriad of veggies, swimming in a fatty dressing, several hot buttered rolls, and a thick steak, lathered in garlic aioli and spices. Leah stared, her mouth watering.

The human placed it in front of Ackerson. He picked up a roll and pulled it apart slowly. He dipped it in the soup and stuffed it in his mouth, savoring each bite. "Sorry about that. I was in a meeting and missed lunch."

Zeke groaned in her mind. *Cliché movie villain.* But as much as Leah didn't like to admit it, it was effective.

"Now," Ackerson said, his mouth still full. "First off, I want to apologize for leaving you both sitting there for so long."

Zeke snapped his head up, glaring, teeth bared. "You want to *apologize* for nearly *starving us to death,* while you stuff buttered rolls in your mouth like a friggin' supervillain? Do you think we'd believe that?"

Ackerson jammed a piece of steak in his mouth, but didn't rise to Zeke's accusation. "Yes, apologize." He spoke with his mouth full, spewing bits of aioli everywhere. "You both are just so far off the radar, I'm afraid everyone just forgot about you. But then Mage's leader showed up this morning, and I remembered I had a reason for bringing him here. Two reasons, I suppose." He swallowed his steak and smiled at them.

Zeke looked like he wanted to rip Ackerson's spine out, and honestly, Leah sympathized. But it wouldn't do to anger him. *Think about your moms, Zeke.*

Zeke's face softened. He glanced off, ears flat.

"Now that I have your attention," Ackerson said. "As you can see, the gears of war demand our full attention. We simply don't have the time or resources to focus on two renegade zyfaunos shirking their duties. However, if you join me and make yourself useful, we'll be much more accommodating."

The message couldn't be clearer. Declining his offer meant starving to death in the cells. Joining him was the only way out.

Trecheon had really believed that the military wouldn't want this man gone? Just wait until she found the right official. Ackerson would hang by his metaphorical entrails if Leah had anything to say about it. She closed her eyes tight a moment and mustered as much strength and power as she could to her words.

"I accept." Not as strong as she wanted, but better than a stutter. She glanced at Zeke.

Zeke waved a hand. "Sure, I guess. I do too."

"Excellent!" He motioned to one of the guards and whispered to him. The guard nodded and left. "Let me get you outfitted and fed, and I'll introduce you to your team leader."

Four new figures, all human, walked in the room soon after the guard left. Two carried trays with the same meal Ackerson was enjoying, and two wore full medical PPE carrying trays with syringes and bottles. A single silver pill sat in a dish in the center of each tray.

Leah leaned back in her chair.

Zeke snarled and glared at Ackerson. *"No.* You are *not* fitting us with those. That program was ended before the war even started. It's *illegal."*

"The war gave us some loopholes," Ackerson said. "And unless you want me to eat all this food myself and drop you back in your cells--"

"You little--"

ZEKE. Leah stared at him.

Zeke stopped and stared back. The smell of rotting eggs hit her nose, overpowering the real food in the room. Anger. Confusion. He wrinkled his snout. "Leah, he wants to put *trackers* on us. *In* us, even. It's placed under the skin, at the base of the skull."

Leah perked her ears in surprise. She turned to Ackerson. "What?"

59

Ackerson waved a hand. "The idea was to keep track of troops and better direct them in battle," he said. "But it had some… unpleasant side effects. About 2% of recipients died for various reasons from poisoning to spine damage. And there was the whole hullaballoo about 'privacy' and 'invasiveness' and whatnot." He leaned on his hands. "But desperate times, and all that."

Leah's fur bristled. That wasn't good. But… she was a Defender. She could get them off-world. Get the trackers out. There'd be nothing Ackerson could do about it. They'd just have to put up with it for now.

"We'll do it," Leah said with more confidence than she felt.

"Leah!" Zeke shouted. "You can't speak for us both like that!"

Leah lowered her gaze at him. *If we don't do this, we'll be thrown back in those cells to die. We both know it.*

Zeke frowned. He opened his mouth like he wanted to protest, but then sighed and shook his head. "Okay. Fine. Go ahead." He pointed at Ackerson. "But you better take these out after the war, or the brass will hear about this."

Ackerson raised one eyebrow and smiled. "Have some *faith."* The two doctors moved behind Leah and Zeke.

Leah's doctor walked behind her. "Take off your jacket, please." Leah did so. The doctor rubbed a gloved finger near the base of her skull. "I'll insert it here. You won't feel a thing." He shaved a little fur, rubbed the area with what was probably alcohol or some other antiseptic, and injected something that made Leah feel completely numb in the area. While Leah couldn't feel anymore, she could watch Zeke's doctor perform the same motions. A little shave, a rub, an injection… then a tiny incision and the little oblong silver object, about the size of a pain pill, was inserted under the skin. Deep. The doctor pulsed a laser over the incision and sealed it instantly. It was like it was never different, aside from the missing fur.

Leah tried not to shiver.

The other two humans then dropped plates of food in front of her and Zeke. Leah's stomach growled and ached more than ever, but she ate her food slowly. She didn't want to make herself sick, but she also didn't want to give Ackerson any sort of smug satisfaction.

Zeke didn't have any such qualms and he shoveled food in his mouth, hardly stopping to chew.

Ackerson nodded to two of the guards, who walked over to Leah and Zeke and dropped a bag by each of them. Leah glanced in. Inside was her effects - Gem, hip holster, staff, and her Defender pendant.

"While you two indulge," Ackerson said. "I'll go get your team leader. Might as well get acquainted while you're relaxed. Then we'll talk about your first mission." As if anything about this situation made Leah relaxed. He touched a finger to his nose. "Best not to mention anything about your minor surgeries here. Wouldn't want to worry him." He left the room with the doctors and servers. The armed guards stayed put.

Leah paused her eating and put on her effects, sliding the holster on and slinging her pendant around her neck, though she left her jacket off. Didn't want to get food on it. Might as well look presentable to this Mage leader. Maybe she'd even get him on her side. Trecheon said that pretty much all of Ackerson's teams eventually turned on him.

Just as she sat down, Ackerson returned with a quilar… and Leah nearly dropped her fork.

Wearing battered Earth military fatigues, with dusty, pure white quills, striking green eyes, and a golden Defender pendant around his neck, was a missing-thought-dead Golden Guardian. Matt's father.

Jaden Azure of the Defenders.

CHAPTER 08

JADEN AZURE

Jaden entered the room, his ears pasted back. Everything felt... dull. Muted. Broken. *Move through the motions, do what you're told, don't question anything.* Maybe somewhere down the line he could find purpose again.

Not likely though. Not on Earth. Not in this military where the only way to get things done is to use corruption like Ackerson did.

Not when the heroes were often just as bad as the villains.

Sometimes Jaden wondered if *he* was one of the villains. What an end for a Golden Guardian. All because he had decided to settle on Earth and raise a family. All because some vicious tribe off the coast decided to ravage and kill a rival village. His settlement.

Curse the damn Omnirs. Curse Theron for manipulating them.

...Curse himself for being unable to let it go.

But who could blame him? Jaden had lost everything that day – his wife, his kids, his sister-in-law, his best friend and partner, his Guardian A.I... his home, both the one on Earth and the one on Zyearth.

His Guardian partner, Dyne, had left behind an X-Zero, the one vehicle on the planet that had the capability to get him home to Zyearth. But... it required Gem shards or a really powerful Gem, like a Black Bound Gem. Jaden had neither. The radio also didn't work – it looked like it had been smashed to pieces. Likely by one of the invading Omnir. He had no way to get home. No way to go back to his old life.

All he could do was move through the motions.

At least under Ackerson he had had some control. Jaden's team was just him and two others. Both mages. Both zyfaunos he could trust. And he didn't think Ackerson could possibly dump more on him. After all, the only natural mages on Earth were the Athánatos, all confined to the safety of the Vanishing Island.

Or the prison, considering what Theron was pulling on them. Lightning and air, what he wouldn't give for the full strength of the Defenders. They'd end him immediately.

And Ackerson too.

Jaden's stomach rolled when Ackerson had told him he had new members for him. He could only imagine what kind of corrupted magic users Ackerson had acquired. He expected cocky, battle-hardened soldiers.

But the two zyfaunos sitting in chairs, looking scared, weary, and angry, were definitely not what he expected.

They both looked very young. The gray and white cat in a plain white shirt was probably no more than twenty. She stared, wide eyed, as if she had never seen a quilar in her life, ears flat against her head. The other looked a little older but--

Wait.

63

His ears. Green interior. Bent back. Those weren't standard quilar ears.

Jaden's whole body buzzed. That... was an Athánatos. A *royal* Athánatos.

His ears rang. *How?* What did that mean for Athánatos? The urgent need to reach out to his teammates clawed at his chest.

"Glad you could join us," Ackerson said. Jaden forced his urgency down. Get through this first. Follow the motions. Questions could come later, without Ackerson hovering over them. Ackerson turned to the two zyfaunos. "This is Jaden, leader of Mage." The Athánatos immediately stiffened up. Jaden flicked an ear back. Ackerson continued. "Jaden, meet your newest members. This is Zeke and, uh. Never caught your name, sweetheart."

"Leah," the cat said. She stood, still staring at Jaden. Something glinted around her neck.

A Defender pendant.

Shock rippled through Jaden's body. A *Defender pendant.* He stared, his heart thumping. Water around him, how--

"Tel rasta separit vasa," Leah said suddenly.

"What?" Ackerson spat. Leah slapped her hands over her mouth. Ackerson turned to Jaden. "What the hell was *that?"*

Jaden thought hard, trying to force down his own panic. "Old, uh, old zyfaunos saying."

Ackerson narrowed his eyes. "Old zyfaunos... or old Zyearthling?"

The Athánatos, Zeke, turned and raised an eyebrow at Leah. She wrinkled her snout but didn't speak.

Jaden shrugged, trying to act casual. "Both, I suppose."

"Hmm," Ackerson relaxed a little. He turned to Leah. "What's it mean?"

"Ah..." Leah flattened her ears a moment. Her fur puffed up. "I-It means 'peace be with you.'"

64

Jaden's ear twitched and he wrinkled his snout, frowning. Weak response. Some soldier. She'd be useless for getting him home. He had to hope she had a superior officer somewhere.

Ackerson raised an eyebrow. "Really?"

"E-Essentially," Leah said. "In spirit anyway. The direct translation might d-differ a bit though."

Ackerson eyed her a little longer, but didn't question her further. "Well. I suppose that means you'll work well together then." He gestured toward the table. "Sit down. We've got a lot to discuss."

Jaden sat. He purposefully chose to sit next to Leah, trying to size her up.

Clearly a rookie. A Defender-Z, by the color of her pendant's Gem. Base level. Black, gray, and white uniform, meaning she was a healer. Perhaps just out of Academy. Probably as young as she looked. Also shaking with anxiety. He flattened his ears. A healer and a DZ. She wouldn't be much help. Good Draso, why were the Defenders bringing rookies here?

The green band on her pendant caught his eye. Not just any healer.

A healer-S.

The kind of healer who could see disease and injury in a body without activating her magic.

His mind swirled with memories of his best friend and partner, Dyne Gildspine. Also a healer-S. The only other healer-S he had ever met in his life. But he had been nothing like this feline was. He was brave. Strong. Powerful. He'd have shaken down Ackerson and made him wish he'd never been born. He would never have let himself be involved in something like this.

His chest ached. What he wouldn't give to have Dyne back by his side again. He needed another Guardian.

He scooted a little farther from her. She frowned and looked away. A twinge of guilt stung for a moment. But only a moment. Because one thing was certain. Leah on Earth meant that the Defenders were also on Earth.

65

He could go home.

Screw Ackerson. Screw this stupid war, this backwater planet, this hell he had been living since the Sol Genocide. None of it mattered anymore.

He could finally *go home*.

CHAPTER 09

THE MISSING ATHÁNATOS

Zeke forced himself to stay calm. Keep his emotions under control. But inside he was screaming.

Mage. The name "Mage" was in his moms' post-mortem files. One of only a few things he could make out, despite Andre's best efforts to crack them. So much of it had been locked down.

But Mage… Ackerson… both names stood out multiple times in the file. These people killed his parents. Perhaps this very quilar.

And Leah. She clearly knew this Jaden by her reaction. Even now she stared at him like she was seeing a ghost. Hell, he stared at her too, his deep green eyes standing out against pure white fur. Did they know each other? Did Leah know what Mage was?

And what the hell was a Zyearthling?

Leah gave him a sideways glance. *That's the worldview shock I'm trying to avoid with you right now,* she said.

Zeke narrowed his eyes, but said nothing more.

Regardless, this team was clearly his ticket to finding his moms. Like it or not, he had to stick it out.

Ackerson snapped at a nearby guard, who walked to the group and dropped folders in front of each of them. Ackerson opened his own, wet his fingers with his tongue, then pulled out a paper. He slid it on the table so everyone could see.

An East Asian gentleman with glasses, tidy hair, and neatly-trimmed facial hair smiled up at them.

"Tao Ying," Ackerson said. "Visiting dignitary from China. As you all know, China has been trying to broker an alliance with us since the war started." He grunted. "Despite the fact that it was China who started the whole problem by drilling illegally in Alaska and bombing Japan for good measure." He pointed a finger at the photo. "Tao is their latest attempt. Right now, he's in negotiations for the Chinese drillers we picked up in Alaska, trying to get them back. We've been asked to take him out. But discreetly. No evidence left behind." He nodded to Jaden. "You know what that means. Just like at Atlas."

Jaden crossed his arms, but nodded.

"He's been making very public appearances in Asgard of all places," Ackerson shook his head. "Why he'd want to be in Montana this time of year and why he thinks he'll get anywhere politically while he's there is beyond me, but regardless, he's staying in the Governor's Mansion. There's some talk that the illustrious Governor Foxworthy may be taking bribes from China. Whether he is or not isn't our business though. That's IntelSec's beat. But, as you can imagine, the place is quite locked down. No one gets in or out, so the reporters are hanging around outside the compound. A *lot* of reporters. Cameras everywhere, mics everywhere, the whole shebang. The place reeks of them."

"With all due respect, *sir*," Zeke said, unable to hide his annoyance. "How are we supposed to take him out discreetly with that many eyes on him?"

Jaden scoffed. "That part is easy. Just get me close." He turned to Ackerson. "I'm more concerned with how we're getting in there."

"I have you all set up as security detail," Ackerson said. "It was easy enough to get you fake backgrounds--"

"What the hell does that *mean?*" Zeke said to Jaden. Jaden and Ackerson looked up. "What good would it do to get this guy close to Tao? Any way you shake it, killing him is going to leave evidence. *Especially* if there's surveillance everywhere."

Jaden lifted a hand and literal ice crystals formed in the air around him. "Trust me. I've got this."

Zeke stared, his spine buzzing. Magic. Actual real *magic.* Just like Leah had said. How?

A smell of perfectly cooked steak entered his nose. Smug. *Told you so.* He glanced at her, and she sunk down. *S-sorry.*

Zeke looked away.

Ackerson's voice devolved into strategies and possible trip-ups as he dove into the mission. But Zeke hardly heard a word until Ackerson slapped the table.

"Alright then, Mage," Ackerson said. "Move out. You have an eight-day window." He turned to Jaden. "Keep the rest of your team out of sight. They stand out too much."

Jaden gave a noncommittal shrug.

Zeke's body buzzed. The rest of them. More of Ackerson's. More... more mages.

Ackerson waved a hand. "Like usual, I'll supply you with basic gear, but you're responsible for getting yourselves there. No connections. Get moving." The man stood. "I didn't get a chance to acquaint you all, what with the pussy-cat speaking in tongues, but I'm sure you'll have a nice chat on the way to Asgard. Take care." He eyed Zeke and Leah. "And watch yourselves."

Zeke gritted his teeth. That little asshole.

Jaden stood and motioned to Zeke and Leah. The guards handed everyone a backpack made of military-grade serge and patterned with jungle camo. Jaden nodded and left. Leah followed without question. Zeke begrudgingly stood and followed too.

The moment they were clear of the building, Jaden led them to an abandoned park full of mangled trees and disused paths and turned to Leah and Zeke.

"Now--"

Zeke cut him off. "What do you know about Estelle and Allanah Brightclaw?"

Jaden raised an eyebrow. "Pardon?"

"The Brightclaws," Zeke said. His voice shook. "Fighter pilots, special forces. What do you know about them?"

Jaden narrowed his eyes. "Why do you care?"

Zeke growled. "So you know them!"

Jaden held up his hands. "I don't, I assure you. I'm just curious why an Athánatos quilar is interested in a couple of mainlanders."

"I don't even know what an Athánatos *is,*" Zeke snarled. "I only heard the term from Leah for the first time three days ago."

Jaden raised both eyebrows and flattened his ears. "How do you not know what you are? Didn't your parents say anything?"

"No!" Zeke shouted. "Assuming they even knew anything. I'm adopted."

Jaden's eyes grew wide. "Really?"

"Yes!" Zeke said. "Why the hell would I lie about that?"

Jaden wrinkled his snout. "That's... something's very wrong with that. How did an Athánatos get on the mainland?" He shook his head. "You know what? Never mind. I don't care right now." He turned to Leah.

Leah sunk down. "Guardian Azure," she said quietly. "If I may ask, how do *you* know what an Athánatos is?"

Jaden perked both ears, his eyes wide. "The real question is how do *you?* The Defenders know nothing of Athánatos."

Leah flicked her gray ears back. "I... I don't..."

Jaden shook his head. "No, you wouldn't. You're just a DZ."

Zeke glanced at her. *The hell is a DZ?*

Worldviews, Leah responded, with the smell of... lime and spaghetti. Confusion. Zeke flicked an ear back. He was getting tired of this.

Jaden snorted. "It's not important. Getting home is. Take me to your superior officer."

"You are *not* leaving me hanging on this," Zeke snapped. "You--"

A snowball smacked him in the face, knocking his glasses to the ground. Zeke shook his head free of snow and glared at Jaden.

Jaden glared back. Sharp ice spikes lined his fur and arms, and ice and snow swirled about him in a tight tornado. He spoke through gritted teeth. "Wait your turn."

Zeke stepped back, holding his hands up. He nearly called for Archángeli, when Leah stepped between them, held a hand out and a shimmer of a shield formed in front of him.

"Stop, *please.*"

"That's not how you speak to a Guardian," Jaden snapped at her.

"And that's not how you treat an ally," Leah said, though she clapped her hands over her mouth. "I-I mean--"

Jaden furrowed his brow, his quills standing on end. "You're a Defender. You clearly know my name."

Leah nodded. "Jaden Azure, Golden Guardian of the Defenders."

Zeke blanked. *What--*

World--

71

Worldviews, I get it, Zeke said. *We need to have a conversation about this sooner than later.*

Jaden stalled a moment, but snorted. "If you know who I am, then you'll know I have only one demand of you." He tensed up, ears flat, eyes glassy almost to the point of tears. "Please... take me home."

HOME

Jaden shook with excitement as he waited for Leah's response. Home. It had been all he could think of during his isolation on Earth. He thought he'd never see it again. But now... now he could. He could see his friends. He could have lunch with his brother Walt. Walk the gardens with Jaymes. Train again with Larissa. Maybe Lance would still be Master Guardian. Surely they had replaced the Golden Guardians by now, but perhaps he could still be one, or at least a consultant for the current pair. He'd have a proper place again, a purpose. Oh, it was so close, he just needed to get his wife and--

"I, uh..." Leah said. "I can't do that."

Every hope shattered in an instant. "What?"

"I can't," Leah said. She rubbed her arm. "...Honestly, I don't know if I'll be able to get home myself."

"What?" Jaden couldn't believe his ears. "Why? How are you even here then?"

"I… I don't know if you'll believe me," Leah said.

"You know what?" Zeke said suddenly. "I'm kind of sick of you saying that. What the hell does that even mean? What does he mean by home? I want answers, damnit!"

But Jaden snapped. "I could ask you that same thing."

Zeke lowered his gaze. "What does that mean?"

"You're seriously telling me you don't know what an Athánatos is?" Jaden said. "You *are* one. What are you doing on the mainland? Why are you in the military? What the hell is Theron planning *now?"*

Zeke splayed his ears. "Who the hell is Theron?"

"Stop!" Leah said. "Just stop fighting. I'll explain all I know, okay? Like it or not, we're stuck together, so we might as well get used to it." She took a deep breath. "Guardian Azure, I'll start with you."

Zeke flicked his tail and formed fists. "You have a whole lot more explaining to do to me, Leah."

Leah winced. "I-I know, but Guardian Azure is more likely to understand it," she said. "I'll explain what I know, and try to fill you in. Okay?"

Zeke crossed his arms, but didn't protest further.

Jaden crossed his arms too and met Leah's gaze. "Talk."

"Zeke and I aren't from this time," Leah said. "We accidentally formed a social bond with our focus jewels and time traveled."

Jaden blinked at her. Any shred of hope he had clung to flew away instantly. He rubbed his forehead. "You really expect me to believe that."

Zeke jerked a thumb at him. "I thought you said he'd be more likely to understand."

Leah frowned at Zeke, then turned back to Jaden. "I-I know it sounds impossible, and frankly I would have thought that too, except that we've already seen the effects of it once when one of our c-current Golden Guardians accidentally bonded his Gem with--."

74

"Jewel bonds don't happen by accident," Jaden said. "Hell, they don't happen at *all*. We stopped that practice generations ago. They're *dangerous*."

"It can and I-I can prove it," Leah said. She turned to Zeke. "Social bonds allow for telepathic speech between the bonded. Zeke isn't from Zyearth." She paused and took several breaths. "A-Ask him a question and I'll give him the answer telepathically."

Jaden crossed his arms. This was a waste of time. But… "Fine." He turned to Zeke. "Give me the full name of Larissa's spouse." Let's see them get that one.

Zeke turned to Leah. They were silent a moment, then Zeke turned back to him. "Viriandia Hobbes. Head of the weapons department." He turned to Leah with an eyebrow raised. "What the hell military are you talking about? Our head is a man and he's definitely not named Hobbes."

But Jaden hardly heard him. His jaw dropped. "How did…?"

"You can drill me more if you want," Leah said.

"But… that…" Jaden gritted his teeth. "That still doesn't explain this supposed time travel."

"Look, I don't get it either," Zeke said. "But I'm Air Corps. I logged a flight just yesterday. May 10th, 2039. Today is--"

"It's 2029 by the Earth calendar," Jaden said. "And that's just some random date. You can't possibly prove it."

"I *can*," Leah said. She pulled up her pendant and pressed her thumb to the back of it. The dragon's eyes lit up and projected a holographic log.

Zeke stepped back. "Whoa, what the hell?"

Jaden squinted at the log. It listed major activity for the last several days with dates. Early dates were Zyearth dates, starting with graduation and moving to mission planning - training, packing, space flights, and mission goals. The last few logs were in Earth dates though… the last being…

"May 11ᵗʰ, 2039," Jaden read aloud. "Left… Left Sol Island for the mainland." He met her eyes, his chest aching. "Why were you on Sol?"

"Because a rip in the Athánatos Veil leads to Sol," Leah said. "The Defenders are here to help restore Athánatos after our Golden Guardians took down Theron and restored the Shadow Cast." She flicked an ear back. "Or… at least they will be here to do that. I'm a part of that team, as a historian."

Jaden stared at the ground. The Defenders took down Theron, just as he had known they could.

And they had replaced the Golden Guardians. He knew they would. He *expected* it. But the moment she said it, a wave of sorrow washed over him.

Zyearth had moved on without him. The Defenders had moved on without him.

Time had moved on without him. And forgotten him.

He wasn't sure he could face it.

Leah twitched her whiskers and leaned forward. "Guardian Azure?"

Jaden looked up. "I don't want to know."

Leah flicked her tail. "What?"

"I don't want to know what happened," he said. "Nothing about Zyearth. Or the Defenders." He pressed his eyes shut. "Especially the Guardians. Not now. Maybe… maybe not ever."

Leah's ears splayed. "But the Guardians--"

"I don't want to know," Jaden said. "It won't help us survive this war." And it'd only serve to remind Jaden that the Zyearth he'd return to wasn't the one he had left. That life really was lost. God, it had been too long. He froze that Zyearth in time and didn't let it go. That was careless.

Zeke crossed his arms. "What about me? I still don't--"

"If you can really speak telepathically, talk about it that way," Jaden said. "Because I don't want to hear it. Not another word." He rubbed his temple. "Why are you even here? How'd you get involved with Ackerson?"

Leah exchanged a look with Zeke. He shrugged. Leah rubbed her arm. "It was kind of by accident."

"That's a hell of an accident," Jaden snarled.

Leah winced and pressed her lips into a thin line. "Guardian Azure... Even if we got here by accident, we've got a purpose. Zeke's parents are going to be killed in a massive battle in July, in... DC?" She turned to Zeke for confirmation. He nodded. "That's our ultimate goal. We need to get to them and save them." She took a deep breath. "And if you can wait eight years... I can get you home."

Zeke gawked. "Do you really think we'll have to live out eight years to get back to our own time?"

"I don't know," Leah said. "But that's the best I can promise right now."

Jaden took a deep breath. Go through the motions. Survive. Maybe there was still something to hope for. Athánatos perhaps. If the Defenders really did clean it out, then that was a victory.

Though it wasn't home.

He had no home now.

He shoved aside all thoughts. Go through the motions.

"Good enough," he said. "Follow me."

ALONE

Zeke followed Jaden down the empty streets of El Dorado through the auto district. It felt so empty. Most shops were closed up. The cafés and donut shops had boards over the windows. No one was around. Trash everywhere. The smell of diesel mixed with the smell of gunpowder and smoking factories. So very different from the district he left behind.

He hoped he'd make it back. Andre would be worried sick.

Good Draso, what the hell was he doing?

A gentle smell of… of crème brulé wafted under his nose. *Zeke?*

Zeke pressed his eyes shut. *I keep hoping that this thought-sharing thing was just a hallucination.*

A long hesitation, almost shameful. *Sorry,* Leah said. *I'll shut up.*

Wait, Zeke said. *Do you know this guy?*

Hesitation again. *I know of him,* Leah said.

You called him a… a "Golden Guardian."

That's his rank in our military, Leah said. *The Defenders.*

Zeke pressed his lips together. *That's the worldview shattering you're trying to avoid with me.*

Y-yes, Leah said. She took a deep breath. *When we have a moment of quiet, I'll try my best to explain.*

See that you do, Zeke said, though quietly he thought she had done a terrible job explaining everything so far. *So who is this Jaden guy?*

More hesitation. The smell of overripe bananas – bruised. Hurt. But it vanished quickly. *Jaden is a top-ranking officer in the Defenders,* Leah said. *Third highest rank in the whole military. But he vanished almost sixty years ago in a big genocide that killed two tribes of Earth natives. The Defenders thought Jaden was dead so… they never looked for him.*

Zeke frowned. No wonder Jaden was so bitter.

Wait. *What do you mean, "Earth natives"?* Zeke asked. *You act as if you're from another planet.*

Leah watched him, ears flat. *We are.*

Zeke stared, wide-eyed. "What?"

"Here," Jaden said, before Leah got a chance to respond. They stopped in one of the big warehouse garages. Jaden unlocked the sliding door and lifted it. A battered, last-gen Humvee stood in the garage. Jaden sighed and turned to Zeke and Leah. "If you're actually going to go through with this, then we need to get to DC by July. And I guess we'll need to find a way to survive a battle so big it has a name." He licked his lips. "That'll be fun." He slipped his backpack off and dug out fresh military fatigues. "In the meantime, we need to do our job and survive. July is a long ways away. Going AWOL now would just get the military police after us, and there's rumors that they're enacting the execution-for-desertion law, and I don't want to test that."

Zeke dropped his jaw in horror. "They *aren't.*"

"They are," Jaden said. "This is a very unpopular war. Citizens aren't used to a wartime life. They're scared, angry, and upset. That, coupled with the fact that we haven't been able to pierce the Desert Wall means every soldier on the field is worried they'll become death fodder. And with good reason, considering they've thrown literally everything at it with no effect. So soldiers are deserting left and right. Thousands upon thousands of them."

"Where do they plan to *go?*" Zeke asked. "Canada shut its borders and Mexico is shooting anyone who steps foot on their soil."

Jaden paused for a long time, staring into the distance as if he was somewhere else, but then shrugged. "I've heard a few have just lost themselves in the woods near Canada's border, hoping they'll get arrested. Better to spend your time in Canada's jails than on the front lines."

"Geez," Leah said.

Zeke was suddenly glad that he managed to escape this during his actual AWOL stint. Probably because he was just a recruit in training at the time. Good Draso.

Jaden slipped his old jacket off and donned the new one. "Get dressed, soldiers. This old Humvee will take us to Montana, but we'll get stopped every ten miles if we aren't in uniform. Leah, do you know how to salute?"

Leah twisted an ear. "Is it different here then?"

Zeke pressed his lips together. Different here. Maybe she was from another planet.

Jaden nodded. He snapped a sharp salute. "You try it."

It took her a couple of tries to get it right, but soon Jaden was satisfied. Zeke split from the group and dressed in his new fatigues and dog tags. He glanced at the tag. Zeke was now under the name Mark Green.

I'm Joan Smith, Leah said.

Zeke pressed his eyes closed and shut her out. Much as he might have questions about this supposed other planet or the Athánatos or this Theron guy, he couldn't focus on that. His moms were more important. He didn't need Leah getting in the way of that focus. Besides, she'd end up being like every other girl he'd met. She'd *want* something and he didn't want to give it.

A smell of... of collapsed souffle entered his nose. Sadness. Zeke flattened his ears.

"Get in, you two," Jaden said, climbing into the driver's seat. "Memorize each other's fake names, but try not to use them unless you have to. You're bound to get it wrong and blow our cover. Understood?" He pointed to Zeke. "You know how to drive this thing?"

"Sure." Zeke eyed the Humvee. "This thing street legal?"

"It is now," Jaden said. "I'll take the first stint out of town. You can take over in a few hours."

Leah climbed into the vehicle behind Jaden. She wouldn't meet Zeke's eyes.

Zeke frowned. Had she heard his thoughts about Leah getting in the way? Or about her wanting something? That... actually, he still didn't care. He couldn't afford to care. Focus on the moment. Focus on his moms.

The collapsed souffle smell returned. He pushed it hard from his mind.

As Jaden drove along through the near-empty streets out of town, the scars of war became even more evident. Homeless families everywhere, scattered throughout the town. Worn down roads. Rations lines. Though somehow the casinos on the beach were still allowed to run. He shook his head. Bread and circuses. Gross.

Leah stared at the floor as they drove along.

Zeke flicked his ears back, guilt biting at him. He forced himself to reach to her. *Leah... I'm sorry.*

You're not really, Leah said, not lifting her eyes. *I can feel it when you speak. But I appreciate you trying, I guess.*

Zeke frowned. *I... I realize this might not be the best time, but, I have to ask... Can we, um... break this social jewel bond thing?*

Leah paused for a long time.

Zeke shifted. *Leah?*

No, Leah said. *But…if… if we ignore it, it'll probably fade until it's useless.* She turned away from him completely now and curled up in her seat. "I'm going to try and get some sleep."

"Might be a good idea," Jaden said. "We've got a long trip ahead of us."

Zeke flicked his tail. He tried poking into Leah's mind again, searching for words, for smells, anything, but he came up short. He sighed. That was probably for the best anyway. The last thing he wanted was a forced relationship. He huddled up on his seat and went to sleep.

It took them nearly four days to get to Montana with all the military checkpoints. More than a few soldiers kept them extra-long for questioning – likely because they were a pack of zyfaunos with high security orders. Humans were always at the top of the pecking order in the army. Classic xenophobia, keeping the minorities at the bottom of the back. Zeke knew that firsthand. Thankfully, though, he could use that knowledge to his advantage and keep his head down and avoid trouble. Don't question things, follow the motions.

Leah had tried time and time again to get Jaden to listen to her talk about what he had missed being gone. But Jaden shut her down every time, getting more and more angry, and turning that anger on her.

By the third day, Leah wouldn't speak at all.

The night before they entered Asgard, Jaden explained their plan in great detail. He laid out a map of the Governor's Mansion. Leah looked over the map, but said nothing.

"From everything I've been hearing on the official channels," Jaden said. "The drill workers Tao is trying to negotiate the release of are being held in Montana. No one is quite sure why – though the rumors suggest Governor

Foxworthy actually bid for them to stay there. He's playing some political game that we know nothing about."

Zeke narrowed his gaze. "He's making himself a big target then."

"Let's hope we aren't called on to deal with that particular mess," Jaden said. He pointed to the map. "Tomorrow Tao is visiting a local theater for some big to-do with Foxworthy and the First Lady."

Zeke scoffed. "People were literally starving during this war, and they're going out to the *theater?*"

Jaden shrugged. "Whims of the rich. Either way, they'll be heading out at about 2PM. We need to be positioned as guards near the gate's exit. I've already confirmed with security detail that we're expected to be there an hour before and relieve the current group. That'll get me close enough."

Zeke eyed him. "So how are you planning on taking this guy out anyway? Just shoot an icicle through his heart?"

Jaden lowered his gaze. "I'm going to freeze his brain."

Leah shuddered, though said nothing.

"It's painless, or so I'm told," Jaden said.

Zeke flattened his ears. "That won't leave any evidence?"

"The brain will defrost by the time they do an autopsy," Jaden said. "And literally no one will suspect a frozen brain, even if they see the evidence for it. It's not possible without magic. They'll write it off."

Zeke pursed his lips. "What about getaway? Or are we expected to stay behind for questioning? You know they'll question everyone there. Us especially, since we're new and we're zyfaunos."

"Being new will probably give us an advantage, actually," Jaden said. "We won't be familiar with the goings on, we won't know anything about the political dealings, or at least that's how they'll see it. Plus, no one thinks zyfaunos are intelligent enough to pull this kind of thing off."

"Guardian Azure," Leah said, her voice quiet and small. It was the first thing she had said in more than twenty-four hours. "…What about our focus jewels?"

"That's always the hard one, isn't it?" Jaden said. "I'll have no choice but to have mine, but I think we'll have to leave yours in the Humvee."

The inside of Leah's ears paled, her eyes widened, and a sharp smell of burning bread entered Zeke's nose. Panic. "Sir, I can't leave it *here*. What if they *find* it?"

Jaden pulled at a panel in the center of the vehicle. A door opened up, revealing a small, heavy duty safe. "Put it here. This panel locks and is basically invisible unless I open it. It'll be safe. I can pass mine off as a lucky paperweight – I've been doing it for years. No one expects a lowly zyfaunos soldier to have something of actual value, and Gems act like glass under their microscopes. Earth technology has no hope in hell to understand its power. But if both of us have one, that'll look suspicious."

Leah flicked both ears back, a smell of hot oil wafting about. Hesitation. But she nodded. She placed the jewel in the box. Jaden locked it up and closed the hidden compartment.

Immediately all the smells felt… muffled. Zeke shook himself, his spines on end. That was weird.

Zeke rubbed the bracelet that held the Ei-Ei jewels, as Leah had named them.

Jaden eyed Zeke, then dropped his gaze to Zeke's bracelet.

Zeke glared at him. "You're not taking these."

"I don't think I need to," Jaden said. "You aren't bound to them. Lucky, honestly, considering this supposed social bond with Leah. Not being bound means your social bond isn't strong. You might escape the worst of the dangers."

Leah frowned. "Social bonds aren't--"

"Don't," Jaden said. "Social bonds were banned for a *reason.* They aren't safe. Especially if they happened on accident, I imagine. There's no control." He turned to Zeke. "I don't think they'll do anything with your bracelet, but you might want to turn it inside out. Draw less attention."

Zeke frowned but did as he was told.

"This isn't going to be a difficult job," Jaden said. "Take out the target, get through questioning, carry out the rest of our watch while we wait for new orders." He eyed them both. "I hope you're up for it."

Zeke responded with a quick salute. Leah followed suit, with a sweeping fist across the chest. But then she frowned and saluted normally instead.

"Good," Jaden said. He passed out blankets, pillows, and some water. "We'll head out tomorrow morning. Everyone get some sleep." He stepped out of the vehicle into the cold snow.

Zeke frowned. "Where the hell are you going?"

"None of your business," Jaden said. "Go to sleep." He shut the door.

Zeke sighed. Asshole. He settled into his seat.

Tomorrow they'd kill a visiting dignitary. Up close. He never expected to do that in the military. It was one of the reasons why he wanted to be a fighter pilot. You didn't have to see the people you had to kill.

"Zeke?" Leah whispered. Zeke looked over. Leah was huddled up on her chair, staring at the floor.

He frowned. Some strange part of him missed the telepathic communication. Though he shoved the idea aside. "Yeah?"

"Have… have you ever killed anyone?"

Good god, that was a loaded question. "Once. And it wasn't something I expected to do. I was flying an exercise with a teammate and an unexpected UFO showed up. Probably trying to steal data. I was told to shoot it down.*"* He fought a shudder. "So I did."

A long pause. "…How did you feel afterwards?"

Zeke breathed deeply. Honestly, he had never spent time thinking about it. In the moment he had been fighting to save Andre's life. Afterwards, he spent weeks recovering from a severely damaged arm and third-degree burns on his feet. In his mind, that invading pilot was just a target to eliminate.

But now that he thought about it, they weren't. They were a person. Zeke didn't know their gender. What country they came from. Whether they were acting alone, as their supposed allies said, or whether they were following orders. Hell, Zeke didn't even know their species.

Did they feel pain? Or was it over so fast they felt nothing? Did they believe in any kind of afterlife? Did they truly think what they were doing was right? Were they even allowed to have such thoughts?

Good Draso, Zeke didn't know anything about a living, sentient being that he killed. And he hadn't even thought about it until now. His eyes and chest burned.

"Zeke?"

"I... honestly, I can't... I don't have words for it." He shook his head. "You'll just have to figure that out for yourself."

"...Tomorrow."

"Yes," Zeke said. "Tomorrow." He wrinkled his snout. "Why are you so worried about it? You didn't hesitate to fight off those thugs at the café."

"That's different," she said. "That was fighting enemies, ones who attacked first. And I was fighting to defend, not kill. This is killing an unexpecting civilian."

Zeke narrowed his gaze. "A politician."

"But not a soldier," Leah said. "And not a personal threat to me."

Zeke sighed. Rookie talk. "He's still the enemy."

"Doesn't make it any easier to kill him."

Zeke stopped himself from rolling his eyes. He glanced at Jaden through the window. He appeared to be talking to someone, though he couldn't see anybody. Probably a comm. Checking in, perhaps. He shrugged. "Well. At least you won't be alone."

Leah stared at Zeke a moment. She flattened her ears, then turned away from him, facing her door.

Zeke stared after her. "Leah?"

She said nothing.

He tried again, in his mind this time. *Leah?*

He got a faint scent of something, though he couldn't place it. No words.

He sighed and turned over, trying to get some sleep.

CHAPTER 12

HIT

Leah didn't want to do this. And frankly, she shouldn't have to. Not with what she knew about Ackerson's corruption.

But she had to convince Jaden of that. And to do that, she had to convince herself to talk to him in the first place.

The next morning they woke up early and got dressed. Leah straightened her American military uniform and Jaden handed her an M4, the same rifle that Ackerson's personal bodyguards had been using. It looked quite different than the comparative Defender weapons, but it fired similarly enough, at least. Thank Draso she had kept up with her firearms training. She also kept her metal staff with her -- could be useful.

Though she longed for her Gem. If someone got hurt, she wouldn't be able to help them. Her one strength.

"We'll get it as soon as we can," Jaden assured her. "Your Gem is safe and no one is going to get hurt." He wafted ice crystals through the air. "Except our target."

Leah shuddered. This was it. Her last chance. "Guardian Azure…"

He looked up at her. "Yeah?"

"We… we don't need to do this," Leah said.

Zeke turned to her.

Guardian Azure raised an eyebrow. He crossed his arms. "Is this going to be an appeal to my morals? Because morals or not, I'm a soldier and this is my job."

"No, no," Leah said. "W-well, I mean, yeah, I guess, but that's not what I mean. This is about Ackerson." Her heart pounded and the Thought Factory ran a thousand miles a minute while she tried to piece together her thoughts. "I-I knew a member of one his teams in the future, who talked to me about him and… h-he's corrupt, he… he…" *Dang it brain, just work!*

Jaden lowered his gaze before she could string together another sentence. "Think I don't know that?"

Leah perked both ears in surprise. "Y-you do?"

"Of course I do," Jaden said. "This whole damn military is. But there's nothing I can do about that."

"C-can't you report him?" Leah said. "Surely--"

"Leah," Jaden said. "This isn't Zyearth. They use corruption here. Reporting him wouldn't do anything. At best they'd just ignore me. At worst, they'd put a target on my back and take me out for daring to challenge one of their top men."

Leah frowned. A target on his back. The same thing Trecheon said.

Jaden's face softened. "Look. I don't like this either. But there's no way around it." He sighed. "At least we're taking out corruption. Tao isn't our ally."

"But he doesn't have to be our enemy," Leah said.

"He does if he's opposing us," Jaden said. "That's what war is."

Leah sunk down. "But…"

"Sorry, Leah," Jaden said. "But we don't have a choice. Not if we want to survive this war. Not if you want to get to DC. Keep your head down. Follow orders. Go through the motions. Alright?" He gave Zeke a knowing look. Zeke glanced off.

Leah frowned. "Sure."

And that was the end of that. She had failed.

Then they drove to the Governor's Mansion. The current guard questioned them for over an hour, and the searches were incredibly humiliating, but they got in.

Jaden was right. They found his Gem almost immediately and asked him what it meant. He shrugged, called it a paperweight good luck charm from home, and they let him have it, though hesitantly. Leah got the faint smell of perfect cookies through her nose – surprise.

Zeke.

She shoved it aside. Zeke didn't want that. Didn't want the bond. So… she didn't either. Her heart ached, but she forced it to shut up.

The guards they were relieving were stationed outside the Governor's Mansion – literally along the high brick wall that surrounded it, right near the entrance.

Leah's heart pumped in her ears, and her whole body buzzed like electricity ran through her fur. Her stomach roiled.

They were about to kill someone. Literally kill someone who was just trying to get their own citizens out of captivity. Who cared if there were some other shady deals going on? Why was that their job to take care of?

Fire and ice, she *didn't want to do this.*

A voice in the back of her head told her it didn't matter. She was a soldier – stuck right now in this sorry excuse for a military, but even when she escaped it, she was still a Defender. Still a soldier.

But healers don't fight. That was what she had told herself all through school. But she knew that was a lie too. It didn't matter that she focused on healing and history. She also had to learn combat. It was why she carried a staff at her side, and why she knew how to use it. It was why she knew how to hold, clean, and fire a rifle, even though the Defenders tended to rely on elemental magic.

But… killing. Draso's mercy, she wanted to escape that.

Zeke stood next to her, his face stoic and calm, though if the smells she got off him was any indication, he was wildly nervous. His ear and tail twitched too, especially since there was a human guard on his other side who kept eyeing them both.

The head of their squad, a human male with neat brown hair, brown eyes, and a thick build named Sharp, stood on the other side of the gate, near the intercom. He sent regular glares at Zeke and Leah, and the occasional one to Jaden through the gate. He hadn't been happy when the three of them showed up for duty, and ran all the questioning himself before he finally and reluctantly found a place for them along the outer wall. "You animals will stay out of trouble there," he had said. Neither Jaden nor Zeke seemed to take the word "animal" well, but neither questioned it. Sharp wouldn't look at them. "The moment the Governor returns, I'm requesting you be relocated. We don't want your kind here."

Fine by Leah. They weren't planning on staying anyway.

Her ear comm buzzed. *"Foxworthy and Tao sighted. They're coming down the drive now. Be alert, soldiers."* Leah resisted the urge to glance Jaden's way. He was positioned right at the entrance to the Mansion, by the gate. A perfect spot, since the car would have to stop for the gates to open. It gave him time to think about how to freeze Tao's brain.

The Thought Factory ran a million miles a minute with every possible scenario. Would Tao feel pain? How would his body react? What about the

91

other passengers? Then the aftermath. What if she cracked during questioning? What if something went horribly wrong and Jaden and Zeke got desperately hurt? What if she needed her magic when she didn't have it? Curse all of this. She tried to stop the shivering, but failed.

Sharp sent Leah and Zeke one more deep glare, then pressed a button on the intercom. "Street is clear."

Then the gate opened.

Leah didn't turn. She couldn't watch Jaden. But she imagined him wiggling his fingers, directing his ice magic up Tao's nose…

She shook the image out of her head. *No!*

The Thought Factory dropped one more thought to her. *If the car stops next to you and they call for help, you better respond.*

Great.

Stay calm, she told herself. *It's not likely we'll have to do anything.*

The long, black vehicle passed through the gate and turned down the street toward her as the gate shut. No sign of movement. No change in pace. How long would it take for people to notice? Did Jaden actually do it? Maybe he didn't. Maybe that'd be better. Maybe--

A muffled scream beat against Leah's ears as loud as a gunshot, and the vehicle screeched to a halt, sending adrenaline rushing through her body. The back door opened and a black-haired man stuck his head out, panicked. Leah moved to help, fighting terror, trying to keep her face neutral. Zeke moved with her.

But when the man saw her, his face turned vicious and he shrieked at her in a language she didn't recognize.

Leah took a step back, flattening her ears. "What?"

The man leapt out of the car, reached for his belt, and brandished a thick knife. He charged Leah.

Leah stepped back and went to shield instinctively, but without her Gem, she couldn't form one. The man stabbed at her. She leapt back, fell to one knee, and lifted her rifle. But he was too close. The man grabbed the barrel, wrenched it out of her hands, and threw her to the sidewalk. She tried bracing herself, but still smashed her head on the ground, sending stars through her vision. The man pinned her down and lifted his knife--

A heavy body smashed into him, ripping him off Leah. She rolled out of the way, snatched the rifle, and got to her feet.

Then Zeke cried out. Leah turned.

Zeke was on the ground, clutching his side and groaning. A splash of red dirtied the sidewalk. A thousand smells assailed her at once.

Leah gasped. *Zeke!*

But he didn't respond.

Dang it, she needed her Gem!

The man turned on her now, brandishing the bloodied knife and snarling at her.

Leah narrowed her eyes, aimed, and in three quick shots to the chest, she took the man down. He fell without another word.

Still clutching her rifle, she dashed over to Zeke, trying to recall his fake name. "Green? You okay?"

Zeke turned over, still gripping his side. His unform dripped red. His body shook, the beginnings of shock. The smells started to fade.

Her heart beat in her ears, and breaths came in ragged gasps. She needed her Gem, she needed her healing, dang it, he was *hurt and she needed her Gem and it wasn't here.*

Jaden was at their side in a moment, with a first aid kit, calling for a medic. He kneeled besides the black-haired man first, though he tossed a roll of bandages to Leah. Frantic, she began wrapping the wound, pushing panic away as much as she could. Zeke could only groan.

93

The car door opened again and a woman in a simple blue dress crawled out, tears streaming down her face. "Mr. Tao isn't breathing!" A thin man with a crisp blue suit and panic on his face came out with her, talking on the phone, likely to emergency services. He glared at Leah and Zeke.

"Green, Smith, Longquill!" Sharp shouted, using the names Zeke, Leah, and Jaden had all taken on. "Back the hell up, now!"

Leah frowned. "Sir, Green is--"

"I don't give a *rat's ass,*" he shouted, waving his rifle at them. "Back up *now!*"

Leah helped Zeke up, but her hand brushed his fur. The pain and trauma from his wounds assailed her – not just the stab in his side, but a dull ache from a previously fractured bone, and painful burns on his feet, which were still healing. A wave of sympathy ran through her.

Zeke turned to her, surprised, a shock of strong lemon flavors wafting about. Leah sunk down. He had figured out she had seen his medical history. A loud voice in the Thought Factory demanded she reach out to him, explain, and apologize, but her shame shoved it away and she muttered a "sorry" instead. She lifted him higher on her shoulders, fighting to keep her knees from buckling, a tremendous feat considering he stood a good half a meter taller than her, but she managed to drag her own feet and pull him out of the way. He hissed in pain. She did what she could to support him.

Jaden padded over to them as Sharp kneeled down by the man Leah shot. Blood seeped from the wounds. Nothing Sharp did for him helped. Leah's stomach churned.

Good Draso, she had just killed someone.

Sharp stood and glared at the three of them. "He's dead."

The sandy haired man on the phone pointed to Leah and Zeke. "Captain, have these beasts arrested."

"Gladly," Sharp said.

Leah flicked her ears back. *Beasts?* "But--"

"You three are under arrest for failing to protect Tao and his translator, and for misuse of a firearm," Sharp said. "Stand up and come with me."

"The man came at us with a knife!" Leah protested. "He stabbed Green for trying to protect me! What the heck was I supposed to do?"

Sharp glared at her. "Die." He yanked her to her feet and zipped her hands up with a zip tie.

TEAMMATES

Leah sat on a bench in an armored car, fiddling with the zip tie around her wrists, fighting her heart and lungs, trying to calm them without success. She rocked back and forth, desperately needing a way to release the excess energy. That went about as bad as it could go.

She, Zeke, and Jaden had been stripped of their weapons and focus jewels just before being thrown in the armored car, going who knew where. A muscle-bound human guard with a strange hat and no smile sat on one end of the car, an M4 waiting in his hands, sneering at the group. From the sounds outside and radio call outs from their guard, she suspected they were in a convoy, probably taking a multitude of prisoners… somewhere.

Jaden seemed strangely unperturbed. He sat in his corner humming quietly, twiddling his thumbs as best he could with his zip ties.

Zeke moaned, gripping his side with both hands, twisting awkwardly. The smells had returned full force, mixing into a conglomerate that smelled more like garbage than food, making Leah queasy.

Leah frowned, turning to his wound. Blood had soaked the bandage now. She reached for it… then stopped. She'd be useless. Worse than useless. No magic. Fire and ice, what she wouldn't give for her Gem. And who knew where it was. The very thought kept her on the edge of a breakdown.

But the bleeding… She pulled on the corner of her jacket and moved closer to Zeke. Maybe she could help stop it.

The guard immediately pointed his rifle at her. *"Don't move, animal."*

Leah shrunk down.

Jaden glared at the man. "He's *bleeding,*" he said. "At least let her try and stop him bleeding out before you take us to whatever horse spit trial you have planned."

The man narrowed his gaze at Jaden. "Like I give a shit if you live or die."

"Your boss might though," Jaden said. He waved his bound hands to Leah. "What's that five-foot kitty gonna do to you, huh? Especially all bound up with zips. Just let her help her boyfriend."

Zeke managed to glare at Jaden, teeth bared, all other smells vanishing in favor of something hot and spicy. A vague feeling ran through her head, anger, with a little shame, but no words. Leah frowned. That was new. Zeke tried to stand, though he winced and sat back down. Leah bunched up the corner of her jacket and pressed it to Zeke's wound.

Her hands brushed his, and she got a solid impression of his ailments.

The wound appeared superficial. Cut through skin and muscle, but nothing major. Just a lot of blood. Far clearer now that shock and trauma wasn't ruling Zeke's emotions and making him think back to his other wounds. Thank Draso he seemed okay though.

It was more than a bit surprising that her magic still worked this far from her Gem. Surprising and disappointing too. If being away from her Gem would mean being away from her power, maybe…

She shook her head. She couldn't escape being a healer-S.

Leah sifted through the other wounds, examining them more closely. Skin grafts on his back and feet. A notch in one rib. A broken bone in his arm, still not fully healed. All around the same age, it seemed. He had been through something terrible. She dug deeper.

And she found that tracker in his neck. She shuddered.

Jaden went back to humming.

The guard narrowed his eyes at him. "Would you cut that out?"

But Jaden ignored him and escalated, whistling instead.

The guard snarled and stood. Leah cowered as he moved up to Jaden. "Listen here, you--"

A muffled boom smashed through the armored car and they screeched to a halt, knocking everyone around. The guard crumpled to the floor, arms and legs tangled together. Jaden snickered.

The guard gritted his teeth and lifted his rifle awkwardly, trying to right himself. "You damn *animal--"*

"Wait," Jaden said, lifting his nose in the air in a dramatic fashion. "You smell that?"

The guard paused. "What?"

Jaden leaned down. "Smells like an escape attempt." He gripped the rifle and smacked the guard hard in the face with the butt, smashing in his nose and knocking him clean out. Blood ran through his nostrils.

Leah gawked. "Guardian Azure! You can't do that!"

Zeke coughed. "The hell are you doing? They've got a whole convoy out there and you've got one rifle. They'll *kill* us."

"More than that!" Leah said. "He's a military officer! We're supposed to follow orders and get out of this the *right* way."

Zeke turned to her. "Do you really think they were going to just question us and let us go free?" he asked. "A dignitary is *dead* and we were the perfect scapegoats. We were headed straight for a firing squad."

98

Leah perked both ears. "But the proper channels…"

Jaden lifted his hands above his head and smashed them into his stomach, snapping the zip ties. He turned the man over so the blood ran out the nose, then pocketed his radio. "Leah, this isn't Zyearth. We're not equals here. For us, there are no proper channels. We need to get out of here or we're dead." He pulled out his pendant. The eyes lit up softly. He smiled. "Thankfully, we're not alone." He used his pendant to cut Leah and Zeke's zip ties.

"We *are* alone," Zeke protested. He growled and gripped his side. "Leah and I are useless to you right now."

Leah frowned and pasted her ears back. She wasn't useless.

Jaden searched the man and found Leah's empty Gem holster in one of his pouches. Jaden shook his head. "Sloppy." He threw the holster to Leah. "They left your staff. Probably because they have no idea how to activate it."

Leah stared. Sure enough, her staff was still there, contracted. "But Guardian--"

"Don't*,*" Jaden said. "You're a Defender. Act like it."

Leah lowered her gaze, glaring. "A Defender *follows orders--*"

"Did they make a mistake bringing you here, or what?" Jaden said. "You're a damn Defender. Fight like one."

Leah's chest burned and she gritted her teeth. "But *Zeke--*"

"The best way to help your boyfriend is to fight," Jaden said.

Leah hunched down. Zeke wasn't her boyfriend. Heck, he wasn't even her *friend.*

The sharp smell of hot spices smashed through her senses again, making her reel back. Zeke stood this time, gripping his side. "She's not my damn girlfriend!" he snarled. "She--"

Another muffled boom sounded from outside and someone screamed.

Zeke turned to the door. "The hell is going on out there?"

"I told you," Jaden said. "We're not alone."

The exit door rattled and burst open, blinding the group with raw sunlight. A quilar stood backlit at the door. It took Leah's eyes a moment to adjust and focus.

Then she stared, wide-eyed.

An Athánatos quilar. *Athánatos.* Bent back ears, long flowing tail, paw-like feet, taller than everyone except Zeke. He was mostly red with streaks and splotches of black all about his fur and around his eyes, like a strange, bizarro version of Trecheon. And he wore an identical US battle dress uniform to Jaden's.

Ei-Ei jewels sat snuggly around the eyes. Zeke stared, and the shock of lemon smell returned.

Instantly Leah had a name. The missing Athánatos Archon – Archon Embrik. He stared at them all with deep, night-blue eyes, landing his gaze on Jaden.

Jaden smirked. "Took you long enough."

"Your signal cuts off in these woods," Embrik said, rolling his eyes. He turned to Leah. "Luckily, I had a second, stronger signal to follow this time."

Leah ran her fingers over her pendant. She stared, torn. Should she say she knew who he was? But that had backfired badly with both Ackerson and Jaden. Should she keep quiet? But Embrik would want to know what happens to Athánatos. Should she--

Another explosion, no longer muffled by the doors. Jaden winced. "She's really going at them, isn't she?"

She. They had another teammate. Another Athánatos?

Embrik lowered his gaze. "She is angry. And you know how she is when she is angry."

"Intimately," Jaden said.

Embrik stared at Zeke, ears pressed back. "Sisters *alive…"*

"Told you," Jaden said. "But we don't have time now. Let's get out of here." Embrik stared a moment longer, then nodded and led the way out of the armored car. They were on a narrow, snowy road in the middle of a forest. Tall junipers and pines lined the road, and despite the afternoon light, darkness bathed the forest floor.

Embrik and Jaden pressed themselves against the side of the truck, while Leah struggled to help Zeke out of the back. A sharp smell of burning stung Leah's nose, though she couldn't tell if that was something in the air or Zeke's emotions wafting through.

Jaden turned to Embrik. "Hostiles?"

"Four armored cars," Embrik said. "An escort up front. Three with prisoners."

Jaden frowned. "They didn't have a rear escort?"

"Well," Embrik said. He nodded to the woods. An armored car lay on its roof, one wheel spinning uselessly. "They did."

"The other prisoners?"

"Our missing Chinese miners," Embrik said.

Jaden narrowed his eyes. "Don't hurt them." He paused. "Did you recover the Humvee?"

Embrik pasted his ears back. "No." Leah shuddered. Her Gem was in that Humvee. The panic began to set in again.

"That's priority number one once we get out of here," Jaden said. "Keep two cars running. Destroy the others." He checked over the rifle. "You find my Gem yet?"

"Kyrie is looking for it."

Leah's fur stood on end. *Kyrie?* That meant--

A hawk squawked in her mind, which she took to be Archángeli. They recognized their partner's name. Zeke could only groan in pain.

"Alright then," Jaden said. "Plan Defender. Take out the hostiles, free the prisoners. They get one car, we get the other. We'll have to scrap the tracking on it."

Embrik nodded to Leah and Zeke. "And...?"

"Achristos," Jaden said, then muttered some string of the foreign language. Leah frowned. Some Earth language. But a second later, the translation flew through her mind, in Archángeli's voice. *Useless. Treat them as civilians needing protection. And don't touch the cat.*

"I'm not *useless,"* Leah snarled. She shook her staff, extending it, and gripped it tightly.

Jaden turned and frowned. "How did you...?"

"Watch yourselves!" a feminine voice sounded. Jaden turned back just as three hostiles whipped around the front of the car, raising their rifles. Jaden lifted his in response.

Then a wall of snow and ice rushed between them and the hostiles, followed by the raspy, deep throated call of a barn owl. Leah shielded her face with her arm, trying to hold Zeke as the flying snow settled.

Standing between Jaden and the soldiers was the final piece of the puzzle. Tall, black with cream accents, wearing the same rumpled BDUs as the rest of them, her barn owl summon at her side, stood Ouranos' missing sister.

Alexina of the Athánatos.

CHAPTER 14

MAKE A WISH

Leah stared. Alexina. The last missing Athánatos royal. Facing down a bunch of soldiers, ready to fight. She leaned down, glaring at the oncoming hostiles, magic of all elements dripping from her hands.

A dozen or so human soldiers faced her, their rifles drawn.

Leah instinctively reached for her Gem. But of course it wasn't there. No way to shield. Jaden didn't have his either. Her chest tightened and she struggled to breathe, making her vision blur. The Prinkípissa was without protection. "Alexina!"

Jaden turned to her, staring, his quills on end. "How did--?"

But Alexina didn't wait. She pounded the ground with her fists and a wall of stone shot up between her and the soldiers. Ineffective gunfire sounded behind it. Kyrie dove for the soldiers, feathers hardened with ice spikes.

Then the soldiers screamed.

Alexina turned to the group. Cream colored fur covered her snout and encircled her bright orange eyes, a stark contrast to her inky black fur.

But the color pattern wasn't lost on Leah. Nor on Zeke, if the sharp lemon smell of surprise was any indication. Nearly identical to his face markings, just a different color. But still a royal color.

Zeke whipped his gaze to Leah.

But Alexina cut them off before he could ask anything. "Embrik! Jaden!"

Embrik nodded. Kyrie soared out from behind the stone wall and dropped something large and shining. Jaden's Gem.

Jaden snatched it out of the air and shielded the three of them. He slammed his fist into his hand, shooting ice spikes in the air around him. "Leah, get Zeke back into the car. We'll take care of this."

Leah frowned. "But--"

"Don't question orders!" He ran with the others behind the stone.

Leah flattened her ears and twitched her tail. She glanced up at Zeke.

He stared wide-eyed, the lemon smell becoming overpowering now. "Those... that... They were..."

"Athánatos," Leah said. "Like you."

"Their jewels--"

"Bound around their eyes, like all Athánatos natives."

"And... that bird..."

Leah shifted. "Archángeli's companion."

Zeke stared at her.

She is correct, Prínkipas, Archángeli confirmed, echoing in Leah's mind.

Zeke violently shook his head. "But... she... who is that?"

Leah pressed her lips together. "That is Alexina."

Zeke's quills stood on end and the lemon smell faded in favor of... of avocado bread, Leah decided. Disbelief. "She... you... you asked me..."

My prince, watch yourself! Archángeli shouted.

A loud boom echoed through the area. Spider cracks ran through the stone, filtering light.

Leah gasped. "Run!" She pulled Zeke behind the truck.

The cracks burst now, shooting stones in all directions. Several smashed into the cars and others vanished into the forest. Dust spilled into the air. Leah coughed. Thankfully the truck protected them.

But it didn't protect their allies.

Jaden, Embrik, and Alexina skidded along the snowy road, covered in sand and dust, having been forcefully thrown to the ground. Leah peeked around the truck.

Their commanding officer from the manor stood there, a riot stick in his hand, glaring at the group. His brown hair was dusted with snow and his white and gray battle fatigues barely contained his thick build.

Captain Sharp.

The other soldiers lay on the ground, unmoving, but Sharp didn't even appear injured. He smacked the riot stick into his hand. "Come at me, you damn fuzzies."

Alexina coughed, but she righted herself and shot a flurry of ice spikes at him, shouting. But the moment they got near him, they shattered to diamond dust and blew away. Leah stared. How had he done *that?*

Embrik snarled now and whipped fire around Sharp. But that vanished in an instant too, leaving nothing but ash to cover the snow. Leah caught a strange reflective gleam in Sharp's eye.

Alexina roared now and shot a wave of snow at him. It rolled toward him, but then stopped mid-roll and turned back on them, smashing into Jaden, Embrik and Alexina, knocking them to the ground. Jaden used his own magic to push the snow off them, but Alexina and Embrik huddled on the ground, groaning.

Oh, if only Leah had her Gem!

Jaden checked on his companions, then stood, but he didn't attack. He lowered his gaze. "Thought something was off about you. You have Wishing Dust in your eye." He bared his teeth. "Your wish negates magic."

Sharp smirked. "You're clever for a damn animal. Though I suppose being a mage puts you above the average beast."

"How'd an Earth native get Wishing Dust?"

"Bold of you to assume I'm a native, Zyearthling." Sharp said.

Leah gasped.

Jaden narrowed his eyes. "Vanguardian then, from the Unus continent. You hold their xenophobic 'values' well." He pointed behind Sharp. "So which one of those was your companion?"

"As if I'd tell you, Zyearth mage."

Jaden snorted. "If you knew I was a mage, why did you station me near Tao?"

"Tao needed to go," Sharp said. "But we couldn't be the ones caught doing it. Your little stunt covered that nicely. We'd take you to trial. Have you executed. Ties up all the loose ends. No harm done." He shrugged. "But things change. Guess I'll have to be the executioner now."

Jaden pulled a small rod out of his pocket and pressed a button on it. It expanded into a sword hilt. He shook the hilt and a long ice blade formed on the end, sending a crisp crackling sound through the area. He held it out toward Sharp. "Try me." Jaden rushed him, bringing the blade down hard.

But the moment it neared Sharp, it shattered, just like Alexina's ice. Sharp smirked and smashed his riot stick into Jaden's side, sending him flying. Jaden yelped and skidded along the snow.

"No mage can harm me," Sharp said, grinning. "'Fraid you're out of luck."

Leah glared. She lowered Zeke down. *Stay here.*

Zeke flattened his ears. "You *can't--*"

Don't try to stop me. She ran around the back of the car.

Jaden still lay on the ground, groaning, as Sharp made his way toward him, still gripping the riot stick.

Leah gritted her teeth and shook her staff into full length. She dug her feet claws into the snow and ground and threw herself at Sharp, smashing her whole weight into him.

She hadn't expected to do any more than just get his attention away from Jaden, but the man was caught so off guard that he flew forward and face planted into the snow. Leah moved between him and Jaden, holding her staff out.

Sharp pulled himself to his knees and wiped the snow off his face. He glared.

Leah stood her ground. "Back. Up."

Sharp stood, looming over her. He chuckled darkly. "What do you think you're gonna do to me, pussy cat?"

Leah let out a feral growl and charged him again. He swung his riot stick, but she ducked and slammed the end of her staff into his stomach. He wheezed, but before he could recover, she whipped around him and smashed the staff into his side, sending him flying again. He tumbled through the snow. Leah leapt on him, claws out on hands and feet, and held her staff under his chin, glaring.

"I'm a *Defender,*" she snarled, showing off her fangs. "I've been training since you were in *diapers.* And I will. Not. *Lose.*"

Sharp bared his teeth. He gripped her staff with both hands and pulled, flinging her over his head. She leaned into his throw, however, and landed gracefully on her feline feet, yanking her staff from his hands. She swung it back down on him, but he rolled out of the way. Sharp sprung to his feet and charged Leah, but she nimbly dodged.

107

They battled back and forth for several minutes. Sharp continually beat her in strength and power, but Leah's agility outpaced him every time.

But then Leah slipped on the snow.

Sharp pounced, smashing his full weight into her, slamming her into a truck. She gasped, lost her grip on her staff, and slid to the snow, groaning.

Sharp picked up his riot stick. "You animals will always be under my boot."

Leah pulled herself to her knees. Everything ached. Her staff was out of reach.

"Say goodnight, beast." Sharp lifted his stick.

No! Zeke's voice echoed through her mind, accompanied with the urgent scent of burning.

A rush of wind blew around her, scattering snow.

Archángeli stood between Leah and Sharp, in full anthro form. Golden brown flight feathers ran down their arms, brushing the snow. Long brown tail feathers lay across the ground, with brown and gold peacock feathers among them. They held Leah's staff in their clawed hands, wind whipping about them.

You will not harm the feline.

Sharp glared, lifting his riot stick. But a rush of brown and white brushed over it and plopped next to Archángeli in a flurry of ice and snow. Kyrie, the barn owl Phonar, stood beside Archángeli, flight feathers also brushing the ground, white, and blue peacock feathers floating about her tail. She held Sharp's riot stick, ice wafting around her, and let out a long, raspy hiss.

"Sisters alive," Alexina said, her voice cracking.

Sharp stared a moment at the two birds. "Mages can't hurt me."

We are not mages, Archángeli and Kyrie said together.

Sharp gritted his teeth, then turned and ran.

Both summons rushed after Sharp, knocking him to the ground, talons out. He grunted once, but then didn't move.

Leah gasped. Did they kill him? She ran after them and checked him over. He had a large, bloody wound on the head, but he was breathing. Not dead, but knocked out. She pressed a hand to his head to get an impression of the wound. Shallow, considering. A mild concussion. But other vitals seemed strong. He'd live.

Leah wasn't sure how to feel about that. She sighed and looked up at the summons. "Thank you." Archángeli nodded and handed her staff back.

Alexina walked forward, favoring one arm. She stared at Archángeli, tears in her eyes. "Archángeli… after all these years… My friend, my companion. Where have you been?"

Archángeli bowed, wind whipping around them. *Apologies, my Lady, but I had another charge to protect.*

"Draso's mercy, Archángeli," Alexina said. "Who else on Draso's Earth could you need to protect?"

Archángeli nodded to the truck Zeke hid behind. *Him.*

Alexina turned.

Zeke hobbled out from behind the truck, gripping his injured side. Alexina brought her hands to her mouth in shock. Jaden walked up to her, favoring a leg, and gripped her shoulder, rubbing it reassuringly, his white fur a brilliant contrast to Alexina's black fur.

White fur.

Like the white tips on Zeke's quills.

Leah pressed a hand to her mouth. *Oh, good Draso.*

Embrik stood now, lowering his gaze. "You two have a lot to explain."

CHAPTER 15

LIKE FATHER, LIKE SON

"I'm telling you," Zeke said, exasperated. "I don't *know.*"

Zeke sat on a bench in a troop-carrying Humvee, still clinging to the wound in his side. Everything ached now, all radiating from the injury like a burn spreading unchecked. Leah had done her best to clean and wrap it with a first-aid kit they found, but the pain meds in the kit had expired and Zeke didn't want to take a chance with them in the middle of nowhere with a rogue team. He was stuck dealing with the raw pain.

Didn't help that they were bouncing along a bumpy, snowy road with the Athánatos named Embrik at the wheel. He stared forward in the driver's seat, but kept one ear perked back, listening to the conversation.

Jaden and his companions, Alexina and Embrik, had piled the unconscious survivors in one armored car, then syphoned most of the gas out of the vehicle, leaving only enough to run the heater for a few hours – enough time for someone to come save them, if they were quick enough. They removed trackers from the other cars and attached them to the one holding survivors.

The dead they had covered with huge snow piles and tarps to avoid animals investigating. Watching Jaden and Alexina use their magic to bury them in snow had been unreal. Literally commanding snow and ice like it was an extension of their own bodies. They left the dead in the safety of the trees, using their rifles as markers. "We respect the dead," Jaden had said.

"Do we respect attempted murderers?" Zeke had said, pointing to the truck with the living soldiers.

Leah stood between him and the truck. "We've killed enough," she said with a tone that shook Zeke to the bone, a sharp smell of hot peppers accompanying her words. No one dared to counter her.

Leah had found the rest of their effects, including Zeke's Ei-Ei jewels, plus the Chinese miners, in the other cars. Jaden got the prisoners out of their zip ties and let them drive off, warning them, in their own language, to stay out of sight. He then slashed the tires of the last car before directing everyone into the Humvee they drove now. Zeke still wasn't sure if that was the right thing to do, but he didn't have the energy to think about it too much.

Especially with the other Athánatos, Alexina, grilling him with questions he didn't have the answers to.

Leah had asked him if his mom was named Alexina back in their cells. He had never gotten the chance to ask more. But now, every time he tried poking into her mind with questions, she shut him down. He supposed that was his fault.

Not that he really needed Leah to confirm anything. Alexina looked so much like him that it hurt to look at her.

She leaned closer to Zeke's face, making him wince. "You are Athánatos," she said. "Royal even, by your colors, though the white confuses me. But I cannot fathom how you have no understanding of your heritage."

"And I keep telling you that I don't know anything," Zeke said. "I was adopted as a baby and only learned about what I am from Leah a couple of weeks ago."

Alexina wrinkled her snout. She turned to Archángeli, who had taken up a perch next to Zeke, their feathers ruffled in agitation. "Archángeli, why have you not explained anything to him?"

Archángeli keened and glared at Alexina. Wind brushed all around them. *I was forbidden from speaking of his past and parentage.*

"By who?" Alexina asked.

The Black Cloak.

Leah gasped and drew her hands to her mouth.

Zeke frowned. "Who the hell is that?"

Alexina stared at Leah a moment, eyes narrowed, before turning back to Archángeli. "We have been searching for the Black Cloak ever since we were exiled from Athánatos," she said, ignoring Zeke's question. "Why has she appeared now?"

It is 'he' now, Archángeli said. *The Cloak needed a new host.*

Alexina frowned. "Why?"

Theron.

Alexina's gaze grew dark. "Did the Black Cloak assign you to Zeke?"

Archángeli shook their head. *No. Tradition did.*

Zeke eyed the golden eagle. "The hell does that mean?"

Jaden leaned back in his seat, crossing his arms. "It means you're Alexina's son."

Zeke's body buzzed. Draso's holy *mercy.* "You know for sure?"

"H-he's right, Zeke," Leah said.

He turned to her. "How the hell would *you* know that?"

Alexina pinned an ear back. "I am curious as well."

Leah furrowed her brow and continued. "I-I'm a historian, with a specialty in summons. They had me studying the Phonar on Athánatos." She took a deep breath. "The Phonar summons are connected to the Athánatos royal family. They'd only move to a new summoner if their current summoner died… or if they had kits."

"But I have never had children," Alexina said.

Leah's eyes widened.

"See?" Zeke said, relief washing over him. But that didn't feel good enough. It didn't feel right. Why did she look so much like him if she wasn't his mother? *Good Draso, someone make sense of this.*

I'm trying to, Leah said, before retreating in shame.

"For once, I'm with you," Jaden said. "Even if Alexina was pregnant *now,* even if you really are out of your own time, something is still screwy. You'd only be eight or nine in your own timeline if you were Alexina's son."

"Jaden," Embrik said from the driver's seat. "If the Black Cloak is involved…"

"If the Black Cloak plans on stealing my future son in order to drop him off with some mainlanders outside of his own time, he's in for a *world* of hurt," Jaden said. "I don't care if you both think he's some omniscient cryptid destined to save the universe. I've already had my family stolen from me once, and I'm not letting it happen again."

"So I guessed correctly then," Leah said. "You and Alexina are married."

Jaden flicked an ear back. He looked up at Alexina, his face softening. She smiled at him and took his hand, squeezing it. He squeezed back and turned to Leah. "My first wife died decades ago. I'm allowed to remarry."

Leah held up her hands. "I-I'm not trying to judge. It's just… interesting, considering, ah, Ouranos' relationship to our Golden Guardians--"

Jaden slammed the side of the truck with a fist, making Leah and Alexina jump. "Not another *word.*"

Alexina pinned her ears back, her tail twitching. "Jaden--"

"I don't want to know, Alexina," Jaden said. "I'll figure it out when... if I go home." He turned to Leah and pointed. "You, however, disobeyed orders, Defender. I told you to stay behind the truck. Instead you recklessly rushed out against a dangerous Wish Duster without even a *Gem--*"

"Hey, hey, *hey,*" Zeke said, glaring. "Don't you start, asshole. Leah saved your sorry tail."

Jaden glared back. "Stay out of this."

"Don't tell me what to do," Zeke said. "You owe Leah an apology for that bullshit. And maybe a thank you, for god's sake."

Jaden snorted. "I don't owe anyone anything. I had things under control."

"None of you could even get a *shot* in," Zeke snarled. "He shut down your supposed world-bending magic like he was turning off a light switch. Leah is a feather-weight compared to Sharp and she knocked him clean on his ass. If he survives the night, he'll be wearing those bruises and broken bones for a damn long time." He pointed to Jaden. "She saved you."

Leah perked her ears. Zeke caught a hint of a smile on her face and the scent of warm cookies in his nose, which he interpreted to mean thank you.

Jaden crossed his arms. "She still lost."

Zeke narrowed his eyes. "So did you."

Jaden bared his teeth, ice floating around his head in sharp chunks.

Leah stood and held her hands out. "Everyone, *please,* let's not fight, alright? I know you're both hot headed after that battle, but please cool it. We all want to survive this war and see our lives restored, but that'll be impossible if we're fighting each other."

Jaden huffed, but he backed down. The ice around his head vanished.

Zeke backed down too, but Leah's comments about hot heads stuck with him. Archángeli once told Zeke he was too much like his father. Zeke didn't know what that meant – after all, he had never known a father.

But looking at Jaden now… butting heads with him… knowing he was married to this woman who was likely his biological mother…

Archángeli nudged him gently. Zeke faced them. The golden eagle eyed him and subtly pointed a wing in Jaden's direction.

Whoever this Black Cloak was clearly didn't forbid Archángeli from hinting. Zeke's fur bristled up.

Alexina furrowed her brow. She turned to Leah. "So Jaden spoke the truth over the radio. Athánatos is saved in your future."

Leah flicked her tail, but nodded.

"You… you speak of Ouranos as a friend," Alexina said.

Leah sat down. "I wouldn't call him a friend, necessarily. I've only known him a few weeks, and we're not close." *Because no one wants to get close to me.*

Zeke shot his head up at that declaration, expecting someone to say something. But no one did. It must have been an internal thought.

His heart ached with the truth of it in his own life. He brushed it aside.

Alexina bent both ears back and frowned.

Leah smiled then. "Don't fret, Alexina. Ouranos is alive and happy. He's still technically a Drifter, but one of our Golden Guardians helped bridge his soul. He's completely himself again, just without the Soul Jewels."

Alexina sighed happily and smiled, her eyes shining. She sat down next to Jaden. "That is a relief to hear. It has been nearly eighty years since I saw my brother as himself."

"I do not suppose you know the fate of the Basileus," Embrik asked.

Leah shifted. "Ouranos turned him into a Drifter with the help of the other Archons," she said. "Then he sealed his Ei-Ei jewels away. As far as I know, the Basileus is in a deep coma."

"Hmm," Embrik said. "Effective, I suppose." He gripped the wheel of the Humvee. "And… Melaina?"

Leah grinned now. "Restored, like the rest of the Shadow Cast."

Embrik was silent for a long time. His voice quavered when he finally responded. "Thank the Sisters."

Alexina patted Embrik's shoulder while he drove. "We will return you to her, Embrik."

"Draso willing," Embrik said.

"Alexina," Jaden said, his voice quiet. "There is one way to determine Zeke's parentage for certain."

Alexina flicked her ears back. "I know."

"If you're talking about doing a DNA test, you can count me out," Zeke said. "We're in a damn war, in case you forgot. We don't have time for that bullshit."

"We would not need a test," Alexina said. She pointed to his wrist. "I would need only to listen to your Ei-Ei jewel's song."

Zeke frowned. "What?"

"The jewelsong," Alexina said. "I can hear it singing now, but I would need to touch them to make out the words. They would sing of your parentage."

Zeke's body buzzed in shock. Draso's holy *mercy*. He didn't... He couldn't... He shook his head violently. "No."

Alexina frowned. "No?"

"No," Zeke said. "I'm not here to learn about some mysterious past that I knew nothing about until recently. I'm here to save my moms. My *real* parents, the ones who raised me." *Not biological parents that I've never known. Not people who clearly didn't care enough to raise me.* He looked away.

The stench of a rotting apple assailed his nose. Hurt. He glanced at Leah, who frowned deeply. But it wasn't Leah's place to tell him what was important to him.

Something in Jaden's pocket beeped. His quills bristled and he pulled up a tiny square, barely bigger than a thumb print. He gave Alexina a dark look before placing it on the floor.

A massive blue-tinted hologram shot out from the center of the Humvee, showing Ackerson's ugly mug. Zeke glared. His wound ached even more.

Ackerson crossed his arms, looking at Jaden. "Could you have made more of a muck of that?" he asked, his voice booming in the tiny space.

Jaden waved a hand. "Blame the rookies."

"I don't give a shit whose fault it is," Ackerson said. He sighed. "But at least it's done, I guess. They've impounded your Humvee, by the way, and I'm having a hell of a time getting it out."

"Impounded!" Leah said. "My Gem is in there!"

Ackerson smirked, his smile full of poison. "Be glad I stopped them before they crushed it then."

Leah hugged herself. "Oh Draso's wings…"

Jaden watched Leah, his ears pinned back, lips tight. He turned back to Ackerson. "Where is it?"

Ackerson shrugged. "Big impound in central Asgard. Good luck getting back in the city though."

"I'm less worried about the car and more worried about the Gem," Jaden said. He turned to Alexina. "Think Kyrie could get it?"

"Of course." She summoned Kyrie, who hovered gently over Jaden's head. Jaden handed her a piece of paper.

"That's the code for the central safe," Jaden said. "Don't lose it."

Kyrie narrowed her gaze at Jaden, but nodded. Two tiny snowflakes floated down from her wings. One landed on Jaden's head, the other on Zeke's.

Don't lose this either.

Zeke frowned. He and Jaden exchanged a look.

Alexina opened a side door and Kyrie slid outside.

"Got a new target for you," Ackerson said. "Rosanna May. I'll send an encrypted file your way."

Jaden raised one eyebrow. "Rosanna May?"

Ackerson narrowed his eyes. "Got a problem with that, furry?"

Jaden's face went blank. "No, sir."

"Good." Ackerson shook his head. "This one will be tougher. Smaller window, higher profile target, though security should be more relaxed. You'll all need to be there. Don't screw it up this time. It's been hell trying to clean up after you. Ackerson out." The hologram blanked.

Jaden picked up the datasquare and pressed his thumb to it. A new holographic interface appeared with files and pictures, including a young, brown-haired woman in a business suit. He thumbed through it, his gaze narrowed in thought. "Thought so."

Zeke lifted a brow. "What?"

Jaden didn't answer him. He tapped a series of buttons on the interface. "Embrik, you've got your ID tag synced to the Humvee, right?"

"I do."

"Good," Jaden said. "I'm sending information about May's location to you. Let's get going. Kyrie will have to be on her own to get Leah's Gem."

Zeke growled. "I'm talking to you."

Jaden dropped the hologram and stared right into Zeke's eyes. "Look here. You want to get to DC by July. I want to figure out how the hell to put my life back together. Both things require us to follow orders and survive this damn war. I don't know if we're related. Frankly I don't give a shit if we are, not with everything else going on. But like it or not, we're stuck working together, especially after those antics with the convoy. So keep your damn head down, do as I say, and maybe we'll both hit our goals. But if we keep going at each other's throats, we're not going to make it. We both know that."

Zeke wrinkled his snout. "Yeah. Sure."

Jaden held a hand out. "For now, we're allies."

"Sure." Zeke said, taking his hand. A shiver ran up his spine. "Allies."

"Fine." Jaden dug through the supplies in the Humvee and found rations, water, and blankets. "We've got another long drive. Drink, eat, rest, and hopefully we'll get through this next mission in one piece."

Zeke took his rations and settled on his bench. Just had to get through this. It'd be fine. He couldn't take any more shattering epiphanies about his past.

But Leah's gaze and the tense smell of cooking steak that accompanied it didn't fill him with hope.

CHAPTER 16

"IF"

Jaden sat in the passenger seat looking through a series of news articles on their target while Alexina drove. They were on the highway now – mostly empty this time of night. The streetlights flickered through the window, making the hologram change brightness with every flash. The others had fallen asleep.

Something wasn't adding up. Rosanna May was a visiting dignitary from the UK. Their ally. A minor dignitary, yes, but still important. So why were they asked to take her out? Why were they attacking allies?

"Jaden," Alexina said softly.

Jaden sighed. "Yeah?"

"You have a Defender in your pack," Alexina said.

Jaden flicked an ear back. He glanced at Leah, curled up like a normal housecat, head leaning on her folded blanket. Jaden scoffed. *A useless Defender.* Nothing like Dyne.

Well. Maybe a little like Dyne. Dyne would have done exactly what Leah did – attack the Wish Duster to protect his pack. No hesitation. No qualms. No holding back.

Dyne would have won though.

But… being the healer, he would have also stopped anyone killing Sharp, even if he deserved death. Kill only when necessary.

Jaden shut his eyes a moment. Water above him. Of all the Defenders he could have met, it had to be Leah.

"Jaden."

He waved a hand, trying to dispel the memories. Keep Leah distant. "Yeah, whatever. Don't touch her, by the way. She's a healer-S. She can read your body's ailments just by touching you, even without her Gem." Just like Dyne could. Damn it all, he didn't want the reminder.

Alexina frowned. "A Defender in your ranks," she said, clearly ignoring his warning. "And yet you said 'if' you go home. As if it was not a certainty."

Jaden's quills stood on end. Damnit, she noticed. He should have kept his mouth shut. "I know."

"My heart," Alexina said, her voice soft. "From the moment we first met, your greatest ambition has been to find a way home. But now it has come to you and you are questioning your resolve?"

Jaden turned off the hologram and sat back in his chair. "The Defenders have moved on without me, Alexina. Leah mentioned new Golden Guardians."

"Was this not an inevitability?"

"It was, but…" Jaden took a deep breath. "I guess it didn't feel real until she mentioned it. I'm having a hard time coping." He shrugged. "Something in my mind hoped I'd be coming back to the same Zyearth. The same job, same friends, same Defenders. But they won't be the same. Nothing will be." He closed his eyes a moment. "Now I'm not sure I'll have anything to go back to at all."

"You could ask Leah," Embrik said from the back. "I suspect she would know."

Jaden turned around and glanced in the back. Embrik eyed him. Jaden narrowed his gaze. "You were sleeping."

"You were brooding," Embrik said. He pointed to Jaden. "Alexina was gentle, but I will not be so. For decades you have spoken nonstop about how you wished to go home. The opportunity is here, Jaden. And you wish to throw it aside? Why? What happened?"

"Time," Jaden said. "Time, and distance, and life, and *change."* He gripped his head. "Damnit, I know I always said I wanted to go home, but I understood I couldn't. Zyearth was a place of my past, a relic, an ideal that I used to fit in to. But things changed. *I've* changed. What if I don't fit anymore? What if I can't go back?" He slumped over.

What if I'm no longer a Defender? What if I've become the villain I always said I'd fight against?

"My love," Alexina said. He looked up. "You have thrown in your lot with Ackerson because this is how this world works. Not by choice, but by necessity. If you go home, you will no longer need to compromise your morals. You can be yourself again. That alone may be reason to go."

But maybe his morals were too corrupted already. Maybe it was too late.

Alexina reached over and took his hand. "But if you choose to stay, no one will blame you. Your home is where you choose it to be. We will support you no matter your choice."

Jaden sighed. He squeezed her hand then let go. "Thank you. That means a lot." He fiddled with his hands. "Honestly, you two are the only home I have right now. I hope you understand that."

Embrik reached over and gripped Jaden's hand too. "We do." He leaned back and glanced at Zeke. "Do you really think it is possible that Zeke is your son?"

122

Jaden turned in his seat and glanced at Zeke. He frowned. He certainly had the characteristics. Athánatos. Royal colors. Alexina's fur pattern.

Athánatos colors were based solely on magic – nothing genetic. Their fur color changed depending on what Archon or royal family they associated with. Those who had no association were pure black.

But no Archon used the color white. Frostrik, the ice Archon, used silver. Bouldrik, gray. But no white.

And yet, Zeke had Jaden's white in his quills. And those characteristic green eyes that almost all Azures had. Not to mention Zeke clearly inherited Jaden's hot headedness.

Worse yet, Zeke's white manifested on the tips of his quills. Athánatos had many color patterns, but tipped quills was not one of them.

But it was common in Jaden's family. His own son Matt had had tipped quills. Blue on white. Blue from Jaden's father Tymon, white from himself.

Jaden shut his eyes. His mind fell back to the last time he saw his son Matt – deep in the bowels of the Inner Sanctum on Sol. Jaden had been battling the Omnir tribal leader Kyo for the unbound Gems the Sol tribe kept, trying to stop him before he destroyed the entire island. Kyo had a bound Gem himself somehow, and wielded fire – the worst enemy to Jaden's ice. He had barely held his own, despite his decades of training. Kyo had been well prepared.

Then Matt, Charlotte, and Dyne's daughter Izzy had showed up in the Inner Sanctum. Kyo turned on them. In the fight to protect the kits, Jaden slipped up, and Kyo had cracked Jaden's Gem, sending him tumbling into the void in a strange and painful teleport, leaving the children behind. He ended up on the other side of the country with a damaged pendant, a barely healed Gem, and a month of lost time. It took him weeks to hitchhike back to El Dorado. By the time he had managed to get back to Sol, it was in ruins. Bodies everywhere. Burned village huts. His own home ransacked and smoldering.

No survivors.

No sign of his kits.

He had found Aurora's body in the garden, barely recognizable. He buried her, and carved a tombstone out of one of the broken fence slabs, tears falling throughout the whole process.

After he had finished, he sat in the garden for hours. It had been the lowest point in his life. Everything was numb. Dead. Ruined.

It was the first time where he considered ending his own life. After all, what else was there to live for? He had lost everything. His family, his kits, his best friend, his way home, and any communication with Zyearth, any support to help him cope with that terrible, terrible day.

Thankfully though, he had met Embrik later that day, and Alexina soon after and slowly started finding purpose again.

But recent events worked to undo all that progress. This damn war. Losing three thousand people when the refugee village Atlas had been callously bombed to hell. Getting stuck with Ackerson and slowly devolving into the villain.

And now seeing Zeke, proof that there was likely more hardship ahead. Another family started and lost.

"Jaden?" Embrik asked again.

Jaden shook his head. "I don't... I don't know." He stared at Zeke again. "In a lot of ways... I hope not. Because I don't want to face whatever it is that takes him from us."

Alexina gripped his hand.

PLANNING

Leah sat opposite of Jaden and Zeke, Embrik next to her, focusing on the harsh bumps in the road as Alexina drove along. They had been traveling for nearly a week, trying to avoid military checkpoints, and were finally nearing their destination. She had changed Zeke's bandages several times during the trip and the wound finally started to look better. She just had to be wary of infection, though so far she hadn't found any with her magic.

But she couldn't sit still. After all, Kyrie could be back with her Gem any minute now. She hoped she would be. The last thing she wanted to do was attempt another mission without her Gem.

Not that she wanted to do this mission at all.

Someone clapped in her face and she jumped.

Jaden waved a hand about. "Earth to Leah. We need to talk about this mission and you need to focus on this if we're going to get through it okay."

Leah glared. Jaden glared back, but she didn't back down. "Guardian Azure--"

"Whatever you have to say has to wait." Jaden put the datasquare in the center of the room and pulled up a map of the capital city of Idaho, their destination. He pointed to a large building. "May is here, the State Congress building. She's moving to the governor's mansion. We need to take her out before she gets to her car." He pointed to a chart. "Security is tight, but not the same level as Tao, since she's an ally, a very minor dignitary, and not considered a risk. Security for Tao was as much about protecting him as it was protecting the American politicians from him."

"How do we get close?" Zeke asked.

Jaden eyed him. "You don't. You're injured, so you'll only be back up."

Zeke flicked his tail, but didn't question it.

"The rest of us will use disguises," Jaden said. "Embrik's got a selection to choose from. I expect there will be a lot of homeless in the area, so that's our disguise. Zeke, you're with Embrik. Alexina and Leah, you're with me."

Leah flattened her ears and snarled. *"Guardian Azure--"*

Jaden turned back to his map, ignoring her. "They're going to be monitoring every electronic form of communication within a twenty-mile radius of May. And we don't have the cover of military this time. We can't risk it. So." He pointed to Leah and Zeke. "You two will be our communication."

Leah jumped a little. "But--"

Zeke crossed his arms in front of his chest. "No. Absolutely not. You don't get to decide that for us."

"It's either this, or we risk getting caught," Jaden said. "And we can't risk that again, especially after that attack. You don't have a choice." He crossed his arms. "Leah, when Embrik first showed up, I spoke to him in the Athánatos' native language. And you understood me."

Leah lowered her gaze, remembering the words. *Useless. Don't touch the cat. Treat them like civilians.* A dark feeling roiled in her gut. "...Yeah, I did."

"How?"

Leah shrugged. "I think Archángeli is translating the words in Zeke's head, and then it transfers to me."

Jaden raised an eyebrow. "Can we test that?"

Leah twitched her whiskers. "Sure, I guess." She shifted in her seat. "But Guardian Azure--"

"Hold. Your. Questions." Jaden shut his eyes a moment, then turned to Zeke and muttered something in Athánatos' musical language. The words bounced around in her mind and slowly made sense, though with a slight lag for the translation. The opening lines for a Zyearth nursery rhyme.

Squirrels climb the branches and birds will fly free
And the winged dragon flutters high over the sea

Zeke gave him a strange look, but repeated the words back to him in English. Jaden turned to Leah.

She glared at him. "Guardian Azure--"

"Did you hear the words or not?" Jaden asked.

Leah sighed. "...Yeah. I heard them, though with a lag."

"Yeah, same," Zeke said.

"Alright, let's see if it works in reverse," Jaden said. "Zeke, cover your ears." Zeke did so, and Jaden continued the poem.

But when the sky darkens and the sun sets to rest,
Squirrel, bird, and dragon return to their nest.

Leah frowned. "I hear it, but it's definitely more laggy on my end."

"Far more," Zeke said, frowning.

Apologies, Archángeli said in Zeke's head, transferring to Leah's. *I can only move so quickly.*

Jaden shrugged. "It'll work for our purposes. For the most part, I'll stick to that, unless I need something more urgent. Now." He sat back. "We're parking outside of town and we'll walk in. Embrik and Zeke from the south, the rest of us from the north. I'm going to try and freeze her brain, like we did with Tao, and Alexina will be backup. Zeke, Embrik, your main jobs will be distraction and confusion if we get caught. I'm sure between Embrik's fire and Archang... er, Zeke's summon, you could do that, plus your summon can get you out of there in a hurry if necessary."

Zeke flattened his ears. "Archángeli couldn't lift even *one* of us, let alone both of us."

"They might surprise you," Alexina said.

Jaden sat back. "We'll try to meet up at the Congress building at 1500. Hope you're all in good shape. We've got a lot of walking to do."

Leah finally had enough. *"Guardian Azure, will you listen to me?"*

Jaden turned on her, glaring. "What?"

"I'm not going to do this mission if I don't have my Gem," Leah said firmly. He glared at her. She winced, but forced the words out. "N-non... non-negotiable." Dang it, that was so pathetic.

Jaden chuckled darkly. "Sorry Leah, that's not acceptable," he said. "Ackerson said we needed all hands on deck, and we've only got an hour window this afternoon because of how long it took to get here, Gem or no Gem."

"But--"

"No buts," Jaden said. "This is war, Leah. You don't have the luxury of saying no."

Leah flicked both ears back and twitched her whiskers. Good Draso, this was such a disaster. "I wish I never would have left my Gem behind."

128

"We did what we had to," Jaden said, baring one fang. "We would have gotten caught instantly otherwise."

"Like that even matters," Leah said, growling. "We still got caught. And we killed even *more* while escaping. Tao, his translator, eleven soldiers--"

"Are you keeping *count?*"

"Of course I am!" Leah said. "Why the heck aren't *you?*"

Zeke frowned at her, ears flat.

Jaden stared at her a moment, then rolled his eyes. "Don't give yourself so much credit. They died because Sharp was running an operation that even Ackerson isn't aware of."

"But they're still *dead.*" Leah's chest and eyes burned. "Over a gone, for what? Do you really believe in this war, Guardian Azure?"

Jaden furrowed his brow, opening his mouth. But he stopped. He gritted his teeth and turned away instead.

"Guardian Azure," Leah said. "P-Please, I'm begging you. We don't have to do this. Ackerson is corrupt--"

"Leah, we've already had this conversation," Jaden said, arms crossed.

"But you didn't let me *finish,*" Leah said. "The team member I mentioned from the future, he said--"

"I don't *care,*" Jaden said.

"I do," Embrik said, turning to Leah. "What did he say?"

Jaden narrowed his eyes. "Embrik…"

Embrik glared at Jaden, his eyes burning. Jaden backed down. Embrik turned back. "Do continue."

Leah shifted. "T-This team member was a part of the team Outlander. He said that Ackerson started using his teams to benefit himself rather than the military, and when the military caught on, Ackerson started cannibalizing his teams. Turned them against each other, trying to cover his tracks. Eventually most of them turned on Ackerson himself and went hunting him."

Jaden frowned, ears pinned back.

Leah leaned forward. "Guardian Azure--"

"Don't call me that," Jaden snapped.

Leah flicked her ears back. "B-but--"

"Don't question me, Leah."

Leah twitched her tail. "Fine… J-Jaden. We can prevent that. We can stop him *now*. We could report him to the proper authorities and explain our suspicions and prevent a lot of hurt."

Jaden pressed his lips together. Embrik turned to him now. Jaden shook his head. "No. I still don't like it."

Leah collapsed, defeated. "Why not?"

Jaden leaned forward. "If everything you say is true, Leah, I promise you a lot of people will die trying to go against Ackerson. Going after him now, proper channels or not, is going to make us targets. And Ackerson is in a position of extreme power. For all we know, it'll just kill us all rather than saving anyone else. We have to put ourselves first."

Leah stared, incredulous. "The Defender Oath--"

"--Applies only to Defenders," Jaden said. "Which… I'm not anymore." He gently tucked his Golden Guardian Defender pendant into his shirt. "I've come to accept that."

Embrik stared, wide eyed. Even Alexina turned her head a moment.

Leah flicked her ears back. Was she really hearing this? Golden Guardian Jaden Azure denying he was a Defender?

What had Earth done to him?

"Jaden," Embrik said. "Even if we refuse to try and stop Ackerson, perhaps it would be in our best interest to disappear. If he is truly on the verge of cannibalizing his teams…"

"You'd have to ditch Leah and I then," Zeke said bitterly.

Jaden raised an eyebrow. "Why?"

Zeke pointed to the back of his neck. "We have trackers."

Jaden's jaw dropped. "He didn't. That program was banned."

"War gave him some loopholes," Zeke said. "Or at least that's what he said."

Jaden sighed. "And there's no way to dig those out safely." He shook his head. "All the more reason to stick with this, at least for now. If we fail, or run, or report Ackerson, we'll be targets." He furrowed his brow. "I'm sorry, Leah, but I don't see any other way."

Leah glared at him. "Y-you're not sorry at all."

Jaden narrowed his gaze… but he didn't counter her.

She leaned her head on her hands. Good Draso. She never should have come to Earth. She never should have gone to the mainland. If she hadn't… maybe all those they killed would still be alive. Some Defender she was.

"Leah," Zeke said suddenly. Leah looked up. He frowned at her. "Don't beat yourself up over what happened."

She scoffed. "Right."

"I'm serious," Zeke said. "You behaved better than all of us. Trying to do the right thing, fighting only when you have to, without intending to kill." He wrinkled his snout. "You could have killed Sharp and you didn't."

She shrugged. "M-Maybe I should have."

"I'm glad you didn't," Zeke said. "Because that says a lot about you."

Jaden let out a tiny, choked sound, and turned away.

She glanced up at Zeke, and pressed her lips together. *Thanks.*

A smell of… habanero and apple crumble hit her nose. Confusion. *Let's… not push it,* Zeke said. *But you're welcome.*

Leah stared at the floor again. Not welcome enough apparently.

I'm sorry, Zeke said. *I know you don't believe me, but I am.*

She looked into his eyes. There was genuine sympathy there. She frowned. If he was sorry, why did he push her away?

131

It's… complicated, Zeke said. He flattened his ears and his tail drooped. *Too complicated. I don't know how to put it to words myself.* Leah felt the truth of it in his words. *So… I'm sorry.*

Leah watched him. *Sure… I appreciate it.* She forced a smile. *Really.*

He managed a smile back, but it didn't look quite right. Better than nothing though.

CHAPTER 18

MAY

I hate this. Zeke's thoughts came through Leah's head loud and clear.

Leah's ear twitched but she didn't respond. The melting, dirty snow crunched under her bare feet, the air bit at her nose, and the silence of a war-torn city on edge strained her ears. The streets were mostly empty, aside from the homeless, who huddled hidden away, far apart from each other. Leah and the others wore ragtag clothes to fit in, but the fake, deceptive feel of the outfits ground on Leah's psyche. Like with El Dorado, Idaho's capital city of Nysa had most of its buildings boarded up, and trash littered the streets.

War ruined everything.

The moment she and Zeke had separated and started walking their separate ways to the Congress building, she got a constant flow of his thoughts filtering through her mind, each one as despondent as the last. Thoughts of the war, the injury in his side, the mission they were about to go on, Jaden's stubbornness, and a constant, underlying feeling of hate – for this situation, for the time travel, for the jewel bond...

For himself.

That last one threw her off guard. She tried chasing it down, tried to learn more, but it vanished quickly.

She stared at the snow. Maybe that was for the best while on a mission.

Kyrie never showed up with her Gem. Alexina assured her that the owl summon would be able to find her way back, but so far, no luck. An ever-present dread hung over her now. What if she never got her Gem back? What if they actually did crush the car?

The Thought Factory went on overload, blasting her with images of the Humvee being crushed into a tiny cube, her Gem shattering with it. She could only imagine the agony of power withdrawal, the psychological horror, the torturous, painful death that she had no chance to stop--

Leah? A gentle, comforting smell of coffee entered her nose. *You okay?*

Leah forced her body to relax. She couldn't let Zeke notice. Or Jaden. She had to be the Defender here, especially if he wouldn't be. *Especially* after all she had done in the Tao mission. She had to prove her worth, make up for the losses, protect her team. *I'm fine.*

You're not, Zeke said. *I can smell it.*

Why do you even care? Leah said, though she immediately regretted it. *...Sorry. I shouldn't have snapped at you.*

A pause. *No. It's fine. I deserved that.*

Leah took a deep breath. *You really don't.*

Another long pause. *So... do you want to talk about it?*

This is neither the time or place, Leah said. She breathed deeply. *But thank you.*

Yeah. Sure. His voice vanished with the smells, making Leah feel empty.

"We're here," Jaden said in the Athánatos language, his voice slightly distant, considering the translation lag. Leah glanced up. A large, domed building towered over them, hidden behind a shoddy chain-link fence topped

with barbed wire. A dilapidated park and garden lay behind the fence – overgrown grass poking through the snow, bushes in bad need of a trim, tree branches strewn about everywhere. Even the building itself didn't look great. Scaffolding covered the front of it, lined with paint and tools, though no workers. A sign in front had details about a restoration project. The sign itself leaned against an unkempt bush. A few policemen stood out front, but seemed quite distracted.

Several cameras lined the gate and street around the building. Jaden wiggled his fingers and froze any nearby until their casings cracked.

While most of the buildings surrounding the State Parliament looked to be worn down government offices, one building across the street looked like a condemned apartment complex. Several homeless entered it, huddled under blankets, avoiding the white glare of the Congress building.

"Parking lot is on the west side, so we'll head that way," Jaden continued. *"Leah, tell Zeke and Embrik to hang out on the east side."*

Leah nodded. She relayed the message to Zeke.

Alexina leaned against Jaden, glancing toward the building. *"Now what?"*

"Now we wait," Jaden said. He sat down across the street by the parking lot and placed an old tin can in front of him. Alexina sat next to him. The pair of them huddled under cheap blankets. He nodded to the corner and handed Leah a blanket. *"Keep an eye out there, Leah."*

Leah nodded and walked down the street before plopping herself on a soft snow pile.

And they waited.

Fifteen minutes passed. A couple of people walked out and poked at the broken cameras, agitated. Leah heard them mumbling about cheap technology and needing to order replacements before they vanished back into the building.

Then a new group of people walked out and headed toward the parking lots. A young woman with her brown hair in a bun, wearing glasses and a long, black peacoat with two bodyguards.

Leah's heart jumped. Their target. Rosanna May.

Rosanna and her bodyguards crossed the street. She pulled out her phone and fiddled with it until they got to the entrance to the lot.

Then she stopped in front of Jaden. Leah flattened her ears.

But Jaden didn't acknowledge her. He huddled closer, shaking as if he was cold, pulling the blanket tighter around him.

Rosanna stared at him a moment, then turned to her bodyguard. "You're sure there's nothing we can do for them?" she asked, her accent thick.

Leah frowned. For them. Not about them. Clearly more concerned for their well-being than the city's image.

The bodyguard shrugged. "You'd have to take that up with the governor, ma'am."

She narrowed her gaze. "That's all I've been doing during this entire visit. I'm tired of being ignored. He's failing his people." She dropped some money in Jaden's tin can. "I'm trying to do more for you, I promise." She walked into the lot.

Leah furrowed her brow. Fire and ice, everything about this was wrong. She... she had to do something. She slowly stood.

But then Rosanna stopped mid-step. Her eyes rolled to the back of her head and she started falling. One of the bodyguards moved to catch her. Leah gritted her teeth. Jaden had already frozen her brain. Too late. Too late! If only she had her Gem, then maybe--

The crack of a high-powered rifle echoed through the buildings and Rosanna's head exploded like a watermelon in a hiss of steam, blood, and flesh. A chunk of her frozen brain lodged itself in one of her bodyguard's shoulders, and he screamed. The body fell cartoonishly fast, splattering remains and blood on the asphalt and snow. The other bodyguard panicked and ran, whipping out his phone and frantically dialing. The policemen in front of the Congress buildings ran for them.

Leah's heart stopped.

Jaden and Alexina stared, jaw slack, before Jaden turned and violently threw up all over the snow. Alexina patted his back, looking around, eyes wide with fear. The policemen ran by, ignoring them all, calling on their radios.

The hell was THAT? Zeke shouted in her brain.

Leah swallowed hard and ran over to Jaden. *Sniper round! Rosanna's head--* she gagged, unable to finish. Fire and ice and *stone,* who did that?

Leah, get the hell out of there!

Trying to! Leah said. Jaden wiped his mouth, then gagged again. He was in no shape to shield them if the sniper decided to eliminate witnesses. She glanced around, frantic, trying to find the source.

Something in the upper floors of the apartment complex caught her eye. A flash of black on red. Leah's breath caught.

Trecheon?

A puma dashed by one window, followed by a black fox, a red quilar, a thin, black-haired human man, and… a quilar with white and blue.

Carter.

Leah! Sirens sounded in the distance.

Leah pulled Jaden to his feet. She and Alexina tugged him away from the scene, and rounded a corner. Alexina covered their tracks with more snow. They moved onto another street just as a police car showed up. *We're out of sight. Meet us at the car. Take the long way around.*

What the hell happened? Zeke asked. *Who the hell sniped our target?*

Leah chewed her lip. *Outlander did.*

CHAPTER 19

CONFRONTATION

"You're absolutely sure, Leah?" Jaden asked. "You saw another of Ackerson's teams?"

The group had managed to make their way back to the Humvee without being stopped or arrested. A miracle in Jaden's mind. He still wasn't sure how they had pulled it off.

His gut still roiled with the image of Rosanna's head exploding. Lightning and *air*. He hadn't seen carnage like that since the Sol Genocide and… and Atlas's destruction. All the blood and brains brought back terrible memories. His stomach still roiled thinking about it. He spent the whole frantic race from the city racking his brain, trying to figure out what the hell happened. Alexina drove for over two hours before anyone spoke.

Then Leah dropped a bomb on them. Another team was there. Another of Ackerson's.

So much for subtle kills.

Leah shuffled on her seat. "I-I can't say for certain…" she said. "But I saw a bunch of figures leaving that old apartment complex, and I'm pretty sure I saw the leader of Outlander, Trecheon." She paused and fiddled with her hands. "He's… pretty distinctive."

Jaden narrowed his eyes. "How so?"

Leah chewed her lip. "H-he's red," she said, looking away. "With black streaks. Unusual." She nodded to Embrik. "A little like Embrik, though with tipped quills, and he's a standard Earth quilar, not an Athánatos."

Jaden's body buzzed. Red quills. *Red quills.* His mind wandered back to the first time he had met Ackerson, right after he had frozen the brains of those responsible for killing the refugees of Atlas. Ackerson had stood over them with two zyfaunos soldiers at his side. A bat… and a red, black-streaked quilar.

And now he had a name. Trecheon. But just a first name. A tiny voice in his head poked at him. *Ask his last name. Ask if he's an Omnir.*

But another voice fought back. *No. It doesn't matter. The Omnirs are dead. They were tricked. Used. They are not your enemy. Theron is.*

Ackerson is, he argued with himself. Jaden shook his head free of the thoughts.

Regardless of how he felt about it, Leah was probably right, much as he didn't want to admit it. He rubbed his temple. "Why would Ackerson send a second team? Especially one so destructive."

Embrik crossed his arms. "Ackerson will apparently pit his teams against one another. He will use them to cover his tracks." He eyed Leah. "We were already warned of this."

Jaden glared at Embrik.

"We did what we had to," Alexina said. "We already discussed that we have very little choice."

"Uh… everyone," Zeke said. "We've uh… we've got bigger problems." He passed a phone to Jaden. It had a news report on it.

Jaden pinned his ears back and pressed play on the video.

"Representatives out of Idaho's capital, Nysa, report that UK Ambassador Rosanna May has been assassinated this afternoon walking from the State Congress Building to her car, prompting the UK to break ties with America. May was with two bodyguards when she was shot in the head. One bodyguard is injured."

Jaden sunk down. Oh, *hell.*

The report continued, giving a summary from the surviving bodyguards, and a breakdown of the weapon that was likely involved – a high-powered rifle firing Lapua Magnum rounds, currently outlawed for civilian use.

"Ammo casings were found in a nearby apartment complex, bearing the name Jackson Ammunition, a US brand munitions company that provides weapons and ammo exclusively to the US military."

Jaden exchanged a glance with Zeke. That was sloppy. The hell was Ackerson thinking?

He leaned on his hands and narrowed his gaze. He checked the time on the phone. It had only been three hours since the attack.

So how the hell did civilian news already have this much information? And why were they allowed to spread it in the first place?

"The UK's Minister of Defense has responded to the situation." The video jump cut to a shot of the Minister of Defense standing at a podium, calmly addressing the crowd. *"'This callous assassination against a peaceful ally was clearly implemented by the US military. This will be treated as an open act of war. As of right now, our alliance with the US is over. We'll be working to get all UK citizens and dignitaries out of the US ASAP.'* The video went back to the original reporter. *Reports from the White House say that the US is trying to mitigate the situation, so far without success."*

"That's circumstantial evidence," Zeke said. "They can't prove that the US military fired that gun. Not with just one casing. Especially since that casing was left there. A good sniper would have picked it up. It could have been planted."

Leah twitched her whiskers. "B-but they did kill Rosanna."

"But the UK doesn't *know that,*" Zeke countered.

"Doesn't matter," Jaden said. "Rumor has it that the UK has been looking for an excuse to break ties with the US for years, considering the current president. This is an opportunity." He shook his head. "And I have a feeling this was planned from the beginning. Perhaps it was a paid assassination even."

Zeke leaned his head on his hand. "Shit." He glanced at Jaden. "I was really out of the loop in my own time during this debacle, so I didn't know what caused the UK to break ties but... I do remember that it led to some serious problems for both countries."

Jaden bared his teeth. "Alexina, find a safe space to pull over. I'm going to talk to Ackerson about this. Privately."

Embrik twitched an ear. "Is that wise?"

"I don't care if it is," Jaden said. "I want answers."

Alexina twitched her tail, but she pulled off the highway and found a backroad by the woods. "Be careful, my love," she said. Jaden nodded to her. He threw open the door and stormed out, leaving the group behind.

Deep in the woods, he found a small clearing, called Ackerson, and threw the datasquare on the snow.

Ackerson appeared a second later, staring at Jaden with a raised eyebrow, his brown hair ruffled. "Well, didn't expect this. You looking for praise or something? The best I can give you is at least you didn't screw up. I'm looking for another job for you. Be patient, furry."

"I have *several questions,*" Jaden said, growling.

Ackerson folded his arms. "Alright then. Ask away."

Jaden intended to ask him about May. Ask why they were taking out allied dignitaries. If Ackerson understood the serious consequences from this. Hell, who was paying him to take out assassination hits. But that's not what came out of his mouth.

"Why did you send a second team after May?"

Ackerson raised both eyebrows now. He leaned on his hands. "I think that'd be obvious."

Jaden narrowed his gaze.

"Jaden," Ackerson said. "You messed up on the Tao hit. And that's not the only example of you screwing around. You're getting sloppy. Not following orders. Allowing yourself to be *seen*. I needed a backup in case you screwed up again.*"

"I follow orders," Jaden said through clenched teeth.

Ackerson eyed him. "This time last year, you would have killed those two rookies for screwing up rather than compromise yourself. Instead, you *protected them,* let yourself get arrested, and went after your fellow soldiers to free yourself instead of letting me do something. Your own damn people."

Jaden snarled. *"They aren't my people."*

Ackerson pointed at the screen. "Well, you better start thinking of them as your people if you want to survive this war."

Jaden sat on a rock and leaned on his knees, his body buzzing. Good. Draso. What the hell had happened to him? Ackerson was right. He would have absolutely sacrificed Leah and Zeke to protect his identity. He would have killed young, innocent zyfaunos in the name of an unjust war and a corrupt commander. The only thing that protected them was the fact that they were useful. Leah for her connections to Zyearth. Zeke for his connections to Athánatos and then later... himself and Alexina.

If they had been anyone else... they'd be dead.

He shut his eyes, as a burning built up behind them. What happened to him? Where was the Defender? The Guardian?

Draso, when did he break so completely?

He couldn't do this anymore.

"For god's sake, Jaden," Ackerson said. "You used to trust me. If you had just waited, I could have talked with Sharp and fixed the whole damn problem, but you're getting reckless."

Jaden glared. "You knew about Sharp. You knew he was a Wish Duster."

Ackerson crossed his arms and leaned back. "I know every mage in this army. Yes, I knew about Sharp."

Jaden growled. "So who's his partner? Are they a goddamn xenophobic asshole too?"

"Don't," Ackerson said. "The other mages in this army aren't your business."

"Are the racists?"

Ackerson rolled his eyes. "Save your breath, Jaden. You know how this military works."

Jaden bared his teeth. "I do, in more ways than one. And I'm done with it. I want out."

Ackerson lifted a brow. "Pardon?"

"When we joined you, you said we could leave any time," Jaden said. "So we're leaving."

Ackerson stared at him a moment, then shrugged. "Fine. You, Alexina, and Embrik can go free. I'll make sure you're fully pardoned for everything. Nice working with you."

"Leah and Zeke too," Jaden said.

Ackerson held up a hand. "Ah, ah. That wasn't part of the deal." He rubbed his chin. "Doubt the two rookies will be helpful in the ways I need them to be. I'll ship them back to Camp Bennett. Likely they'll go straight to the front lines--"

"You can't do that!"

143

"I can, and I will," Ackerson said. "They weren't a part of our original agreement. They're uncontrollable. Out of line. Risky. Can't have that in my team without someone to balance them out."

Jaden snarled. "They'll *die.*"

"Hmm, yes, like so many *fuzzies* before them," Ackerson said, emphasizing the slur. "Luck of the draw, I suppose." He eyed Jaden. "Strange time to develop a conscience over two total strangers." He leaned in. "Perhaps there's something going on that I don't know about, eh, Zyearthling?"

Jaden gritted his teeth and pinned his ears back.

Ackerson tilted his head. "Tells me all I need to know." He pointed to Jaden. "If you really want to protect them, you'll stay. I can't guarantee their safety if you don't."

Jaden's whole body shook with a poorly contained anger. How dare he. Treating them like pawns. Blackmailing him.

But this was the Ackerson he knew. He should expect this. And Leah warned him...

He really shouldn't have gotten involved with this asshole.

But what could they do about it? Nothing. There was nowhere to go. Not with Zeke and Leah's trackers. Not with Leah's Gem missing. Damn all of this.

"...Fine."

Ackerson smiled slyly. "Good." He sat back. "After the last two hits, you all clearly deserve a break. Take a week. Get a hotel. Sleep in a bed for once. In the meantime, I'm going to find a simple hit for you. Something where you can work with another of my teams – knowingly this time." He eyed him. "This is your last chance to prove you're still worth something to me, or I might terminate this relationship myself and put the bastard pilot and pussy cat on the front lines anyway. Understood?"

Jaden leaned his head on his hands. "...Yes. Understood."

"Good to hear," Ackerson said. "Go relax. I'll contact you in a week. Ackerson out." The hologram vanished.

Damn it. Damn it all! He should have left this alone. He never should have confronted Ackerson. He wasn't going to give them a week off. He was going to hunt them down. All of them. Jaden had essentially painted the targets himself.

He needed to get out of there. He needed to protect his team. And he needed to do it alone. He couldn't panic them. Leah might have a heart attack hearing Ackerson was after them.

He paused. She probably wouldn't actually. She'd go after Ackerson herself. Like Dyne would. Even though neither of them were equipped to fight him. Healers weren't fighters.

Fire and ice, what he wouldn't give for Dyne at his side. But he didn't have Dyne. He only had himself.

And only he could do this.

DISTANCE

"Leah," Zeke asked. "What happened to Jaden all those years ago?"

The group of them sat huddled in the Humvee with blankets and water, still fighting off the shock of Rosanna's assassination. Zeke had only seen the shot second-hand through Leah's memories, but the blast to his system was just as bad as if he had been right there. The wound in his side ached even thinking about it. He had to put his brain elsewhere.

Leah looked up, one ear flat.

Zeke shrugged. "You said you'd explain when you had a moment, and with everything going on, now's probably as good a time as any. Especially with Jaden not here."

Leah waved a hand. "Y-yeah... you make a good point." She leaned back. "I mentioned before that Jaden was a high-ranking Defender. For context, the Defenders are a military from the planet Zyearth. Zyfaunos originate from Zyearth actually. They all left in a mass exodus during a catastrophic world war. Like... like this one." She shook her head.

"Why Defenders?" Zeke said. "Most militaries don't have like, proper names. They're just a country's military."

Leah leaned forward. "The Defenders were created to protect the zyfaunos leaving Zyearth during that mass exodus. Some left with the fleeing citizens, others stayed to help get the planet back on its feet. This used to be the core of the Defenders. Altruistic work helping war- and natural disaster-torn civilizations function again. But it… changed, after the Sol Genocide. The Defenders thought their Golden Guardians, Jaden and Dyne, had both died. It was a massive blow to everyone, and Master Guardian Tox reacted poorly. The altruistic work stopped. Master Guardian Tox basically shut all intergalactic efforts. He decided it was better to stay on Zyearth and protect the citizens there. We had a few missions here and there, but more and more, they ended in death, even when they were peaceful. My dad was one of those."

She shut her eyes a moment, then continued.

"The senior Defenders believe that's why the Master Guardian didn't replace his Golden Guardians until last year," Leah continued. "The Golden Guardians were always at the forefront of those altruistic expeditions. No Guardians, no missions." She sighed. "Master Guardian Tox lost two Golden Guardian pairs in his time in the position. That was unheard of. He was afraid to lose another."

Zeke frowned. "But Jaden didn't die, obviously. So what happened?"

Embrik took a deep breath. He took a sip of water. "It is complicated. But on the surface, as I understand it, Jaden had married someone in an Earth tribe called Sol and was living with them. When his oldest child was eight, a rival tribe, the Omnirs, attacked Sol and destroyed the whole village, including Jaden's entire family."

Leah narrowed her gaze. "The Omnirs were innocent."

Embrik scoffed. "They were coerced, but 'innocent' is too kind a word, considering they murdered an entire people without thought. But yes, they were tricked into attacking by the Basileus. And they paid the price for that gullibility as well. The Basileus destroyed them all trying to force the leader of the Omnirs into a Black Bound bind with their stolen Gems. Jaden and I witnessed it first-hand."

Leah gawked. *"That's* what killed them? That's awful…"

Zeke raised an eyebrow. "What's a Black Bound?"

"A… very unpleasant form of binding to Lexi jewels," Leah said. "Most who start the process don't survive."

Zeke winced. "Yikes."

"Yeah," Leah said.

Zeke frowned. "So Jaden lost everything then."

"He did," Embrik said.

"But," Zeke said. "He still has you two."

Alexina and Embrik exchanged glances. Alexina fiddled with her hands. "Jaden holds us at arm's length," she said. "Yes, I am his wife, and yes, Embrik is like a brother to him, but after the emotional trauma of losing everything in the Sol Genocide, he… struggles with emotional connection."

"That puts it too lightly," Embrik said.

Leah chewed her lip. "He didn't lose everything."

Alexina glanced at Leah. "What do you mean?"

Leah sat up straight. "His kids survived."

Embrik's eyes widened and Alexina let out a gasp. She brought her hands to her face. "They did?"

"Yeah," Leah said. "Matt, Charlotte, and his partner's daughter Izzy. Matt and Izzy are our new Golden Guardians actually. Guardian Azure… Matt… He handpicked me to come on this mission because I'm an expert on summons."

Alexina frowned deeply. "But he has not let you talk to him about this."

"I've tried," Leah said. She pulled her blanket closer. "I really have. You've seen it. I've been t-trying every chance I get, since the moment we met. B-but he pushes me away every time I try, so I've given up for now." Her face grew bitter and a smell of raw cranberries hit Zeke's nose. "He'll figure it out eventually."

"He should know *now,*" Embrik said.

"Then you tell him," Leah said, her voice thick. "Because I can't."

Embrik exchanged a glance with Alexina. They opened the Humvee's door and rushed out. Zeke frowned and followed, Leah on his tail.

Just in time too, apparently. Jaden walked through the trees toward the Humvee. Alexina ran for him. "Jaden--"

He held up his hand. "Let's... let's not. That was an emotional roller coaster there. But I explained we're all shaken up by what just happened. Ackerson is... giving us a week off. We're gonna get some tents and go camping, away from everything. He'll contact us in a week."

Embrik frowned. "A week off."

Jaden pressed his lips together. "Yeah."

"This is not the kind of job that permits time off," Alexina said.

"Then think of it as a sabbatical," Jaden said. "He said we needed the break."

Embrik glanced at Alexina, then turned to Jaden. "But Jaden--"

"Later," Jaden said. "I just... I need to drive and get my mind off things." He smiled, but even Zeke could see how fake it was. "Let's just go. In silence for now, okay?"

Leah stepped forward. "Jaden..."

"Please," Jaden said. "Just for a little bit."

Everyone looked at each other. Zeke stared at Jaden, trying to process all he had learned about him. He looked different, in that light. Like Zeke could see the cracks behind the mask.

"Let's give him his time," Zeke said. "We've got a week."

Leah looked at him. He tried smiling at her, though it probably looked fake. *Let's try to be understanding, okay?*

You're talking to me willingly?

Zeke shrugged, though his ears grew hot. *Sometimes it's necessary.*

Leah watched him a moment. "Yeah." She entered the Humvee again. The rest of them piled in, leaving Zeke standing outside.

Jaden walked up and opened the driver's side door. "Thanks," he said, though he wouldn't look at Zeke. He pulled himself in.

Zeke took a deep breath and entered the Humvee.

CHAPTER 21

WISHING DUST

They spent the next two days driving, taking winding roads and staying away from all major cities. Along their trip, camping equipment kept randomly appearing in the vehicle – tents, air mattresses, thick blankets, pillows, big brown tarps, piles of food, cooking utensils, fancy first-aid kits, everything. The Humvee grew cramped with supplies.

For some reason, Jaden was sneaking out while they rested and buying equipment without anyone seeing or helping.

Zeke didn't like it.

By the time they stopped moving, they were high up in a set of wintery mountains, far from any roads, buried in a tiny clearing surrounded by thick trees and snow. No one anywhere. Zeke didn't have a clue where they were. And it was clear that that was the point.

"We'll camp here," Jaden said.

"Not much of a vacation spot," Zeke muttered.

Jaden ignored him. He got out of the Humvee and started clearing snow with his magic. "Zeke, can you have Archángeli do a sweep of the perimeter for us?"

Zeke exchanged a glance with Leah. She frowned, but nodded. He flicked an ear back. "Uh, sure." He sent Archángeli into the woods around them.

They set up the rest of the camp in silence. One tent each, camouflaged in white and gray, all in a semi-circle around a rocky firepit, with heavy logs around it. It looked like one of those picturesque camping postcards with "Wish you were here!" blazoned across the top. It could almost be peaceful except for the overarching sense of dread. Embrik started a fire, which strangely didn't produce smoke, and started preparing food on the camp stove.

Jaden sat on one of the logs, fiddling with his hands. "We need to talk about Wish Dusters."

Zeke glanced up. Embrik paused with the food, and even Alexina raised an eyebrow.

Leah frowned at Jaden. "Why?"

"Because there's likely going to be more than one," Jaden said. He turned to Zeke. "What do you know about focus jewels?"

Zeke flicked an ear. "Practically nothing."

Jaden sighed. He clapped his hands. "Alright. Focus jewels 101, speed run edition. Focus jewels are typically bound to users through two ways – physical and spiritual. Most use only one. Vanguardian Continuum Stones are physically bound, our Lexi Gems are spiritually bound. Some use both, like the Athánatos Ei-Ei jewels. With me so far?"

"Sure, I guess," Zeke said.

"Wishing Dust though, is very different," Jaden said. "It's bound psychologically. To get the dust, users grind a focus jewel into a fine powder and drop it into the eyes, while making a 'wish' in a ritual. That wish is bound to the user's psyche. Wishes are essentially very specific magic spells that do one thing really well."

"Like what?" Leah asked. She took a plate of food from Embrik and bit into a hotdog. Her face suggested it wasn't terribly tasty.

"Usually relatively simple things," Jaden said, taking his own plate from Embrik. "Illusions, telepathic communication on a limited scale, being able to see in the dark, lifting small objects with your mind, that kind of thing. Rarely anything physically destructive or elemental. Wishing Dust is a low-power focus jewel, so it can't handle anything bigger. Wishes come with consequences, usually some catch or loophole in the wish, based on the language used to make it, so Wish Dusters need to plan out their wish very carefully to make sure nothing goes seriously wrong."

Leah flicked her ears back. "W-What do you mean by seriously wrong?"

"Death by self-destruction," Jaden said. "The psychological load is too much to handle and they physically rip themselves apart, skin and flesh, and nothing can stop it. Rituals fail when a Wish Duster wishes for something too extravagant and the loophole is too big to compensate for, and it unfortunately happens often. The deaths aren't pretty."

Leah shuddered.

Jaden continued. "By intergalactic law, Wishing Dust is illegal because it's so deadly. So naturally there's a big black market for it. Planet Vanguard has the greatest concentration of Wish Dusters on the continent Unus, though they can be from anywhere. Also, Wish Dusters have terrible reputations and most of them turn to a life of crime."

Embrik flicked his tail, poking at the food on the camp stove. "Why would any use this Dust if the consequences are so dire?"

Jaden shrugged. He sipped at his water and adjusted his seat on the log. "Desperation. Power. Greed. Who knows. But to help increase the chances of success, Wish Dusters usually have a companion. Two Dusters with wishes that complement each other. It helps them bear the psychological load."

Leah twitched her whiskers, frowning. "Then Sharp has an accomplice."

"Very likely, yes," Jaden said.

Zeke lowered his gaze. "So Sharp's wish…"

"I obviously don't know the exact language," Jaden said. "But it was clearly something about immunity from mage magic."

Zeke flicked his tail, swishing snow off the log he sat on. "A mage's worst nightmare."

"If they have no other way of fighting, yes," Jaden said. "Honestly, he wished well. Better to wish for immunity than to try and wish for control over a mage's magic. That'd be almost impossible to survive."

"Hmm," Alexina said, rubbing her chin. "He may have a good wish, but there still must be some loophole, as you have said. Is there any way to predict that?"

Jaden waved a hand. "There's roundabout ways to guess, but nothing is definitive until tested. But they tend to work like the old genie wish standby, where the language is interpreted literally and the result isn't what you expect. Like wishing to be an only child and rather than being the only child in your family, you're the only child in the world. Or asking to stop world hunger only to find that anyone who's hungry is now instantly dead, because hey, no more hunger."

Leah winced. The shadows on her face from the firelight exaggerated the expression, making Zeke feel queasy. "Could a wish really do that?"

"Because Wishing Dust is on the low end of the power spectrum, no," Jaden said. "That's why they often fail. The dust can't handle that big a wish. Wishing for protection against mages though… that'll be hard to predict the exact effects and loophole."

"Is there any way to recognize a Wish Duster?" Zeke asked. "In case we might run into one."

Jaden leaned on his hand. "You can, but it's very difficult. Wishing Dust will add specks of color to the eye that are almost unnoticeable, unlike most focus jewels which tend to be large or very out in the open. It takes a trained eye. Lucky for us, I'm trained in it. But when we're in the heat of battle, there's only so much I can do."

"One more question," Embrik said, passing a cup of coffee to Jaden. "Is there any way to predict his partner's wish?"

Jaden's gaze grew dark. "All I can say is, expect that their wish does something to our magic." He bit into a burger.

Zeke lowered his gaze. He took a plate from Embrik. All this magic stuff ate at him. He glanced at the Ei-Ei jewels on his wrist. Maybe if he actually bound to these things, he could get his own magic.

But that'd also mean giving Alexina access to the jewels. That meant knowing for sure if Alexina and Jaden were his biological parents.

He didn't need anything else to unpack with everything going on. It just wasn't the time.

"Why tell us about this now?" Leah said. Zeke flicked his ears forward.

Jaden flicked his ears back, pausing midbite. "Well… it's important."

"But why?" Zeke asked. He eyed him. "Leah makes a good point. Why now? Because of something Ackerson said?"

Jaden pressed his lips into a tight line but said nothing.

Zeke wrinkled his snout. "It is, isn't it? And you don't want to tell us what."

"I've got it under control," Jaden said.

Zeke shook his head. "Draso's damned wings, Jaden, can't you be up front with us for once?"

Alexina eyed him, frowning.

Jaden narrowed his gaze. He shook his head. "I've got it under control," he repeated. "Trust me."

"Give me a *reason* to then," Zeke said.

"Jaden," Alexina said. Jaden turned to her. She lifted her chin and looked at him firmly. "You have shut us out for too long. Let us help."

Jaden stared at her a moment, then looked away. "I've got it under control."

Alexina narrowed her eyes. "If you truly did, you would not have to repeat it so many times." She stood and took her food into her tent.

That was the end of that conversation. They finished dinner in silence.

After dinner, Leah offered to rebandage Zeke's injury. They sat in Zeke's tent while Leah peeled back his shirt and changed his bandages. He winced while she ripped off old medical tape. *Good Draso, that hurt. Are you trying to wax me or what?* He tried to keep the tone light.

Leah glanced up at him, an eyebrow raised. He tried smiling at her. She smirked back. *Next time I'll just get the electric razor.*

You'll have to fight me first.

That got a little chuckle out of her. She went back to the bandages, gentler this time.

Zeke smiled. That... felt good, to act like a friend with Leah. Though some form of panic fought the dopamine. Should he really let her in? What if that was a mistake? What if she really did have some hidden agenda, like everyone else?

Draso's holy breath, why was this so damn hard?

Leah continued quietly for a moment. *Jaden's hiding us.*

Zeke frowned. *Yeah. Whatever Ackerson said clearly wasn't good.*

He expects Ackerson to come after us, Leah said.

Zeke fiddled with his fingers. *You nervous?*

A little, Leah said. *But prepared. Ackerson won't win.*

Yeah. Zeke breathed deeply. *Ackerson will try to surprise us.*

Then we better make sure he doesn't, Leah said. *Let's take turns keeping watch. And keep Archángeli on high alert.*

Mmm, Zeke said. *Good idea.*

Leah finished up his bandages. "All set. It's healing slowly, but at least it's not infected."

He smiled at her. "Thanks."

"Get some sleep," Leah said. *I'll take first watch. I'll come get you in a few hours.* She left.

Zeke stretched and climbed under the warm blankets on the air mattress, careful of his wound. First decent bed in weeks, he realized. Over a month. No wonder he was so stiff all the time.

He pushed the thoughts aside and forced himself to rest. Just a few hours of sleep. He needed to relish it.

Almost a week passed with no incident, each day blurring into the next. They woke up. They ate. Most of their daily activities were done in total silence. A light snow fell most nights, though Zeke couldn't tell if that was natural or if it was Jaden's doing. It was cold, but not unbearable, especially with all the extra blankets. The woods were inviting and quiet, though Jaden wouldn't let anyone go off alone.

Zeke could understand that.

He tried to exercise when he could. Leah continued washing his wound daily. Kyrie still hadn't shown up with Leah's Gem. Constant food smells followed him everywhere, betraying her worry, both for her Gem and for the battle they all knew was coming.

Zeke warred with how to handle the situation. Afraid to let Leah in… afraid to let her wallow in fear alone. In the end he pushed aside his own discomfort and kept her close. Much as he hated to admit it, they both needed the support. That seemed to help her.

Jaden spent most of his time near the edge of the camp, staring off into the woods. He looked more tired and anxious with each passing day. More than once, Zeke had caught him packing things up in his tent, muttering to himself, before unpacking it all again and talking about "making a stand" and not getting caught off guard.

Alexina, Embrik, and Leah had tried more than once to talk to Jaden about his kits, but he constantly waved them off. None of them could get a word in. Leah stopped trying on the second day.

So far Archángeli hadn't reported anything, which was almost worse. The tension grated on everyone. They all knew what was coming, even if Jaden still hadn't said anything outright.

On the seventh night, Zeke woke up early for his shift. He sat up in his tent, letting the cold air wake him up, and trying to force the tension from his body.

Then he heard footsteps outside. Adrenaline shot through him and he peeked through the tent flap.

It was Jaden. The white quilar paced back and forth in the snow, wearing a path, murmuring quietly, before finally sitting down on a log. He looked like a ghost in the empty moonlight.

Zeke frowned. He looked like he hadn't slept in days. This had to stop. Zeke slipped out of his tent and sat next to Jaden. "Hey, you doing okay?"

Jaden jumped. He frowned at Zeke a moment, before turning and staring at the snow. "Fine. Just keeping watch." He faltered. "You know, for… bears and such."

"Shouldn't you sleep?" Zeke said. "You look like death warmed over."

Jaden's brow furrowed slightly, but he shrugged. "I'm fine. I can handle it." He took a deep breath.

"Do you always shut out your support network when things get tough?" Zeke blurted.

Jaden eyed him. "What?"

Zeke crossed his arms. "You heard me."

Jaden glared. He shook his head and poked at the snow with a stick. "I can handle it."

Zeke sighed. "Hell, Jaden. You have worried people all around you. Let us help, for Draso's sake."

"I can *handle it.*"

Zeke narrowed his gaze. He gave Jaden a gentle shove.

Jaden fell with a dramatic "Whoaaa!" and landed shoulder-first in the snow. He righted himself and glared, wiping snow from his fur. "What the hell was that?"

"I barely pushed you," Zeke said. "And you fell over like a truck hit you. You aren't handling this."

Jaden stood up and brushed the snow off his pants. Zeke noticed he didn't use his magic. Jaden glared at him. "What are you trying to prove?"

"Jaden," Zeke said. "We're in danger. We all know it. But you're killing yourself trying to protect us instead of letting us *help.*"

"I don't *need* help."

Zeke wrinkled his snout. "Do you really think you're protecting anyone by pushing people away? Least of all yourself?"

Jaden stared at him. He opened his mouth as if searching for an answer, but nothing came out.

"You know you aren't," Zeke said. "You're just making things worse. For yourself, for us, for this situation. You're surrounded by people, and yet you're incredibly isolated."

Jaden leaned on his hands. "Do you even understand *why?"*

Zeke closed his eyes a moment and sighed. "Because you're afraid to lose people. Because of what you've already lost."

Jaden turned to him.

Zeke met his gaze. "You keep people away because you think it'll hurt less if you lose them. But Jaden, I promise it won't. It'll hurt more. You'll live your life thinking about all the things you wished you did. Isolation isn't the answer."

"And how would you know?" Jaden said.

Zeke hesitated. *Because I do it myself. Because I've lost so much and I'm afraid to lose more. Because I'm afraid to let people in because people have agendas. Because… because I'm too much like my father.* His eyes burned. Hopefully Jaden wouldn't notice in the dark. "I just… I just know."

Jaden scoffed. "You don't--"

"Wait." Zeke held up a hand and stood. His ear twitched.

Something in the woods. He mentally reached for Archángeli. One word shot through his brain from the bird.

RUN.

Jaden suddenly stood and spread his hands, shielding them both. The shield glowed green, but never vanished like Leah's did. Jaden strained, his eyes flashing.

"Zeke!"

Zeke's heart seized and he glanced around, frantic. "Mom?"

"Zeke, over here!" another voice cried.

"Mama?" Zeke whipped about.

And there they were. His two moms walking up to him from Alexina and Embrik's tents, big grins across their puma snouts. Mom with her shining blue eyes, and Mama with her soft gray ones.

Zeke stared, his heart swelling. They found him. They were *alive.* They--

A gun cocked. He turned.

Jaden raised a pistol that Zeke didn't know he had and fired two shots through his moms' foreheads.

CHAPTER 22

CHAOS

Zeke's whole world slowed to a crawl, focusing every element in sharp, excruciating detail. The echoing sound of the gun. The whizz of bullets flying. The sickening thud as they hit their targets, piercing fur, flesh, and bone. Blood flying through the air. Moonlight making each drop sparkle. The unnaturally fast way his moms' bodies collapsed to the snow, splattering more blood on the ground, the trees, the rocks, the tents. Jaden, holding the weapon, his face devoid of emotion.

All other sounds faded, and Zeke's vision blurred at the edges as his body went numb, staring at his dead moms. He fell to his knees. Emotions ran haywire, filtering through all of them at once - anger, fear, shame, despair, hate, trying to settle on one and failing. He pushed at his body. He had to move. Had to do something. Check his parents. Get the gun from Jaden. Even screaming would be better than freezing.

But he couldn't move. He completely shut down.

He had lost everything.

161

"Hey, handsome."

Zeke blinked, and managed to lift his gaze.

Leah hovered over him, smiling seductively, twitching her tail. "Now that everyone's gone, maybe we could have a little fun?" She leaned down and purred, running her tongue over her teeth.

Zeke stared. What the *hell?* Jaden just *murdered his parents* and Leah chooses *now* to reveal her sudden attraction to him? Draso's damned wings, he knew it, he shouldn't have let her in, she had a romantic agenda just like the others, she--

Wait. He shook his head. That… wasn't Leah. She didn't feel right, didn't move right. No smells accompanied her terrible flirting. In fact, he got an entirely different smell -- burning jalapeños. Anger. Solid, unfiltered, focused anger.

Leah's image glitched out of existence and suddenly she was several feet away, collapsed staff in hand, furious furrowed brow, screaming something in bursts that he couldn't catch. Then she was back near him, flirting again. Then far away. Then back.

Zeke stared. This… something wasn't right. Wasn't *real.*

And if that wasn't real, maybe none of it was. He turned back to his parents' bodies.

One second they were his moms, lying in pools of their own blood. But in an instant, they flashed away, revealing Embrik and Alexina, sitting on the snow. Embrik glanced around, frantic, tongues of fire surrounding him. Alexina held herself tight, wailing, tears streaming down her face.

Each one trapped in their own personal hell, screaming about family, the Basileus, Shadow Cast, and who knew what else. Trapped. Broken.

Just like Zeke.

Then they flashed back to his dead moms.

162

He turned to Jaden now. He appeared stoic, holding the gun out, but then faded. The real Jaden huddled on the ground, cheeks wet with tears. "No… please… not Zeke too… Not Alexina… not another family… I can't lose them again, I can't, I can't, *I can't…*" He switched back and forth between the broken Guardian and the stoic soldier.

Thoughts battled for attention in Zeke's mind. His eyes darted around, trying to focus the reality, trying to push aside what wasn't real. He still saw flashes of his parents, flashes of Jaden as the murderer, flashes of Leah, flirting. He couldn't focus, couldn't fight.

Leah appeared several feet away again, shouting something. He tried concentrating on the words. He couldn't make them all out with his ears, but his connection with her filled in the rest.

"I don't know *what* the heck is going on," Leah said through clenched teeth. "But you aren't fooling me. I'm not alone. No one has abandoned me." Her next words echoed in his ears and his head, like a megaphone. "*I can feel Zeke, you rotten, disgusting filth, I feel his pain, and if you've hurt him or the others in any way, you'll--*" She stopped suddenly, her tail twitching. One ear flicked in the direction of a bush. She let out a feral growl, shook her staff to its full length and dove for a bush like a wildcat after prey.

Someone shrieked and tumbled out of the bush. A blue and white otter in snowy military fatigues. She scrambled to her feet, but Leah pounced again, knocking her down. "A Gem user," she said, pinning the otter to the ground and pawing at her left thigh. "Thought so. Cloaker."

"Get your grubby paws off me!" the otter shouted.

But Leah ignored her and pulled at something. She lifted it into the air. A Gem. She glanced up. "Archángeli!" She threw the Gem in the air.

Archángeli swooped down and snatched it in their talons, then flew off.

The moment the eagle took to the air, two feminine humans also in fatigues showed up behind Alexina and Embrik, though his teammates didn't seem to notice them. Both humans had shocked looks on their faces.

Zeke pointed. "Leah, there, *there!*"

Leah looked around, but she didn't seem to notice Zeke's screaming. "Not cloaked. Cloaking your own team then?"

The pair of humans flashed in an out of existence. Dead moms, no humans. Alexina and Embrik, humans hiding behind them.

Magic. Wishing Dust.

And those humans had to be the Wish Dusters. Jaden had said a common Wishing Dust power was illusion. That had to be what was going on.

Leah, behind you, by Alexina's tent! Leah whipped around now and found the two humans. She narrowed her eyes, then darted after them, staff out. The otter reached for her but missed.

One of them, a stocky, broad-shouldered redhead with her hair in braids and shaved sides, Viking style, growled and pulled out a tactical knife, rushing Leah.

Leah spun her staff about and smashed the knife from the redhead's hand and knocked her to the ground. Immediately all the visions faded. Alexina and Embrik widened their eyes, glancing around, confused. Jaden stopped too, blinking the tears from his eyes.

Leah pulled the redhead to her feet and shook her. "Ackerson won't win."

"Neither will you," the woman said, and she headbutted Leah, forcing her to let go. Leah groaned and stumbled back. The redhead moved to tackle.

Then Alexina snarled. She blasted an angry bombardment of snow and sand at the redhead, burying her.

The other human, a nimble, short woman with razored, blonde hair, pulled out a pistol, but Embrik knocked it free with a fireball, sending it flying into the woods. The woman screamed and thrust her burning hand into the snow. Embrik moved to comfort Alexina, tongues of fire all around them.

Zeke stood, gripping his side. He glanced around. No way Ackerson only sent two illusionists and a… a "cloaker" after them. Not with all the elemental magic they had. There had to be more. But where were they? If only he had his own magic! What a thing to wish for.

A tiny buzzing sounded by his ear. He turned.

A miniature black drone hovered by his ear. He recognized it immediately. A Paper Wasp Nano. Military surveillance.

He snatched the drone out of the air, ignoring the pain from its spinning blades smashing against his fingers. He crushed the propeller as best he could and threw it into the woods. "Watch out, we've got Nanos!"

The tiny drone smashed into a tree… and immediately exploded. The blast ripped through the trunk, scorching through wood, bark, and snow, sending embers and flames into the air.

Zeke shrunk down. Since when did they make Nano *bombs?* He searched wildly for more.

One hovered near Alexina and Embrik. Zeke waved a hand. "Alexina, Embrik, there's a Nano, *move!"*

Alexina and Embrik dove in separate directions away from the drone, but too late. It exploded and sent both of them crashing through their tents, setting the fabric on fire.

"No!" Zeke scrambled to his feet and ran for the tents. Leah ran for them too.

Someone crashed into him, knocking him away from his teammates. Zeke snarled, fighting tooth and claw with his assailant, a red wolf. "Let me go, asshole!"

"Yeah, don't think I will," the wolf said in a stony voice. "At least not without a parting gift." He smashed something into Zeke's side and rolled off, yipping and laughing.

Zeke pawed at his side. Something round stuck to it.

A *Nano.*

Adrenaline rushed through him and he pulled at the Nano, with no effect. It was stuck fast to his jacket. He pulled the jacket off, but the stickiness seeped through all the way to his fur. He couldn't pull it off his skin. The jacket hung at his side.

No, no, *no!* "Archángeli!"

I'm with you! Archángeli dove down and gripped the Nano in their claws. With a mighty yank and a rush of wind, they ripped the bomb off, taking Zeke's shirt and a patch of fur and skin with them, and took to the air. *My prince, remember to--*

The Nano exploded, and Archángeli with it, in a flurry of feathers and sparkly dust.

Zeke stared, slack jawed. No. *No. "Archángeli!"*

The red wolf walked forward, arms crossed. "Hmm. I thought those damn summons were more resilient than that." He shrugged. "Welp. Something to keep in mind for the future." He turned to Zeke with a toothy grin. "Now though…"

Zeke turned on him, snarling. "You're *dead."* He rushed the wolf.

But the wolf leapt aside and pulled out another Nano. Zeke skidded through the snow, the cold stinging his raw skin. The wolf licked his teeth, grinning. "Ah, ah, ah, can't have that." He pressed something on the drone and held it above his head. "Welcome to Chaos, you bastard son of a--"

A sharp ice spike ripped through the wolf's left shoulder, cutting him off as he gasped for air at the sudden pain. A dozen more ice spikes flew after him, but they caught in a shield, protecting him. He leaned over, nursing the injured shoulder, his left arm swinging uselessly at his side. He dropped the Nano and weakly kicked it outside the shield. It exploded and knocked him down, though the shield held.

Damn it!

Zeke growled. The wolf didn't have a Gem that Zeke could see. That meant the otter was back up and had her Gem again. Shit! Zeke had never felt so powerless.

Jaden dashed toward Embrik and Alexina, bathing the burning tents in snow. "Zeke, help Leah!"

Zeke ears grew cold. *Leah.* He turned.

Leah hadn't made it to Alexina and Embrik. The two humans had gone after her, and she had her hands full keeping them busy. Both humans had long knives, and Leah was barely able to keep them away with her staff. They were skilled.

"I don't have magic!" Zeke called. "Can't you freeze their brains?"

"They're moving around too much!" Jaden said, sliding in the snow next to his teammates. "You've got to help, but for the love of god, don't get yourself killed!"

Zeke cursed and ran for Leah, that helpless feeling overwhelming him. He tried calling Archángeli.

Nothing.

They were gone.

Zeke pushed his legs as hard as they could go in the snow. He wasn't going to lose anyone else. *Leah, I'm coming!*

Then the blonde found her gun again. She aimed it at Leah.

Watch out!

Leah turned, but too late. The woman fired, hitting Leah's forehead point blank. She fell in a spray of blood.

Zeke stopped, another wave of shock rushing through his body, making everything feel weak. "No! *Leah!*"

I'm here, Zeke, Leah said, her voice breathy and tired. *I'm here. Whatever you're seeing isn't real.*

His brain rejected Leah's words. She still lay on the ground. Still dead. He was hallucinating. He couldn't hear her.

Zeke, listen to me! Leah said, emphasizing the words. *Embrik's flames damaged the pistol. I don't even know where it is, but I doubt it could fire. They're showing you your fears, Zeke. Focus elsewhere. Focus on my voice.* A gentle, soft smell of citrus entered his nose. *Let the scent ground you.*

Zeke forced shut his eyes a moment, trying to fight back the adrenaline, then opened them, concentrating on the citrus smell.

Still a dead Leah. But only for a second. Then she glitched into real space, still fighting the humans. Then she was dead. Then she was fighting.

But one thing remained the same. The humans didn't move.

Tackle the redhead! Leah called.

Zeke rushed forward and crashed into the redhead, knocking her down. Leah's dead body vanished in favor of the real Leah. Relief washed over him.

Something stung his side, sending searing hot pain through him, blinding him, making it hard to breathe. The redhead had stabbed him, right above the old wound. He collapsed to the snow.

The woman hovered over him, knife in hand.

Leah rushed forward and swung her staff into the woman's chin, sending her reeling back into the snow. Then she was on her knees by Zeke's side in an instant, ripping off her jacket. "Hang on, Zeke, hang on, I'm here." Though his mind was bombarded with her deep desire for her Gem.

Zeke tried to speak, but he spat up blood instead.

"Don't move," Leah said.

I'm dying.

"Don't say that," Leah said. "You're fine, you're right here, don't move." She pressed the jacket to his new wound.

Then the blonde rose up from the snow, shouting, knife above her head. Leah held up her staff, but there was little she could do while kneeling.

A flash of white and blue crashed into the woman, shoving her aside. The cold, icy scent of deep winter filled the air, and in a flurry of fur and feathers, a gryfon stood between them and their enemy.

Zeke stared. A gryfon. A real life, honest-to-Draso *gryfon.*

Leah gawked. She didn't speak, but one word ran through her mind and into Zeke's. *Rashard.*

Despite the pain and his blurred vision, Zeke couldn't help but stare. The thing was the size of a horse, close to six feet tall, with a wingspan at least double his height. He spread his large, blue-tipped white wings and let out a rumbling lion roar, making Zeke's ears throb.

The blonde stood her ground. "Caster! A little help!"

"Kind of bleeding out here, Theophania!" the red wolf shouted.

"Not an excuse!" the woman screamed back.

Caster growled and dug into his pocket.

Jaden snarled now though and waved a hand, raining a thousand tiny ice spikes on Caster. He rolled left, the shield still holding, and threw the drone Jaden's way. Jaden shielded, but it still remained stubbornly green.

A blur of red and black rushed after the drone and snatched it up – another gryfon, just as large as the previous one. It flew into the air with speed that would rival even Archángeli, holding the drone in its talons. In a dramatic flip, it threw the drone, spun upside down, and slapped it high into the air with its feathered tail. The drone zoomed up and exploded harmlessly.

Leah stared. "Kjorn," she muttered.

The gryfon landed hard in the snow between Jaden and Caster, screeching at the latter with a high-pitched eagle sound.

169

Caster backed up. "Kitta, little help here?"

"On it." The otter appeared now, and the two of them vanished.

Zeke groaned. Shit. His vision blurred further.

Zeke, stay with me! Leah shouted in his mind. *Don't you dare give up, we haven't saved your folks yet, I'm not going to let you die.*

But Zeke couldn't muster the strength to respond.

And the red-haired woman took advantage of it. She rushed the pair of them, knife out.

But the knife stuck fast in the air. A figure moved between Zeke and the redhead. Kyrie, Alexina's summon, sat on their shoulder.

The figure was draped in a long, black cloak.

CHAPTER 23

MEMORIES

Leah stared at the cloaked figure, her mind reeling from everything that had happened.

The Black Cloak. Here. And with Jaden's father's summons.

Rashard and Kjorn.

The Thought Factory worked on overload, flashing visions of her room growing up, plastered with posters, figurines, plushies, and 3D art of the two gryfons.

And their summoner. Golden Guardian Tymon Azure.

But Tymon was dead. He had died on Erdoglyan during his final mission as a Golden Guardian, just before Jaden and Dyne had become Guardians.

Which meant Rashard and Kjorn had taken a new oath with a new summoner.

The Cloak stood stoically next to Zeke and Leah, his piercing green eyes glaring at the red-haired woman behind a full-faced silver mask.

Green eyes. Green eyes and Tymon's summons. It was like looking at Tymon's ghost.

Jaden had to be freaking out.

The Cloak lifted a chin, eyeing the woman. "There's nothing you can throw at me that would trap me in fear. I've lived too long to fall for it." He narrowed his gaze.

Leah strained her ears, cycling his voice through her mind, trying to match it to Tymon's. But his word reverberated inside his metal mask, muffling the sound. Leah shook herself. That couldn't be Tymon. Tymon was *dead*.

Kyrie raised her wings, rasping at the woman, ice and snow swirling around them. Rashard responded, mimicking her in pose and magic, magnified five times.

The woman backed up, teeth gritted. "Kitta!" she called. Then she and the other woman, Theophania, vanished.

Theophania. Kitta. Caster. Names Leah wouldn't forget.

Zeke groaned. Leah peeled her gaze away from the Cloak and turned back to Zeke, wordlessly pressing her jacket to his wounds. Good Draso, they were awful - deep, bleeding terribly, one lung punctured…

She shook her head. *Can't focus on that. Can't let him hear.* She just had to save him. Oh, if only Kyrie had come back with her Gem… "I need a first aid kit…"

The Cloak turned and kneeled beside her. He pulled something from the long robes. "Here."

Leah's Gem. The color had faded, but it was still shining.

She stared at him, eyes wet. Relief warmed her bones as she took it from him. The color flooded back, full strength. "Thank you."

He nodded.

172

She pressed the Gem into her hip holster and turned to Zeke. He lay unmoving next to her, barely breathing. She reached for him. *Hang on. I'm here. Hang on!* She pressed her hands into his fresh wound. Lungs first. Then blood. Then flesh.

Her mind wouldn't stop moving. Zeke, Black Cloak, Rashard, Kjorn, summons, Golden Guardian, it all moved so fast she couldn't focus on one thing. But she had to, she had to focus on *something* or she'd wander too far away and she'd lose Zeke. *Focus on Zeke.*

Rashard moved close and gently nudged her, though he didn't speak.

She glanced at him briefly, staring into his deep green eyes. At home, on Zyearth, during a bad incident involving a broken tree and a bully, Rashard had shown up to help her. Maybe. She still couldn't tell if what she had seen all those years ago was real or not.

But now Rashard stood by her like an old friend.

A gentle, cold snowflake landed on her nose. *Concentrate on the Prínkipas.*

She glanced down. Zeke's wounds were nearly healed… but he remained stubbornly unconscious.

Panic ran through her. *Don't you dare let go!*

Zeke didn't respond.

"Zeke, *please!*" she screamed.

The Black Cloak gripped her shoulder. "You have a social bond," he said. She whipped her head up. He smiled with those green eyes of his. "Use that to your advantage. Dig deeper and call him."

Leah frowned. She dug deep into his mind, pulling everything she could to the surface. *Come on, Zeke. It can't end this way. Come back to us. Please!*

Nothing.

The Thought Factory raced through ideas. Maybe… maybe she needed to give him something to live for. An image. A memory. But of what? His

173

family? Friends? Something to ground him? Dang it all, she didn't know enough about him to do this!

She pressed her eyes shut. She'd just have to find out more. She pushed everything she had into her mind and dove into Zeke's subconscious.

She landed first on a memory of his moms – a gentle scene when he was a kit, playing in the snow, falling off a sled, hugging his parents and laughing. But that quickly turned sour. He grew older, and while hugs were still frequent, they were less and less about love and more about comfort, like a heavy sadness haunted him.

Then they were gone, and the hugging stopped.

She shook her head. Different memory.

She caught him playing with friends as a kit. Same interactions. Hugs, shoulder grabs, holding hands. Then they got older. Hugs stopped. Hand holding was only for romance. Friends shunned all touching.

Then they were all gone too.

Leah's heart ached. But he still didn't respond. She needed another memory, the right one. Maybe more recent.

Flight school. Taking classes alone. Flying alone. Testing alone. She almost gave up when she caught one word, which immediately brought the warm smell of cookies to her nose.

Andre.

She dove after it.

A man appeared in her mind's eye, a human with dark skin, bald, nearly Zeke's height, with a wide, welcoming grin and calming brown eyes. And once again, Zeke sought hugs with him. Reluctant at first. But they grew comfortable quickly.

Leah's heart ached again, for herself this time. She wanted this more than anything. Someone she could be close with, as friends.

174

But then… it slowed. Not stopped, but slowed. A vague memory followed. Zeke telling Andre something she couldn't make out. Andre's sad smile. They remained close, but touching became a thing of the past. But Zeke still clung to Andre, and Andre to him, just without the physical side.

And behind it, a longing.

The bitter, striking smell of fresh lemon drew her out of her memory trance and into the real world, and she suddenly found herself staring deep into Zeke's green eyes. He sat up, staring at her, all his wounds healed.

She slumped forward, the tension finally leaving. He was *alive.* She smiled and reached for him. "Zeke--"

Zeke recoiled. "The hell was *that,* Leah?"

She stared. "What?"

"Rifling through my head?" he said. "Going through all my deepest memories? Why the hell did you do that? What is *wrong* with you?"

She frowned, her eyes wide. "I-I wasn't trying to rifle through your thoughts, I--"

"Well, you sure did a damn good job for not trying!" he said.

"I was trying to bring you *back!"* Leah said. "Trying to find something for you to reach for!"

"So you went through all my *darkest memories?"*

"No!" Leah said. "I mean, I wasn't *aiming* for that, I just--"

"Don't try to excuse it," Zeke said.

"I'm not!" Leah reached for him again. "Zeke, I promise--"

He pulled back. "Don't touch me. Don't even get near me." He got to his feet and walked off, rubbing his arms.

Leah scrambled to her feet. "Zeke, wait, please, I'm sorry!"

"Leah!" Jaden called. "Embrik needs healing, *now!"*

Leah stood, frozen, watching Zeke walk off. She chewed her lip, her whole body shaking with adrenaline.

175

"Leah!"

She turned back. Jaden had Alexina in his arms, eyes wide, heaving breaths through his open mouth. Alexina sobbed, holding her arm. Embrik lay unmoving in a burnt tent.

The Cloak gently gripped her shoulder. She stared at him, his figure blurry in her teary eyes.

His gaze looked sad. "I don't know what happened, but I'll make sure he's taken care of. Go help the others." He turned and followed Zeke, Rashard at his side, bounding through the snow in great leaps.

Leah watched them a moment, then hugged herself and jogged to the others, feeling numb.

CHAPTER 24

DYNE

Jaden held tight to Alexina, unable to take his eyes off the Black Cloak. The urge to chase after him while he followed Zeke was nearly unbearable. The Cloak couldn't be allowed to hurt his family, no matter how Jaden felt about Zeke.

Of all the times for the Cloak to show up. Jaden didn't need any more anxiety.

But his team was hurt. Alexina had minor injuries, but Embrik was worse off, lying on the ground, struggling to breathe, unable to move. Jaden was afraid to move him or even touch him – he needed a healer *now*. He patted Embrik's limp hand as gently as he could and rubbed Alexina's shoulder while she nursed an injured arm. She got off light considering they leapt away from an explosion.

In all honesty, he wasn't sure if he could do much anyway. Exhaustion glued him to the spot. Zeke had been right. Staying up all this time keeping watch had been sloppy and dangerous. Now they all paid the price for it.

Alexina groaned next to him.

He leaned into her. "Hold on, help is on the way." His voice shook as he spoke. He gently kissed her forehead.

Alexina nodded and buried her face in his chest, shaking. She gave Jaden a dark look. "Embrik."

Leah jogged up, kneeled beside Embrik and began working on him wordlessly.

"He'll survive," Jaden said. *I hope.*

"Those humans," Alexina whispered.

"Wish Dusters," Jaden said.

"And their magic," she said, her voice trembling. "Preyed on our fear."

Jaden flicked his ears back. Wish Dusters often specialized in illusions. More effective and easier to handle than something physical. These two apparently could make illusions based on fears. And a Gem-wielding otter kept them cloaked.

He hadn't expected to find another Gem user on Earth. Also sloppy.

In the strange vision, he had seen Alexina pregnant. The Black Cloak appeared and took Zeke, as a baby, from them. Then Kyo, leader of the Omnirs, killed them both. It had been so frighteningly *real.* Even though he knew it couldn't possibly be real, he hadn't been able to pull himself out of it. He still got chills thinking about it.

And then the real Black Cloak appeared. Saving them. Carrying his father's summons. God, carrying Tymon's *summons.* There could hardly be a worse kick to the gut.

Then he went after Zeke. Jaden shook with a poorly contained energy. But he couldn't leave his wife. Couldn't fight.

Embrik groaned and turned over as Leah healed him. Jaden relaxed. He'd be okay. Alexina sighed and leaned more into Jaden.

Jaden turned to Leah. "How's Zeke?"

"He's…" Leah flicked her ears back. "I healed his wounds."

Jaden wrinkled his snout. "And he's okay."

Leah didn't respond. She continued working on Embrik's injuries.

The Black Cloak walked toward them, Rashard next to him. Zeke stood not far away, ears pinned back, huddled in on himself, a deep frown on his face. He refused to look at Leah.

Jaden stood immediately, pushing through the exhaustion as every muscle groaned at him, moving between the Cloak and the rest of his team. He formed ice spikes around them in a protective cage, though they were tiny, translucent, and clearly weak. But he stood his ground. "Back the hell up."

The Cloak raised his hands. "I didn't--"

"Back the hell up," Jaden said. "You're not touching my family, do you hear me?"

The Cloak lowered his gaze. "I'm not going to hurt anyone. I'm a healer. Let me heal Alexina."

"How do you know her name?"

The Cloak's eyes narrowed. "I'm an honorary denizen of Athánatos. It would be unbecoming of me to not know my Prinkípissa." He nodded to her. "Are you going to let me heal her or not?"

Leah stared at him, one ear pasted down, looking confused. She glanced at Zeke. He huffed and turned away. Leah's whiskers twitched and she turned to Jaden, staring at him blankly. "She's hurt. Embrik will take time. Let him, please."

Jaden glanced at her. Her words were terse, robotic. That wasn't like her. His mind shot straight to the very realistic and unsettling illusions from earlier. Was this really Leah?

But she remained where she was, still healing Embrik. No broken illusion. Not like before, when he started to break through the vision. He glanced around. No humans either.

179

Alexina shifted, still clutching her arm. "My love, please…" She shook.

Jaden's ears flattened. "Okay… okay, you're right, I shouldn't look a gift horse in the mouth." He glared at the Cloak. "But you'd better not try anything."

The Cloak's gaze softened. "Hurting any of you is the furthest thing from my mind." Jaden huffed, but he waved the ice spikes away. Not like he had the energy to keep them up anyway. The Cloak leaned down and began work on Alexina's arm.

Jaden fell to the ground again. He stared at the Cloak, memories flooding him like a cold rain in his belly. He could practically be looking at his father. Green eyes. Rashard and Kjorn at his side. Even the healing.

But Tymon was dead. Jaden had seen it himself. It had been his first mission as a Golden Guardian – retrieving his father's body from the bloody, violent planet of Erdoglyan where Tymon had died on what was supposed to be his final mission as a Guardian. He still remembered holding his father's cold, dead Gem, reading the monitors matching what little DNA they could extract from Tymon's charred body to his DNA signature.

Water above him… he could almost hear his father speaking now.

"Jaden, shield, now!"

Jaden's insides froze and he whipped around. That voice. *"Dyne?"*

And there he was. His partner, his best friend, his Guardian companion. Golden quills flowing down his back, healing uniform rumpled and stained, bright blue eyes, just like his daughter's, staff in hand, ready to fight.

Dyne Gildspine.

Jaden's heart stopped.

Dyne waved a hand and in a flash of green and purple, he formed a shield in front of them. "Protect yourselves!" Dyne rushed forward.

Jaden held out a hand, shielding instinctively, though the shield immediately collapsed, sending wisps of Lexi acid in the air. "Wait, Dyne, *don't!*"

But Dyne ignored him. He held out the staff. "Rashard, give me a burst of ice!" Rashard keened and waved his wings in Dyne's direction. Ice shards flew through the air and formed a thick spear on the end. Dyne held the spear over his head and rammed it into a bush.

A shot rang out, tearing through Dyne's shoulder, blasting away fur, quills, and flesh. A basilisk lizard in gray and white fatigues tumbled out of the foliage.

Dyne fell to the ground, unmoving.

"No, Dyne, *no!*" Jaden scrambled up. This couldn't be happening. He couldn't watch his best friend die again.

Again.

That made him pause.

That couldn't be Dyne. He was dead. Gone. Murdered. That couldn't be him.

He turned back to his team and counted. Alexina. Embrik. Black Cloak. Zeke running toward them.

That left Leah. Another illusion. Probably the whole thing was an illusion. She hadn't been shot.

Then Zeke's panicked, screeching voice rang out. *"Leah!"*

The Cloak waved his hand. "Rashard, Kjorn, get the cloaker, chase off the Wish Dusters!" The gryfons keened and took off into the air, surrounded by their elements. The Cloak sprang to his feet and ran toward Dyne.

Jaden turned.

Leah's staff stuck out of the basilisk's neck, ice crystals splashed red with blood. A rifle lay next to him.

And instead of Dyne, Leah lay on the ground, unmoving, blood pooling under her.

Jaden's breath hitched. "No, no, no!" He ripped his jacket off, ran for Leah, and pressed it to her wound.

The Cloak slid in next to them and immediately ran healing magic into her shoulder and neck. Everything was slick with blood, staining Jaden's jacket and the Cloak's gloves. The Cloak spoke shakily. "Pendant, unlock, Defender access override, 57213."

Jaden stared at him. Defender access?

"Access confirmed," the pendant beeped.

"Show biosigns," the Cloak said.

The pendant's holographic interface appeared, displaying Leah's biosigns. Not good. Fast heartrate, short breaths. Bright red splotches appeared on her shoulder, neck, and head where the injury was.

"Damn it," the Cloak muttered. "She's going into shock. I'm not a great healer." He pointed to the wound in her neck. "Jaden, press your jacket there, stop the blood--"

Something beeped. Jaden's datasquare. He exchanged a glance with the Cloak.

The Cloak locked his gaze with Jaden. "Ackerson."

Jaden snarled. He went to turn the datasquare off.

The Cloak grabbed his wrist. "Don't. He's going to send you on a mission with team Hunt. Don't question it. Don't bring up what happened here."

"Why the hell *not?"*

"I can't heal Leah," the Cloak said. "I can stabilize her, but I need help. Hunt can provide that help, but I don't know where they are. Ackerson does. If you challenge him here, he'll never give you that information and Leah will die."

Jaden growled. "What the hell are you?"

The Cloak huffed. "Put simply, I'm a time traveler."

"*I know that,*" Jaden said. "How the hell didn't you predict *this?*"

"I don't know *everything,*" the Cloak said. "Broad strokes, yes, certain events in time, but I have to follow specific steps, and I can't predict all outcomes." He glared. "And we don't have time to argue this."

Jaden stared at him, his ears burning. "Fine. Fine, I'll do it." He turned. "Embrik?"

Embrik coolly took Jaden's spot and pressed the jacket to Leah's shoulder. "Jaden, please, do as he says. I promise you, the Cloak is not our enemy."

Jaden took a deep breath. "I don't know who my enemy is anymore." He stood and walked off. Alexina and Zeke slid in next to Leah while Embrik and the Cloak worked on her. Jaden's belly roiled leaving his injured teammate behind.

Leah had put herself in this position saving them. Saving him.

Again.

Jaden pressed his eyes shut. Damn all of this. This was his fault.

Maybe he was his own enemy.

He found a secluded spot and activated the hologram.

Ackerson looked surprised that Jaden answered. Predictable, considering he had just sent Chaos after them. Jaden schooled his face. He wouldn't let Ackerson know anything was wrong. "Azure reporting for duty."

Ackerson coughed. "Well then. Good to see you look well rested." As if. "Finally got the job set up for you. You'll be working with Hunt. They're good at what they do, and are far less... sloppy than Outlander." He smiled. "Think your team is up for it?"

"Absolutely, sir," Jaden said. Full obedience. No cracks.

"Good," Ackerson said. "I'll be sending coordinates to your datasquare. Get there ASAP. The faster the better."

He had no idea. "Yes, sir."

Ackerson saluted, which Jaden returned, despite the shaking. "Ackerson out." The hologram faded.

Jaden frantically typed at the hologram's interface, looking for coordinates. He got them and plugged them into the nav.

Canada. He wanted them in *Canada.* Good Draso. Canada's borders were completely shut off. Ackerson had asked for the impossible.

And Ackerson knew it. But they didn't have a choice. He dashed back to the group.

The Cloak was slowly knitting through Leah's open wounds, but she still wasn't conscious. Jaden leaned down and checked her vital signs. Thankfully her breathing looked more normal. Her heartrate remained the same high number though, and now blood pressure had dropped. On top of that, the red splotches on her body diagram hadn't really changed. Shock. He frowned. "She's lost a lot of blood."

"I know," the Cloak said. He hissed and shook his hand, a tiny cloud of Lexi acid in the air. "But I'm at my limit. I have to rest."

"Is she stable?" Zeke said, speaking way too fast. "Tell me she's stable."

Jaden frowned. Her clothes were soaked through with blood, staining her white and gray fur. "Are the wounds closed up?"

The Cloak frowned. "Well enough, on the outside anyway. I've done all I can to stop the bleeding. But it might be good to put bandages on just the same. Prevent infection."

"Here," Alexina came to them with a first-aid kit. One corner of the kit was melted from fire. "We will have to make do." She and Jaden bandaged Leah as best they could.

Jaden looked over the pendant interface. "Biosigns look decent." He turned to the Cloak. "Think I could pick her up?"

The Cloak nodded. "But be careful."

Jaden gently pulled Leah into his arms. Zeke stood close to him, his face contorted with worry. Leah flopped like a housecat that didn't want to be held. Jaden pulled her close to him to steady her. Draso, this was all his *fault*. Some Guardian he was. He gathered up the rising panic attack and shoved it into a corner of his mind. He had to stay clear for Leah. "Gather up everything you can, but quickly. We don't have the time."

"Where are we going?" Embrik asked.

"Canada," Jaden said. He nodded to the Cloak. "And you're coming with us."

CHAPTER 25

GUILT

Zeke huddled in his seat in the Humvee, wearing a fresh set of BDUs, his mind on overload.

A weird feeling since his mind had felt so blank since Leah had gotten shot. It was like she wasn't there at all. Like he couldn't even find her. The absence hurt far more than he would have imagined. Like a part of his own mind vanished the moment she fell, blood flying everywhere. Like a part of him was missing.

Right after he had yelled at her too. Yelled at her for saving his life. It didn't matter what she had seen to do it. He shouldn't have screamed at her. God, he was terrible. He stripped off his glasses and held his head in his hands.

The mad dash down the mountain felt like an out-of-control roller coaster, bumping around, trying to keep Leah steady. They couldn't lay her flat, so Embrik and Alexina leaned up against her tightly, holding her in place. Her breathing and heartrate seemed to improve, but she still refused to wake up. They took turns cleaning blood off her fur with wet wipes, but neither felt comfortable changing her clothes. The deep, iron smell of blood filled the Humvee quickly. Her bloodied glasses sat in a recess near the front seats.

And Zeke still couldn't feel her. Draso, what he wouldn't give for the gentle smells of food from Leah again.

The Cloak had tried multiple times to activate his healing powers again. Nothing worked. They were stuck.

"It's ten hours to Canada's border," Jaden said, his voice quiet. "Then who knows how long to try and get past the border patrol. But we've got time. Your magic will come back soon and you can work more on her. We'll keep her safe until we get to Hunt."

Hunt. Another of Ackerson's teams. Why they were actually following orders and working with another team after what happened with this team Chaos, Zeke couldn't fathom. For all they knew, they were walking into another death trap and Hunt would murder them all while they were looking for help.

Alexina kept her gaze trained on the Black Cloak, her brow furrowed. He calmly stared back and gently waved a hand. "You're free to speak, my Lady."

"Where were you?" Alexina spat, her voice shaking. "Theron has destroyed Athánatos. Created Shadow Cast. Separated our family. You were supposed to *be there* if a royal lost themselves chasing the Cast, and *you were not there.*"

The Black Cloak bowed. "Apologies, my Lady, for what little good it might mean. But the Black Cloak *did* go after Theron, just before he turned Melaina. He killed her, took her Gem, and used it to complete the process for Shadow Cast creation." He lowered his head. "The Cloak itself took time to find a new host, and… problems arose."

"I can see that," Alexina snapped, though her voice lost some of its bite. "But it should not have taken that long. Daisy's line--"

187

"--Is ended, my Lady," the Cloak said. "The previous Cloak was the last of Daisy's family and the Daisy's Gem is lost. I'm not of Daisy's line."

Alexina's eyes grew wide.

The Cloak breathed deeply. "I am sorry I couldn't be there when you needed me. I'm also sorry that I can't drop everything now and go after Theron. But," he waved to Leah. "You already know he'll be taken down in the future. This was by design. If you don't trust me now… trust the outcome."

Alexina lowered her gaze, but said nothing.

"Theron has already set his fate in motion," the Cloak continued. "So I'm here, protecting his family until the right time to strike. Because you'll need all the help you can get."

Zeke lowered his head. He was right. Oh, if only he had *magic*.

The Ei-Ei jewels on his bracelet caught his attention. He frowned at them. Maybe he could. "Alexina," he said softly. "Is there a way I could get healing magic?"

Alexina frowned. "Not with the Ei-Ei jewels, no. They do not provide healing magic. Even if you could, you can only access their magic if you are bound to them."

Zeke cursed.

"Have you tried reaching for her like she did for you?" the Cloak asked.

Zeke stared at him. Dressed head to toe in black, with a full faced silver mask, revealing only deep green eyes. So strange.

Jaden clearly didn't trust him. Alexina clearly knew what the title meant, but she wasn't exactly thrilled with his presence, which made Zeke's feelings toward him even more conflicted. He saved Leah, though he couldn't heal her completely. He had saved the group of them with summons, but still let Chaos get away. He knew this Theron person was a threat, but was waiting for "the right time" whatever the hell that meant.

Zeke wasn't sure he could trust him either.

188

The Cloak lowered his gaze. "Zeke."

"I've been trying since I felt her get shot," Zeke said, his voice cracking.

"Try again," the Cloak said. "It might be the only thing that saves her."

Zeke frowned, his body buzzing, filling his mind with a million questions about what would happen if Leah died. He closed his eyes and reached into her subconscious again, trying to mimic what she had done to him. He shook his head. For him. She hadn't been trying to hurt him. And he wasn't going to hurt her. He just... needed a memory.

Just like before, he got nothing. At least nothing of value. Vague, fuzzy images similar to what he had seen when they first bound their jewels. A gray lioness. A lion with a feather mane. Their faces so blurry that he couldn't even make out eye color. Both family, he thought, but no friends, no coworkers, no other anchors. Nothing of use.

"Any luck?" Alexina asked.

Zeke shook his head. "Nothing. Just vague, unrecognizable images." He leaned forward. "I don't know if that's just because of the injuries or because she blocked me out for yelling at her." No more than he deserved.

The Cloak lowered his gaze. "I'm sorry. I pushed her to seek a connection with you and save you that way. I didn't know she'd invade something personal."

"Not your fault," Zeke said. "But thanks, for what it's worth."

"We have time, Zeke," Jaden said. "We'll save her."

He could only hope.

They rode along in silence. Zeke's mind clung to the memories Leah resurfaced.

Good Draso. Why those ones? Why now? Especially everything with Andre. They had been so close. Hugs with abandon. Leaning into each other when they laughed.

Then Andre started flirting with Zeke.

189

And Zeke didn't know how to handle it. He let Andre's flirting go on far too long, simmering in that fear of losing the first true friend he had had in years. He couldn't tell Andre that he had no desire for romance.

But he had to.

When he had finally approached Andre about it, he fully expected Andre to leave, to abandon him for leading him on for so long. He could recall that tearful explanation in excruciating detail. Even thinking about it now made his chest hurt. He truly thought he was going to lose his only friend.

But Andre didn't leave. He stayed. It took some time, but the flirting eventually stopped and they settled into a deep friendship. But when the flirting stopped, the hugging stopped too. All the physical parts of their relationship ended. Zeke didn't even lean into Andre anymore when he laughed.

Not that he laughed much these days.

Zeke desperately wanted their old relationship back. But he didn't know if he could ever get it back.

He buried his face in his knees, his chest aching. God, why was he like this? Wanting intimacy, without romance or sex? What was *wrong* with him?

He took a deep, shuddering breath. War was not the place to be exploring these feelings.

He looked up, trying to focus on anything other than Andre. "Alexina… what… what *would* happen if I was bound to the jewels?"

Alexina frowned at him. "I had thought you uninterested."

"We've faced mage after mage since I got to this time," Zeke said. "And I'm powerless to fight them. It might be something to consider if we're going to keep at this." He glanced at her. "Would the jewels grant me magic like you all have?"

"Very likely," Alexina said. "If we are correct about your parentage, you are a prince of Athánatos. The Ei-Ei jewels will grant you control over all seven elemental magics."

Zeke's eyes widened. "Really?" He flicked an ear down. "That's a lot of power. Would I even be able to control it?"

"When a focus jewel is bound physically, magic comes more naturally to the user," Embrik said. "You should not have trouble learning it."

Alexina nodded. "Though… the jewels do more than just grant magic."

Zeke lowered his gaze. "So there's a catch."

Alexina exchanged a glance with Embrik. "Not a… catch, necessarily, but… side effects. The biggest being your lifespan."

Zeke raised an eyebrow. "My lifespan? Is this going to take years off my life?"

"Exactly the opposite," Embrik said. "The jewels grant you eternal life."

Zeke's heart sank into his stomach and he stared, mouth open.

Embrik readjusted Leah on his shoulder. He wiped blood off her whiskers with care. "Most choose not to live forever. We have a ritual to end our lives when we choose. It is peaceful and painless. But until you make that choice, your body essentially stops aging. You will look and function the same as the day you bound to the jewels, barring injuries or accidents."

Zeke's body buzzed. Living *forever?* That was terrifying. "Do all focus jewels do that?"

"Most focus jewels change lifespan to some degree," Jaden said. "Our Gems grant about four hundred years of life, give or take, depending on the planet you're on. Wishing Dust changes lifespans individually, depending on the wish, usually decreasing it rather than increasing it. Continuum Stones change lifespans depending on what Time magic they have."

Zeke stared at Jaden. "So how old does that make all of you?"

Jaden shrugged. "Hard to know the exact year, since I was counting by Zyearth years and I've spent the last fifty years of my life on Earth, but I'm well into my second century."

"Embrik and I are near the same age, in our third centuries," Alexina said. "Though after we come of age at twenty, most Athánatos do not keep track. The years blend into one another." She shifted. "That changed when the Basileus started his campaign with the Shadow Cast. The last seventy years have felt longer than all the rest of my life."

Zeke turned to the Cloak. "And you?"

One of the Cloak's eyes widened, which Zeke took to be an eyebrow raise, a curious look through the mask. "That's not for me to disclose."

Zeke stared. "Alright, fair, I guess." He looked at Leah. "And... Leah?"

Jaden flicked an ear back. "Her pendant is a Defender-Z pendant. First year Defender. That'd make her at least forty. Barely a young adult on Zyearth."

Zeke slumped down. He suddenly felt very, very young at only twenty-eight.

Leah, like him, was in her prime. And she was dying here.

Zeke leaned his head in his hands.

"There's one other problem," Jaden said. "Your social bond. I meant it when I said they were dangerous. There's a reason why they were nearly universally banned by intergalactic law. You've been protected from that by not being fully bound. I don't know exactly what binding to your Ei-Ei jewels would do to your bond, but there's no doubt that it would strengthen that bond and open you up to those dangers in a major way."

Zeke flicked his ears back. "What dangers?"

"Lots," Jaden said. "Thought invasions. Loss of privacy. Physical control over your bonded partner." He breathed deeply. "Energy stealing. The history

192

tells of some bonded pairs that killed their partner through energy stealing. And most of these are accidental. Uncontrollable. Bonds can be deadly."

"They don't have to be," the Cloak said.

Jaden glared. "You'll forgive me if I'd rather take the word of thousands of years of Zyearth recorded history over the protest of one mysterious cryptid."

The Cloak glared back, but didn't counter him.

Alexina reached out and gripped Zeke's hand. She smiled. "Hopefully you will be able to reach her without having to bind to your jewels," she said. "Or the Cloak can heal her. None of us want you to put yourself in danger to save her. Least of all Leah, I would think."

Zeke blinked at her. He squeezed her hand back. She smiled at let go, then grabbed another wet wipe to clean Leah.

Zeke stared at his bonded partner. *None of us want you put to yourself in danger.* But Leah had put herself in danger several times to save them. Shouldn't he be willing to do the same?

Assuming anyone would be willing to bind the jewels to him. He'd have to see what the Cloak could do for her.

The next ten hours felt like a lifetime. They continued in almost total silence, with only Jaden's occasional promptings to the Black Cloak to try and heal Leah more. Seven hours in, he was able to make the magic work for a couple more minutes and stop the internal bleeding, though Leah still didn't wake up. Zeke tried several more times throughout the trip to reach her, but nothing much changed until the Cloak was able to heal her a little more.

In the fog of Leah's mind, Zeke caught one more vague image. A tall, short quilled quilar. White, with blue tips and strangely familiar green eyes. He held the image for as long as he could, searching for anything identifying.

Then one name came to him. Matt Azure.

Zeke's heart seized. Azure. Jaden's son. Zeke's... Zeke's half-brother. That was why the green eyes looked so familiar. Zeke had the same eyes.

He dug further. Leah didn't really seem to have a romantic relationship with Matt. More like she admired him, in a mentor-like fashion. But he couldn't get more than that.

They finally stopped near the border as the sun started setting, having driven all day long. Like before, Jaden directed them into the woods and they camped, far from civilization, with Alexina at the wheel. Jaden had spent the last several hours helping Embrik hold Leah up, snoozing lightly. Snow caked the ground. It was like they hadn't even moved anywhere, despite the long ride.

"We'll have to rest here," Jaden said, sounding exhausted. "I don't know how to get into Canada, but there's no way we're attempting it while we're all this tired." Embrik and Alexina nodded. They got up and started pulling equipment out. The Black Cloak gave Leah a sad look, then followed them.

Zeke sat next to Leah and helped Jaden hold her up. "Any ideas about how to get in?" he asked.

Jaden sighed. "None. Not yet." He crossed his arms and stared up at the ceiling.

Zeke narrowed his gaze at Jaden. "We've been driving for ten hours. I can't imagine you haven't thought of *anything.*"

Jaden glared at him, but shook his head. "I had briefly considered just letting border patrol find us. They'd take Leah to a hospital and get her fixed up and we wouldn't have to rely on Hunt. Except... Hunt is out there. Chaos is out there. And you two have trackers. Canada won't take them out and risk injuring you, and I don't think they'd put a lot of resources into protecting us from assassins." He shook his head. "I absolutely hate this... but I don't see another choice."

"Can we actually trust Hunt?"

Jaden shrugged. "The Cloak trusts them."

Zeke lowered his head. "Can we trust the Cloak?"

Jaden flicked an ear back. He turned and looked out the tiny window. Zeke followed his gaze. The Cloak helped Alexina and Embrik set up the few tents they had left. But at one point, when the two of them were busy with a tent, the Cloak turned his head, summoned his two gryfons, and sent them off into the woods.

Jaden winced. "I don't know."

CHAPTER 26

PARTNERS

The group was short two tents, so they had to double up. Jaden and Alexina took one tent, Embrik took another, and they placed Leah in a third. The Cloak said he'd sleep outside next to his summons on one of the brown tarps.

Zeke offered to sleep in the same tent with Leah. He couldn't stand the idea of her being alone. With Alexina's help, he got her ruined jacket and shirt off and cleaned the rest of the dried blood off her fur and undergarments. The Cloak had managed to close up the wounds, but they weren't fully healed, leaving her with angry red scars, pink skin, and no fur around the injury. Zeke rebandaged them, just in case they opened again. Alexina got a long-sleeved shirt on her and they tucked her onto an air mattress, buried under blankets.

She looked almost… normal. Breathing normal, Heartrate normal. Wounds cleaned and closed.

But she wouldn't wake up. Zeke prodded her brain again, but the images were muddier than ever.

He set up his air mattress and lay down, desperate for sleep. But it wouldn't come. Every time he shut his eyes, his brain roared at him, reliving the events from the last few days – dead parents, dead Leah, stabbed side, memory invasions, real, actual wounded Leah, the frantic rush to save her.

He pulled the blankets over his head, trying to drown out his own thoughts. Draso, he was going to break. Leah had healed him completely, but everything ached, especially his chest. He turned back to Leah.

No change.

He couldn't stand it. He threw the blankets off and walked outside, leaving his boots behind. The frigid snow and air did nothing to help his mood, but it at least grounded him.

The Cloak sat on a tarp on the ground, leaning against the white and blue gryfon's side, looking like some fantasy cowboy resting with his horse after a long day of cattle herding. The summon lay on the ground like a big cat, feathered tail wrapped around its body, head resting on its taloned front feet. Its massive wings folded neatly against its back, and its ears twitched with every tiny sound. The red and black gryfon lay down nearby, its head up, glancing around, though still sitting in that casual cross-paw pose, like a giant housecat.

The Cloak poked at the fire with a stick, coaxing more flames, then turned to Zeke. "Can't sleep?"

Zeke rubbed an arm. "No." He frowned. "Aren't you cold?"

The Cloak's eyes crinkled in a smile. "Naw. Big warm gryfons at my back, heavy black cloak on my person. Couldn't ask for a better bed." He patted the brown tarp next to him. "Come sit. I'm sure you'll agree." The blue and white gryfon lifted its head, its beak parting in an almost smile, its solid, shining green eyes inviting him. The Cloak stroked the gryfon's feathers. "Don't mind Rashard, he's a big softy." Rashard snorted a stream of snowflakes through his nostrils.

Zeke breathed deeply and sat down. Rashard nuzzled Zeke gently, pressing his beak against the side of his head. Despite the ice all around them, he was quite warm, smelling of the soft, silent world of deep winter. Comforting. More little snowflakes fell. *Courage, Prínkipas,* Rashard said, his voice airy and musical in Zeke's head. *Everything will right itself.* Rashard lay his head on his front claws again.

It should have been reassuring. But it brought Zeke that much closer to breaking. He leaned against Rashard's folded wing, pressing his eyes shut, fighting back the pain in his chest and the pumping in his ears. "God, what I wouldn't give to have Archángeli back…"

"They'll be back," the Cloak said.

Zeke snapped his head forward. "They will?"

"Sure," the Cloak said. "Summons can't die. But that explosion scattered Archángeli's energy. It'll take them a couple of days to pull themselves back together, but they'll be back. No worries."

Zeke heaved relief. A heavy weight fell off his chest and he could breathe easier. *I'll see you again, old friend.* That pulled him back from the edge a little. Maybe he'd be okay after all.

Well. As long as Leah survived. He reached over and gently stroked Rashard's neck feathers. Rashard purred. Zeke stared at the Cloak. "So. Who are you?"

The Cloak raised a finger and winked. "Ah, that'd be telling."

Zeke narrowed his gaze. "I meant more about your title than your identity."

The Cloak chuckled. "Fair." He lifted a part of the cloak's long cape. "Put simply, if any of this is simple, I'm one of the Keepers – four guardians formed to prevent the creation of Shadow Cast and stop a terrible summon from taking over the universe."

Zeke raised one eyebrow. "That's... I don't... where do you even start with that?"

The Cloak laughed. "Don't think about it too hard, it's an inflated title. I am tasked with preventing Shadow Cast creation, but the idea that we're fighting a universe-destroying summon is definitely exaggerated."

"Alexina mentioned them," Zeke said. "The hell is a Shadow Cast?"

"The Athánatos call them 'stolen warriors,'" the Cloak said. "Basically an invincible, sentient puddle monster."

Zeke blinked. "Puddle monster."

"Don't be fooled by the simple description," the Cloak said. "They're quite deadly."

Zeke shook his head. A brief image flashed in his mind, from when he and Leah first bound their jewels. A black puddle with three glowing blue orbs for eyes. He shuddered. "Alexina said you hadn't prevented their creation."

"Alas, no," the Cloak said. "We failed there. Ask any of your teammates. Most of them had to fight Cast at some point in their lives. But thankfully a certain set of Guardians in the near future will take care of that for me."

Zeke leaned further into Rashard's warm feathers. Alexina hadn't thought that was good enough. This Cloak character was so strange. "So what's wrong with your healing magic?"

The Cloak lifted a brow. "Pardon?"

"You admitted yourself that you're not a strong healer," Zeke said. "But Leah is. What makes the two of you different?"

"An excellent question," the Cloak said. "For one, Leah has an advantage. She's a healer-S. She can see damage far more clearly than I can, which guides her magic. For two... she actually likes healing. Most healers hate their powers, and while no one can really prove that that has any effect on a healer's strength, I certainly think it does."

Zeke frowned. "Leah likes being a healer? But she hates her healer-S magic."

"She does," the Cloak agreed. "But there's a big difference between hating the effects of being a healer-S and loving what you can do with your magic." He shrugged. "Most healer-S's hate that part of themselves, no matter how they feel about the magic itself."

Zeke narrowed his gaze. "So do you hate your magic then?"

"As I said," the Cloak said. "Most do."

Zeke frowned. "Why? I'd kill for proper healing powers right now. Anything to save Leah."

The Cloak shrugged. "Seems counterintuitive doesn't it? I should add the caveat that most *Defender* healers hate their magic. It's a social thing. Defenders are Zyearth's most powerful soldiers, but healers are considered support, not frontline soldiers. It's the elemental users that get the spotlight. Even cloakers, as much as they're also support, are important parts of the battlefield. But healers are on the sidelines, and are only useful after someone's been hurt. So there's a social stigma that they just aren't as good as the other soldiers. Never mind the fact that history says different and that many of our best Guardians have been healers." He shook his head. "Healers start out excited about their powers usually. They're the first to break their magic, the first to show off their powers. But as their elemental peers leave them behind, they learn to resent healing for not being 'good enough'."

"But Leah's different."

"Leah was already stigmatized for being a healer-s," the Cloak said. "In a way, that saved her. No one could spoil her love for her magic because no one cared to try when they had already given up on her. But that doesn't mean she didn't fall for some of the same traps healers do. It's one of the reasons she's so adept at battle. Most healers are, as 'compensation' for their magic."

Zeke flicked his ears back. "That's kind of despicable. Healing shouldn't need compensation."

A gentle snow fell on Zeke's head. *Dyne Gildspine felt the same way,* Rashard said. *But it was easier for him to be confident in his magic.*

Zeke glanced at him. "Why?"

He had a supportive partner, Rashard said. *In Jaden.*

Zeke frowned. "And then Jaden lost his partner… now he's a mess."

The price paid for a deep connection with another, Rashard said. *But a price worth paying.* Rashard chuckled, a deep, melodic sound. *You should have seen them in their prime. Inseparable in training, there for each other in the best and worst of times. They traveled the universe together, handling missions that would run your blood cold, while having the time of their lives doing it.* Rashard lowered his head, his ears flat.

A tiny, cold ember landed on Zeke's nose and he glanced up. The other gryfon, Kjorn, nodded to Rashard. *He could have something like that again,* he said, his voice harsh and gravelly. *Not exact, because that kind of love is irreplaceable. But similar.*

But he's afraid to, Rashard continued. *Because of the price he paid for losing Dyne, and his family.*

Zeke frowned. He fiddled with his hands, staring at the snow.

Prínkipas, Kjorn said. Zeke lifted his head and met the deep blue eyes of the gryfon. *The price paid is worth it. What would our lives be if we lived them alone for fear of a broken heart? Our existence is made richer by the company we choose to keep.* He lifted his head and nodded to Rashard. *Right, Wingbrother?*

Rashard gave Kjorn that subtle smile again. *As long as I draw breath.*

We will never fly alone, Kjorn said. *No matter where we find each other, summon or otherwise.*

Zeke watched them a moment, then turned his gaze to the ground again. Jaden was afraid of a relationship like this, because he was afraid to be hurt again. It was why he kept Alexina and Embrik at arm's length.

It was why he pushed Leah away.

And Zeke was the same way. He had been afraid to open up to Andre, and when he did, their relationship changed, like he feared it would. He was afraid to open up to Leah for the same reasons. She could be just like Andre – romantically interested. He was afraid of getting hurt again. Better to push her away before she ever got the chance to hurt him, or at least that was what his brain told him.

Draso's mercy, he really was just like his father.

And he shouldn't be. He needed to talk to Andre when… if he got back. Explain what he missed. See if they could fix it. Andre… he'd like that. He'd understand.

And he needed to stop pushing Leah away.

He stood. "Thanks for the talk," he said. "All of you."

The Cloak's eyes wrinkled in a smile. "Any time."

Zeke managed a small smile, then walked back to his tent. He sunk into the covers again, watching Leah. She still didn't move. He carefully checked her breathing and pulse. Normal. She could be sleeping except that she wouldn't wake up.

He tried poking in her mind, one more time. It was more blank than ever, and yet… something was there. Something sad. Distant. And it got more distant the more Zeke reached for it.

Damn it all.

Leah, Zeke said. *I'm… I'm sorry.*

A tiny, twinkling light shot through his mind, and some faint smell of tea hit his nose. But it was gone in an instant. He waited a moment longer for more, but nothing came.

He flicked his ears back. "I really am sorry, Leah… Just… come back. Please." He frowned. "We… we need each other." He chewed his lip. "We each need a partner."

Nothing.

Zeke sighed. He took his glasses off and huddled deeper into his blankets, hoping for sleep he knew wouldn't come.

CHAPTER 27

CROSSING BOUNDARIES

Everyone slept past noon the next day. Everyone except Zeke, who spent most of the night and morning lying awake on his bed, trying and failing over and over to reach into Leah's mind and bring her back. It wasn't healthy, he knew, but he had to do something. He had to fix this.

Someone tapped on his tent. He slowly sat up and ran a hand down his face.

The tent flap unzipped slightly and Jaden peered in. "Hey, you awake?"

I never slept. "Yeah," Zeke said. "What's up?"

Jaden frowned. "How's Leah?"

Zeke shook his head. "No different." He pulled his knees up to his chin. "Draso's mercy, Jaden, what the hell am I supposed to do?"

Jaden flicked an ear back. He pulled the zipper further down and sat inside, meeting Zeke's gaze. "I don't... I don't know."

"I could bind to my Ei-Ei jewels."

"Putting yourself in danger isn't the answer," Jaden said.

"And why the hell isn't it?" Zeke said. "It's what Leah did for me. And you."

"Zeke," Jaden said. "This is too big a risk. You might end up killing both of you instead of saving Leah. I can't emphasize enough how dangerous social bonds are." He shifted. "It might even be worse for you two. You don't have the same focus jewels. Who knows what problems you might face with two different jewels."

"So I have to sit here and watch Leah fight for her life, alone," Zeke said bitterly. "Someone who was only trying to be my friend, who I screamed at and pushed away." He held his head. "Goddamn it."

"Give it time," Jaden said. "The Cloak's magic will come back. Hunt… Hunt should help. We'll save her. You don't have to risk yourself to fix her. That's not your responsibility."

But wasn't it? Leah had risked so much for them. And no matter how you looked at it, they were already bound in a social bond. It didn't matter that Zeke had worked so hard to push her away. It changed nothing. They were stuck together. He should be embracing it, damn it.

But after everything he had done to Leah, he doubted she'd want anything to do with him anymore. Maybe that was why she wouldn't come back.

Maybe it was Zeke's fault.

"I should never have pushed her away," Zeke said. "She needs a partner."

Jaden shifted. "I'll admit, healers do better with good partners."

"Like you and Dyne," Zeke said.

Jaden lifted a brow. "Where did you hear that name?"

Zeke hunched down. Oops. "You uh, you mentioned when Leah went after that basilisk. I assume you saw Dyne in an illusion."

Jaden eyed him a moment, but then shrugged. "Alright, fair. Yes, like me and Dyne. Leah needs that kind of partner."

Zeke scoffed. "But I've ruined those chances. I've been terrible to her." He picked at a loose thread on his blanket. "Hell, we both have."

Jaden narrowed his gaze. "What does that mean?"

Zeke waved a hand. "Being so critical of her. Analyzing her every move, calculating her every act, always worried about what would happen if you bonded with her because of what you've lost in the past..." He leaned his head on his hands. Good Draso, he really meant himself, didn't he? Calculating every damn move, expecting her to turn on him at any moment. That was the fear the Wish Dusters put on him. How the hell was he supposed to help her when he couldn't force himself to see past his own irrational fears? "I'm sorry, Jaden, I--" He glanced up and stopped.

Jaden stared at Zeke wide eyed, his inner ears darkened in a flush.

Zeke's eyes widened and he frowned. "Oh Draso, Jaden, I'm sorry, I didn't--"

"No, it's..." Jaden stopped. He shook his head, rustling his quills. "There's food waiting for you outside if you're hungry," he said suddenly. He moved to leave.

Zeke frowned. "Jaden, I didn't-- I just wanted you to-- I've been doing the same thing to her and--"

"This conversation is over," Jaden said. He left.

Zeke flopped back on the bed and covered his face with his hands, his eyes burning. He lay that way for a long time before finally pulling the blankets over his head again, desperate for sleep.

Leah stayed perfectly still in her bed.

It was afternoon before Zeke finally peeled himself off the air mattress, aching, hungry, exhausted, and heart sick. He checked Leah. The scars hardly looked different. He gently took her hand. Limp, but warm. But that was it. He squeezed it gently. "Leah. Please come back."

Nothing.

206

He closed his eyes. All he had to do was open up. Let Leah in. He had to push past his own fears and pull her back. He could bring her home even without binding to his jewels. His hands shook, trying to let go of the fear. *Leah. Please. I'm sorry. I'm here. You're not alone. Please, come back...*

Still nothing.

He stared a moment longer, then growled, and stormed out of the tent, feeling helpless.

The rest of the group sat around the fire, chattering quietly. Zeke glanced up. Clouds hung low overhead, darkening the sky. The gryfon summons were missing, but Kyrie sat on the ground near the Cloak, preening her feathers. Zeke slogged through the snow and sat next to the Cloak too.

Jaden wouldn't look at him.

Embrik perked his ears. "Finally get some sleep?"

"No," Zeke said. He twitched his ear. "Maybe a little." Alexina handed him a mug of coffee. Zeke sipped at it, letting the hot liquid burn his tongue. He turned to Jaden. "Jaden--"

"We're trying to find a way to cross the border," Jaden said without looking at Zeke. "No great suggestions yet. Let me know if you have any ideas."

Zeke twitched his tail. "But Jaden--"

"Focus on the task, Zeke," Jaden said. "Leah's life depends on it."

Guilt stabbed through Zeke's heart, making everything ache. "Yeah. Sure." He sipped coffee. "What do we know about the border patrol?"

"It's mostly drones in the area," the Cloak said. "Out here in this thick forest, they don't really expect many attempts to cross illegally. Too dangerous. Especially tonight – looks like the area's gonna get a late season snowstorm."

Zeke looked up again. "Can we use that to our advantage?"

"If you think we're going to just mosey across the no-touching zone between borders in the middle of a freakin' snowstorm, you've got another thing coming," Jaden said. "That'd be suicide. The storm would get us before the Mounties would. Especially having to carry Leah."

"Jaden is right," Embrik said. "None of us are truly prepared for the cold. And we cannot take most of our equipment – the Humvee will have to stay here."

"You're all mages," Zeke said. "You gotta have *something*. What about having Embrik blast away snow with his fire?"

"Inefficient at best," Embrik said. "And at worst, it would serve only to create sloshy piles to slog through. Even if Alexina and I worked together, we could not combat a full storm. Also, the fire would be a beacon for drones to find."

Zeke slumped forward. "What about Jaden's ice?"

"No good," Jaden said. "I can move stationary snow, and perhaps could combat a light dusting, but not a full snowstorm. I'm not strong enough."

"All these suggestions ignore the biggest problems," Alexina said. "How do we get Leah across? Carrying her will be difficult in the best of times, but it will be far harder while fighting a snowstorm and keeping watch for drones. Also, what do we do when we get in? We have to leave our supplies here and trek through raw wilderness. No food, no tents. That cannot be good for Leah even if the rest of us could stand it."

Zeke leaned on his knees. This was hopeless. Regret ate at his belly.

Kyrie hopped up to Zeke and nuzzled his elbow. He absently reached over and stroked her feathers like he had done so many times with Archángeli. Then his eyes grew wide. "The gryfons."

Jaden lifted his head. "Pardon?"

Zeke turned to the Cloak. "Could Rashard and Kjorn make it through a snowstorm?"

The Cloak rubbed the chin on his mask. "Possibly."

"And could they carry Leah?"

"They could…" The Cloak frowned. "But we risk someone seeing us. Rashard and Kjorn aren't exactly small."

Zeke pinched the bridge of his snout and pushed his glasses closer to his face. "Okay… what if rather than keeping the snow away from us, we use it to hide ourselves? We have at least three people with ice magic. We have camouflage. We could put Leah on Rashard's back with our supplies and create like… a snow vortex around us. Push the snow back while also hiding us. We'll have to really bundle up and make sure Leah is nice and warm, but it might be doable."

"Hmm," the Cloak said. "That might be worth exploring."

Jaden sighed. "It's as good a plan as any." He stood. "Let's pack what we can and give this a shot."

Over the next several hours, the group sorted through their supplies, picking the absolute necessities and stowing the rest in the Humvee. The worst part was trying to secure the supplies to the gryfons and figure out how to strap Leah safely across Rashard's back. She fit snuggly between his wings, but moved too much when he tried to fly. Plus, the moment she was out from the tent, she started to shake with cold. In the end, they wrapped her in blankets, mummy style, and strapped her to Rashard, deciding that the only way to do this was to walk across the border. This left almost no room for supplies, and definitely amped up their chances of being caught, but they did what they could.

By the time they settled everything, it was true dark, and the snowfall had already started, making it difficult to see, though it did give them a chance to test out Zeke's snow blinding technique. Between Jaden, Alexina, and Rashard, they were able to create a convincing snow whirl, though their outfits still stood out behind the snow. It simply wasn't enough camouflage.

But they were running out of time. They had to get going.

"Wait," Jaden said. "Where's the Cloak?"

"Here," the Cloak said, walking up to the group. He held a lot of white objects – jackets, beanies, blankets, even a rope.

Jaden eyed him. "Where have you been?"

"Whitefish," the Cloak said. "Local ski town."

"Dressed like *that?*" Zeke asked.

The Cloak only winked. "Take a guess." He walked past them and looped a rope around Rashard's neck. "I'll tie all of you to this rope around Rashard so you don't get lost in the storm. You'll wear those white cloaks, masks, and beanies. You weren't blending well enough. I'll get you all settled with Rashard, then I'll cross over with Kyrie and Kjorn. Kyrie will help protect us from the snow. We'll be your eyes in the air, take out any drones we see."

"If you can see anything in a snowstorm," Jaden said.

"You'd be surprised," the Cloak said. He reached over Leah and activated her pendant, showing her vitals.

No change.

He shook his head. "I don't like it, but we need a way to communicate that the drones and Mounties can't interpret." He slipped her pendant off and turned to Jaden. "I'll use this and contact you if I need to. They'll pick up a signal, but it's not likely they'll be able to pinpoint the signal or hear us. They'll dismiss it."

Jaden wrinkled his snout. "...Yeah." He pulled up his datasquare and activated the map. He showed it to the summons, pointing out the coordinates Ackerson gave them – looked like a small clearing deep in the woods just on the other side of the border. "Meet here. Be careful."

Zeke frowned. "How are we going to monitor Leah without her pendant?"

Rashard turned and snorted. *Climb aboard, Prínkipas,* he said. *You will monitor her.*

210

Zeke pressed his lips together. "Are you going to be able to hold me with all those supplies?"

Have faith.

Zeke sighed, but nodded. He climbed up on Rashard's back and settled himself, then took one glove off. Wouldn't be as accurate as the pendant, but he could at least feel if she got too cold.

Goddamn all of this.

They did one more quick check, then tied themselves to Rashard and headed for the border.

Despite being huddled in the blankets and supplies next to Leah, Zeke never felt such biting cold before. Snow whipped at his face, cutting through his fur and stinging his skin. His ears felt ready to fall off, even with two beanies on his head. His glasses nearly flew off twice – in the end, he took his and Leah's and shoved them in his deep pockets, which he should have done in the first place. Not like he could see anything in the dark anyway. None of them could. They had to rely on Rashard's night vision.

Leah still never moved, but at least she had stopped shaking. Zeke kept checking her temperature, making sure she was warm enough. His hand ached with cold, but he didn't have a choice.

Zeke wasn't quite sure how long it took them to trek north. Hours probably, but it dragged on until it felt like his life would never be different. Like they'd never stop freezing to death. Like Leah was lost, forever, fighting for her life while Zeke did nothing.

But eventually the storm slowed. Zeke's hand felt less numb. Leah seemed to settle. And as the clouds cleared, the moon appeared, giving the fresh snow a haunted, glowing look. The Black Cloak and his summons had long vanished into the night sky.

"Just a little further," Jaden said, though his voice was muffled in the new snow. "We're almost there."

211

"Actually, this is as far as you go," a deep voice said. Jaden whipped around and bathed the group of them in a shield. Rashard leapt around too, hissing and spitting, knocking Zeke clean off his back. He whipped out his glasses and scrambled to his feet and searched for the source of the voice.

A black zyfaunos fruit bat with green streaked wings and fur stood before them, arms crossed, wingtips brushing the snow, barely more than a colorful shadow in the moonlight. And at his sides were a black alicorn and a black and white striped lion/zebra centaur, both with pupilless eyes.

Summons.

The fruit bat snapped two elongated fingers and the summons attacked.

CHAPTER 28

HUNT

Zeke could only duck as the black alicorn leapt into the air and dove on them. Rashard roared at the summon, mantling his wings over Zeke. A sharp cracking sound echoed in Zeke's ears. But only one thing ran through his mind.

Leah.

He pressed against Rashard's wing, trying to get free, though he couldn't even hope to budge it. "Rashard, back up, let me get to Leah!"

Peace, Prínkipas! Rashard said. *I have you protected.*

Zeke pushed through anyway and managed to poke his head through Rashard's flight feathers. Rashard had formed a thick ice shield over them.

But the alicorn wasn't backing down. Its yellow-orange eyes glared at them, and it snarled and snorted at them, fogging the ice with its hot breath. It reared up and stomped at the ice, wings flared, blocking what little moonlight they had. The ice cracked with every hoofbeat.

Rashard let out a long hiss and tramped a back foot in the snow. Ice spikes spit out of his ice shield, aimed at the alicorn's belly. But the spikes cracked and splintered the moment it hit the alicorn's hide.

Rashard growled. *Stone element.*

"Shit," Zeke said.

Can you summon Archángeli? There is little they could do, but they could at least be a distraction while we flee.

Zeke reached for Archángeli, but still couldn't quite reach them. Their voice sounded in Zeke's mind, distant and flat. *I need rest…*

"They're still out for the count," Zeke said. He reached up around Leah and pulled her collapsed staff out. He shook it to full length. "Make me an ice spear like you did for Leah."

Rashard turned to him. *You cannot hope to fight it!*

"I have to do *something!*" Zeke said. "Leah has risked herself over and over again for us and I'm not going to let her get hurt again, damnit!"

The summon is made of stone, Prínkipas!

"Not all of it is," Zeke said. He slipped out from under Rashard's wing. "Let me out and keep it distracted!"

Rashard eyed him. He turned back to the alicorn and blasted spike after spike of ice at it, while opening a small hole in the ice shield for Zeke. Zeke slipped out while the alicorn was distracted then stood, iced spear in hand. Echoes of his teammates shouting and something crashing through the trees bombarded his ears, as flashes of fire and ice burst through his peripheral vision, but he pushed them out of his mind.

One shot.

He raised the makeshift spear and threw it as hard as he could at the alicorn's face.

The spear hit its mark, piercing the alicorn's eye. It reeled back, howling, beating at the now stuck spear with its wings. In its panic, it slipped down the

214

side of the ice shield in a pile of flailing legs and feathers, throwing bits of stone in the air.

Relief washed over Zeke. He'd done it! He'd--

Someone crashed into him, knocking him deep into the fresh powder. Zeke tried to scramble out of the snow, but before he could get his legs under him, his whole body lifted into the air. He got one quick glimpse of his attacker – another bat, black, with orange, red, and white streaks – before he was flung away by some invisible force. He crashed hard into Rashard's ice shield. Pain ripped through his side, as if his ribs had exploded.

Rashard squawked and turned to him, but the alicorn leapt to its hooves and sprang back on the ice shield. It let out a terrifying bellow and half a dozen ice spikes exploded from its wings, smashing against Rashard's ice. The spear still stuck fast in its eye - glowing yellow-orange blood ran down its muzzle and in its mane. Rashard turned back to it turning Leah away from it. He thickened the ice shield and hurled spikes at the alicorn, though it did little to stop it.

Zeke tried to stand, tried to move and get back in Rashard's ice shield, but the pain threw him off balance and he slipped on the snow.

Both fruit bats walked up to him now, with the zebra-striped centaur walking between them, towering over them, its big lion paws padding soundlessly on the snow. Zeke gripped his side and backed up against Rashard's ice.

The black and green fruit bat crossed his arms. "Hmm. You'd think a group named Mage would have more mages in it. Ackerson is getting sloppy."

Zeke growled and tried to speak, but failed, coughing up blood instead.

The bats stared at him, frowning. The black and orange one lifted his head. His expression morphed from confused to fear and he held up his hands just as a massive ice spike bore down on them. The bat pulled his hands apart and the ice spear shattered to diamond dust.

Jaden rushed in front of Zeke, sword hilt in hand. He shook the hilt and a long, thick ice blade formed on it. He gritted his teeth. "If it's a mage you want..." He waved a hand, surrounding himself with sharp icicles and rushed them both.

The bats dove aside and centaur leapt forward. He held his hands out and shot two glowing orbs of purple and blue energy at Jaden.

Jaden gasped and shielded, but the orbs ripped through his shield and threw him against Rashard's ice shield. He slid down next to Zeke.

Embrik roared now and set the air on fire around him and rushed forward. But a strange pink and white doe dressed in all white slipped around him with impressive speed and caressed a hand around his Ei-Ei jewels, smiling at him. "Ah, ah, not so fast."

Embrik's fire immediately blew out. The doe moved quickly, wrapping an arm under Embrik's chin and pulling him down to the snow. He struggled, but apparently couldn't manage any more fire.

Alexina growled now, filling the area with fire and ice. "Let him go!"

The centaur turned on Alexina and fired two more orbs of energy at her. Jaden tried to sit up and warn her, but he could only manage a squeak. The orbs hit Alexina's back, knocking her into the snow. Three more does, all identical to the one who held Embrik down, rushed for her. The centaur turned back on Jaden and Zeke.

Zeke tried to move, find the hole in Rashard's ice shield, do *something,* but the pain was unbearable, ripping through his entire midsection. Ice and snow rained down on him from the alicorn's stone magic beating against Rashard's ice.

The black and green bat stood and brushed snow off his fur and clothes. He walked up to Zeke. "Not bad, considering," he said. "Now--"

In a flash of fire and snow, Kjorn barreled out of the sky, crashing into the centaur, knocking it into the woods in a tangle of limbs and elements, sending the bats tumbling. The orange and black bat vanished into the snow, and the black and green bat slammed into Rashard's ice next to Jaden.

The Black Cloak landed on the ground between Embrik and Alexina, Kyrie at his side. He held his hands out. "Everyone, *please--*"

One of the pink doe leapt up and charged the Cloak with a wide-bladed dagger. He whipped out a staff similar to Leah's and raised it to defend.

Jaden tried again to stand, but only managed to get to all fours. He coughed blood on the snow while his Defender pendant hung loose around his neck.

The bat groaned and turned to Jaden. He blinked several times, then his eyes grew wide. "Silver Tailwind, that's..." He shook his head and waved a hand. "Ari, Pathos, Lysander, everyone *stop!*" He pointed to the centaur, who vanished in a flurry of purple and white sparks, leaving Kjorn standing confused, fire all around him. The doe all stopped and glanced at the bat. He turned to Jaden. "You have a Defender pendant. A Golden Guardian one even."

Jaden turned to him, one eyebrow raised. He coughed. "How do you know what this is?"

"Am I right?"

"Yes, but--"

"Oh my god, I am *so sorry,*" the bat said. "I assumed you were one of Ackerson's."

Jaden stared at him. "We are technically, but..."

A flurry of ice hit the backs of everyone's head. *Call off your alicorn!* Rashard's voice.

"Sorry, sorry!" The bat scrambled to his feet. "Magna, back up, they're fine!"

A pebble bounced off Zeke's head. *That rat stabbed my eye!*

217

"Then go into standby and heal up," the bat said. "He was just trying to protect--"

"Leah," Zeke said, pushing through the pain and standing. He pounded on the ice. "Rashard, let me get to her!"

The alicorn, Magna, snorted into the ice and stepped off. Rashard pulled the ice shield down, snorting back at Magna.

Zeke hobbled over to Leah, gripping his side. *Please be okay, please be okay!*

Leah still lay there, though she had started shaking uncontrollably. Zeke put a hand to her forehead. "Draso's wings, she's burning up…" He pulled back the blankets to see her injury. The fabric clung to the wound, peeling back pus. The skin was hot and bright red. Damn it!

The black and orange bat walked up now. "One of your companions is injured?"

"Gravely," Jaden said.

"We need your help," the Cloak said. He coughed. "It's the least you can do for attacking us unprovoked."

The black and green bat narrowed his gaze. "Blame Ackerson."

"We don't have *time* for blame," Zeke said, also coughing. "We need to help her *now.*"

"And what do you expect us to do?" The four pink and white doe walked up to them. They might as well have been clones or illusions, they looked so alike. Zeke couldn't tell which one of them spoke. All of them wore identical white snow outfits. They looked strangely familiar too, but Zeke didn't have the energy to figure out why.

The Cloak could tell them apart apparently though. He pointed to one. "Ethos. Your Wish allows you to enhance objects."

The second doe in the group raised an eyebrow, but nodded. "Not sure how that helps a dying teammate."

The Cloak pulled out a Gem. It was encased in a tight, matte black pouch. "You can enhance this."

The doe eyed him. "You seem so certain."

"We don't have time," Zeke said. He gripped his side and groaned. "Can you help or not?"

The doe flipped her long ears back. "I suppose I can try. Give me the Gem."

The Cloak furrowed his brow at Zeke. "Zeke, you're injured." He moved closer.

"Leah first, goddamnit," Zeke said. "I'll live. She may not." He pulled himself back up Rashard's back and hung on to his neck feathers. "Please."

The Cloak lowered his gaze. He nodded to Jaden. "Help him stay up. I'll work on him next."

Jaden twitched his ears, but nodded. He stood, favoring his left side a little, and pressed himself up against Zeke.

The Cloak reached over Rashard's shoulders. "Zeke, reach for her while I work, okay?"

Zeke nodded. "Hurry."

The Cloak pressed his hands to Leah's wounds.

Zeke dove into her mind with renewed vigor. *Come on, Leah. Come back. Come home.*

The same images floated through Zeke's mind again. The gray lioness. The lion with a feather mane. Zeke's apparent half-brother Matt. As the Cloak healed her, the images grew sharper, but no matter how hard Zeke tried, he couldn't coax any other anchors out of her mind.

But then, a new image, faint and gray, slowly came into focus near Matt. A tall, fully black Athánatos quilar with soft, pupilless teal eyes and a gentle walk. He walked next to Matt and the two of them shared a smile. His name floated through Zeke's head.

"Ouranos," Zeke said aloud.

Alexina gasped. "My brother."

My uncle, Zeke thought. Why would he show up in Leah's mind? He focused on the image, trying to make sense of it.

Ouranos put a hand on Matt's shoulder and the pair shared a sideways hug, and started chattering excitedly, though Zeke couldn't make out any words. There was something... different about their bond. Almost like...

Then everything vanished, forcing Zeke back into reality. He glanced around frantic. "What happened? Is Leah okay? The images all went away!"

"She's fine," the Cloak said. "But... she's still not awake."

"What?" Zeke turned to Leah.

The Cloak pulled back the blankets where her wounds were, revealing perfectly healed flesh. Fresh fur, soft skin, no sign of injury. Her Defender pendant lay on her chest with the hologram activated. All readings perfectly normal. She didn't even appear to be very cold.

But she wouldn't wake up.

Zeke frowned, his heart and side aching. His eyes burned. "Damn it all... What's wrong with her?"

The Cloak met Zeke's gaze. "We need something stronger to pull her back."

Zeke flicked his ears back. "Then I need to be bound to these jewels."

Jaden snarled. "Zeke--"

"Don't," Zeke said. "She needs me, and she's worth the risk." He turned to Alexina. "I need to be bound."

Alexina frowned, but nodded.

BOUND

"I don't like this," Jaden said.

Zeke turned to Jaden, frowning. After the Cloak had healed all their injuries, with Ethos' help, Hunt led Zeke and his team to their original meeting point, a derelict Mounties station in the middle of the woods. The outside was rotting and disgusting – no paint, peeling wood and roof shingles, boarded up windows, and the whole thing appeared to lean to one side. Absolutely no signs of life.

The inside was an entirely different story though. Everything was clean and well kept. A fancy electric heater sat in one corner. Big comfy couches lined two walls, and oversized bean bag chairs filled each corner. A hallway led off to what Zeke suspected were bedrooms. It was homey.

The two bats, Angus and Ronan, had made everyone breakfast and coffee. Both teams ate in silence, all of them wary of each other. A smell of fresh toast, bacon, and cooked eggs filled the room, making Zeke long for the comforting smells of his bind with Leah. That was… unexpected, to say the least. After their tremulous beginnings, who would've thought he'd actually miss it? Damn, he wasted so much effort pushing her away.

Jaden sat stiffly on one of the couches next to Embrik, his meal sitting untouched on the coffee table. "We should wait and see if she wakes up. She's healed. Give her time."

"Her mind went *blank*," Zeke said. "She's trapped in there somewhere and I have to get her out."

Jaden narrowed his gaze. "Zeke. This bind is *dangerous*. Social binds weren't banned lightly. No one would expect you to go through with this. Not even Leah. I know you earthlings can be foolhardy but--"

"Don't start," Zeke snarled. "Don't even. I'm not going to listen to your bullshit." He glanced at Leah. They had placed her on one of the oversized beanbags near the electric heater and wrapped her in a blanket, but she still didn't respond. Zeke was no closer to finding any new anchors in her mind either. Everything was entirely black. If she hadn't been breathing, Zeke would have thought her dead. He glared at Jaden. "We've been here for several hours and she hasn't changed. We can't wait any longer. She needs me." *And… I need her.*

Jaden glared back. "Zeke, the risk--"

"--Is worth it," Zeke said. "This is my choice. You don't get a say in it."

"If I may ask," one of the doe said. "Why is this bind necessary to save her, and why is it dangerous?"

Jaden narrowed his gaze. "Why do you care?"

"Safety," the doe said. "And curiosity. I'll admit, I'm interested in watching the bind. I've never seen jewels of his type bound before. But I'd like to know why you think it's dangerous. I dare say none of us would like to be here if this puts us at risk."

"It only puts Zeke at risk," Jaden said, his voice cracking. He glared at Jaden. "These binds invade privacy and steal energy and magic at best and kill at worst. They--"

"Jaden, just *stop it,*" Zeke snapped. "I get it already!"

"You clearly *don't--*"

"I beg to differ," the doe said. "He clearly understands the risks. Let him make his own decisions." Jaden bared his teeth, but the doe ignored him. She nodded to Leah. "What happened to her that a jewel bind might save her?"

Zeke glanced over at the doe. All four of them sat on one couch, blending into one another. Zeke wasn't sure which one to address. "We were attacked by one of Ackerson's teams."

The doe on the far end nodded. "Ah. Chaos, correct?"

Jaden raised an eyebrow. "How did you know?"

"They attacked us recently," Angus said. He ran three fingers through a black, green streaked tuft of hair on his head. "It's kind of why we attacked you. Chaos is hunting Ackerson's other teams."

Ronan sipped at his coffee, a black, orange and yellow fur tuft falling in his face. "Ackerson denies it, but we've spoken with Guardian, and they've lost members to Chaos now. We got a hold of Outlander and warned them. Hopefully they'll come out okay." He shook his head. "We're lucky we escaped it. But we had advance warning." He twisted his pointed ears. "You were the only team we hadn't been able to get a hold of before now, so we were wary when Ackerson said he had a job he wanted us to do with you."

Embrik nodded. "Your caution is warranted," he said. "We had the same concerns, but with our companion down, we had no choice."

"Forgive my intrusion," one of the doe said. "But this still doesn't answer the question. Why do you think binding this Athánatos to his focus jewels will bring her back to consciousness?"

Alexina lifted a brow. "You know of Athánatos?"

All four does exchanged looks with each other and settled uncomfortably. "We... specialize in focus jewels," one said. "It's pertinent for us to be familiar with all of them."

Zeke stared for a moment, then all his quills stood on end. "Wait. Now I know why you all look familiar. You're a part of the Fawn Family!"

Jaden gripped the arm of the couch and pressed his ears flat against his quills.

The does exchanged glances again, all of them flattening their ears. One spoke. "Yes. But not by choice. We were born into it and pressed into service by our current Matron... our older sister."

Zeke stared. The Fawn Family was a notorious mafia in El Dorado, working under the business name Triple Fawn. They controlled most of the casinos in Zeke's time, and were well known for their brutality. Zeke had heard dozens of rumors about them in his short time on the new base. Their lead assassins, the Triple Danger, were the best of the best. No one could touch them, not even the police. "Beware pink doe," the rumors said. "She'll take you home and use you to practice making it look like an accident."

While it was never confirmed, for obvious reasons, rumor had it that the Triple Danger were related. Triplets, probably.

And yet, he was staring at quadruplets.

"If you're members of the Fawn Family," Jaden asked, his voice tense. "Why are you working for Ackerson? And what does the Fawn Family have to do with focus jewels?"

"That ignores the question at hand," one doe said.

Jaden glared. "I don't--"

"Jaden," Alexina said, glaring at him. "Not the time." Jaden snorted, but she shrugged it off. She turned to the doe. "Leah and Zeke share a social bond with their focus jewels. Zeke needs to be bound to his jewels for their bond to be strong enough for him to help her."

224

The doe raised her eyebrow. "Social bonds, hmm? Weren't those banned?"

"Yes," Jaden said bitterly.

"It happened by accident," Zeke said.

The doe raised the other eyebrow. "Some accident."

"I know," Zeke said. He leaned his head on his hands. "But we're stuck, and I can't break it, even if I wanted to. And I *did* want to at first, for stupid, selfish reasons and I treated Leah terribly because of it, but the more I think about it, the more I *don't* want to break it. I've wanted something like this forever, but I don't even know if Leah wants this anymore after I screamed at her, but she's also in serious trouble and I have to *do something.*" He paused and took a deep breath, his eyes burning. "So I have to do this."

The doe leaned forward, a gentle frown on her face. "Tell me," she said. "Are you doing this because you really want to, or because you feel obligated?"

Zeke turned to Leah. "I'm doing this because... we need each other and it's about time I admit that."

The doe smiled slowly. "Good reason."

Jaden looked off, his ears flat.

Alexina gently gripped Zeke's shoulder. "I agree. So shall we begin?"

Zeke closed his eyes a moment, then nodded.

Alexina stood. "Come." She kneeled in the middle of the floor, sitting on her feet. "Kneel in front of me."

Zeke did as he was told.

Alexina lowered her gaze. "I am going to ask for your Ei-Ei jewels now," she said. "But remember what I said earlier. Once I touch them, I will hear their jewelsong. We will know for certain who your biological parents are." Jaden crossed his arms and looked off, frowning sadly. "Are you okay with this?"

Zeke pressed his lips together. "Yeah, I guess. Don't really have a choice." He slipped the bracelet off and passed it to Alexina.

She held the Ei-Ei jewels close to her chest for a moment, eyes closed. Several minutes passed in total silence. When she opened them, they shined with tears, though she managed a small smile.

Zeke frowned. "…Guess I don't have to ask."

"It is… as we expected," Alexina said. She shook her head. "Though I do not know what that means for our future."

Jaden turned to the Black Cloak and glared. "You're going to take our son from us."

The black and green bat Angus tilted his head and exchanged a glance with his brother. The orange and black bat just shrugged.

The Cloak narrowed his gaze, but said nothing.

Jaden stood now. "That's it then, huh? That's what you plan to do?"

"I'm not allowed to discuss my future or past actions as the Black Cloak," the Cloak said, his voice firm, almost challenging. "But I can assure you, nothing I do is with the intent to harm."

"Horse spit," Jaden said, but he sat back down. He wouldn't look at Zeke.

Ronan flicked a pointed ear back. His wings twitched. "There's some subtext here that I really don't understand."

"It's a long story," the Cloak said. "Another time."

Alexina reached out and gently took Zeke's hand. She smiled at him. "No matter our hardships in the future, I am glad to know you now, Zeke. And I am proud you have chosen this path." She squeezed his hand. "Your moms would be proud of you too."

Zeke's ears grew hot. "Yeah… thanks."

She flashed a slight grin, then let go of his hand and turned to Embrik. "Embrik, come be a guardian for Zeke."

Zeke glanced at Embrik. "Guardian?"

226

Embrik nodded and kneeled next to Zeke. "Binding will put you into a vulnerable state. Guardians are there to protect you while you are bound, though it is more for ceremony than necessity." Embrik smiled, though his ears were flat. "Since you are Alexina's son, that makes me your uncle, by marriage. I hope you will allow me to be your guardian. Though… you should have two guardians."

Zeke frowned. He turned and looked at Jaden.

Jaden slumped forward. "You can't mean me."

Zeke twitched his tail. "Why not? I mean… you're… you're my father."

Jaden's eyes shimmered with unshed tears. Zeke's chest tightened and he swallowed hard. Jaden chuckled darkly, but it rang of pain. "Right. Some father."

"Then this is an opportunity to start over," Zeke said. He held a hand out to Jaden. "I mean that. You're a Guardian already, right? You should be my guardian now. As my father."

Jaden stared at Zeke's hand for a long time. His gaze wandered to Alexina. She smiled at him encouragingly, her own eyes shimmering, and she nodded. "My love… let us lead our son into this new life together."

Jaden watched her, brow furrowed. He took a shuddering breath. "…Yeah. Okay." He took Zeke's hand, then kneeled next to him.

Alexina nodded. She held up Zeke's bracelet. "This yellow jewel is the Mind Jewel. It will keep your mind sharp while you are bound. The red jewel is the Body Jewel, and will keep your body strong. The final jewels are the Soul Jewels. Once bound, they'll take on your eye color. This keeps your soul connected to your body. Together this grants immortality. Do you accept this responsibility?"

Zeke breathed deeply. "I do."

Alexina plucked the yellow jewels off his bracelet. "Once I start the binding, you will go into a deep trance. The jewels will show you bits of our history – your family, living and dead, the jewels' previous owner, and possibly even far back to the time of the Four Sisters, though this is a rare occurrence."

Zeke tilted his head at Jaden. "Will it show both sides of the family?"

Alexina chewed her lip. "I am unsure. Athánatos jewels are kept among our people. Pure Athánatos only. This is the first time an... outsider has received them, to my knowledge."

Outsider. What a loaded word.

Alexina squeezed his hand. "My son, you may be an outsider, but you are also like me. A bridge, representing both secluded Athánatos and mainland zyfaunos. You represent hope."

He frowned. "Quite a thing to live up to."

"We will do so together." She smiled.

He smiled back. That felt right, even if he wasn't sure what that meant yet. He took off his glasses and placed them by his knee. "Alright then. Let's get started."

Alexina pressed the first set of jewels to the fur around Zeke's eyes.

Instantly Zeke felt like his body faded from reality, leaving only his soul. He felt lighter than air, floating through darkness. Somewhere in some distant reality, Alexina sang, in some unknown language, though a vague translation floated through his mind in Archángeli's voice.

Memory clings to truth
Truth clings to memory
They are distant relatives
Struggling to trust
The Mind Jewel offers a bridge.

Figures formed all around him in the darkness. Some he recognized – Alexina, Jaden, Ouranos, Matt. Others, not so much. A tall, feminine Athánatos with a cream-colored snout. Another next to her with pale dots over one eye, and burnt-orange on her ears. A white, blue streaked quilar with long quills running down the side of her head.

Some figures stood farther back. A feminine one with cream and burnt orange. A masculine one with angry pale eyes and orange streaks over his brow. A fully azure-blue quilar who shared Zeke's striking green eyes.

The last one was the hardest to look at though. A massive feminine Athánatos with angry orange eyes, and vicious streaks of color through black fur, hovering over all of them, staring at them greedily, like they were a meal. Four feminine Athánatos stood below her, their faces cracked like pottery, all wearing frowns. The others seemed ignorant of her.

Zeke almost called out a warning, but then everything vanished. Alexina's singing shone through again.

Flesh clings to bone
Blood clings to flesh
Melded together
Forever bound
The Body Jewel offers them life.

Flashes of Athánatos history ran through Zeke's mind. A village, well kept, surrounding a massive airy palace, filled with adults and children alike, playing and laughing, all with colorful fur against a sea of black, each eye color unique and pleasant. Then battles raged – The angry masculine Athánatos from Zeke's own bloodline led a war with strange, pupilless soldiers. Black puddles with glowing blue eyes ran under their feet. *Shadow Cast.*

229

On the opposite side, normal Athánatos stood scared but determined, with nothing but scythes, staves, and pitchforks in their hands. They charged after the soldiers.

And Ouranos led the charge. Two phoenix summons similar to Archángeli charged with him.

A surge of power ran through Zeke's body and he held out his hands. *Wait, stop!*

Then it vanished again.

O Soul of Zeke
Wary, cautious, curious
Loving, and also loved
Seeking a place
Within Mind and Body
The Soul Jewels offers refuge.

Only one image accompanied this part.

Leah.

She stood still in the center of darkness, blankly staring forward while tears ran little rivers down her face. Silent.

Zeke held a hand out to her. *Leah!*

But she didn't respond.

Zeke ran to her. *Leah, please, I'm here, come back!*

Leah blinked and turned her head. Their eyes met.

Then a jolt ran up Zeke's spine and he was suddenly fully in reality again, his whole body buzzing. He glanced around.

Little elemental motes floated around his head. He stared at them a moment, and held up a hand. The motes weaved around his fingers. A marble of lightning. A ball of fire. A swirling sphere of water. Floating pebbles, swishing dirt, a miniature tornado… and a single, perfect, oversized snowflake.

He tapped the snowflake and it popped into a stream of thick diamond dust, like he had seen Jaden use so many times. He waved his fingers and the stream of ice followed. A smile crossed his face, his heart swelling. He twirled his finger around, spinning the ice into a glittery circle, before forming a quick fist, dissipating the magic entirely.

Unreal.

"A natural," Embrik said, gripping Zeke's shoulder and grinning.

Jaden smiled too, his eyes shining, though he didn't say anything.

Alexina gripped Zeke's hands, her eyes glimmering. "Welcome home."

Zeke gripped them back, taking in their warmth. Home. What a nice feeling. "Thanks." He stood. "Now… let's see what I can do for Leah."

CHAPTER 30

ANCHOR

Getting into Leah's subconscious was remarkably easier now that Zeke was bound to his Ei-Ei jewels. The world inside her mind felt so real, though it was nothing but solid darkness. Cold seeped through his feet, adding to the emptiness of it all. He glanced around.

The four figures he had seen so frequently came into sharp focus around him. The gray lioness - Leah's mom. Dressed in a pale green hospital gown and carrying a roaming IV. *Dead...* Zeke thought. *Cancer.* The lion with the feather mane walked alongside her. Leah's uncle. Seemed like he and Leah were close, but it wasn't the relationship Leah wanted – family couldn't provide what she sought. She wanted a peer. A friend.

A partner.

Then, Matt, with Ouranos by his side. Still distant from Leah's family, but extremely close to each other. They shared words and laughs, though silently. Zeke watched them closely.

Something clicked. *They have a social jewel bond.* Just like him and Leah. A Lexi Gem and Ei-Ei jewels.

But nothing indicated danger. They seemed perfectly content and happy. Safe. Comfortable.

This wasn't a friend that he could use for Leah's anchor. This was an ideal and a goal. It was Leah's greatest desire.

Deep, solid friendship in an unbreakable bond.

Zeke furrowed his brow. *Leah. We could have that. I want that. I know you want it. You just have to come back.*

He glanced around. Surely he'd find more anchors now. More reasons for Leah to come back to them. They had the clarity.

But… there was nothing.

He called out to her. *Leah?*

Still nothing. Just darkness as far as the eye could see, bathed in intense cold.

Zeke flicked his ears back. Was this it? Was this all she had?

An ache worked its way through his heart. Alone. Like he had been for so much of his life. He breathed deeply.

Then it was up to him.

He'd be her anchor.

He called out. "Leah! Leah, it's Zeke! I'm here, it's safe, you're healed, you're home." He chewed his lip. "I'm sorry I shouted at you. I should never have done that. It doesn't matter what you saw in my head - you saved me. Let me save you."

Something white and gray huddled in a pocket of darkness, far away from the figures around him. It sniffled gently.

Zeke perked both ears. Leah. He ran for her.

But a new figure sprung up between them. All black with a white outline, a burnt orange snout, and solid green eyes. Tendrils of moving blackness flittered off the edges of the figure, like it was having a hard time keeping itself together.

He paused. That... was him. But it was dead. Cold. Flat.

Zeke narrowed his gaze at it.

That couldn't be right. This nasty blob of a monster. That couldn't be him. Could it? Did she really see him as a faceless, distant shadow?

The figure lifted his head, looking off, crossing his arms like he was closing himself off. The colors and shapes faded even more.

Leah curled away from it.

God. That was how she saw him. A hateful, angry, distant monster. He gripped his head. What kind of person was he? He couldn't let that stand. He inched his way around the dead figure, its eyes following Zeke as he did, then he kneeled in front of Leah. "Leah."

She lifted her head. He tried smiling at her, but it didn't feel right. She narrowed her gaze a moment, then lifted a hand to his face, pressing her fingers to the jewels around his eyes.

"...You bound your jewels."

Zeke opened his mouth to speak, but then Leah jerked her hand back and huddled away from him. "Zeke doesn't want me touching him."

"Leah, it's okay--"

"No, it's not," Leah said. "Zeke doesn't want the bond. He doesn't want me. You're an illusion. You're a dream." Zeke's silent doppelganger glared at him, arms crossed.

Zeke reached out and gently took her hand. She turned back to him. "Leah, I promise you, this isn't a dream."

"Then why are you bound to your jewels?" Leah asked. "Zeke wanted nothing to do with them."

"Because you got hurt," Zeke said. "Because I needed to save you."

Leah scoffed. "Because you felt guilty." The doppelganger laughed darkly.

Zeke flicked an ear back. That was a kick to the gut. "...That's part of it, yeah."

Leah's eyes narrowed. "So did this make you feel better?"

Zeke frowned. "No. Because this doesn't make up for the way I've treated you. I shouldn't have chased you away." The doppelganger shrugged and turned away now.

Leah glanced up at it a moment, then turned to Zeke. "Then why did you?"

Zeke's tail twitched. His stomach churned, drawing his fear to the forefront of his mind. Fear he had buried for longer than he could remember, and yet it felt as fresh as it ever had. "Because... I was scared."

"Of *me?*"

"Of relationships," Zeke admitted. It should have been a relief to admit that finally, but it only burned his throat. "Because I lost my moms and I don't know if anything can fill what they left behind. Because people always *want* something from me, that I'm not willing to give. Because... because I'm too much like my father."

The doppelganger turned back, meeting Zeke's eyes. It looked almost... sad.

Leah furrowed her brow. "Like Jaden."

Zeke nodded. "But I'm done running. I should never have run in the first place." He squeezed her hand.

Though his hand still shook with tension, still gripping his fear, holding it back.

She frowned and pulled back her hand. "I... I still don't believe it. You don't want this bond. You don't want anything to do with me." She pressed her eyes shut.

The doppelganger turned away again. Darkness slowly encroached on them, pushing closer, like wisps of cloud, solid and cold. Whispers Zeke couldn't make out floated like gusts of winds around their heads.

Leah choked on a sob. "Just once... just *once,* I want someone to hug me with abandon... without feeling like they have to ask first or feeling worried that I'm going to see some deep personal secret. I want to feel *wanted...* " She leaned on her knees. "...I hate my magic."

Zeke reached forward, his heart seizing. *You are wanted. I want you.* But then he stopped, recoiling his hand. If he wanted her, why couldn't he tell her out loud? What was he so damn afraid of? The doppelganger stared at Zeke, judging him. Damn it all. *Damn* it all. He sat down next to Leah instead, tucking his knees against his chest.

Leah sniffled. The whispers grew a little stronger, their words, clearer.

Ugh, a healer-S. Don't let her touch you.

Useless with that magic.

Why can't the healers do *anything?*

No one wants you. You're not good enough.

Zeke glanced around. But the whispers faded again, just slightly, mumbling. The darkness pressed closer to them, thicker now. The words hit Zeke's ears, buzzing angrily.

Were these the thoughts Leah heard all the time?

She curled tighter into her ball.

Zeke stared at her. He took slow, deliberate breaths, trying to dig into his mind, find the right words, something, to bring back the light.

His brain chose something strange though.

"My moms were the hugging type," he said suddenly. Leah turned. So did the doppelganger. A soft smell entered his nose – some kind of fancy coffee. Curiosity. The first smell he had gotten from their bond since her injury. Though the moment he noticed it, she turned away and squelched it.

236

But he continued anyway, despite the swirling heat of fear in his belly.

"You saw that when you were in my head," he said. His chest burned thinking of his moms. "Every kind of reward, every kind of comfort, every kind of greeting or goodbye involved hugs, high fives, back pats, whatever, especially when I was little. As a result, I was the same way with my friends.

"But then we hit high school and suddenly every physical touch meant romance or sex to them. And I didn't want that." His vision blurred, tears pulling at the corners of his eyes. "It turned back on me too. I suddenly lost this connection with my friends because I didn't want what they wanted. I couldn't even connect with it as a joke."

The burning in his stomach made its way to his throat, catching there, gripping his vocal cords, strangling his words. He held his hand out and called on his newfound magic, desperate for a distraction. A tiny stream of glittering diamond dust wove around his fingers. He focused on it, forcing the burning back down his throat, though it didn't go away completely.

The doppelganger stared at him, brow furrowed.

"I just wanted to hug my friends again, and I couldn't. Not like before. So they abandoned me and I was alone."

Leah flattened her ears. "…Like me. When my powers broke." A fruitcake smell mixed with the coffee smell. The doppelganger squatted down now, staring at the ground.

Zeke paused. "Yeah… like that." He shook himself, his eyes burning now. *Keep going. Don't stop.* "It… didn't help that I didn't have a name for it. But even after I found a name – asexual, aromantic – it made me feel worse. I was still different." He shrugged. "A lot of people feel comforted when they can put a name to their identity, but it just further isolated me. There was a constant pressure to ignore that part of me and just do what everyone else did, but I couldn't."

Leah reached her hand out, but stopped. She pulled back and stared at the darkness in front of her. A smell of something baking, but unfinished, wafted by his nose.

The darkness tightened around them, and those tiny, whispering thoughts beat against his ears, like tiny bees, looking for a target.

Zeke formed a tight fist, trying to drown Leah's thoughts and force the words out. *Don't. Stop.* His voice cracked as he pushed through. "It only got worse as I got older. Because I started to see what they meant. Adults have a reason for touching. An agenda. I was different. Exotic, whatever the hell that meant. People saw me as a prize. They *wanted* something from me, something I didn't want. No one understood that. Hell, no one even tried to understand. No one *cared.*"

Leah pulled into a tighter ball. The doppelganger copied her. The thoughts grew louder.

Broken.

Ruined.

Strange.

Unwanted.

"It only got worse when my parents died," Zeke said, trying to ignore the thoughts. "The only two people in the world who didn't have an agenda when they hugged me. I lost everything when I lost them. Even my will to live for a time." God, that was the core of it, wasn't it? It was hard enough losing his friends, but when he lost his moms too, everything crashed down. He threw the ice away, and sparked fire instead, as if trying to burn away the fear. But it only mimicked the burning his throat and belly. "So I pushed people away too. I wouldn't let anyone get close."

"But you have Andre."

The sickening feeling in his gut doubled. The thoughts grew louder, the darkness, thicker.

Leah had no one. But Zeke had Andre. Except… "I hold him away from me." The bitter words felt like acid on his tongue. "I love Andre to death. He's the only thing in the world that keeps me going and I can't imagine my life without him. But he also had a crush on me for years."

Leah glanced up.

Zeke balled up his fists, letting the fire engulf them. "His touches and hugs had an agenda, just like everyone else. Flirting. Hinting. Hoping something more would come of our friendship. But I couldn't tell him I didn't want that. It chased everyone else away. I worried it'd chase him away too." He leaned down. Another effort wasted. Another relationship broken because of his fear.

Leah glanced up. "Did it?"

"No." Zeke glanced off. "But it put a strain on us. Once he really accepted that about me, he made a conscious effort not to touch me at all. Something was lost. Something I don't know if I can get back." *Something I caused. Something I should have fought for and I didn't because I'm a damn coward.* He leaned on his knees, letting shame mix with fear in a swirl of heat and ice in his gut.

Leah turned to him. A smell of some kind of sweet bread. Zeke took it to mean sympathy. He didn't know whether to feel relieved or worried. "Why are you telling me this?"

Zeke turned to her now. "Because you're the first person I've had any relationship with since my parents who didn't have an agenda. Who wasn't trying to get something from me except friendship. But I kept pushing you away because I couldn't believe that was real. I couldn't believe that you didn't have some romantic agenda at heart. For all I knew, you'd want something too, and leave me or break our friendship when you couldn't have it."

"W-we have a jewel bond," Leah said, her voice cracking. "You can see t-that I didn't."

239

The whispers changed now. Swirling darkness became physical figures, hovering over them, their voices growing.

See? No one wants you, even when they see you.

No one will let you touch them, so why wish for it?

You're not good enough. You never will be.

Leah sobbed quietly. The words pierced Zeke's heart like an ice spear. He held up his hands.

Ice formed on their tips.

He pressed his lips together and guided the ice, covering them in a dome, like Rashard had done. The darkness pounded on his shield, but at least the words were muffled.

Leah glanced up. Ice chilled him to the bones.

Zeke pulled the words out of his mind, forcing them through his mouth. "That's the problem isn't it?" he said. "I'm literally in your head. I could *see* that you didn't have that agenda, and yet I couldn't let it go." He flattened his ears. "That was *wrong*. Hurtful. All you wanted was a friend and I pushed you away like an ass because I was afraid of my own damn feelings. I don't want that anymore. I want this bond." He held a hand out to her. "It's what I've been seeking ever since my friends left me. And I can't let my fear push that away anymore. I can't… I can't stand hurting you." His voice hitched and his throat tightened, but he pushed the words out, quiet and broken. "I want to start over. Make this right." he choked. "I want you."

Leah furrowed her brow, but didn't speak. The shadows banged on his ice shield.

But still, Leah said nothing.

Ice lanced his belly now, all his fear coming to a head. It had been too much. He pushed her too hard. He lost her.

No! Fight for it!

"Leah…" Zeke spoke softly. "We both should have something to live for."

Leah looked down at his hand. Carefully she slid her hand into his and squeezed it tight. He squeezed back a moment before releasing, then cautiously pulled her into a sideways hug. She hesitated a moment, then leaned into him.

The banging stopped. The whispers faded. The icy feeling in his veins vanished, melting his ice dome with it, leaving the pair of them to each other. She leaned deeper into his hug, shaking, but warm.

A gentle smell of cinnamon buns wafted past his nose. The smell of comfort. He leaned his head on hers and closed his eyes. His chest ached. His eyes burned. All the emotions, the touch starvation, the fear of letting someone hug him again rushed through his mind, making his body buzz.

But in his mind, Leah's soft friendship. It was weird, feeling it. So devoid of romantic agendas. And yet, it was so real. Draso, he should have seen it sooner. Andre probably had that same thing. He just wanted friendship. But Zeke had pushed him away.

He couldn't do that anymore.

The doppelganger leaned back against Leah and Zeke, for just a moment. *He'll leave you. Like everyone else.*

Leah stiffened up next to him.

"I *won't,*" Zeke snapped at the figure. "I won't. You're not me."

The figure stared a moment, but didn't move.

"You really want to be my partner." Her soft voice cracked.

He gave her a squeeze. "I do. I really do."

Leah sighed. "I want that too."

Zeke's doppelganger stood now. It walked off into the distance, taking the last of the heavy darkness and whispers with it. Zeke sighed with relief and pulled Leah closer.

They sat there together for several quiet minutes. No more encroaching darkness. No more figures. Just peace. In the moment.

"It's hard," Leah said. "Living in one moment. I don't... I don't really know how to."

"I know," Zeke said. "It's too easy to dwell on the past."

"And give up on the future." Leah squeezed him. "So... thanks... for giving me the space to live for right now. Even if it's just one time."

"I hope it'll be more than once."

"Yeah..." She sighed. "I'll come home. Be there for me."

"Always," Zeke said. "I mean that."

Leah squeezed him once more, then everything went fully black.

CHAPTER 31

RECOVERING

Leah woke with a start, not in a tent, like she expected, but in a warm cabin on an oversized bean bag chair, surrounded by blankets. She tried to force her eyes to focus. No glasses. She sat up, glancing around.

There was no way that vision had been real.

"Here." Zeke's voice. He handed her glasses to her.

She took them gingerly, shaking, but she didn't dare look at Zeke. That wasn't real. Just a fantastic, wonderful, unrealistic dream.

It was real, Leah.

She stared at the wooden floor, her chest aching. She put her glasses on, and shut her eyes tight.

"Leah?"

She breathed deeply and slowly opened her eyes.

Zeke sat on a chair in front of her, staring intently. The Ei-Ei jewels glinted around his eyes in yellow, red, and green.

Draso's horns. He had actually done it. She reached for them... but stopped, curling her fingers back.

"It's okay." He smiled. No hesitation. No worries. No fear.

She chewed her lip, but reached back out and ran two fingers over the Ei-Ei jewels, careful not to touch his fur. This was real. He had really bound to them. "...You did this for me."

"I did it for us," Zeke said, his voice cracking.

Us. *Us.* He had bound his jewels for them. For their bond. Because... because she was worth it. Could she admit that?

Zeke's smile grew. Leah's chest warmed. She could admit that.

Zeke's eyes shined with tears. He reached over and drew Leah into a deep hug. "I'm so glad you're okay..." His voice trailed like he wanted to say more, but he just held her instead.

Her mind flooded with his recent injuries. The stab in his side he got while saving her from Tao's translator. The second stab he got from one of the Wish Dusters, fighting alongside her. More recently, a near frozen hand and cracked ribs, both paired with some distant memory of desperation and fear. For her.

And then... their social bond. When Matt had touched her unexpectedly months ago, she had gotten a sense of his social bond as an ailment. But this was the first time she felt her social bond with Zeke. Fresh, new... warm. As she focused on it, all his other injuries faded, leaving her with this deep, deep connection, intertwining their very essences. A delicate smell of chocolate chip cookies wafted past her nose.

Home.

Leah wrapped her arms around him and pulled him close, fighting back tears. Home. *Home.*

Thank you... she whispered in his mind.

Always, he said. *I mean that.* She almost laughed. It wasn't a dream. All of that had been real.

Something beeped, and the sudden realization that they weren't alone made Leah's ears grow hot. She broke the hug and glanced around.

Jaden sat on a couch nearby, Alexina and Embrik near him, staring at his datasquare. Two zyfaunos bats and four identical does she didn't recognize filled the other seats, but they all stared at the datasquare too, tense. One of the doe snorted, glaring at the device. Jaden flicked his ears back and dropped the datasquare on a thick coffee table.

"Before you activate that and start screaming at Ackerson," the Black Cloak said, standing in the corner of the room. "Listen to him."

Jaden snarled. "Can't you just out with it instead of being so vague?"

"Would you actually listen to me if I was blunt?" the Cloak said. He eyed Jaden with his striking green eyes. "You and I both know the answer to that."

Jaden narrowed his gaze. "I really hate that you know me so well."

The Cloak paused a moment. He glanced off. "Curse of the job."

Jaden sighed. He pressed a button on the datasquare.

A hologram formed from the center, revealing Ackerson's glowing form. He glanced around at everyone, then raised an eyebrow at Jaden. "You made it."

Jaden crossed his arms, his face blank, but he said nothing.

It took all of Leah's willpower not to shout at Ackerson. *Yeah, we made it, no thanks to you.* But she trusted the Cloak, even if no one else did.

I'm with you there, Zeke said. He gripped her hand. She gripped it back, warmth running through her fingers. Gentle lemon tea scents wafted through her nose.

"I assume you found Hunt," Ackerson continued.

"We did," Jaden said, his voice flat.

"All of them?"

"I can only guess," Jaden said. His anger tensed his voice. "Why, are you surprised by that?"

Ackerson narrowed his gaze. "No. I expect it."

"Do you have a job for us, Ackerson?" Jaden asked, teeth gritted. "We're all ears."

Ackerson furrowed his brow. Leah kept her ears perky, unsure if he could still see her, wondering if he got the subtext.

"I do," Ackerson said. "Hope you fuzzies are up for it, because it's a doozy." Zeke winced at the word "fuzzy" – Leah got the impression it was a slur. Ackerson smiled slyly. "But I think you'll like it, considering."

Jaden raised an eyebrow.

Ackerson grinned, his expression dripping with poison. "I'm sending you to take out Captain Sharp."

No one spoke, but the shocked looks on everyone's faces said everything. Sharp meant something to Leah's team, sure, but also this other group, apparently. The doe in particular. One wore an angry scowl, but the other three cowered. Both bats crossed their wings, and the black and green one growled.

A sharp smell of some strong cheese hit Leah's senses, though it mixed with the scent of… coffee. Cheese coffee. Confused. Disoriented. Like Zeke didn't know how to respond. She squeezed his hand in reassurance and the coffee smell faded.

Only Jaden seemed completely unfazed. He crossed his arms. "I thought I was supposed to treat him as one of my own."

Ackerson waved a hand. "Yeah, well, when it turns out that one of your own is running a focus jewel smuggling ring, it changes perspectives."

One of the doe yipped, though Leah couldn't tell which one.

Jaden lowered his gaze. "You want to send two small black ops teams to take down an entire *smuggling ring?"*

"We'll do it," all four doe said at once. Jaden looked up, but all of them stared at him, daring him to contradict them.

Ackerson smirked. "Alright then. Get some rest. I'm still putting together the rest of the briefing, but I'll have everything for you by this afternoon." He leaned on his hands. "Be careful. Ackerson out." He shut off the hologram.

Jaden snatched up the datasquare. "Subtle, Ackerson." He stood. "Pack up. We're not safe here." He glared at the doe. "I don't appreciate you accepting this job for all of us."

"There's a reason for it," one of the doe said. "I'll explain as we leave. You'll understand when you hear it, Guardian."

Jaden snorted. "I'm not a Guardian anymore."

"You can't deny what you are," another doe said. "You're here for a reason, even if you don't know it yet." Jaden crossed his arms and looked away. She turned to Angus. "We should get to work."

"Agreed," the green and black bat said. He turned to Leah and Zeke and smiled. "Glad to see you made it through alright." He pointed to Zeke. "Hold on to him, okay? He risked a lot to save you." He nodded to the other bat. "Come on, Ronan."

The orange and black bat nodded back. "We'll be ready in fifteen." They headed down a long hallway.

The doe stood as one and did the same. One turned to Jaden. "Guardian."

Jaden flattened one ear.

"I don't know where the Defenders have been all these years," the doe said. "But I'm glad to have you here now. We'll need it." She followed the other doe.

Jaden furrowed his brow and flicked an ear back.

Alexina stood up once they left. She sat next to Leah and gently took her hand into both of hers, a big smile on her face. "I am so glad you are safe now." Embrik sat beside her too and gripped her shoulder, grinning.

Leah filtered through the impressions of their injuries as they held her – burns, cuts, cracked ribs…

247

Zeke rubbed his thumb over the top of her hand. She met his eyes and he smiled. She stared a moment, all the impressions of their injuries fading in favor of their touch. They grounded her, keeping her present, chasing away everything else. The Thought Factory ran a million miles a minute, but if she focused on Zeke's thumb, Alexina's hands, Embrik's grip, her thoughts focused too. One rang out loud and clear.

They aren't afraid to touch me. Zeke answered with the comforting lemon tea smell again.

Tears built in her eyes and she smiled at them. "Thank you all…"

Jaden stood. "This is all well and good, but we really do need to get going. Ackerson isn't as subtle as he thinks he is with his threats." He turned toward the hallway.

"Jaden," Zeke said.

Jaden turned. Zeke eyed him. The tension in his body manifested as the smell of mushroom risotto for some reason. Complicated.

Jaden frowned. He met Leah's eyes. "I'm glad you're okay. But next time… think before you go running after a rifleman alone." He turned and continued down the hall.

Zeke furrowed his brow and moved to stand, but Leah gripped his arm. "Don't bother, Zeke. It's fine."

"It's not *fine,* Leah--"

"Zeke," Leah said. "Please. We don't have time right now."

Zeke sighed. "Okay, you're right. But I don't like it."

The Black Cloak stood. He walked over and patted Leah's hand, though Leah couldn't feel anything about him through his gloves. He smiled with his eyes. "I'm glad you're okay, though I'll admit, I already knew you would be. One way or another."

She smiled. "I figured."

The Cloak turned to Zeke. "Give Jaden time. He'll need it."

Zeke rolled his eyes. "A long damn time."

The Cloak chuckled. He pressed something into Leah's palm. "Also, thanks for letting me borrow this, even if you weren't aware of it." He walked down the hall.

Leah looked down. Her Defender pendant. But the green stripe on the tail that marked her as a healer-S had been mostly wiped off. She ran a thumb down the pendant. Maybe that was a good thing. She slipped the pendant over her head.

Zeke shook himself and pawed a little at the Ei-Ei jewels. "How long before these stop feeling weird on my skin?"

Alexina giggled. "It varies person to person, but most feel normal again after a few days."

"Training with your magic will be a good distraction," Embrik said. "Alexina and I will help guide you while we travel, if you are willing."

Zeke paused a moment, then smiled. "Yeah, I'd like that."

"Then let us get ready." Alexina stood and she and Embrik followed Jaden.

Leah stood and gave Zeke another big hug. Zeke hugged her back, again with no hesitation. She smiled and took it all in, though her brain still fought the idea that this was real. She broke the hug. "Are you sure you want this?"

"Absolutely," Zeke said.

"No strings attached?"

"No strings attached," Zeke said. He tapped his chin. "Well, except for the fact that I'm gonna come running to you every time I have a cold from now on."

Leah smirked. "Healing magic doesn't work on colds."

"It doesn't?"

"Viruses are stubborn," Leah said.

"Thinly veiled metaphor understood," Zeke said, smirking. "Stubbed toes then."

She laughed. That felt good. They followed the rest of them down the hallway.

CHAPTER 32

SMUGGLER'S REACH

Jaden helped pack as quick as he could, trying to avoid Leah and Zeke. The four doe had gone into one room to pack supplies, and Ronan had already taken his supplies to the living room with Alexina and Embrik, leaving Jaden to pack with Angus.

Draso's horns, he felt like such an asshole. Why the hell had he gone after Leah like that? What good did that do? She was alive, damn it. He should be happy. He should have hugged her, like the others.

Dyne would have done the same thing Leah had. Run after the enemy to protect his team. That was what the Wish Dusters preyed on. He knew it. Yet here he was still pushing her away and critiquing her every move. He should be encouraging her. Training her even. She could be every bit as good as Dyne was, with practice. Jaden didn't like to admit it, but it was the truth.

Zeke's accusation about Jaden treating Leah like garbage wasn't unfounded. Jaden snarled to himself. He quickly zipped up a full backpack and began rolling a sleeping bag to go on top.

Zeke and Leah laughed from the living room. Strangely that hurt. It shouldn't. Good Draso, it should be a source of joy for him. Leah finally had her partner. Zeke was, in fact, his son, and thriving, despite whatever it was that was going to break apart the family down the road.

But all it did was remind him of what he had lost when Dyne passed.

"So where's your Guardian partner?" Angus asked suddenly.

Jaden's knee buckled and he dropped a sleeping bag.

Angus held his hands up, flexing his three long fingers, his leather wingtips brushing the floor. "Sorry, did I speak out of turn?"

"How do you know I have a partner?" Jaden asked. "More to the point, how do you know what Guardians are at all?"

Angus smiled sadly, his large ears drooping. "I'm a refugee from the big smuggling ring bust on Vanguard in UX 5788."

Jaden's eyes grew wide and lightning ran up his spine.

Angus strapped a rolled up sleeping bag to one of the backpacks. "So you know it then."

"How are you still alive?" Jaden asked, though he was already forming a theory. "That raid was almost a hundred years ago by the UX calendar. You don't look a day over thirty."

Angus pulled on his ears, revealing a smooth, radiant green jewel attached to the skin in one ear, and a deep purple jewel on the other.

"Continuum Stones." Jaden flattened his ears. "Not from Unus then."

"Born and raised on Tribus," Angus said. "But my family was on the Unus continent when the raid happened. Got caught in the crossfire. Both my parents were killed, leaving Ronan and me alone. I was only six."

Jaden winced. Six. The same age Matt had been when the Omnirs killed him.

Angus strapped another sleeping bag on a backpack. "The Defenders saved us. More specifically, a set of Golden Guardians. I don't remember much about them – just glimpses of those golden dragon pendants, which I'd never forget."

Jaden patted his Guardian pendant under his shirt. The pendant weighed heavier than ever.

"The Guardians dove between us refugees and a bunch of the smugglers and fought them off," Angus continued. "You know how vicious they got trying to flee the galactic Interpol."

He did indeed, because he had been there, in one of his early missions as a Guardian. The whole incident played over in his mind. Galactic Interpol's ring busting attempt. The vicious, year-long war that followed. The Defenders' frantic, unexpected, unplanned missions trying to get refugees off the planet as fast as they could. Dyne put himself in charge of healing and rescue, but that required more one-on-one battles with the desperate smugglers than he anticipated.

If Angus had seen what he thought he had, then it had been Dyne and Jaden who saved him and Ronan. Dyne, diving in to battle against impossible odds, trying to save innocents.

Just like Leah.

Lance had warned Interpol to wait and get more intel. Their hasty decision cost thousands of lives. Much like the bad decisions Jaden had made over the years with Sol and Atlas that had similar results.

Jaden shook his head of it. "How did you two end up on Earth?"

Angus' wings drooped. "Bad luck is all. A nice couple adopted us after the war, but Ronan has always been restless, especially after losing our parents. Once we came of age and got our parents' Continuum Stones, Ronan joined up on an intergalactic freight ship and I just followed along. Ronan wanted to take an extended vacation here, but then we got caught up in the war and lost contact with our freighter." He grinned. "Maybe with the Defenders here, we can get in contact with them again and get off this hellhole of a planet."

"Can't help you there," Jaden said. "I'm stranded too. Have been for decades."

Angus' face fell. "Damn. Sorry about that."

Jaden snorted. "Sorry I'm not what you expected."

Angus shrugged. "Don't worry about it. We'll figure it out."

"So what magic do you have?" Jaden asked.

"Both of us have telekinesis for space powers," Angus said. "Ronan's stronger than me, so he can lift more, and he has a knack for dissipating magic with it. I have scrying for time powers, but I'm terrible at it, so don't ask for much. Ronan has healing. Good for healing himself at the very least, but after that bout with Chaos, he's still a little outside time."

Jaden winced. Time mages healed themselves by reversing time on their own bodies. Do it too much and you risk time glitching. Some mages took years to get their whole bodies back in sync. "I haven't seen him glitching."

"It's his left wing," Angus said. "Still not fully in sync yet. Watch real close and you'll see it blink. He'll right himself in time." He flashed a grin. "And hey, I have Magna and Lysander, so it makes up for it. They'll help us carry things. Along with your gryfon summons, I suspect."

"Are you two done yet, or what?" Ronan stuck his head in the room. The orange tipped tuft of fur fell in his face and he brushed it aside, smacking his wing on the doorframe. It glitched and blinked, just like Angus said. "We're running out of time."

"Coming," Angus said. Ronan huffed and walked off. Angus hoisted a bag gingerly on his back, careful of his wings.

"So," Jaden said, grabbing two more bags. "What about the doe? Their eyes sparkle. They look like Wish Dusters to me."

Angus gave Jaden a dark look. "Best let them come to you with that information." He walked out. Jaden sighed and followed.

The whole group stood in the living room in heavy winter gear, most wearing packs, silently waiting. Jaden passed a pack to Embrik and shouldered the other one.

Zeke shifted uncomfortably. "Is there a reason we're leaving in such a hurry?"

Jaden narrowed his gaze. "You heard Ackerson's threat."

"Yeah, but what good does it do to run?" Zeke said. "Leah and I still have trackers."

One of the doe let out a little gasp. "Did he really stick you with those horrible things?"

"Unfortunately, yeah," Leah said.

"Well, that won't do." The doe waved to them. "Drop your packs, please. I'll take care of this."

Both Zeke and Leah took steps back. Zeke flattened his ears. "No offense, ma'am, but I don't even know your *name--"*

"It's Pathos," the doe said. She pointed to each of the four doe. "Ethos, Pathos, Logos, and Ari."

Ari's ears flicked back. "Pathos…"

"Hush," Pathos said, with all the authority of a mother hushing her child. "How can we expect them to trust us enough to work together if they don't know our names? They'd learn eventually." She turned to Zeke and Leah. "I'm a Wish Duster. I can use my wish to break the trackers. You'll never be in any danger."

Jaden stepped forward. "Hold on. How do you intend to do that?"

"My wish allows me to degrade or destroy objects," Pathos said. "One touch and I can ruin the electronics. No more trackers."

Embrik twitched his tail. "So that is what you did to my Ei-Ei jewels."

Pathos nodded. "The wish isn't as permanent or effective on focus jewels, but it works to a degree."

255

"I should be grateful for that," Embrik said. Pathos smiled cheekily.

Jaden didn't trust it. He moved between Pathos and Zeke. "And they won't be harmed."

Pathos smiled, eyes half lidded, and raised a hand, clinking her hoof-tipped fingers together. "You have my word."

"We'll do it," Leah said, stepping forward.

Jaden wrinkled his snout. "Leah--"

"It's our bodies, Jaden," Leah said, though she wouldn't meet his gaze. "L-let us do what we think is best."

Jaden growled. "But--"

 "Who'd like to go first?" Pathos smiled.

"Me," Zeke said. "Leah's put herself in danger enough."

Jaden's whole body seized up and he fought the urge to pull Zeke away from the doe.

Pathos furrowed her brow at Zeke's declaration, but she shook her head. "You shouldn't feel a thing." She ran her fingers across the base of his skull. "Oh, yeah, it's there. One moment." She pressed against his fur and one brown eye sparkled with blue glitter for a quick moment. "There, done. How do you feel?"

Zeke rubbed the back of his head. "Exactly the same. Are you sure it did anything?"

"It shouldn't feel any different," Pathos said. "I just want to make sure you're not in any pain. Sometimes degrading an object can have unintended consequences." She turned to Leah and repeated the action. Leah's shoulders drooped and her tail dipped down, no longer so rigid. Pathos shook her tail and tapped her foot. "There. Much better. That'll give us more time to get away from whatever Ackerson has planned for us."

"Thank you," Leah said. Pathos nodded to her.

Jaden lifted his chin. "Assuming that actually did anything."

"Have faith, Guardian," Pathos said.

"Hard to have faith in people I don't even know," Jaden said, his eye twitching at the word Guardian. He turned to Leah and Zeke. "Ackerson is going to realize the trackers aren't working."

"He won't know why though," Pathos said. "Those things are terribly unreliable in the cold. Guess the snow storm was too much, huh?" She winked.

Jaden narrowed his gaze. "Right. So do all of you have Wishing Dust, or were you planning on keeping that a secret?"

"We do," Ari said, crossing her arms. "Are you always this rude to people you don't even know?"

Jaden lowered his gaze, ignoring her accusation. "Why do you have Wishing Dust?"

"Because the focus jewel smuggling ring we're going to take down," Ethos said. "Is run by our sister, Matron Fawn."

CHAPTER 33

RING RUNNERS

Jaden walked alongside Ethos as the group trudged through the new snow, headed anywhere but the cabin, waiting on Ackerson's orders. They aimed to put a few miles between them and the cabin and avoid running into border patrol or whatever nasty surprise Ackerson hinted at. Angus' summons, the alicorn and the centaur, walked alongside Rashard and Kjorn, each of them carrying blankets and backpacks, though Jaden had talked them down from carrying too much, in case the group needed to ride them. Both Archángeli and Kyrie flew above them, keeping watch.

"So you've been fighting this smuggling ring for generations," Jaden asked Ethos.

Ethos nodded. "Grandmother Fawn learned about it first, when they set up a base here and started hocking their damn Wishing Dust in her casinos," she said. "Grandmama wanted nothing to do with it. Drugs had killed her husband and she saw this as just another drug. But there's little you can do to fight an intergalactic smuggling ring when you're stuck on one planet and have no magic of your own."

"She fought anyway though," Logos said. She carefully weaved around a thick bramble bush. "Even to the point of giving in and getting Wishing Dust herself. She created a whole damn army of Dusters. If you can't beat them, join them, or whatever crap."

Jaden perked his ears. He turned behind the group and covered their tracks with snow. "How'd she manage that? Wishing Dust has such a high mortality rate."

"Not if you pick the right wish," Ethos said. She tested the depth of a snow mound with a stick, then walked around it. "Most of them are body morphers. Effective for many forms of magical combat and comes with a more bearable psychological load than most combat-ready wishes."

Jaden winced. "Bearable while binding, but not always when using it," he said. "You can kill yourself pushing it. You might morph your hands into shark heads, but the cost could be exploding your spine out your back. It's entirely unpredictable."

Logos nodded. "They learned that the hard way. But we have lots of training to help prevent that problem now."

"I can only imagine what needed to be done to get that training," Jaden said. He brushed away a large snow mound with his magic. "I assume your grandmother never beat them back."

"She slowed their attempts," Ethos said. "But never fully chased them offworld. When Grandmama died, she passed the torch to our mother, who fought them with a renewed vigor, even getting her hands on a spaceship. Some Defender plane. She couldn't make the damn thing fly, but she was able to use it to contact another planet to try and get help."

Jaden flicked his ears back. "Did it work?"

Ethos turned her gaze on Jaden, glaring. "No. She got a hold of the Defenders. But they told her they wouldn't be coming back to Earth any time soon." She snorted. "They abandoned us. We had to fight on our own. Mama dropped the ship on one of the Trinity Islands after that, to try and prevent anyone else from taking it."

Leah frowned and flicked her tail. "How long ago was that?"

Logos walked in step with Leah. "About fifty years ago, I think. Long before we were born, though Mama spoke of it as if it was yesterday up to the day she died. It left her really bitter."

Leah frowned. She turned to Jaden.

Jaden kicked at the snow. Fifty years ago. Right around the Sol Genocide. Why would Lance do that?

"Lance was really broken up by your loss, Jaden," Leah said quietly. "He was trying to rebuild a shattered life. Try to give him some slack."

"There's no excuse, Leah," Jaden said. "We're the *Defenders.* Emotions have no place in our jobs. That was *wrong.*"

Leah eyed him. *"We're* Defenders, huh?"

Jaden glared at her. The pendant pulled at him, digging into his fur. "Don't start." He covered their tracks again, then turned to Ethos. "How'd your sister get involved?"

Ethos growled, a deep throaty thing that set Jaden's fur on end. She dug her walking stick deep into the snow, with a purpose. "She decided she liked money more than people's lives and cultivated the business instead. Mama died just after our eighth birthday. While there's no way to prove it, we all think the Matron killed her, because things changed immediately after the funeral. Loyalists to my mother were killed, admin changed, and the Matron ordered us four to be trained as assassins and isolated. We were sent to a 'school' if you want to call it that." She snarled and kicked at a snowbank. "When we 'graduated,' she forced us to take on the Wishing Dust, and forced

260

our wishes too, based on what she wanted. Then she took on a Wish Duster companion and made a wish to be able to track magic." She rubbed her arms, brow furrowed. "Her reach is… limited. This far from home, she'd have a hard time pinpointing us. But she always knows where we are."

Zeke twitched his tail. "Then destroying the trackers was useless."

"Not really," Pathos said. "Ackerson and the Matron aren't working together. He just happened to snatch us up not long after the war started and the Matron let him. Helps our 'training.' But she isn't interested in hunting us down and hurting us – just keeping us in line."

Leah brought her hands to her snout. "That's awful…"

"Who's her companion?" Jaden asked.

"Sharp is," Logos said. "Matron's power keeps us within her sights. Sharp's power keeps us from being able to use our powers against them." She snorted, rough and angry. "Total control."

They walked in silence for a moment. The heavy snow crunched under their feet, though the forest was devoid of sounds. Quiet, dead. Not even any bird sounds. The cold pierced Jaden to the core.

"If you don't mind me asking," Zeke said. "What are your powers?"

Ethos pulled out a knife. With a quick flip, she turned the knife into an ornate sword. Zeke and Leah jumped back. "I can enhance items I can hold, but if it's too heavy or if it's stuck fast to something, I can't enhance it. It only works if I hold it in my hand. I also can't make it go back to the way it was." She passed the sword to Pathos.

Pathos twirled the sword, and it turned into a butterknife. "I can degrade items, with similar limitations. Also, I can't change it back. Only Ethos can if she enhances it again." She passed the butterknife to Logos.

"I can see an item's history," Logos said. "Where they've been, if they've been enhanced or degraded by my sisters. Images are sharp, but I'm barred

261

from seeing names or faces attached to that history." She passed the butterknife to Ari.

Ari took it. "I make up for that by getting names and dates associated with an item's history. But I can't see images the way Logos can." She passed it back to Ethos, who turned it back to a normal knife and sheathed it.

Zeke flattened his ears. "Not the kind of magic I'd expect from a mafia."

"You might think differently if you saw me turn a pistol into a bazooka," Ethos said. "Or watched Pathos turn rifles into water guns. Saves tons of money on supplies, and makes weapons untraceable."

"The Matron uses my and Ari's powers to track rivals without traditional espionage. Makes it impossible to get caught," Logos said.

Jaden rubbed his chin. "Clever. Insidious, but clever."

"The Matron to a T," Ethos said.

"So then," Embrik said. "How do we take down an intergalactic smuggling ring against such odds?"

"I honestly don't know," Ethos said. "But our mother believed the Defenders were the answer." She eyed Jaden. "The fact that we have a couple now gives us an advantage that she did not have."

Jaden slowed his pace, staring at the snow. He could feel Leah staring at him.

No one spoke after that.

They walked for another four hours, exchanging only small talk when Jaden's datasquare beeped. He pulled it up and frowned. "Got our mission brief. Let's stop and rest and I'll go over this."

The group set up places to sit and passed out food and water. Angus and Ronan leaned against Magna's side, and the four fawns leaned against Lysander. Jaden's team followed their examples with Rashard and Kjorn. The Cloak stood, staring out into the woods.

Jaden watched them all a moment, then sat among the trees to pull up the briefing.

There wasn't as much as there should be, considering the Fawn's elaborate history. A location, some names, including Matron Fawn and Sharp, and some basic information about the jewels they were smuggling. Mostly Wishing Dust, though he also saw Jewel Shards, Continuum Stones, and even the rare Blood Crystals on the list. No Lexi Gems though, strangely.

Sharp ran their Canadian connections. Matron Fawn ran their US connections. The two rarely saw each other. There was nothing about extraterrestrial connections, or about its size or strength.

The briefing said their only job was to take out Sharp, but the Fawns clearly had other plans. Jaden breathed deeply. It was tempting to leave them to their own devices. They weren't his pack, and he had a... a family to protect. And Zeke still wanted to try and save his moms.

But hearing the Fawn family's struggles with this smuggling ring woke something in Jaden. He couldn't abandon them. He'd be just as bad as Lance had been leaving them in the dust.

Damn you, Lance.

Maybe he was just as bad as Lance. He'd already renounced the Defender moniker. Leah's judgmental look haunted his mind. He pressed his lips into a thin line, then glanced back over the briefing, trying to distract himself. Then he noticed the location they needed to get to.

Redbridge, Ontario.

Ontario. East coast. When they were in Alberta.

He flicked his ears and put the town into the map. The path laid out gawked at him like an angry red scar. It crossed nearly the entire continent. That battle that killed Zeke's moms was in July – they were cutting things close with this long journey. His ears burned and he almost put in a call. But he stopped. Last thing he wanted to see was Ackerson's nasty face. He typed out an angry message instead.

AZURE: Redbridge? ONTARIO? Seriously?

ACKERSON: Something wrong, fuzzy?

AZURE: You did NOT just throw a slur at me. You're supposed to be above that.

ACKERSON: I'll call you whatever the hell I want. Answer the question.

Jaden snarled. That asshole. He typed away.

AZURE: That's at least five or six weeks of travel. Don't you have any other teams? We don't have a car and we have to be discreet.

ACKERSON: Then you better get started.

Jaden growled, his fur heating under his jacket.

AZURE: How the hell are we supposed to supply ourselves? Stay safe? Hidden? Warm? Fed?

ACKERSON: Not my problem. That was part of the deal when you signed up for this. Supply yourself and get the job done. Sooner than later if you know what's good for you. You know what those smuggling rings do to people.

Damn it all. The message was loud and clear. Ackerson didn't expect them to do this, but he did expect them to run themselves ragged trying to.

ACKERSON: Also, take everything Hunt says with a grain of salt, especially the fawns. I've been wary of them for a while now. Can't trust them.

And sowing distrust too. Asshole.

AZURE: Noted. Azure out.

He'd show that bastard. That smuggling ring was going down. Finish what the Defenders should have started decades ago.

Time to end this.

BONDING

Leah followed behind Jaden and Embrik, sticking close to Angus' alicorn, Zeke at her side.

Learning they had at least five weeks of hard travel to get to their next destination should have worried Leah, but instead, she relished it. Five weeks in a peaceful country with good company where she wasn't expected to fight or kill anyone sounded like a vacation after these last few months, despite what waited for them at the end of the journey. Besides, Jaden had pointed out several cute looking towns where they could rest and replenish supplies. And for once, she wasn't alone. They could take it easy.

Well, Zeke said. *We might have Chaos on our trail.*

I'd like to see them go up against all of us, Leah said. *Especially now that you have magic. And with the summons.* She turned to the alicorn.

Angus' summons fascinated her. Magna was happy to walk alongside Leah and answer questions, even letting Leah stroke her hide and run a hand

266

over her long flight feathers. Pegasi and unicorns were common summons, but alicorns were far less so. Her stone hide was especially interesting, as it made her invulnerable to a lot of common attacks.

Except in the eye, apparently.

"I said I was sorry," Zeke said, eyeing Magna. He turned to Leah. "I was trying to protect you."

A tiny pebble bounced off Leah and Zeke's heads. *No apologies, Athánatos,* Magna said, her rough voice rolling through their minds like thunder. A smell like hot sulfur followed her as she walked. *You put yourself at risk to save your partner. We should all be so lucky to have partners such as yourself.*

I second this idea, Rashard said in a flurry of ice. He shook himself, sending tiny bits of white and blue down into the air, though he eyed Magna suspiciously. Magna lifted her head and whinnied playfully at him.

Leah smiled. Zeke smiled back and squeezed her hand.

Getting used to Zeke's physical contact was… well, it was harder than Leah expected. She had wanted it her whole life, especially after her Gem broke, but after a lifetime of avoiding contact with others, she found the habit hard to break. She still jolted a little every time Zeke gripped her hand or touched her shoulder or hugged her. It didn't help that she still got little impressions of his recent injuries.

A smell of… burnt toast, Leah decided, wafted under her nose and Zeke moved to pull away, but she gripped his hand back and smiled at him. *It's fine, Zeke. Really. I'm just not used to it yet.*

Zeke relaxed and the burnt toast smell faded in favor of strong coffee. *Sorry. I guess I'm not really either.*

We'll figure it out together.

Lysander, the lion/zebra centaur, was less willing to speak and stuck to the edge of the traveling group, keeping his eye trained at the woods around

267

them. Leah admired him from afar though. His bottom half was a lion with a zebra tail, and his top half was the body of a zyfaunos lion with a thick mane. His fingers had tiny hoofs on each tip, like a stag zyfaunos, and his entire coat was zebra striped, including his mane. He carried the smell of sharp electricity, like the air just before a lightning strike.

There were plenty of hybrid and centaur summons – her textbooks had dozens of examples – but there was nothing like seeing it in person. Absolutely fascinating.

Angus told Leah that Lysander tended to keep to himself. Magna called him a stick in the mud.

"You get the dynamic," Angus said with a smirk. "But give Lysander time and he'll open up."

Angus was chatty and friendly, full of stories about his time as a crewman on an intergalactic freighter, though his brother Ronan was quiet and reserved, interjecting only occasionally. Neither had the social stigmas surrounding Leah's healer-S status, which felt nice. Angus occasionally grabbed her shoulder when a particular bout of laughter threatened to knock him over. While Leah had healed all their injuries, their stress still surged through her body at his touch, but as time went on, and as Leah got used to their touches, she slowly learned to push the stress aside and not allow it to take over her mind. She hadn't known healer-S's could do that. Perhaps the Defenders didn't either, considering how isolated healer-S's were. Something to take home, maybe do some research on.

The Fawn sisters were the most mysterious of them all though. They often moved as one, falling into step next to each other, turning their heads to look around in unison, never speaking unless spoken to, and even then, they had very little to say.

Leah relaxed more the longer they walked as they approached the Alberta border, though it was still a little concerning that they hadn't met any border patrol yet. She kept her ears perked for any sounds of movement. They were probably two or three days from their first stop, a little town just past the border called Pincher Creek.

The terrain, their big party, and their heavy packs made them slow-going. The further east they headed, the more snow had started melting, leaving patches of mud, budding grass, and puddles behind. While the mud still made things difficult, it was easier than trudging through snow. Jaden assured them they were making good time.

That night they made camp in a small clearing surrounded by thick trees. Everyone paired up to use the tents, aside from the Black Cloak who politely refused. It was still cold, but this was the first dry patch they had found since the start.

"We'll keep watch in groups of three," Jaden said. He assigned Leah and Zeke the third watch with Ari, one of the doe.

Zeke made himself comfortable on a sleeping bag, buried under blankets. "Finally, I can get some decent sleep," he said. "No more keeping myself up worrying."

Leah snuggled under her covers too. "Sorry I worried you."

"It's not your fault," Zeke said.

Leah frowned, flicking her ear back. "One could say it is, considering." She leaned on her pillow. "...For a while, I wasn't sure I wanted to come back."

Zeke turned and faced her, frowning.

Leah pulled the blanket over her snout. "Zeke, I really am sorry for what I saw in your head. I wasn't trying to scrounge through your memories."

Zeke held up a hand. "You don't need to apologize. I should apologize for shouting at you. You were just trying to help."

"It doesn't excuse what I saw though," Leah said. She breathed deeply. "We're going to save your moms, Zeke. I'm going to do everything in my power to help them."

Zeke's face fell a little, and a gentle smell of strong coffee filled the tent. Awareness. Zeke leaned back on his bed. "I've gotten so caught up in all this, I almost forgot that was the end goal." He ran a hand down his face. "It's early June. That gives us a little over six weeks to get to DC."

Leah's eyes grew wide. "That's a tight schedule if we're really going to go after Sharp."

"I know."

Leah reached out to Zeke. He reached back and they held hands a moment. She tried to smile, hoping it came off well. "We'll get to them, Zeke. I promise."

Zeke stared at her a moment. *Don't promise what you can't keep.*

Then take this as a sign that I'll keep it. She squeezed his hand then buried herself in blankets again. "Goodnight."

"Night." He turned over.

It took Leah a long time to fall asleep. They had to get Zeke's moms. It wasn't a choice.

She'd save them.

And she'd save Outlander too. She had to. It was why she was here in the first place. Save Trecheon's arms, save Neil from his PTSD, save Carter from whatever fate he faced.

And take down Ackerson.

Leah was still groggy by the time Jaden gently tapped on their tent to wake them up for their watch. She and Zeke woke and stretched, then exited the tent.

Jaden stood outside, arms crossed. He pointed to the doe sitting by a fire, Ari. "I'm sure it's just Ackerson causing problems, but watch her, okay? Just in case. We really don't know anything about them." He went into his own tent.

Leah exchanged a glance with Zeke, then walked over to the fire.

Rashard and Kjorn lay on the left and Magna and Lysander lay on the right, each pair eyeing the other. Ari sat on a tarp surrounded by blankets and pillows, leaning against a rock and staring at the fire. Archángeli stood near her. The Black Cloak and Kyrie were nowhere to be seen though.

Ari looked up and smiled. "Ah. I have company." She nodded to the two of them. "There's coffee and tea if you'd like some."

"Please," Leah said. She made herself a cup of tea and sipped it gently. She sat back against a log, pulling blankets around her. "This really is a vacation after everything we've gone through."

Ari nodded. "I agree."

Zeke made himself a cup of coffee and sat next to Leah. "I'll regret this later."

"But you'll love it right now," Leah said grinning.

Ari glanced over the two of them, smiling. "You two have a wonderful bond."

Leah's tail drooped. "Well, we do *now.*"

"And we will in the future," Zeke said. "I promise that."

"That's what matters then, right?" Ari pointed to Leah. "Do I see a Defender pendant around your neck?"

Leah shifted. "Yeah, though I'm the bottom of the barrel," she said. "Jaden's the real Defender."

"He doesn't seem to think so," Ari said.

"He's… been through a lot," Leah said.

"Hmm," Ari said. "Based on what little I've heard, I think I shouldn't pry further." She glanced at the pendant. "If you wouldn't mind, could I see your

271

pendant? After everything my Mama has said about the Defenders, I feel it'd be disrespectful not to."

"Uh, y-yeah, sure." Leah pulled her pendant off and passed it to Ari.

Ari glanced over it. "Very intricate design. Why a dragon?"

"There's a lot of symbolism in the pendant," Leah said. The Thought Factory worked correctly for once, drudging up the early lessons of her time in the Academy. "Legless dragons – Quetzalcoatl – are symbols of peace on Zyearth because the Dragon Seers who care for and bind Gems are usually Quetzalcoatl. The neck is tucked in a sign of defense, to prevent choking. Wings open are a sign of welcome." She paused, glancing down at the fire. "And the Gem is a sign of power." Her voice was quieter than she intended.

Ari turned the pendant over, then met Leah's eyes and twitched her black nose.

Leah shook her head. "Sorry. It does mean power, but it's probably an overexaggerated symbol. Not all Gem users have great power. Not even all Defenders, really. Most of us are healers and cloakers, not elemental users. They--"

"Your pendant is outside of time," Ari said suddenly.

A shock ran up Leah's spine in surprise and she sat straight up. Zeke did too. She flattened her ears. "Uh, what do you mean?"

"I can read an object's memories," Ari said. "And this pendant has memories years into our future." She lifted the pendant and let it spin on its chain. "There are… familiar names. Trecheon. Ackerson." She squinted. "Members of Chaos. And Angel." She tapped the pendant. "Vera. Theophania."

"Theophania!" Zeke said. "One of the human Wish Dusters from Chaos."

"Seems this pendant will cross paths with her far in your future."

Leah shifted. "I-I think I saw her and her Wish Duster partner back before I met Zeke. Just passing by."

Ari eyed her. "If your pendant is outside of time, does that mean you are as well?"

Leah exchanged a glance with Zeke. He flicked his ears back and gently held her hand. Food smells mixed with the smell of the burning wood. "You uh, you could say that."

Ari shook her head. "Time travel then."

Leah sunk down. "…Yeah."

"Not intentional," Zeke said quickly.

Ari smirked. "Unintentional jewel bond and unintentional time travel. You two have a terrible habit of getting involved in accidental world changing problems." She leaned on one hand. "If you truly have time traveled, why are you here? Shouldn't you be trying to find your way home?"

Leah glanced at Zeke. "I'm… not sure we can get home. At least not through time travel. Besides we have a reason for staying."

Ari raised an eyebrow. "Sounds like you have a noble plan to stop this war."

"Nothing that elaborate," Zeke said. He stared at the ground. "I'm going to save my moms. In July, there's going to be a massive battle in DC. Unnatural winds, scrambled communications, and terrible dogfighting killed every pilot in that battle, my moms included." He wrung his hands together. "I saw their files though. They were highly classified. The only reason I was able to get them, let alone open them, was because of a friend of mine. He was able to get a hold of the files, but he couldn't decrypt much of it. Except photos." He paused and took a deep breath. "I had been told my parents were killed in crashes like all the other pilots. But their photos showed them both with bullet wounds in their foreheads."

Leah drew her hands to her face. "Oh my gosh, Zeke."

"Yeah," Zeke said. He sighed. "I know the plan has been to save them from crashing, but I don't even know if that will save them."

273

Ari eyed him. "You are willing to change the course of time for two people," she said. "No regard for the consequences of changing literal history."

Leah flattened her ears.

Zeke eyed her back. "If it was your mom, wouldn't you?"

Ari's eyes widened. She shook her head and smiled. "Alright, you got me. I would." She leaned back a little. "Mama was a solid rock for us. She fought for us, and taught us how to survive in a world that hates zyfaunos. I want to be a mother someday, to honor her, and pass her lessons on." She snorted. "Our sister's blatant dismissal of all our mother taught us is an insult to her memory. I don't know what caused the Matron to stray so far from what we've worked so hard for, but she deserves the consequences coming to her."

Zeke flattened his ears, and the smell of hot peppers wafted under Leah's nose.

Ari glanced back at Zeke. "Do you have a plan for finding them in the midst of a dogfight?"

Zeke's eyes grew wide and he perked his ears. A smell of something burning bit Leah's nose. Panic. "Oh, *hell.* I didn't even think about that."

Leah frowned. "I-I didn't either."

Ari waved a hand. "Then let me ask you this. Have you considered contacting them now and warning them? You might not have to put yourself in the battle at all."

Zeke frowned. "That's a good point, but... It's not like they have cellphones that I can just call up. I wouldn't even know how to do that."

Ari smiled slyly and pulled out a small datasquare. "Thankfully, I do."

CONTACT

Zeke lunged to his feet at Ari's declaration, his heart beating against his chest. "Are you *kidding me?*"

"This isn't something to kid about," Ari said.

Zeke sat hard on the ground. *"How?"*

Ari lowered her gaze and smiled. "Black Ops datasquares are notoriously time consuming to program, especially when putting in call numbers individually. They're not like normal phones. It's assumed they're preloaded with specific call numbers and departments, but it's more time efficient to preload everything on it at once and have their in-house AIs block access based on the users' needs." She spun the datasquare on the tip of her hooved finger. "It takes very advanced software to crack those blockers. Something usually only the deepest spy networks in world superpowers have, if they have anything at all. But." She raised both eyebrows. "Nothing can stop my magic. I can see this thing's history and access all the numbers."

Leah stood straight up. "Really?"

275

"It's how we contacted Outlander and Guardian," Ari said. She held the datasquare in both hands. "Tell me their names, please?"

Zeke stared hungrily at the datasquare. "Estelle and Allanah Brightclaw."

Ari's eyes lit up with tiny orange sparkles, and her hands glowed. Then she passed the square to Zeke.

He took it gingerly. "How secure is this?"

Ari waved a hand. "Considering how many blockers I had to go through, very. Seems like they're extra top secret. No one will be able to pick this up."

Zeke stared at the datasquare. That made sense. And yet it didn't. As far as he knew, his parents were ordinary fighter pilots. Yet Andre's deeply encrypted files suggested something deeper. It was strange to think of his moms as actual spies.

Though, perhaps not entirely out of the realm of possibility. After all, look where he ended up, totally by accident.

He took a deep breath. "I'd like some privacy while I do this."

"Woods that way," Ari said, pointing. "Take your bird summon for protection. You never know what's out there."

"Yeah." He stood.

Leah gently touched his elbow. He glanced down at her. She flattened her ears. "You sure you want to do this alone?"

Zeke pressed his lips tight. "I have to."

"You don't," Leah said. "You have support."

Zeke blinked, then smiled. "Yeah, I know. But it's been over nine years since I last spoke with my moms. I need to do this alone." Assuming he could get through it at all. Even trying to remember their voices threatened to break him.

Leah stared at him a moment, then forced a smile, which came as a smell of unwanted vegetables. "I'll be here when you're done."

"Of course." He gripped her hand a moment, called for Archángeli, then headed into the woods to find a quiet spot.

Archángeli perched on Zeke's shoulder. *Are you sure you can trust the doe?*

"No," Zeke admitted. "But I have to try. You understand, Archángeli."

I do, Archángeli said. They puffed up their chest feathers. *But I will remind you that our enemies wield our love like daggers.*

Zeke tensed. "I know. But I still have to try."

Caution, Prínkipas, Archángeli said. *Shield your heart.*

Zeke sighed. He sat on a log, the fire at his back, and with shaking hands, he put the call through.

It connected quickly, and a pair of puma faces appeared in the hologram. Mom's blue eyes shining against soft tan fur with long black tear tracks. Mama's gray eyes and her excessive white fur around her snout. Both of them wore confused looks, though his Mom, Estelle, brought her hands to her snout. *"Zeke?"*

A sob caught in Zeke's throat. His eyes burned and watered, blurring his vision. His moms, alive. Talking to him. He tried finding words, but only managed a squeak.

Though he didn't feel Leah's presence in his head, he did feel her warmth run through him, calming him, bringing a gentle scent of lemon tea with it. He took a shuddering breath. *You have support.*

"Honey, what on earth are you doing on this channel?" his Mama, Allanah, asked. She craned her neck. "And where in Draso's name are you?"

Keep calm, keep the tears back, focus on Leah's support. "It's… a very long story. I'm just… I'm calling you with a warning. There's going to be a big battle in DC on July 14th, and it kills all the pilots in the area and you have got to stay away from it, okay? Don't get caught up in it."

277

The pumas exchanged looks. Estelle turned back. "Real cryptic, honey. How do you even know this?"

God, that'd be impossible to explain. "I just do. Please, Mama, you gotta understand--"

"How did you even find us?" Estelle asked. "Our mission has us off the grid."

"Estelle!" Allanah said.

Estelle waved a hand. "He clearly *knows* if he was able to find us."

"I'm… I got roped into black ops," Zeke said.

Estelle eyed him. "You're just a recruit. You haven't even finished boot yet."

Zeke shrugged, trying to be nonchalant. "I don't understand it any more than you, but that's where I'm stuck."

"Is that how you found out about this planned battle?" Estelle asked.

It was as good an excuse as any. "Maybe."

Allanah narrowed her gaze. "Hun. Who are you working with?"

Zeke pressed his lips tight, his ears growing hot. "I'm not at liberty to say."

"Is it Bob Ackerson?"

Zeke's eyes widened and adrenaline sent his heart pumping.

Allanah snorted. "It is, isn't it? Zeke, you need to get out of there *now*. Go to a superior officer and turn yourself in. Don't do anything else for him. Ackerson is *corrupt.* He's got blood on his hands and I don't want your blood mixed in with that.*"*

"How do you even know who he is?" Zeke asked.

The pair of them exchanged glances. Estelle tucked her ears back. "I'm not sure I should say--"

"Mom, I have to know, *please.*"

She twitched her whiskers and furrowed her brow. "How secure is this connection?"

Zeke pushed his glasses up on his nose. "Very, or I wouldn't have called."

Estelle paused a moment, then took a deep breath. "We're investigating him. His teams, specifically. We're in the UK right now chasing two teams down--"

"You're in the *UK?*" Zeke said.

"Zeke, listen to me," Estelle said. "He's cannibalizing his teams. We've just witnessed the results of that. One of his teams ripped apart another. Two of their teammates are now *dead* and another is MIA."

Zeke's body buzzed. "Who? Which team got hit?"

"Would you even know it?"

"Please, Mom."

She flicked her ears back. "Outlander."

Zeke formed a fist. Damn it! "And Chaos attacked them."

Allanah gasped. "How did you *know?"*

Zeke looked away. "They attacked us recently."

"Zeke!" Allanah exclaimed.

"It's okay," Zeke said. "We won. Even took out one of their members. We're safe."

"Wait," Estelle said. "How recently?"

Zeke frowned. "A couple of days ago."

"Shit," Allanah said. "That confirms it. There's two Chaos teams. Damn it all, we're behind."

Zeke's ears rang. "Wait, there's *two teams--"*

"Zeke," Estelle said. "You have to get out *now.* I don't want that happening to you, do you understand?"

"Even if I wanted to, that's not possible," Zeke said.

"Why not?"

279

Zeke shook his head. "It'll take far too long to explain. Just promise me you'll stay in the UK. Promise me you won't go near DC. *Please.*"

Allanah frowned. She looked at Estelle and the two of them gripped each other's hands. "We'll do our best, hun," Allanah said. "But you need to protect yourself too, okay?"

"I will." Zeke fiddled with his hands. "This whole thing, this team I'm in... Draso, I wish I could explain why, but they've been good for me. Really." He took a deep breath. "And we know Ackerson's corrupt. We know what he's doing. We're staying safe. Okay? Ackerson can't hurt us."

Both his moms smiled. *Smiled.* To see them, alive, smiling again... God, he was going to break.

But then Estelle frowned. "Honey, what's that around your eyes?"

Zeke froze. Oh *shit.* He had his Ei-Ei jewels on. "They're... uhh..."

"Are those the jewels from your bracelet?" Allanah asked.

Zeke shrunk down. "Yeah, they are."

They both went silent for a moment, then Estelle smiled. "Finally found their purpose then. That must mean Ackerson put you in Mage."

Zeke's jaw dropped. "You know what these *are?*"

Estelle shook her head. "We didn't, not until the war started and we got involved chasing Ackerson's teams. But we've seen a handful of real mages on this trip. It's been an out of this world experience honestly. Outlander has at least three, though not everyone on the team is aware of it. We intended to talk to you about it when the war was over." She flicked one ear back. "What um, magic do you have?"

He furrowed his brow and held out his hand. Zeke hadn't called on his magic once yet, except in that strange dream state in Leah's head. But might as well test it. He closed his eyes and pictured the little elemental motes that first appeared when he was bound. Something tugged at him and all the elements returned – the orb of lightning, the ball of fire, the marble of water, and all the rest. He slowly twisted his hand and glanced back at his parents.

They stared for several moments. Allanah cleared her throat. "Well then. Elemental."

Zeke forced fire through his hands and formed a floating orb of it in his palm. "Yeah. I have some people in Mage who can teach me how to use it properly. They've been mages far longer than I have."

"Good," Allanah said. Her gray eyes sparkled. "Good." She smiled. "We're so proud of you, hun."

Zeke smiled back, his eyes watering. "I know."

"We'll try to stay here," Allanah said. "If you say there's trouble in DC, we'll stay away from DC as best we can."

Zeke frowned. "That's not exactly a promise."

"It's not really something we *can* promise," Estelle said. "Not with our jobs. But we'll try. Best we can do."

"But that's not *good enough,*" Zeke said. "If you go to DC you'll *die.*"

"You can't predict that, Zeke--"

"Mom, Mama, *listen to me.*" Zeke said, speaking too fast. "If you really believe in magic, then believe this – I'm from the future, from nine years after the war ends. *You die in the Battle of DC and I'm here to stop that.* Please, for the love of everything, throw your duty to the side, for one day, and stay away from DC. Please…" Tears built in his eyes. He tried forcing them back, but a couple stained his fur. "I-I can't lose you again. Please…"

Both his moms stared at him, wide eyed. Estelle shook her head. "The future? But how?"

"You just have to trust me. Please Mom… I wouldn't do this if I wasn't serious."

They glanced at each other again. Allanah twitched her snout, then turned back. "Zeke. These people in your squad. These mages. I don't suppose they're…" She paused, and shook her head. "Actually, never mind."

Zeke's tail twitched. "Are they what?"

"Never mind," Allanah said. "I don't want to know more than we have to. If you trust them, I assume there's a reason. A very good reason."

Images of Alexina and Jaden appeared in his mind. His parents. That was a good enough reason. Wasn't it? "I mean, yeah."

"Okay… okay." Allanah smiled. Estelle's face fell, but she managed to keep her smile up. Allanah gripped her hand "We're prepared. We'll do as you ask." She took a deep breath.

Zeke's heart seized. "Prepared for what?"

"We love you, honey," Estelle said, smiling. Her eyes sparkled. "More than we could ever say. Thank you for the warning. Take care, okay? The war will be over sooner than we think. We'll stay away from DC and see you again."

"But--"

"Target's moving," Allanah said, turning her head. "Gotta make this quick, Zeke."

Zeke frowned and reached for them, but stopped. Draso, what he wouldn't give to be able to hug them again. "I love you both." His voice cracked. He needed to turn off the datasquare. Go back to the camp. Move on, and hope for the best. He needed to let them go… just in case. But he couldn't make himself turn it off. It'd be losing them all over again.

Estelle turned her head. "We're going to lose them."

"We've got to go, hun," Allanah said. "Love you. We will see you soon, I promise."

Zeke's heart cracked. "Mom, Mama, please--"

"See you soon," Estelle said. And the call dropped. The hologram faded.

And Zeke was left alone in the dark. He took off his glasses and rubbed his forehead, fighting the tears.

A gentle gust of wind brushed his neck. *Prínkipas.*

"N-not… not now, Archángeli," he said, his voice cracking. "Just let me be."

A pause. Then, in a gentle wing flap, Archángeli took off.

Zeke sat there, stewing in his own emotions. His whole body felt heavy and cold. His chest burned and he struggled to breathe. God, why did that hurt so much? He should be happy. He passed his message on. They'd stay away from DC. That was more than he could hope for. But the whole conversation left him feeling raw and open, like he had just had his heart ripped out and laid in front of him for the world to see, and there was nothing he could do about it.

That could have been the last time he ever spoke with his moms. Who knew how seriously they'd take his warning.

God, if only his chest would stop hurting…

Someone touched his shoulder and that gentle lemon tea smell returned. Leah. He wouldn't look up.

She moved in front of him and kneeled, hands on both his shoulders now. He pulled his hand away from his face and glanced at her. She wore a sad smile. "Did you get the message out?"

Zeke could only nod.

She gently stroked his shoulders. "Zeke… It's okay to cry about it."

He stared at her… and let out a quiet sob. Tears ran down his cheeks.

Leah wrapped her arms around his neck and held him tight. He held her back, acutely aware of the fact that she was the first person since his parents who allowed him to cry on their shoulder. He buried his face in her jacket and let the sobs take over.

CHAPTER 36

SHIELD YOUR HEART

"You contacted your parents?" Alexina exclaimed.

Zeke shifted on a log. The group sat around the remains of their fire, eating breakfast. Jaden had vanished into the woods early that morning to scout around while everyone ate. Zeke must have looked terrible, because Alexina didn't even finish sitting down before asking him what was wrong.

No one liked the answer, apparently. Everyone stared at him. Leah moved closer to Zeke, as if she was trying to protect him, though Alexina didn't seem angry.

Zeke shrugged. "Ari suggested it, and she made good points."

Alexina pulled her coffee cup to her lips, ears back. "Are they... well?"

"As well as could be," Zeke said. "And far away from DC. They're in the UK chasing Outlander and Chaos."

"Whoa, whoa, *whoa*," Angus said, shaking his wings. "Chasing *Outlander?* Whatever for?"

Zeke wrung his hands together. "They're investigating Ackerson, apparently."

"Not surprising," Embrik said. "We were already warned of this."

"We were." Zeke turned to Leah. "They said something to me that didn't make sense. Are there really three mages in Outlander?"

Leah perked both ears. "T-three? Not that I know of. The only one I know for certain is Trecheon, and he wasn't even bound during the war."

"Trecheon," Ronan said suddenly, his voice deep and suspicious. "Red quilar, black streaks through the quills, blue eyes?"

Leah shuffled her feet. "Y-yeah. Why?"

"Hmm," Ronan said, shaking his wings. "He was with me and Ackerson when we were hunting down the Atlas survivors."

Alexina's eyes widened. "Sisters alive. That is why I find you so familiar. You helped Ackerson recruit us after Jaden killed Atlas' murderers."

Ronan looked away, his big ears twitching. "If I had known what Ackerson would become, I wouldn't have. Sorry."

"You cannot be faulted for it," Embrik said. He tapped his chin. "But come to think of it, the quilar you describe was with you that day, was he not?"

"He was," Ronan said. "Leader of Outlander. Honestly I should have recognized his voice over the comm, but it has been a long time. But he's not a mage, to my knowledge."

Leah twitched her tail. "W-well, like I said, he wasn't bound and didn't really have access to his magic. As far as I know the first time he'll use it is in DC."

"You keep talking in future tense," Angus said, eyeing them both. "Is there something you're not telling us?"

Zeke turned to Leah, frowning.

Ari nodded her head. "Might as well tell them. It'll get out eventually."

"She's right," the Black Cloak said.

Zeke jumped. The Cloak had leaned against Kjorn's hide and blended in, to the point where Zeke forgot he was there. He sighed. "Okay. Leah and I are time travelers. Accidentally. I know that sounds impossible but it's true."

Angus laughed. "Brother, Ronan and I are literally time mages. Time manipulation is difficult, but not impossible." He winked. "Not sure how you did it, but I believe you."

Ronan huffed, but he nodded.

Ethos leaned back and took a sip of coffee. "So all these references to DC…"

Zeke leaned on his knees. "There's going to be a big battle in DC around July 14th, which absolutely destroys the city and kills every pilot fighting in the air. Including my moms."

"B-but we also know Ackerson will be there," Leah said. "And several of his teams use the battle as a distraction to hunt him down." She shifted. "Including Trecheon. He'll lose both his arms in that battle." She glanced down. "I… I want to prevent that."

Zeke turned to her and frowned. "Can you?"

"I can try," Leah said. "Like you're planning to try and save your moms."

Everyone grew quiet.

"You are playing a dangerous game," Angus said, his voice dark. "Messing with time."

"I know," Zeke said. "But I have to try."

"I don't suppose you have the survival statistics of the Battle of DC," Logos said.

Zeke shook his head. "Not offhand. But it's not good. I meant it when I said the city was flattened. Took a long time to repair things. They're still working on getting back on their feet nine years later."

"It's very bad," the Cloak said. "Takes nearly twenty years to fully recover. Tens of thousands dead."

Logos eyed him.

The Cloak lowered his gaze. "I'm a time traveler too, though more experienced, and I can do it on purpose."

Angus smirked at him. "You'll have to share your secrets with me."

"Not on your life," the Cloak said.

Angus raised both eyebrows. "Good answer."

"What about for Ackerson's teams specifically?" Pathos asked.

Zeke turned to Leah.

Leah stared at the ground. "I really only know what happened to Outlander."

"And?" Ari asked.

"C-crushed," Leah said. "Like I said, Trecheon lost both his arms. He gets shot by sniper rounds, resulting in a double arm amputation. Neil has terrible PTSD and tries to kill himself. And Carter goes MIA. Trecheon still hasn't found him to this day." She twitched her tail.

Ari turned to the Cloak.

He shrugged. "Sorry. Not at liberty to say anything more."

The four does turned to each other. "Perhaps this is a battle we ought to avoid," Ethos said.

Pathos nodded. "Agreed."

"I suppose there's at least one silver lining in this," Logos said. "Chaos is in the UK. We're probably safe."

Zeke lowered his gaze. "Probably not, honestly. For one, my moms think there are two Chaos teams, considering how close the attack on us and the attack on Outlander in the UK were."

Leah winced. "Y-yeah, I could see that."

"For two," Zeke said. "We might face Angel. There's a saying in the military. Fear the Angel. Unknown and unnamed assassins working for who knows who." He sipped carefully at his coffee. "But based on Ackerson's teams and what little I got from my moms' files, I think Angel must belong to Ackerson."

A dark silence fell over the camp.

A few minutes later, Jaden wandered back. He glanced around, one eyebrow lifted. "What a lively bunch we have today. What happened?"

Zeke waved a hand. "Just tired. I was talking about what happened when I contacted my moms last night and--"

"You did *what?*" Jaden shouted. Everyone jumped. Angus dropped his coffee mug, splashing everywhere.

Zeke flattened his ears and shrunk down. "I used Ari's datasquare to contact my moms."

Jaden glared at Ari. "Are you *trying* to reveal our location?"

Ari lifted her chin and raised one eyebrow, eyeing Jaden. "I was trying to help him."

"Help him do *what?*" Jaden said. "Get us all *killed?*"

Zeke held up his hands. "Jaden, don't blame Ari. I'm the one who contacted them. Ari just gave me the means."

"And you didn't think about our safety first?"

"It was perfectly safe," Ari said. "I wouldn't have given him the means otherwise."

"I didn't ask you," Jaden said. "Zeke, for Draso's sake, I thought you had more sense than that."

Zeke glared, heat building under his collar. "More sense than what? Is it not sensible to want to save my moms? That's literally why I'm still here instead of hiding from this damn war until I catch up with my own timeline."

Jaden snorted. "I thought the idea was to get to DC--"

"And do what?" Zeke said. "They'll be in *fighter jets,* Jaden. How the hell am I supposed to protect them? Thank God Ari pointed that out to me. This was the only way to make sure they're safe."

"So what, you told them you were a time traveler?" Jaden snapped.

"Of course!" Zeke said. "What else was I supposed to say?"

"And they *believed you?*" Jaden said. "No one on this planet knows about magic. For all you know they're reporting us right now--"

"They already know about magic!" Zeke snapped back. "They're chasing down Outlander who has *three mages.* Hell, I showed them some of my own magic--"

"What mages?" Jaden said. "Outlander doesn't have mages."

"Trecheon Omnir is a mage," Ronan said.

Jaden froze, his quills all on end, and his eyes wide. Alexina gasped and Embrik let out a dark, choked sound. A sharp smell of some rotten fruit stung Zeke's nose. Panic. Fear. Leah shrunk down next to Zeke. The Cloak stood, tense.

Jaden turned slowly to Ronan. "Did you say Omnir?"

Ronan raised an eyebrow, crossing his arms. "I did. Trecheon Omnir. He met you when Ackerson first recruited you. With me there too. Thought you looked familiar but couldn't quite place it. Sorry."

Jaden turned to Leah. "You didn't tell me Trecheon was an Omnir."

Leah flattened her ears. "He's not part of the tribe that attacked Sol. He's two generations removed."

"The hell difference does that make?" Jaden snarled. "He's still a damn *Omnir.* And he has a Gem? Where the hell did he get it? Does he have one of Sol's Gems?"

Leah moved closer to Zeke. "I-I honestly don't know, but maybe--"

The Cloak took a step forward. "Jaden, calm yourself."

"Are you *serious?*" Jaden said. "Do you know what they *did to me?*"

Leah stood, forming fists. "D-don't start. Theron was responsible for that, not the Omnirs. Besides--"

289

"Don't," Jaden said. "I don't want to hear another word. You know what the Omnirs did to me, to Sol, and you kept that from me. Unacceptable. Shut your damn mouth."

Leah shrank down, those spoiled food smells coming back.

Zeke stepped forward. "Don't talk to her like that."

"You have no room to protest," Jaden said. "Putting us all in danger for something like--"

"Don't you dare finish that sentence," Zeke said. "These are my *moms.* My only family. I *lost them* and now I have a chance to save them, so I'm going to do whatever it takes to do so."

"I lost my family too!" Jaden said. "To the damn Omnirs!"

"So wouldn't you do everything in your power to bring them *back?"* Zeke retorted. "Why the hell is it a problem when I try to do that for my family? Are they not as important? Or are you so caught up in your own grief that you can't believe anyone else faces it?"

Jaden stopped, his ears flat.

Zeke narrowed his gaze. "You would, and you know it. Even if that meant putting others in danger. Which I *didn't* by the way. Don't come after me when I know you'd do the same thing."

Jaden turned his gaze to the pine needles on the ground, his eyes unfocused and glistening as he stood frozen in the melting snow.

Zeke's ears pinned back. That might have been taking things too far. But he snorted. He didn't feel sorry at all. Jaden was out of line, acting like Zeke's moms didn't matter. Damn double standards.

Silence permeated the air for several minutes, then Jaden shook himself. "Pack up. We're leaving." His voice was thick and heavy.

Leah took a step forward. "Jaden--"

"I said pack up," Jaden snarled. "If we hurry, we can get to the first town by nightfall and restock. And keep silent. We're too close to the border here."

Leah wrinkled her nose, her brow furrowed. Some exotic fruit smell pierced Zeke's nose. "But--"

Jaden turned and glared at her. "No buts," he said through gritted teeth. "Get moving." He entered his tent.

Leah frowned and turned back to Zeke.

Zeke huffed. "He had it coming to him." He turned to his tent to start cleaning up, trying to ignore his own guilty conscience.

CHAPTER 37

TRAINING AND TRUTH

"More power!" Embrik shouted, bracing himself with a wall of ice.

Zeke growled, dug his feet in the pine needle-covered ground, and formed a bigger fireball, though it was hardly larger than a baseball. He threw it hard against the wall of ice, cracking it into embers and steam.

Jaden leaned against a tree, arms crossed, taking in the warm weather and watching the whole thing from afar. They had been traveling for five weeks and were almost to their destination. Tomorrow they'd enter Redbridge and start reconnaissance.

The group was antsy with anticipation and each one did what they could to mitigate it. Angus and Ronan took turns climbing trees and gliding down to stretch their limbs and wings. The doe worked on sharpening and cleaning various bladed weapons. Jaden didn't even know they had so many, but he supposed it made sense considering their Wishing Dust. The Cloak had vanished into the woods with Rashard and Kjorn, checking out the area.

For Zeke, that meant training. And for Jaden, it meant only watching, trying to process the last several weeks.

He had to admit – Leah was right. The rest of the team had seen this as a vacation, and acted accordingly. Travel was easy, especially with the summons keeping border patrol off their tails, and even camping wasn't that hard with the solid summer weather at their backs now. They had ditched the winter gear ages ago. Alexina and Embrik were relaxed in ways that Jaden hadn't seen in years, laughing and chatting with their allies. And time with Hunt proved they were, indeed, allies. Jaden discovered that it actually had been him and Dyne who had come to his and Ronan's rescue all those years ago, which made Angus extra chummy. The black and green bat spent a lot of time with Jaden, talking about news from inhabited planets and showing off his magic.

A good distraction while Jaden pretended nothing was wrong.

Ronan was more reserved, though he had muttered a thank you at least. Angus told Jaden that he was older when the whole thing had happened and more traumatized by it. He didn't like talking about it.

The does had become far more relaxed, showing more of their individual personalities and making it easier for everyone to tell them apart. Ari in particular had developed a close friendship with Leah and Zeke and spent all her night watches with them.

Jaden had caught Ethos openly flirting with Leah every chance she got, but Leah seemed oblivious. Whether that was on purpose or by accident, he wasn't sure.

Leah and Zeke though, that relationship was something else. They walked alongside each other, ate together, and laughed a lot even while walking, though a lot of their conversations were in their heads. They had their hesitations. After all, they were trying to repair the cracks from the early parts of their relationship. But overall they did nothing but grow closer. They seemed almost like two halves of the same person. Leah seemed to gain more

293

confidence as they continued on – she didn't falter so much when she spoke, she sought out conversations with the other members of their team, and she even did some scouting missions. Just like Jaden had predicted. She'd needed a good partner.

The whole thing reminded Jaden entirely too much of his friendship with Dyne. That should be a good thing. His son, having a friendship like Jaden had had for so much of his life. What could be better? But it only made his stomach churn.

He had lost Dyne. His partner, his best friend, one of his major anchors to life. And he lost him to the Omnirs. Which made it that much harder knowing that at least one Omnir had survived to make offspring.

He knew he shouldn't hate them. It had really been Theron who ran that shit show. But every time he closed his eyes now, he saw his village, his friends, his children, calling out to him, begging for help he couldn't give. It made sleep difficult, and he hardly ate.

It didn't help that the walking and bouts of silence gave Jaden too much time in his own head. While everyone else's mental health seemed to be at an all-time high, his was dropping with every passing day, as it was getting harder and harder to live in the present. His mind kept wandering to the past.

Another reason to focus on Zeke's training. *Stay present.*

It'd be easier if he was doing the training, admittedly. Zeke had a knack for floating pretty magic around his fingers, but actually trying to use it in battle eluded him. But Zeke hadn't spoken to him since their fight over him contacting his parents. Almost no one had spoken to Jaden, in fact, aside from Alexina and Embrik, who stood by him no matter what, and Angus, who seemed to miss the social cues from everyone else. He wasn't sure if he should be relieved or angry about the isolation. Probably a bit of both. Or maybe neither at all.

The Black Cloak seemed to take particular interest in ignoring him. Though that could be because he was isolating himself in general. That stung terribly, but he couldn't put to words why.

So far, Zeke contacting his moms didn't seem to have any negative effects – they hadn't been attacked or reported, like Jaden feared they might. He should extend the olive branch and apologize to Zeke.

But he couldn't convince himself to. Not while mentally living so firmly in his past the last few weeks. He couldn't focus on anything with the guilt of Sol taking over every waking moment.

He shook his head. *Stay present, damn it.* He forced his vision to focus and watched Zeke again.

Alexina pulled down the wall of ice and Embrik stepped out again. "Fire does not appear to be your strong suit," she said.

Zeke frowned, staring at it. "That's the one that seems to come most naturally though. I just can't make it very powerful."

"We should try another element," Alexina said. "We can come back to fire another time."

Zeke sighed and crossed his arms. He kicked at a pile of pine needles. "So what do you suggest?"

"We should try ice," Alexina said. Jaden perked his ears. Alexina gave him a quick look, then turned back to Zeke.

Zeke glanced at Jaden, but immediately turned away. "Yeah. Sure." He held out his hands. Tiny ice crystals formed around his fingers, flittering about like glitter in the air.

Embrik formed several tiny fireballs around him. "Try to hit the fireballs with your ice. Your aim is to obliterate them."

Zeke narrowed his gaze. He shot a stream of ice at one fireball. It smashed into the flames with a hiss of steam, though the fireball remained. Zeke growled and threw a larger, less focused blast of ice. It steamed up the fireball, but didn't destroy it.

"Take your time," Embrik said.

"We don't *have* time," Zeke snarled. "We go into town tomorrow."

Jaden nodded. "Form a circle with your hands, then force the magic through that circle. That will concentrate the stream, making it more powerful, and will get you used to focusing your magic through your fingers." He held his own hands together in a circle and guided his magic through it.

Zeke glared at him. He formed a fist instead and punched an iceball through the air. It smashed into one of the fireballs, doing more damage than before, but still not completely eliminating it. Ice crystals dusted the pine needles on the ground.

Jaden wrinkled his snout. "I said--"

"I didn't ask for your help," Zeke said. He threw another iceball at the flames, though the effect wasn't much different. "Damn it!"

"Perhaps a different tactic," Embrik said, holding his hands up and eyeing Jaden and Zeke. He nodded to Leah. "Your staff has channeling abilities, yes?"

Leah perked her ears. "Yeah."

"Come here then," Embrik said. "You two are stronger together."

Leah smiled at that and stood, brushing pine needles off her pants.

Jaden shut his eyes a moment. The rejection punched him in the gut. "Embrik…"

"We do not have time for squabbles," Embrik said. "The training is more important." He motioned everyone back, creating a wide circle. He waved a hand and a dozen or so fireballs appeared in the air around Leah and Zeke. "I will throw these at you a few at a time. You two will deflect them. No shielding unless absolutely necessary. Rely on each other. Protect each other. Your power is greater when you have the proper motivation."

Leah held up her staff, a smirk on her face. "Just like training at home." She turned to Zeke. "Toss some ice my way!"

Zeke did so. Leah swirled her staff around his magic, catching it in a churning twister of snow.

For a brief moment, Jaden saw himself in Zeke's place, and Dyne in Leah's, standing in a circle while Master Guardian Lance threw snowballs at them. He shook his head of the memories though they crowded around the edges, clamoring for his attention. His gut roiled.

He should feel happy. He should be excited to see their relationship grow. Why the hell wasn't he?

Embrik tossed the first fireball. Leah smashed her staff into it, demolishing it, disbursing ashes harmlessly among the trees. He threw two more. Zeke heaved a massive snowball at one and another at Leah's staff, which she used on the second. Both vanished in clouds of steam.

Embrik grinned. "Excellent! Use that connection." He threw three fireballs this time. Leah and Zeke caught two of them, but the third smashed into Leah's side, catching her uniform on fire.

Leah transformed into Dyne, trapped in a battlefield, burning to death. Jaden held out a hand, his heart pumping, magic forming at his fingertips. *"Get that fire!"*

Water splashed on Dyne and he transformed back to Leah. She blinked, standing there looking dumbfounded, soaked head to tail.

Jaden blinked rapidly, trying to make the image of Dyne vanish. His heart thumped against his chest.

Zeke frowned and whipped up wind around Leah, drying her uniform and fur. She laughed. "Okay, okay, I'm dry." She crossed her arms. "I guess you *can* produce solid magic with the right motivation."

"If you're not the right motivation, I don't know what is." Zeke glanced over the uniform. "No damage. You sure you're okay?"

"It caught on my shield," Leah said. She eyed Embrik. "Gotta do something to protect myself."

Embrik crossed his arms and smirked. "Cheater."

"Only in the best way," Leah said, grinning. "Let's try again." She held out her staff.

And she transformed into Dyne again, back-to-back with Jaden, grinning. Jaden violently shook his head and beat his skull with the heel of his hand. *Stay! Present!*

"Love?" Alexina said. "Are you okay?" Her voice sounded distant, muffled, like it wasn't really there.

"I'm fine," Jaden said. He blinked hard, trying to chase away the ghosts. But they gripped his mind like talons.

"Three more!" Embrik shouted. "Brace yourselves!"

Jaden whipped his head back just as a fireball smashed into Zeke's side. Adrenaline rushed through him. Not another family! *"Zeke!"*

The fire slumped off Zeke's side making Leah's shield around him ripple reflections. It vanished with a hiss against the ground. He sighed relief. "I'm fine."

"You're not fine!" Jaden said, his breath ragged. "Leah, you're leaving him way open. You should be protecting your partner, damn it!" *Or you'll lose him like I lost Dyne!*

Embrik flattened his ears. "Jaden, she was doing fine. Zeke twisted strange and left himself open."

Jaden growled. "Don't blame Zeke." He turned to Leah. "You should be making up for each other's weaknesses. Remember that."

Leah flicked her tail, but didn't say anything. "Embrik, try four fireballs this time. Zeke, give me more ice!"

Zeke wove a long ribbon of ice and snow around Leah's staff as the four fireballs shot at them. Zeke held his hands, palms out, and smashed through two of them. Leah pounded the others with her staff.

And she was Dyne again – strong, determined, fast. The ache in his chest returned tenfold.

Imaginary Dyne turned to Jaden. "How was that?"

Jaden shook his head. Dyne became Leah again. Leah looked at him expectantly.

Jaden glared. He pushed through the aching in his heart. "You still left him open. One of those fireballs almost hit his foot."

"I got it though, didn't I?" Leah said. "Close call or not, he's safe."

"That's still not *good enough,*" Jaden snarled. All his times with Dyne pushed to the forefront of his mind, so real it was almost like Dyne's ghost settled next to him, whispering, longing. Jaden formed fists, wishing for the thousandth time he could reach Dyne. Didn't they get it? They'd lose each other if they didn't work harder. They had to *push.* They had to be of one mind, one body, as much in battle as they were casually, or else--

"Did you treat Dyne this way?"

Jaden shook his head and stared at Leah, Dyne's ghost fading. Electricity ran up his spine and his ears burned. The sharp smell of pine stung his nose all of a sudden. "What?"

"Dyne." Leah flattened her ears and her snout wrinkled. "He was a healer, too. A healer-S even, just like me. S-So did you hold him at arm's length? Tell him he wasn't good enough? Constantly criticize everything he did?"

"Of course not!" Jaden said.

"Th-Then why are you doing it to *me?"*

Jaden looked taken aback.

"Answer the question, Jaden," Embrik said slowly. "She deserves to know."

Jaden watched him a moment, ears flat. The words stuck in his throat. How could she understand? She hadn't lost everything like he had. No one had.

"My love." Alexina gently gripped his shoulder. "They should know."

"I know... I know." He took a heavy breath and turned to Leah. "It's... it's because you remind me of him. Of Dyne." Jaden's eyes burned now. "I can't stand it, Leah. I can't stand the constant reminder. I need to keep you at arm's length." He shook his head. Everything ached now. All the images of Dyne from training to Guardianship to his death ran through Jaden's head again, his ghost hovering near Jaden's head, threatening to break him. His stomach churned, his heart pounded in his ears, his breath ran shallow. "He's *dead. I lost him, damn it.* I lost Aurora, Solana, Matt, Charlotte, Dyne, Izzy -- *I lost everything, and you'll never understand that."* He held his head in his hands. "Draso's wings... no one understands it. No one else has lost everything like I have."

Leah frowned. "Jaden. You didn't lose everything."

"Oh, don't start," Jaden said. "Everyone's *dead."*

"But they're not," Leah said. "Matt's *alive."*

Jaden stopped. His eyes grew wide and shock froze him in place, stinging his ears. He met her gaze, his vision blurring with tears. "...What?"

Leah rubbed her arm. "Matt's alive. Matt, Charlotte, and Izzy. T-They survived. The Defenders picked them up and took them back to Zyearth after the genocide. Matt and Izzy were inducted into the Golden Guardianship just last year." She furrowed her brow. "Matt is friends with Trecheon."

Jaden's breath hitched.

"Yes, the Omnir," Leah said. "They worked together with Natassa, Melaina, Ouranos, and what was left of Outlander to help bring Theron down and save the Cast late last year." She shook her head. "The year before I arrived

300

on Earth. Matt and Trecheon are extremely close – I've seen it myself. It's a bond I always wanted."

Zeke slipped his hand into hers. She gripped it back.

"Matt also has a jewel bond with Ouranos," Leah said. "Like Zeke and I have. An accidental one like ours, but a strong one. They consider each other brothers because that's…" She stole a glimpse from Zeke. He smiled at her and she smiled back. "That's what jewel bonds are supposed to do."

Jaden stared, trying to find his voice. Alive. *Alive*. His children were alive! And thriving even. His voice finally came out in squeaks. "Why… why didn't you tell me sooner?"

Leah threw her hands down. "I've been *trying,* Jaden, and you know it." She hugged herself, her ears flat. "You've shut me down every time I even hinted at talking about Zyearth. Heck, you're so busy hating yourself and wallowing in death and guilt and depression that you don't think you have anything to live for." She frowned deeply, brow furrowed, tail puffy. "We're about to go fight an intergalactic smuggling ring. Just two little teams against a massive operation. And if we survive that, we'll be headed straight to DC where tens of thousands died. We'll be lucky if we make it, and by *Draso,* I am not going to let you go into that battle thinking you have no reason to live."

He stared at her, unable to speak. Adrenaline buzzed through his body, his brain, throwing images of his kids as children at him, trying to imagine them as adults, trying to imagine them *thriving* but he couldn't picture it. Draso's damn *mercy,* they were alive and he couldn't even make himself believe it. Pain he couldn't name built in his chest and worked its way through his body up to the tips of his ears.

Leah shook her head. "You have a lot to live for. You have a family waiting for you on Zyearth. And you have family *here.*" She waved to Alexina, Embrik, and Zeke. "This is your family and they all care deeply for you. You're not alone." She met his eyes. "Don't throw that away."

301

Jaden flicked his ears back. He glanced at Alexina and Embrik. Both of them frowned, clearly hurt. Zeke rubbed his arm, though he kept his gaze on Leah. His eyes glistened.

Jaden stared at them all a moment, then rubbed his eyes. "I just... I need..." He stopped. He didn't know what he needed. It was so much. Too much.

Space. He needed time, space, room, fewer eyes staring at him. Quiet from the raging thoughts in his head. He had to *run*. He shook his head and turned toward the woods.

Then Zeke moved in his way and stopped him.

RECONCILIATION

Jaden met Zeke's eyes. "What are you doing?"

Zeke pressed his lips together, one ear twitching. His brow furrowed, as if uncertain, not quite sure how to respond. But he stood firmly in place. Silent.

Jaden snorted. "Out of my way."

"No," Zeke said. "Jaden, you have been running from your emotions and guilt from the moment I met you, and I assume longer. You can't… you don't get to do that this time." He formed fists, though his soft expression betrayed compassion. "You have a team. You don't have to do this alone. You shouldn't do it alone. You…" He breathed deeply. "You have to stop running."

"And that's our cue to make ourselves scarce," Ethos said suddenly. She waved her sisters into the woods, and nodded to Angus and Ronan. Angus flicked an ear back, hesitant, but Ronan tugged on his arm and they followed the does.

That left Jaden alone with his team. And his stewing emotions. Emotions he had been running from for so long he had forgotten life before it. He turned back toward the camp, snapping twigs under his feet, kicking up dirt and pine needles, trying and failing to ground himself in the loud sound of his tread. His legs felt like jelly, his head burned with thoughts and images, unable to focus on a single one. Eventually he sat on one of the logs surrounding their dead firepit from last night. Moving hurt. Thinking hurt.

The rest of his team exchanged glances with each other, then took their places around the other logs.

Zeke sat close to Jaden. "Take your time. Organize your thoughts." He folded his hands in his lap. "We can wait."

They couldn't though. They should be training Zeke. Prepping for the battle ahead. Doing reconnaissance. Anything but sitting here exploring Jaden's guilt and fear like some kind of group therapy session with drum circles and singing.

Damnit, he should be *running*.

"Jaden," Alexina spoke softly. He glanced up at her, sitting on his left. She gently took his hand. "It is time to stop running."

Jaden gripped her hand and shut his eyes, letting the soft sounds of the wind in the trees and the birds singing away ground him. Just a moment of silence. Of peace.

But his mind started in immediately.

Draso... why? His kids were alive but God, why did that hurt? *Why?* Rather than repairing his broken heart, it was like trying to put pieces back that didn't belong anymore. He had lived the last fifty years thinking they were gone. What was he supposed to do now that he knew they were alive?

Draso, who *does* that? His children were alive, damn it. He should be shouting with joy. Instead, a strange emptiness entered his belly.

He was broken. It was the only explanation.

Zeke coughed. Jaden opened his eyes and watched him, his heart aching.

Zeke was another family lost. Two families and he wasn't even allowed to raise them. Maybe that's what was so broken.

His team was silent for what felt like years.

Finally Zeke spoke. His voice was like a canon, signaling the start of battle. "So. How do you want to talk about this?"

He didn't. Draso's mercy, he had no desire to ever speak of this again. He wanted to shrink away, vanish from sight, from shame, from fear, from guilt. He was so broken he couldn't even be happy his family was alive. It couldn't drive away the agony. He held his head in his hands, fighting panic, as Zeke's words dissipated into the woods.

Silence. And yet his mind was filled with screaming.

"You don't have to if you're not ready," Zeke said, his voice still booming. But... soft. Softer anyway. Giving him permission. For whatever it was he needed.

He needed to talk. He knew it. He should. He had been running for too long. Draso, he didn't want to, but he needed to. For... for Leah. For Alexina, and Embrik.

For Zeke.

He couldn't do it for himself. So he needed to do it for them. For the second family he'd lose. Because he hadn't lost them yet, and now they were here, reaching out, wanting connection and Jaden was squandering it. Assuming he could make a connection at all.

Broken people couldn't make connections.

But he pushed anyway. Searched his brain for words, any words, and forced out the first thing that came to mind.

"I lost everything when I lost my family," he said. Zeke watched him, crunching his feet through the forest floor debris. "I seriously considered killing myself."

Leah let out a tiny gasp.

Jaden steadied himself and continued. "What was the point of living? Burying my wife, my best friend's pendant, and my children's toys was the hardest thing I've ever had to do. It was like burying *me*. I swear, I could have died from sadness alone. I don't know why I didn't."

Zeke didn't say anything, but he moved a little closer to Jaden. Alexina still held tight to his hand.

Jaden pressed his eyes shut tight and spoke through his shuddering voice. "I should be happy that they survived, that I have something to look forward to but I just feel empty inside." He leaned his head on his hand, shutting his eyes. "Alexina… Embrik… You've been so good to me. You gave me a family again. But all I've done is treat you like fragile trinkets that could break at any moment. Like… like you're ghosts instead of the solid rocks you have been. I can't seem to get past that." His eyes burned and he leaned down. "Have I really become so consumed with guilt and grief that I broke?"

Zeke shrugged. "You know, the good thing is, broken things can be mended."

Jaden scoffed. "Maybe."

They sat in silence for several minutes. So much for a connection. He couldn't even get the words right. Couldn't fix this. Couldn't *be* fixed. Nothing would fix this. No one would understand.

Zeke folded his hands, breathing deeply. "When I got the news that my moms had died, I was AWOL."

Jaden looked up.

Zeke twitched his ears. "Yeah, AWOL. I was supposed to be in boot, but like so many others, I ran. Everyone in this war was dying. I didn't want to join them. My buddy Robert convinced me to leave. He vanished after we ran and I haven't seen him since." He shook his head. "But hearing about my moms' deaths encouraged me to reenlist."

Jaden wrinkled his snout, his heart aching. "You're braver than me."

306

"I'm not at all, and that's the point," Zeke said. "I didn't reenlist in some noble attempt to make them proud or do what they couldn't do, or any such nonsense. I reenlisted so I could join the Air Corps and die in the air like they did."

"Oh, Zeke..." Leah gripped his hand. He smiled gently at her, and wrapped an arm across her shoulders, holding her close. She leaned into his hug.

Jaden perked his ears, frowning.

"They were all I had," Zeke said. "And I couldn't take their loss. I thought I'd get into the Air Corps and take every dangerous job I could in some kind of heroic suicide. Then the pain would stop." He shook his head. "They were the only people who let me hug them without making a big deal about it. I didn't know how to survive without that."

Leah wrapped her arms around his torso now, holding him. His shoulders relaxed and a soft smile found its way to his mouth.

Jaden furrowed his brow. Images of Atlas ran through his mind, along with all the times he put himself in danger trying to protect it. No fear for his own life. "What changed?"

"Andre did," Zeke said. "Not at first. It took years for him to get under my fur and force his way into my life. But he gave me a chance to thrive again. He gave me a reason to live." He flattened his ears. "Then he developed a crush on me and our relationship hasn't been the same since. Yeah, maybe I'm not looking for heroic suicide anymore, but I've found myself not caring if I die. I'm a test pilot. We die every day. I accept that. Andre and Archángeli keep me from fully throwing myself into complete apathy, but it's a tight rope I walk over a deep chasm." He glanced at Jaden. "I'm broken too."

A twinge of anger mixed with guilt and beat at Jaden's chest. He didn't understand what broken was. Not with a partner. "You have Leah now."

"Yeah, *now,*" Zeke said. Leah leaned closer. "But you saw how I fought that bond."

So what? Jaden wrung his hands together, watching the light filter through the trees and draw spots on his fur. *You still won. You still repaired each other. I'm hopeless.*

"I fought her," Zeke repeated. "Because I didn't want a reason to care anymore. I didn't want to dare believe that I could have peace and happiness again. That someone could really and truly fill the hole my parents left behind. Because everyone has an agenda."

Jaden winced. Ackerson's words about protecting strangers ran through his head. Because even he had an agenda protecting them, didn't he? Draso, he was terrible.

Zeke perked his ears. "But Jaden... that's where you are right now. Where you've been since the Sol genocide. Thinking that no one could fill the hole of your family. But you already have people trying to fill that hole. Alexina, and Embrik, and even Leah and me. But you're pushing back and covering up with grief and fear because you don't want to believe you can have happiness again. That you *deserve* happiness again."

But do I?

"Jaden, you *do* deserve happiness." Zeke breathed deeply.

"He is right, Jaden," Embrik said. Jaden turned to him. Embrik offered a smile. "I have said that since the moment I met you. Your tragedy has no right to define you, or deny you happiness."

"You are allowed to be happy," Alexina said, leaning closer. "You are not alone. You can fill that hole in your heart again."

"And you know what?" Leah said. "That hole isn't even as deep as you thought it was. Your family is waiting on Zyearth. If you only reach for it." Leah smiled at him. "But you have to reach for it first. You deserve to."

Zeke held out a hand to him.

Jaden stared at Zeke's hand. What right did they have to say that Jaden deserved anything? Not being so broken. He pressed his lips together. "Is anyone going to want someone this broken?"

"I do," Zeke said.

Jaden's heart leapt, spreading unexpected warmth through him. "Why?"

"Because you're my family, damn it." He stretched his hand closer to Jaden. "Because I'm broken too. Because broken things can be mended. They deserve to be mended." He nodded encouragingly at him. "It just takes time, and a little love."

Jaden frowned. Broken things can be mended. But he had been broken for so long. Could he really be mended? After all this time? Who could want something this broken?

I do. Zeke's voice warmed him again. Two simple words. Who knew they had such power.

"Jaden," Leah said. "I want you too." She held her hand out next to Zeke's.

Embrik reached out and laid a hand on Jaden's knee. "As do I."

"And me." Alexina leaned against him now, nuzzling her face into his neck. "I made that clear when we took our wedding vows. You deserve to be wanted, my love."

Jaden took it all in. Alexina's soft nuzzles, Embrik's gentle grip, Zeke and Leah extending themselves toward him. He paused a moment, then reached out and took Zeke's hand. Leah placed her hand on theirs. Zeke smiled.

Jaden sighed. "Am I really worth fixing?"

"If my moms are worth saving," Zeke said. "You're worth fixing. That's what family is."

That's what family is. Jaden's eyes burned. "Family…" Tears clung to his fur. "*Family*… Everyone, my kids are alive…" He wiped at his eyes. "God,

309

they're *alive*. I can't even believe it." He brushed tears off his cheeks and sighed. "But I'm not sure where I'm supposed to put them in my heart."

"Good thing you've got lots of years to find out."

"If we survive this."

"We'll survive," Zeke said. "I refuse to die in this damn war. Not after everything I've survived up til now."

Jaden wrung his hands. *Now's the time. Apologize. Speak out. For Draso's sake, don't leave Zeke hanging. That's what a Defender would do.*

But you told Leah you're not a Defender anymore.

That stung. Because he had. And he still hadn't rescinded that.

Maybe I'm not a Defender… But I am a father. It's what a father would do.

No pushback from that one.

But easier said than done. He gently pulled back from his team and stood, pacing back and forth, trying to get the words out. "Zeke… I am so sorry for how I've treated you. You never deserved any of it. I… I just…"

"You don't have to say anything right now, Jaden."

"No, I really do," Jaden said. "I… just need a minute…" He continued pacing, staring at the ground, listening to the birds in the trees, following the light filtering through the leaves. "Zeke… seeing you, as an adult, never having known you as a baby…" He shook himself, his quills standing up in anxiety. "You… represented another broken family to me. And in some ways you still are."

"Yeah, I know," Zeke said. "I wish I knew what to do about that."

A rustling sound hit Jaden's ear and he turned. The Black Cloak walked through the woods and leaned against a tree, as if on cue. There was… sadness in those deep green eyes of his. But he didn't speak.

In some sense, Jaden wanted to throttle him. In another, he knew it wouldn't do any good. The Cloak wasn't acting maliciously. Perhaps taking

Zeke away was a necessary action. He couldn't know, not yet. But it hurt looking at him.

The Cloak probably knew this. He turned away, arms crossed, silent.

"I do too," Jaden said. He shivered. "Draso's mercy, I sincerely wish I did. If anything just to… prepare." He shoved his hands in his pockets. *Look at Zeke, for Draso's sake. Look at your son.* He turned.

Zeke smiled encouragingly.

Draso. His son. His son with a new wife. A new life. Proof that good things can come from tragedy. That warmth returned, giving a little life to Jaden's words. "But that's no excuse. I can't. I can't let my grief and worry affect that. *Especially* if I don't get to see you grow up. I need… I need to enjoy the time we have now, as much as this war will let me." He pinned his ears back and glanced quickly at the Cloak. The Cloak nodded, still silent. Jaden pressed his lips together and turned back to Zeke. "I squandered that. I'm sorry."

"Well," Zeke said. "Maybe we can start over. For real this time. Now that you have a reason to survive."

Jaden turned to Alexina and Embrik, guilt eating at his chest. "I've had reasons to survive already, and I ignored them. I need to stop that."

"Then let's start with us." Zeke smiled.

Jaden slowly smiled back. "Yeah. Let's do that." He sat back down on the log. "I have to survive this war. See my kids again. Find out where they fit in my heart now."

Zeke gripped Jaden's shoulder. "Sounds good… Dad."

Jaden's eye twitched. "Yeah, too weird, let's not do that."

Zeke laughed. "Considering I've never had a dad, yeah, that doesn't come natural at all. Just Jaden then."

Jaden forced a chuckle, but his chest burned. Just… one more thing. "You know… you and Leah… your friendship remind me of my friendship with Dyne."

Leah smiled. "Really?"

"Really," Jaden said, his heart aching. His eyes burned again. "It's why it's been so hard watching you. It's… a reminder of what I've lost."

Leah's smile faded. "Jaden, I didn't mean to. That's not our intention at all."

"Of course it's not," Jaden said. "It's me being unable to let go. But… it's time I stop seeing that as a bad thing. It's time to let go, no matter how hard it is." He pushed back the tears and said a silent apology to Dyne. "Instead, I'm going to see it as a blessing. The torch… passes."

Zeke smiled slightly again. "We're happy to carry it. I mean that."

"Yeah," Jaden said.

Leah flicked her ears back and she pulled her tail into her lap, picking at the little hairs on its tip. "Jaden, I really am sorry I didn't tell you sooner about Matt, I should have just pushed through and said something, maybe we wouldn't be in this situation now, and--"

"Leah," Jaden said, holding up his hands. "It's okay. It's not your fault. I'm the one who stopped you every time you tried."

"But if I had just been more forceful--"

"What's done is done," Jaden said. "No point in dwelling in the past. I've been doing that too much anyway." He turned to Alexina and Embrik, his heart pounding. Zeke nodded to him. He took a deep, calming breath and forced the words out, before he lost the opportunity to say them. "I have been terrible to both of you. Especially as of late. I let my grief and guilt eat me up and I wouldn't let you two pull me back out like you've always been good at. That was wrong." His voice cracked. "I am so sorry…"

Embrik stepped forward and pulled Jaden into a hug. Warmth ran through him, but he also felt like he was on the urge of breaking too. He gripped Embrik tight. Embrik spoke calmly, soft, but solid as he always had. "As you have said. It is all in the past. But I am glad to have my brother back." He pulled away and pressed his forehead to Jaden's. "I know I cannot replace Dyne. It would be cruel to even try. But I hope you can find solace in me regardless."

Jaden gripped Embrik's shoulders, relief washing over him. He hadn't lost his best friend. "You're right that you can't replace Dyne, but that doesn't mean we can't have a friendship like I had with him. I need to let Dyne go and let you in."

Embrik smiled. "It would be an honor."

Jaden drew Embrik into an embrace, taking it all in. His strong hug, his gentle demeaner, his solid grounding. No more taking this for granted. He couldn't afford to.

Then he turned to Alexina. His wife. He opened his mouth, but the words stuck and he only managed a squeak instead.

But that was enough, apparently. She smiled at him, eyes glassy, then threw her arms around his neck and drew him into a deep kiss. A kiss he hadn't shared with her since they first got married. Draso, he missed that. How could he have let it go?

Alexina pulled back after a moment and held him close. "Welcome back, love."

Love. He held her tight, his mind fighting the idea that he deserved that love, that gentle kiss, that beloved nickname.

Zeke smiled and gave him a thumbs up. A reminder. *You deserve happiness.*

He shoved the doubt into a corner of his brain. Doubt would come later. Now he needed strength. He gave Alexina a squeeze, then kissed the side of

313

her head. "Glad to be home. Now that I finally recognized where it is." He kissed her forehead. That felt right, finally.

He didn't have to think of Embrik and Alexina as replacements. They weren't. They were something new. A new family, a new heart. And he could make room for the old and the new.

Finally, he turned to Leah. Leah perked both ears.

The words stuck again.

"You've got this, Jaden," Zeke said.

Jaden glanced at him. "Yeah." He shook out his hands, smoothed down his ruffled fur, and forced himself to look into Leah's eyes. She needed this and he was the only one who could give it. "Leah, I'm going to say something to you that I have never and maybe will never say to anyone else." Leah frowned and tilted her head. Jaden wrinkled his snout. "You are Guardian material."

Leah's ears perked and her eyes widened. "What?"

Jaden wrinkled his snout. "…This is really hard to admit, so bear with me, but…" He ground his teeth together, and pushed his brain to work. "I was dead serious when I said you reminded me of Dyne. Somewhat in personality, but far more in strength and skill."

"Me?"

"Yes." Images of Dyne floated through his head again – Dyne healing on the battlefield, Dyne fighting the enemies on Vanguard, Dyne demanding they respect life, Dyne working side by side with Jaden, working their magic together – but this time he grasped for them, using them to guide his words. "You are a master of your weapon, you battle well with others, you understand how to use magic that isn't your own, and you're fearless. You've leapt into battles to save your teammates, you've put yourself at risk, and… and you fight to defend, not kill. You try to keep the death count low. Because you're a healer at heart."

314

Leah's mouth slowly curled in a smile.

Jaden's heart ached, identifying one hole that wouldn't ever be filled again. Except... maybe it could be. Maybe there was room for Leah there. He pushed aside the fear and guilt and searched for pride instead, remembering Leah's battles, her determination, her similarities to the best friend Jaden had always looked up to.

"Dyne was the same way in all forms," Jaden continued. "Like you, he liked being a healer. It was a source of pride for him. The only thing he had that you don't yet is his experience." He rubbed his arm, as a little guilt made its way back to the forefront of his mind. "And you're right, honestly. I didn't always treat Dyne the best because he was a healer. Despite him being my best friend and partner, I still hoisted a lot of the stigma on him. Like I did with you." He forced himself to meet her eyes. "I'm sorry. I hope you can forgive me."

Leah stared at him, seemingly dumbfounded. Her ears flushed and she lowered her gaze sheepishly. "You really mean all that."

"I do," Jaden said. "And... if we manage to get out of this, I'd love to train you." He swallowed hard, trying to choke down a sob. "Dyne would want me to."

Leah pulled at the tip of her tail again. She nodded slowly. "Honestly... I'd like that. Really." She stared at her tail a moment, then dropped it, wringing her hands together instead. "And I forgive you." She walked forward, arms out, but then stopped.

Jaden stepped forward and drew her into a hug. "No stigmas. No hesitation. No one should feel unwanted. I'm sorry."

She hugged him back. "Thanks. Seriously."

He stepped back. "So... Matt's a Golden Guardian?"

Leah grinned now. "Here." She pulled out her pendant and pressed her thumb to the back of it. In a moment, the profiles for the Golden Guardians showed up, complete with full 3D models of Matt and Izzy. As adults, in full Defender uniform. Jaden held a hand out toward the models, his chest swelling with pride. Tears ran down his face. His children. Golden Guardians. Leah flicked her tail excitedly. "They chose to be Golden Guardians because of you and Dyne. And their grandfathers too, but mostly because of you."

The Black Cloak let out a quiet choked sound. Jaden turned to him, where he stood in the shadow of a birch, but he wouldn't meet Jaden's eyes.

"I could tell you more about them if you wanted," Leah said.

"Soon," Jaden said. "I need to let this settle first. Besides." He turned to Angus, Ronan, and the fawns, who had quietly edged themselves back into the clearing. "We have a smuggling operation to take down."

CHAPTER 39

NOT ACCORDING TO PLAN

Leah fidgeted with her wide-brimmed straw hat and followed Ari and Zeke as they entered Redbridge, trying her best to look like a tourist.

To help keep suspicions down, the group dressed in civilian clothes, split up into four teams, and entered at different intervals and entry points throughout the day. It was a cute little town, built right on the shore with colorful buildings, clear water, dense forests, and high rocks all around. Signs everywhere advertised a sunken ship that was a local favorite for divers. Pamphlets spoke of hiking trails, grottos, and beaches. It looked untouched by the war.

Zeke led their team to the hotel Jaden had booked for them. Locals wandered the streets unafraid and friendly. Almost overly friendly – several called out to Zeke like he was a friend, and multiple people encouraged them to come visit their shops or get an ice cream, or whatever. Considering what war could do to a tourist town's economy, Leah wasn't too surprised, though it was all a bit unsettling. She didn't like how much her team stood out.

They entered their hotel, a quaint boutique in a pale pink building. The receptionist, a human woman, glanced up and greeted them. Zeke checked them in and they entered their room. The window overlooked the harbor and had a plush red seat under it, long enough to sleep on comfortably. Probably a good thing, considering there was only one antique four-post bed in the room.

Zeke rolled his eyes. "No wonder the receptionist winked at me. Showing up with two cute girls to get a room with only one bed."

Ari batted her eyes at him, popping her foot up in the air and faking shyness. "Golly, Zeke, you think I'm cute?"

Zeke ran a hand down his face. "Let's not, please."

"Only teasing," Ari said. "You're not even my type. You'd kind of have to be interested in sex and romance first."

"Funny," Zeke said.

Leah frowned. "I didn't even notice the receptionist winking. They really do infer a lot on Earth. Guess that's what you mean by agendas."

"Yeah," Zeke said. He turned. "Wait, what do you mean on Earth? Is Zyearth different?"

Leah shrugged. "Yeah. We don't infer stuff like that, and we don't emphasize labels. Your gender, sexuality, and romantic interests are assumed to be a blank slate until you say something otherwise."

"Really?"

"Really," Leah said.

Zeke pressed his fingers to his lips, thinking. "Maybe I should move to Zyearth."

Leah grinned. "My suite has a spare bedroom with your name on it. Just say the word."

"Something to think about," Zeke said. He opened their big picture window and summoned Archángeli. "Let the other teams know we got in no problem."

318

Archángeli nodded and flew off.

Zeke plopped on the bed. "I need a shower."

"We all do," Leah said, sitting on the bed next to him. "So don't use up all the hot water."

"Noted," Zeke said, and he headed for the bathroom.

Ari sat on the window seat, dropping her bag next to it. She smiled. "It's so nice to be near the sea with forest all around. My favorite environment." She turned to Leah. "So. Rest, shower, sleep, and meet up with the others after dark to get a feel for the town. We take down Sharp and dismantle the ring, and then what?"

Leah checked the clock by the bed. The date read July 13th. They were really cutting it short. Hopefully Zeke's parents really decided to stay away like they had promised. "Go to DC. Zeke wasn't too confident that his parents would steer clear. And I need to try and save Trecheon's arms. If you could feel his trauma…" She shook her head. "Jaden suggested we use the summons and fly in, but we're all worried we won't make it in time. It took longer to get here than we expected, and who knows how long we'll be working on this smuggling operation. The other alternative is to steal a couple of cars from here, which I suppose we could do in a pinch, but it doesn't feel right."

"That's something I can help with." Ari pulled out her datasquare and played around with it. "Here. Nearby Canadian Air Force Base." She tilted her head. "Hmm. Says here there's a US division that works with them here. Bet they don't anymore." She chuckled. "With all of us working together, shouldn't be too hard to get transport out of there."

Leah winced. "Bit risky."

"Anything would be," Ari said. "But we need to get there fast. The summons are too slow. You need something with power."

"True," Leah said. "We'll see what Jaden says." She sighed. "Is anyone here going to recognize you?"

319

Ari waved a hand and scoffed. She put the datasquare in her bag. "It doesn't do your mafia much good if people can recognize your assassins."

"Zeke recognized you."

"Zeke is from the future," Ari said. "Where I assume our reputation will get the better of us, if we stay on this path. Right now, we're ghosts."

"Fair enough." Leah flopped down on the bed. "Is the Matron going to know you're here? What with her tracking magic and all."

"Unless she's in town, the only thing she'll know is that we're in Eastern Canada," Ari said. "It's not pinpoint by any means. Trust me – we've tested that."

"Good," Leah said. "Any idea where to start looking?"

"The Matron likes to hide things in plain sight," Ari said. "At home, she uses the casinos. Tourist attractions are good covers."

"So she'll pick something touristy here then."

"Likely," Ari said. "I predict the grotto, or perhaps the sunken ship."

Leah shuddered. "It'd have to be places with water."

Ari smirked, her short tail wagging playfully. "What, kitty afraid of water?"

"Nothing so stereotypical," Leah said. "But I've never used scuba equipment before."

Ari leaned on her hands and smiled slyly. "I have. I'll teach you. Private lessons and all. I kind of hope we do end up using it. You'd look cute in scuba gear."

Leah's eye twitched. She sat up and met Ari's soft brown eyes. "You are totally flirting with me aren't you."

Ari laughed. "Okay, you found me out. Took you long enough." She sat on the bed and gently placed her hand on top of Leah's, stroking her fur. Brief images of Ari's medical history ran through her brain – torture as a child, cuts and bruises during assassin training, emotional anguish. That was a new one.

But somehow it didn't overwhelm Leah like Trecheon's trauma had. Perhaps all her time with Zeke had helped ground her better than she had realized.

"Are you okay with touching me?" Leah said.

"Only if you're okay with me touching you," Ari said. She moved her hand away.

Leah took her hand back. "It's fine... nice even. To pretend like I'm normal."

"You don't need to be normal to be desirable," Ari said, moving closer. "Unless you're like Zeke and not interested in that kind of thing."

Leah's ears grew warm, though she didn't move her hand. She twitched her tail nonchalantly. "Like I said, we don't really use labels on Zyearth, but if I had to describe it, I'd say I'm not really interested in romance."

"Intimacy doesn't necessarily need romance," Ari said, running a finger up Leah's arm.

Leah's face grew hot now, but a warmth ran through her chest and down her legs, sending delicious shivers up her spine. Her tail puffed.

A soft smell of brewing coffee tickled her nose. Curiosity. Leah squelched her libido, her ears flushing with embarrassment. It hadn't even occurred to her that Zeke would feel that. But of course he would. She'd definitely have to learn how to block that from their bond. "True. But I'd rather not attempt this now." *Zeke could feel everything...* She shifted. "Because... um... we've got this really tense mission and all."

Ari winked at her. "Fair enough. Just had to test the waters if you will." She smiled softly, moving her face close to Leah's. "Perhaps after the mission?"

Leah stared into Ari's eyes. She leaned close too, trying to mimic Ari's sly smile. Flirting was harmless, right? Zeke wouldn't notice that. Maybe. But she probably failed. She never was that great at flirting, and they didn't have any practice blocking big emotions like that.

Ari didn't seem to care about her terrible flirting though.

And Zeke stopped responding. Maybe he was trying to block it himself. Perhaps… she could test that. "I'll take you up on that."

"I look forward to it," Ari said. She gently nuzzled the side of Leah's head, her wet nose sending pleasurable shocks through Leah's body.

Leah's mind swam, trying to drink in her body's responses, block them from Zeke, but also try to go gauge if he was trying to block them himself. It came out as a jumbled mess. She leaned her head back, encouraging Ari, wanting more. "Been waiting long to do that?"

"Since the moment I laid eyes on you," Ari said, her hot breath teasing Leah's neck. Leah shivered, and the Thought Factory leapt into full production. *Drink it in, block it, test it.* Ari buried her snout in Leah's fur. "But the last thing I wanted was to make Zeke uncomfortable with all this silly flirting, so I refrained from the physical. But… gotta take the opportunity while I have it. And beat Ethos to the punch."

Leah chuckled. "Her too?"

"Yes, but she's a lot less subtle," Ari said, running a hand over Leah's thigh. Leah's fur stood on end. *Drink it in, block it, test it.* No more smells, but a lingering discomfort sat at the forefront of her mind. She couldn't tell if that was from Zeke or from herself. Ari moved her hand to Leah's hip, which chased the discomfort away. "I think you're not used to being hit on though, because she's been commenting on your butt and especially your tail pretty much the whole trip."

"That's what I get for not paying attention," Leah said, breathless.

"But I win," Ari said mischievously. "I'm the one who gets to get you all hot and bothered." She gently licked along Leah's jaw.

Leah let out a soft moan. Her body buzzed and a heat built in her belly and between her legs. *Drink it in, block it, test it.* But *drink it in* was winning out against *block it* and *test it. Might as well get used to it, Zeke.* Thankfully no smells hit her nose. "Your timing's terrible."

"This mission's terrible," Ari said. "So let this be motivation to live through it." She licked a long stripe up Leah's neck, then stood and settled down on the window seat.

Leah lay back on the bed, letting the waves of pleasure run through her. Good lordy, it didn't take much, did it? She hoped to Draso that Zeke had been successful in blocking that, because she certainly hadn't been. "Curse you."

"Sorry, not sorry," Ari said grinning.

Leah pointed up. "I'm going to survive this mission if it's the last thing I do."

Ari laughed now. "Glad to hear it."

"I'm dead tired," Leah said. "And also frustrated, and it's your fault."

"Still not sorry."

"Don't be," Leah said. She turned over on the bed. "I'm gonna nap. You can shower next. Have Zeke wake me an hour before it's time to go."

Ari nodded. "Will do. Maybe I'll enjoy myself in the shower if I can't enjoy you now."

Leah's ears flushed brighter. "Thanks for the mental image."

"You're so very welcome." Ari smirked.

Leah curled under the sheets and slept sounder than she had in months, dreaming of Ari.

It felt like only minutes had passed when someone shook her awake and she heard Zeke's voice in her head. *Leah! Wake up! We have a problem!*

Leah woke groggily to a very dark room. The moon shone through their shaded window. Zeke and Ari both stood by the bed, brows furrowed. Leah frowned. "What's wrong? What happened?"

Ari huddled in on herself, her fur puffed up and her tail and ears slumped, a very different doe than the flirty one Leah had seen right before her nap. "Ronan, Ethos, and the Black Cloak are missing."

Leah leapt up. "*Missing? How?*"

Zeke sat on the bed next to her. "They never reported in. Angus is worried sick."

"Dang it." Leah threw the blanket off and stood. "What's the plan?"

Zeke shifted. "Well--"

Ari put her fingers on both their lips, shushing them. She turned toward the door and pressed her ear against it.

Leah's ear twitched. There was a tiny *click, click* sound right outside. Her eyes grew wide.

Ari waved frantically. "Out the window! Go, *now!*" She grabbed her bag and ran for it.

Leah snarled. She shielded the three of them and ran for the window. Zeke blasted a fireball at it, smashing it, and they leapt out.

A high-pitched whistle struck Leah's ears just before they hit the ground and the room behind them exploded. Leah's shield protected them, but she still felt the heat of the detonation on her back as they went flying haphazardly through the air. Leah and Ari managed to tuck into a roll and save themselves, though Zeke crashed hard on his stomach. Leah could sense bruising on his body – that was a new sensation – but nothing more, thankfully. Leah righted herself and helped Zeke to his feet. Ari moved close to both of them.

The side of the building was trash – bits of concrete and rebar hung loosely in a massive hole, and flames consumed the four-post bed and dresser. A figure with brown hair and a thick build walked through the smoke, seemingly unaffected by the blast.

Sharp.

He grinned at them unnaturally, with too wide a mouth, teeth that looked sharpened, and eyes gleaming with red and orange speckles.

"Boo."

CHAPTER 40

WISHING DOUBLE

Leah stared, adrenaline rushing up her spine. How had Sharp found them? Their trackers were broken, their plans so carefully laid out… and if Sharp had them here, that had to mean he had people after the rest of their team.

But the fact that *both* eyes sparkled with Wishing Dust was far more concerning.

Zeke snarled and thrust both hands forward, throwing fire and ice streams at Sharp. But Sharp waved a hand and the magic vanished instantly. He chuckled.

"Forgot I can't be hurt by mage magic?" he said.

Zeke stepped back, gritting his teeth.

Sharp grinned again. Leah hadn't been imagining things. His teeth really were sharpened. "Want to see my new trick?" He opened his mouth and his pointed teeth grew longer and longer, spreading his mouth and stretching his face – nose, skin, hair, eyeballs, and all, blowing up his head to twice its normal size, and his mouth even more so, making him so misshapen it was hard to recognize him as human. The teeth stretched forward out of his mouth almost like they were reaching for them.

A smell of hot vomit hit Leah's nose, and Zeke gagged.

As Sharp's mouth and teeth grew, his left leg ballooned, literally blowing up around his calf and thigh like it could explode at any moment. He hobbled toward them, chomping with unnatural speed.

Ari leapt back. "Body morphing! Watch out!"

Leah leapt aside too, just barely missing Sharp's attack. She shook her staff into its full length, frantically searching for an escape. "To the left! Run, go!" Zeke and Ari ran left and Leah followed, keeping one eye on their enemy. She threw shields over all of them, for whatever good it would do.

Sharp's leg made him slow, but his strange, elongated mouth-trap gave him range, and he snapped at Zeke. Zeke leapt back, but Sharp grabbed ahold of Zeke's shield and crunched at the magic like glass. Zeke's fear manifested as rotting meat in her nose, making Leah gag.

Leah strengthened the shield and pulled it away from Zeke, trying to distract Sharp. *Zeke, get out of there!* Zeke scrambled out of the way.

Sharp jerked his head to the side, sending rippling rainbows through Leah's shield before shattering it completely. Zeke ran toward Leah, but Sharp reached out and stabbed one of his strange teeth into Zeke's leg. Zeke screamed.

Leah dove forward and smashed her staff against the elongated tooth, destroying it and getting Zeke free. Zeke hissed and fell to the ground, holding his bleeding leg. Leah stood between him and Sharp, staff out, but she had no idea if she could do anything to keep Sharp at bay. One broken tooth wasn't enough to keep him away from them.

But they weren't alone.

Ari reached into her bag and pulled out throwing knives, which she hurled into Sharp's ballooning leg. The flesh popped, spewing rivers of blood. Sharp howled and his leg and mouth snapped back to their natural size and shape. The knife fell out of his thigh and hit the floor, leaving a tiny cut inconsistent with the big wound it should have left. One of his teeth was chipped where Leah had hit it.

That was their window. Leah held out her staff and charged Sharp.

But he whipped his head about and threw his arm forward. It stretched, growing massive bulges on it and wrapping around Leah, holding her in place. Leah dropped her staff with a clang, and Sharp pulled her toward him, his mouth growing large again. His other arm and leg both ballooned, making him list to one side.

Leah held her head back, refusing to scream, though her heart pumped like it was trying to escape. She gritted her teeth, struggling to get free.

Shield yourself, Leah! Zeke shouted. He threw ice spikes at Sharp, though each one vanished in a cloud of diamond dust when it neared him. He laughed, dark and gagging, unlike any creature Leah had ever heard.

Draso's mercy, it was enough to drive someone off the brink. She shielded all of them and focused on Zeke instead. *Zeke, you're injured, save your power, you can't hit him!*

I know, Zeke said, throwing fire at him now and glaring. *That's not the point.*

Ari whipped around Sharp now, a thick, jagged dagger in her hand. She dug it deep into Sharp's shoulder.

Sharp howled like a wounded animal. His stretched arm sunk back into his shoulder, whipping about like a retracting tape measure, flailing everywhere. Leah shielded and shrunk down to avoid it, but Ari wasn't as lucky, and she got hit with his thrashing hand. She slid backwards with a yip.

Zeke held his hand out and called Archángeli now, who bore down on Sharp, shrieking. Sharp waved at the bird, snarling, then stretched his fingers so they grew long and thick. His left ear expanded and grew to the size of his

328

torso, making his head dip to the side, but he didn't seem perturbed. He snapped his hand around Archángeli, trapping them. "I'll show you," he said, his voice distorted and distant. He tightened his grip.

A rush of wind brushed Leah and Zeke's necks. *Prínkipas! Remember the alicorn!*

Zeke frowned, scooching back. "What?"

Your training, the ice spear--!

Leah's heart pounded. Ice spear in the eye. But… "He's protected against mage magic!"

Zeke held out his hand, and Archángeli vanished. He pulled himself forward and snatched up Leah's staff. *We just have to trust them. Take this!* He threw the staff.

Sharp grabbed it with his hand-cage. "Ah, ah." But a kunai flew through the air and dug into his hand. He dropped the staff, screaming.

Leah seized the staff back. "Zeke!" Zeke held his hand out and formed a ridged spear head out of ice on the staff's tip. She rammed the blunt end of the staff into Sharp's stomach and knocked him to the ground. He wheezed.

She pinned his arms and legs, then held the staff above his eye.

Sharp spat up blood. "You can't hurt me with that," he said, his voice breaking up like a corrupted audio file. His face reached forward, becoming the mouth-trap again, though much slower now.

Leah lifted the spear. "You can't be hurt by a mage's magic, but that says nothing about *borrowed* magic." She stabbed the eye with orange specks in it, hoping it was the right one.

Sharp wailed, and his body instantly reformed back to its normal state. Leah sighed relief.

But Sharp grabbed Leah's shirt collar and slammed his head into hers. Stars blinded her vision and she wobbled, listing to one side. Her ears rang, drowning out all other sounds.

A pair of hands grabbed her before she hit the stone harbor. Zeke. Instantly the smell of warm cookies and hot chocolate filled her nose, pulling her back, steadying her. His stomach was covered in bruises and his leg was still bleeding, but he seemed okay otherwise. She groaned.

Ari dove on Sharp the moment Leah was out of the way, pressing her thick knife at his throat. "A *second wish?* What the hell is the Matron planning now? She's going to kill off her entire army making them do multiple wishes."

Sharp chuckled, blood trickling out of his mouth. "Maybe that's her goal. I don't pretend to know what goes on in her head."

Ari narrowed her gaze. "How long have you had a second wish?"

Sharp managed a sly smile. "Since the Matron made a deal with Ackerson to put you in Hunt."

Ari's eyes grew wide. Leah gasped.

Sharp laughed now. "You think Ackerson managed to pick up four highly trained assassins by accident? Naw, he's been a part of this since Vanguard proposed an alliance with Four Fawn." He coughed again. "The Matron doesn't get her hands dirty. She has assassins for that. After all, who do you think actually killed your mother?"

Ari bared her teeth. "You disgusting little *rat!*" She raised the knife.

Leah gripped her wrist, feeling Ari's bruised rib and extreme stress wash over her. "Ari. Don't."

"After all he did to us?" Ari said. "You want to leave this little stain *alive?"*

Leah turned to Sharp, Jaden's voice running through her head. *You remind me of Dyne. He also valued life.* She shook her head. "We don't have to kill him."

"Are you serious?" Ari growled. "Leah, please--"

"I don't want to kill anymore," Leah said. "I'm a healer."

"Then let the assassin do it!" Ari said.

Leah narrowed her gaze. "The assassin who was made one against her will."

Ari flicked her ears back. She turned away.

Sharp laughed. "You Defenders and your stupid morals."

Leah glared. She stepped on Sharp's wrist and held him in place, her ice spear at his throat. Zeke carefully crawled over and kneeled on Sharp's legs, frowning. Leah brought her face close to Sharp's. "Just because I'm not willing to kill you doesn't mean you escape punishment."

Sharp rolled his one good eye. "What, you're gonna turn me in? Where? To who? Ackerson owns this military. He'll get me free."

"Yeah, we figured that out," Leah said. "But there's other ways to make sure you can't harm anyone else." She nodded to Ari. "Hold his arms down." Ari dug her knees into his chest and held his arms down, glaring, daring him to move.

Then Leah took her spear and dug the tip into his other eye.

He screamed, trying and failing to jerk out of Leah and Ari's grip. Leah pulled the spear out, leaving a bloody gash. "There. No more Wishing Dust."

"I swear to every god in this universe, I will hunt you down and *destroy everything you love,*" Sharp said through gritted teeth.

Ari hissed hot air in his face. "Try me."

"Try the Matron first," Sharp snapped. "She's *here.* In Redbridge. You don't stand a chance."

Ari sat back, her jaw slack in surprise. "No... she..."

"Better get the hell out before she gets to you," Sharp said. "You're *replaceable.*"

Ari glanced around, frantic, as if the Matron could show up at any second. "No, impossible, impossible!"

Sharp tried laughing, but it came out like a melted gurgle.

Ari snarled at him. She pushed Zeke off his legs, pulled Sharp to his feet and dragged him to the water. With a quick heave, she tossed him in the drink. He screamed, flailing about and floundering, pawing at his injured eye sockets as sea water splashed them.

Leah flicked her ears back.

"I followed your prerogative," Ari said. "Didn't kill him. Let him find his own way back to shore. But we need to get out of here *now*. Mission aborted."

Leah's pendant beeped. She twitched her tail and pulled it up. "Jaden, we found Sharp--"

"Got a problem here!" Jaden said. "We found Ethos. Kyrie still can't find the Black Cloak, and we're in dire need of healing!"

Adrenaline ran through Leah's spine. "Wait what? What happened? Where are you?"

"Follow the pendant signal!" Jaden said. "Hurry!"

Ari moved into the picture. "Are Logos and Pathos with you?"

"They are," Jaden said. "But what--"

"Tell them to get out *now*," Ari said. "The Matron is *here*."

Tinny gasps sounded over the pendant.

"We'll be there soon, Jaden," Leah said. "Leah out." She glanced once more at Sharp flailing about and wiping at his eyes, but shook her head of it. Incapacitated. Not dead, at least not by her hand.

Fate could decide now, because she didn't have time to. She turned and ran, Zeke and Ari at her heels. She had a life to save.

TRAITOR

Jaden kneeled by Ethos and examined her as best he could, trying to assess all the damage. Broken bones, head injury, slash across her chest. More than enough to put her out of commission, but not enough to kill her.

This was a trap and he knew it.

They had found Ethos lying on the jagged rocks near the entrance to Redbridge's famous grotto, dripping blood and unconscious, with no one around her, not even Ronan. She was barely recognizable in the moonlight. Angus left Lysander with the team and flew off with Magna, trying to find any sign of his brother. Alexina sent Kyrie to find the Black Cloak – he had come in his own way, and Kyrie was the only one who had a hope of knowing what he looked like without the cloak on.

Jaden wasn't sure Ethos would make it. Leah had a long way to get here.

He had tried convincing Logos and Pathos to leave like Ari asked, but they were having none of it. They stood by Ethos' side like guards, glancing all around, each carrying a long knife, ready to spring at any moment.

Alexina had taken off her jacket and pressed it to the wound on Ethos' chest, hoping to staunch the blood. She kept opening her mouth like she intended to say something, but nothing came out.

Embrik shifted from foot to foot, little embers flittering around his head. "Jaden--"

"I know," Jaden said. "But I can't move her. We have no choice. We have to wait."

"So *noble,*" a voice said. "Mama was right about you Defender types. Too bad she couldn't get you to actually help her, huh?"

Jaden whipped about, shielding the others.

A golden doe with deep green eyes, a gray pantsuit, and silver earrings lining her ears stood apart from the rest, leering down at them. "Hello, sisters. Although I suppose I should call you traitors."

Jaden narrowed his eyes. "Matron Fawn, I presume. Thought you'd be taller."

The Matron waved a hand. "Didn't expect a Guardian to give into stereotypes."

Logos and Pathos shouted angrily and leapt forward, knives aimed at Matron Fawn's throat. Jaden hastily shielded them, but they didn't get far. Matron Fawn held out a hand, manifested several throwing knives in her fingers, and tossed them toward her sisters.

The first knife cracked Jaden's shield, and the second shattered it. The knife spun haphazardly through the air before it finally found its mark in Pathos' thigh. She shrieked and fell. Logos dashed past her sister and swung her own knife, but the Matron held up her arm and a round metal shield formed on it, blocking Logos' weapon. The Matron smashed the shield into Logos, sending her flying.

Jaden snarled and formed an ice wall between the Matron and her sisters. Alexina held her hands out and strengthened the wall. Lysander dashed up, silent as a cat, and snatched up the injured does. He got them a safe distance away, then turned back to the Matron with a glowing green energy orb.

She manifested a long spear and threw it at Lysander. It met its mark in his eye, digging deep into his head. He let out a loud lion roar, dropped the two does in a pile, and vanished in a swirl of colorful smoke.

The Matron leaned on her knees and wheezed.

Jaden dashed between the Matron and her sisters, then bombarded her with ice, pulling on every atom of power. Alexina and Embrik stood in front of Ethos, throwing every element they could, bathing the doe in erratic plasma. The elements clashed and exploded, sending smoke, fire, steam, and wind flying into the air in a churning tornado of magic.

Alexina gave out first, collapsing to the ground, her magic fading away. Embrik followed, his fire dying. Jaden spent the last of his magic and leaned on his knees, huffing, as Lexi acid vapor blew away in the sea breeze. But that had to be it. There was no way she could survive that.

The smoke cleared slowly revealing not Matron Fawn but Ronan. He held his hands out, a determined look on his face, his wingtips brushing the floor. Matron Fawn sat behind him on a rock, the picture of dignity despite labored breathing, clapping slowly.

"Fantastic," she said. She wiped blood off her nose with a delicate handkerchief. "Amazing what telekinesis can do. Well done, Ronan."

"Ronan!" Logos shouted. "How could you?"

Ronan snorted. "I admit, I was on the fence about it when the Matron proposed an alliance to me. But then *he* showed up." He nodded to Jaden.

Jaden stared. *"Me?"*

Ronan glared. "You damn Defenders. Acting all high and mighty like you think you do so much good. But you *don't*. You don't stop the wars, you just show up last minute to clean up if it benefits you."

Jaden narrowed his gaze, though his head swam with confusion. "Where the hell did you get that idea?"

"You didn't stop Galactic Interpol from invading Vanguard," Ronan said. "It's your fault my parents were killed, my home destroyed. Then you swept up survivors and sent them who knows where to whatever benefits you."

Jaden pinned his ears back. "Is that what you think we do? Ronan, we *saved them.*"

"You certainly didn't save my mother," the Matron said. "She could have really used your help. Instead, you left her to defend *herself.*"

Jaden stepped back, though guilt ate at him. "I didn't--"

But Pathos pulled herself to her feet, favoring her injured leg, and glared at the Matron. She hobbled near Jaden. "You have no place to speak about Mama like that. You had her killed, joined the enemy, and used your own family." She waved at Ethos. "Your sister is *dying* and not only do you not care, you ordered it!"

The Matron raised one eyebrow. "You're replaceable."

Logos snarled, ready to charge her when Ronan suddenly glanced to the side. In a flash, the Matron passed him a manifested knife, and he threw it to his left.

A shocked gagging sound followed. Jaden whipped his head about.

Zeke, Ari, and Leah stood there.

And Ari had a knife in her throat.

Shock ran through Jaden's body, setting his quills and fur on end, pumping adrenaline through his veins.

Leah gasped. *"Ari!"*

She fell forward, gagging and shaking. Logos and Pathos ran for Ari as best they could with their injuries. Zeke caught her, and Leah went to work with her healing magic, but Jaden had seen enough death to know there was no saving her. Alexina and Embrik held hands out, trying to call on their magic, but both of them fizzled out. They hovered over Ethos instead, protecting her.

Jaden turned to the Matron, snarling. "Your own *sister.*"

The Matron shrugged. "Replaceable." She waved a hand. "Take them out, Ronan." She turned.

Jaden rushed forward, rage fueling him.

But Ronan slid between him and the Matron and blasted Jaden with a telekinetic blast. Jaden held his hands out and shielded, the blast pushing him back while the Matron walked off.

Jaden gritted his teeth. He pulled out his sword hilt. "Try me." He shook it.

But no ice appeared. Just a faint cloud of Lexi acid.

He was spent.

"Jaden!" Zeke shouted.

Jaden turned his head. Leah still worked on Ari, who lay under her, convulsing. Zeke held up Leah's staff and tossed it to Jaden. Jaden caught it, and Zeke weaved fire around the ends of it. Jaden brandished the staff, turning to Ronan.

Ronan laughed. "Do you really think you'll take me down with borrowed magic?"

Jaden spun the staff forward and shot one of the fireballs at him. Ronan blocked it with his telekinesis, but while he did, Jaden ran up and slid under him, smashing his stomach with the other side of the staff, setting his fur ablaze. Ronan howled and threw Jaden back with his mind, patting his fur to put out the blaze.

Jaden shook himself free of Ronan's telekinesis. "Zeke!"

Zeke threw ice at the staff now, creating a double headed spear. Jaden threw the spear at Ronan. The orange and black bat snarled, caught the spear with his mind, and threw it back. But Jaden caught it, spun around, and threw

337

it again, using the momentum from Ronan's throw to speed it up. It pierced right through his left wing, leaving a massive hole in the leather. The wing glitched and flickered, still out of sync with time. Ronan took in a sharp breath, but Jaden was on him before he could scream. Jaden pressed him against one of the rocks.

"Make no mistake, Ronan," Jaden said, wedging his arm under Ronan's chin. "The Defenders may have been created to save others, but I am a war-hardened *Guardian.* My job is to remove obstacles and aggressors. You will not take me down."

Ronan bared his teeth. "Maybe not now."

"Not *ever,*" Jaden said. "I promise you that."

"We'll see." Ronan blasted Jaden back with his telekinesis and took to the air, wobbling about on his injured wing.

Jaden cursed. "Zeke, we need Archángeli now!"

Zeke threw his hands out and Archángeli took to the air after Ronan. Ronan twisted around and blew Archángeli back. They smashed into a rock and shrieked, favoring a wing before vanishing in light motes. Jaden formed a fist. Damn it all!

"Jaden, help, *please!*" Leah's frantic voice cracked.

Jaden growled. He turned away from Ronan and ran back to Leah.

Ari still convulsed, but her open brown eyes were blank and dead. Leah had removed the knife and healed most of the wound, though a stubborn hole still remained and blood soaked the doe's pink and white fur, caking on her lips and nose.

Leah pressed her hands to the injury, tears streaming down her face. "I-I can't make it close, I-I can't *feel* it anymore, Jaden, what do I do? Are my powers broken? I h-have to save her, I…" Logos wouldn't look at Ari, though Pathos leaned over her, begging her to come back.

"I can't get through to her," Zeke said.

338

"I have to save her," Leah said. "I-I'm the healer, it's my *job, my life--"* Her voice dissolved into sobs.

"Leah," Jaden said. "Let her go. Ethos still needs help. Don't lose them both."

Leah sobbed. "B-but…"

"Part of being the healer is knowing when to let go," Jaden said.

Leah met Jaden's eyes, her fur soaked in tears. She blinked at him, then turned to Ari. Her body was perfectly still now. Leah sniffled, wiping at her tears. "I'm sorry…" She closed Ari's eyes. "I'm so sorry…"

"Leah," Jaden said softly.

"I know…" Leah stood. "Zeke, watch her for me."

Zeke nodded. Leah nodded back and ran over to Ethos, with Pathos and Logos on her tail.

Jaden and Zeke sat in silence. Jaden didn't bother hiding the tears. He was done hiding his emotions.

Zeke stared at Ari's lifeless body. "Sharp attacked us."

Jaden furrowed his brow. He wiped at his eyes. "I thought I heard Leah mention him. Where is he now?"

"Who gives a shit?" Zeke said. "Leah blinded him. He had two wishes and she took out both of them."

"He had *two* wishes?"

"Apparently a lot of the Matron's army does now."

"Shit." Jaden frowned. "I think that explains the Matron. Looked like she did too."

"Yeah."

Jaden took a shuddering breath. "You didn't kill him?"

"Leah said she needed to be the healer."

Jaden paused. He turned to Ari.

Zeke waved a hand. "Ari threw him into the harbor before we left. With saltwater in his wounds and no eyes to see how to get to shore, he might have drowned. But I doubt it."

"At least he can't harm anyone with magic anymore," Jaden said.

A flap of leather wings sounded in Jaden's ear and he whipped about. Angus alighted the ground, Magna by his side. He stared at Ari's lifeless body, his eyes glassy. "Oh Great Zephyr…" He turned to Jaden. "Who did this?"

Jaden narrowed his eyes. "Ronan."

Angus' big ears perked straight up. "You can't be serious."

"He's working with the Matron," Jaden said.

"And they're all working with Ackerson," Zeke said bitterly. He waved a hand to Ari, tears in his eyes. "He did this. He did this, damn it!" Zeke pounded the ground. "We couldn't stop him."

Jaden narrowed his gaze at Angus. "Ronan blamed me for Vanguards' destruction. Said the Defenders are opportunistic predators."

"That egotistical *asshole,*" Angus formed fists, a fire in his eye. "Where'd he go? I'll kill him myself."

Jaden frowned.

"You think I won't kill my own brother?" Angus snapped. "I will. That damn *traitor.*"

"Angus," Jaden said. "You'd be on your own. You can't go after him."

"Point me in the direction, Jaden."

"Angus," Jaden said. "You want to go against Matron's entire army alone? We're hurt, physically and mentally. We can't fight. Besides, someone needs you here." He nodded behind him.

Leah had healed Ethos it seemed, as well as Logos and Pathos, though Ethos still limped slightly as she approached Ari's body. All three had tears streaming down their faces. Logos and Pathos kneeled next to Ari, though

Ethos stood still, rubbing her arm. Leah walked up behind her and hugged her. Alexina and Embrik both kneeled by Jaden. He wrapped his arms around them.

Zeke twitched his tail. "I never told you but, in my time, the Fawn Family assassins are called Triple Fawn."

"Well, that part of your history is about to be *erased,*" Logos said, her voice deep and angry. "We're never working for the Matron again."

"Or Ackerson," Logos said.

"Or anyone but ourselves," Ethos said. She held her hands out to Logos and Pathos. "Sisters. It's time the Fawn Family changed leadership." They held her hands. She turned to Angus. "With us?"

Angus furrowed his brow and nodded. "Always."

"But first," Ethos said. "We have an unpleasant job to do." She turned to Zeke, her eyes pleading with him.

Jaden looked at him encouragingly.

Zeke stood straight and nodded. He lifted Ari off the ground.

CHAPTER 42

BURIAL

Zeke held Ari's body close to him while the group encircled a small clearing in the woods overlooking the harbor. The moon provided chilly, dead light. Leah stood next to him, pressing her side against his, shaking. The only feeling he got from her was cold, hard ice, running through his mind. Silent tears ran down her face as Alexina used her magic to dig a grave.

Leah shook her head. "She deserves better."

"Ari would love nothing better than to rest under the trees in the great mist of the sea," Ethos said. "It's the resting place she deserves."

Leah sniffled. "She deserved to live."

Zeke leaned against Leah.

Ethos wiped at her eyes. "I know. But the Matron stole that from her." She turned to Leah, a sad smile on her face. "Thank you for all you did for her."

Leah shuddered. *Not enough.*

You put everything you had into saving her, Leah, Zeke said. *No one could ask for anything more. It's enough.*

Leah only sighed.

Alexina stepped back. "It is ready."

Zeke stepped forward and with Jaden's help, they carefully lowered Ari into the grave. Embrik spoke over her body in the Athánatos language; a musical last rites poem sending her into the afterlife. Leah wrapped her arms around Zeke's torso, and he held her close with an arm across her back.

Then Ethos, Pathos, and Logos stepped forward, faces stained with tears, though fire lit their eyes. Each one held a bare-bladed dagger. Logos ran hers across her palm and dropped it, bloodied, in the grave. "For our grandmother."

Pathos followed her example and dropped the blade. "For our mother."

Ethos did the same, her head high, anger wafting off her body. "For you, our sister."

"We vow revenge," the three said together. Ethos nodded to Alexina.

"Wait." Angus stepped forward, brow furrowed in anger. "One more." He turned to Magna. She lowered her head so the sharp tip of her unicorn horn was pointed at Angus' chest. He ran his hand across the tip of her horn, then let his blood dip in the grave. "By the Great Zephyr, I vow revenge with these three Fawns."

Ethos gently pressed her forehead to his. "Thank you."

Alexina sighed, then covered the grave with a thick stone slab and forest debris. "She will rest safe. No one will find her."

Leah picked up the first-aid kit and frowned. "You're sure you don't want me to just heal your hands?"

"No," Ethos said. "We will carry these scars as a reminder of our vow."

Leah twitched her whiskers, but nodded and set to work bandaging everyone's hands.

343

Jaden watched, arms crossed, brow furrowed. "It seems the Matron has a second wish."

"Metal manifestation," Ethos said, keeping her eye on Leah's work. "Another of Grandmama's wish inventions, though only a few choose to take it now, considering the cost."

Jaden raised an eyebrow. "What's the cost?"

"The metal manifestation robs the user's own blood of metal," Pathos said. "Iron, specifically. Not all of it, mind you, but enough that only a few manifestations in a short period of time would make the user anemic."

"Or dead," Logos said.

Ethos flexed her hand when Leah finished. She turned to Jaden. "I don't know where the Matron is now, but while she's away from our home, now's the time to strike. We're going to return to El Dorado as quick as we can. We couldn't break the ring here, but we will at home, our way. What will you do now, Guardian?"

Jaden formed fists. "Go to DC. Save Zeke's parents if they're there. And Chase Ackerson down. He's hurt too much." He flattened his ears. "And save Outlander while we're at it. Trecheon. It's what Leah wants."

Leah dipped her tail. "Thank you."

"Without the Black Cloak?" Alexina asked.

Jaden scoffed. "He abandoned us here. I don't give a shit if he joins us now."

"But without him, we don't have enough summons to fly to DC," Leah said. "Ari... Ari had found a nearby military base. It should be on her datasquare. That might help us."

Pathos nodded, looking over the datasquare. "We can use it to get transportation to our respective destinations."

Zeke flicked his ears back. "Are we seriously thinking we're going to walk up to a military base and steal a car?"

344

"Better than trying to steal a car here," Ethos said. "Canada has closed borders, so they won't let civilian cars through customs. Military vehicles though…"

"We can work together on a distraction and get transportation," Embrik said.

Ethos nodded. "We just can't accompany you to DC, or we'll miss our window. We might miss it anyway, but we have to try."

"Please take care of yourselves," Leah said. "I don't want to lose anyone else."

Ethos hugged her. "Thank you. Come find us in El Dorado when this is over, okay? We'll have things settled."

"I'll bring the Defenders," Jaden said. "It's the least I can do after they shunned your mother."

Ethos nodded. "We appreciate it."

The base was only about thirty miles away, though it still took nearly three hours to get there with their heavy, slow-moving convoy. By the time they did, the dawn was just barely blushing across the sky.

They dropped near the far end of the tiny base, by the backs of the large hangars. Zeke kept the group hidden behind the trees. "There will be cameras."

Jaden growled. "Can't reach them from here. I'll get caught."

"Not to worry," Alexina summoned Kyrie. "She can take out the cameras when we are ready to advance."

"Magna and Archángeli can cause the distraction," Angus said. Zeke nodded and summoned Archángeli. "Preferably near the front of the base. Draw people away from this area."

Leah flicked her ears back. "But which hangars have what we want?"

A drop of snow landed on Zeke's head, followed by a cold ember. *Mage, Hangar 10. Hunt, Hangar 12.* Rashard and Kjorn ran around the group and leapt into the air. *Keep up!*

345

Jaden cursed. *"Now* he shows up."

Magna whinnied and followed, with Archángeli at her tail. An explosion on the far side of the base sounded a second later, in a plume of fire, then the sirens started. Soldiers from all over ran for the source of the fire.

"Now, Kyrie!" Alexina said. Kyrie flew out and banked along the fence, freezing the cameras.

"Quickly!" Angus said. Lysander held his hands out and blasted twin bolts of energy at the fence, tearing it down. The group ran for the hangars.

"Don't get yourselves killed!" Ethos called. "I better see you in El Dorado!"

"You can count on it!" Zeke shouted. Ethos waved, and Hunt vanished into Hangar 12. Zeke turned the corner and led his group into Hangar 10. And he gasped.

The lights were already on. And the only vehicle in the hangar was a troop transport hovercraft.

A Raven.

It looked like a massive drone – four large turbines attached at all four corners to an enormous fuselage, with a small cockpit sticking out. The whole plane was painted black. Zeke's shoulders slumped.

This was the very plane he and Andre had flown right before meeting Leah. The one he had crashed.

"Don't worry," a voice said. Zeke turned. The Black Cloak. He smiled at Zeke with his eyes. "This isn't the experimental one. It'll fly just fine. Oh, and I already ran safety checks and fueled it."

Jaden snarled at the Black Cloak. "Where the hell were you? Ari is *dead."*

The Black Cloak's shoulders slumped. "I know. I've paid my respects."

"So care to explain?" Jaden snapped.

The Black Cloak glanced off. "I can't."

Jaden narrowed his gaze. "You can't."

"No," The Cloak said. "Part of the--"

"Part of the job, I get it," Jaden said, rolling his eyes. "Always the excuse."

"What's the good of being a time traveler who knows the past and future if you can't even prevent your allies from dying?" Zeke growled. "Ari didn't deserve that."

The Cloak crossed his arms and lowered his head. "I can't get you to understand, but I promise you, I did everything in my power to try and stop that. But there was nothing I could do. Her death started too many dominos that wouldn't fall on their own. I'm sorry, for what it's worth."

Leah glared. "Not worth very much."

"I know," the Cloak said. "Trust me I know. It's the worst part of this damn job. But I'm sorry just the same."

"We do not have time," Embrik said. "How do we fly this plane?"

"You don't," Zeke said. He took a deep breath. "I do." He pointed to the sliding door. "Everyone inside. Leah, you co-pilot."

Leah stepped back, her ears flat. "I don't know how to pilot this thing!"

"I know, but we're connected," Zeke said. "If I really had to, I could teach you."

Panicked shouting followed another explosion.

"Everyone on, *now,*" Zeke said. "We're running out of time." He ran for the hangar door controls, smashed the button to open them, then dashed back to the plane and took his spot in the pilot's seat. Leah sat next to him, frowning. Zeke began launch procedures and locked the doors. The hanger opened slowly. "Buckle up. We're bound to hit resistance. Summons would be helpful here." He called Archángeli. "I'll need you extra today, buddy."

Archángeli keened. *You are protected as always, Prínkipas.*

"Rashard and Kjorn are on their way," the Cloak said. The group buckled in.

Zeke gripped the plane's yoke, took a deep breath, and started the engines. The turbines spun, shooting huge amounts of dust into the air. Zeke stared forward.

"Here goes nothing." He engaged the lift.

The plane lifted with ease and Zeke guided it out of the hangar and into the air. A few soldiers noticed, pointing and shouting, but then a Humvee blasted out of Hangar 12, scattering them. Hunt. Zeke could picture Angus whooping and hollering. Zeke turned away from the base, and headed for the trees. *Archángeli?*

If you are looking for someone to conceal you, you already have the gryfons helping with that, Archángeli said. *I honestly could get used to their help.*

Maybe don't get too comfortable, Zeke said. *Just let me know when we're in the clear.*

Will do.

Leah fiddled with her hands. A smell of some complicated dish, perhaps a souffle, wafted around Zeke's nose. Uncertainty. She turned around and faced the rest of the group. "It's morning. And we're heading to DC."

"Yes?" Jaden said. "That was the plan."

"To the Battle of DC," Leah continued. "On July 14th. In a plane. Where all the pilots that day died."

Zeke's insides froze.

"I... think we have to," Embrik said.

"I know," Leah said. "But just in case we don't make it, I'm going to explain to you all I know about the future. You deserve to know."

"Give me time to get us settled," Zeke said. "Then we're all ears."

Leah nodded.

EXPLANATIONS

Jaden listened patiently to Leah's description of all that he had missed since the Sol Genocide – Matt, Charlotte, and Izzy all surviving, the Defenders picking them up, Matt and Izzy determined to become Guardians to honor their dads. It was like something out of a fairy tale – the orphans facing tragedy, yet overcoming their obstacles and hitting their goals. It even had a happy ending.

And to have Jaymes Fogg raise them. Jaden couldn't ask for a better foster parent. He loved his brother Walt, but he never was great with kids. But Jaymes and his wife were unable to have kids of their own. This was a good alternative. Jaden would have to thank him when he got home.

Because now he was determined to get there.

But one thing shocked him – their relationships with their Gems. Matt and Izzy Black Bound. Charlotte without any Gem at all, having to Gem share with Jaden's brother Walt who was now dead. His chest ached with the news, but he pushed the matter into a corner of his mind. They were heading into battle. Mourning had to come later.

"So, Matt has wind magic?" Jaden asked.

"Yeah," Leah said. "One of very few who do. He likes being really unique though."

Jaden smiled sadly. "And Izzy?"

"Healing," Leah said. "Though she had to fight to get her Gem to break."

Jaden flicked his ears back. "Trauma training."

"Yeah," Leah said. She folded her hands in her lap. "She and Roscoe, the stag who would eventually become her husband, both underwent trauma training. He nearly died in that training. Izzy really hated her magic for a while, until she saved Natassa's life with it."

Alexina gasped. "Oh no."

"It's okay," Leah said. "She's perfectly fine now."

Alexina sighed relief. "Natassa always had a habit of putting herself in danger."

"Specifically for Ouranos," Embrik said. "Especially during the war."

"Izzy's married then," Jaden said. "What about Matt and Charlotte?"

Leah waved a hand. "Both single. I don't pretend to know their preferences, but as far I know, Matt hasn't ever had a partner. He could be like Zeke and be, uh, what was the term again?"

Zeke smiled. "Ace/aro."

"Yeah, that."

Jaden chuckled. "Fair enough." He wrung his hands together. "Have their Black Binds affected them at all?"

"We've learned a lot about Black Binding since they got their powers, actually," Leah said, and she described some of the basics. "And yeah, it has affected them individually. Izzy can push beyond a normal healer's ability, since she can actually give the person being healed extra energy. She also has

350

a strange quirk. Healing works by giving energy and speed to a target's cells, commanding them to heal. Well, Izzy can activate her Black Bound powers and command a cell to die instead."

Jaden perked his ears, his eyes growing wide. Alexina gasped.

"She doesn't like to use the power offensively," Leah said. "But she can if need be. It's extraordinarily powerful."

"And Matt?" Jaden asked.

"Matt's power is basically limitless," Leah said. "While I don't know all the details, rumor has it that that was quite a problem for him when he first broke. But as a result of that, he has control like no one I've ever seen." She smiled. "He's a fantastic Guardian. Both of them are. They faced a lot of prejudice for their whole lives for being Black Bound, but rather than make them bitter, it made them more aware of others who faced prejudice. Matt is a fierce advocate for healer-S's in fact. He stood up for me on Athánatos." She shifted. "I kind of wonder now if that's why he picked me to come along. Yeah, I have that dissertation on summons, but I also face a lot of stigma because of my magic, just like he did. Maybe he was making a statement."

Jaden smiled, taking it all in. "Sounds like they've done well for themselves. I'm proud of them." His smile faded. "Hopefully I'll get to tell them that someday."

"You will," Leah said. "I'll make sure of it."

Jaden smiled again. "Thanks." He sat back. "So he really made friends with an Omnir, huh?"

"He did," Leah said. "He has a habit of befriending his enemies. That's how he befriended Ouranos too." She twitched her tail. "Though from what I understand, he and Trecheon had a much rougher start, involving a sword near the pier of a place called Casino Beach in El Dorado."

Zeke turned to her. "Casino Beach? That place is derelict."

"Which is why it made the perfect spot to hide the X-Zero planes they used to get to Earth," Leah said, grinning. "We have one there now, or at least we did when I left. It's kind of a joke among the Defenders."

"Hmm," Jaden said. "If it's that well known among the Defenders, then maybe that's where we should meet if we get separated or if you two somehow make it back to your own time without living it out." He eyed the Black Cloak, but the Cloak just shrugged, then laid his head back and pretended to sleep. Jaden rolled his eyes, then turned back to Leah. "If I don't see you two there, I might meet another Defender."

"It's a pact then," Leah said. "By the old pier on Casino Beach." She flicked her tail. "I hope it doesn't come to that though. I'd rather stick together."

Zeke twitched an ear. "On the one hand, I do too, but on the other, I really don't want to have to live out nine years to get back to my own time," he said.

"Well, you've got a lot more years to live now," Leah said. "And at least you're not living it alone."

Zeke turned, then smiled. "True."

Jaden leaned forward, staring at the ground. "And then there's Lance, cutting altruistic programs and shutting the Defenders away." He couldn't hide the bitterness in his voice.

Leah shifted. "Jaden, you have to understand. Lance has lost a *lot*. His wife, two sets of Golden Guardians... it's a lot for a Master Guardian to deal with. He didn't even want to elevate Izzy and Matt. He made them go through all kinds of extra training and still denied them three years in a row. Even after the Assembly approved them." Her nose wrinkled. "DD Hobbes threw a real stink about it, actually."

Jaden pressed his lips together. So Lance was really falling apart. No wonder he had stopped the altruistic work. Maybe if Jaden returned, he wouldn't feel like such a failure. Maybe he'd start back doing what the Defenders were meant to do.

That meant Jaden had to survive this war.

"And you met Zeke because you just happened to be in the right place at the right time," Jaden said.

Leah shrugged. "Seems that way." She eyed the Black Cloak.

He held up his hands. "I promise you, I had nothing to do with that."

Jaden crossed his arms. "You'll forgive me if I don't believe you."

"I don't think it matters much who had a hand in it," Zeke said. "What happened happened."

Leah shifted uncomfortably. "I saw Vega and Theophania from Chaos before I actually met Zeke," she said. She glanced off. "Ari confirmed that when she held my pendant. Said it was outside of time." She lifted her head. "But we were attacked by a rabbit and a stag."

"The rabbit had a Brooklyn accent," Zeke said. "And the stag was Russian or Ukrainian or something. We haven't seen either of them, so I assume they're a part of the final rogue team – Angel."

"I think that's fair to assume," Jaden said.

Embrik rubbed his chin. "So they spoke with you then. Anything useful?"

Leah flicked her ears back and turned to Zeke. "Now that I think about it… they had a name for us. The 'dynamic duo of DC,' whatever that means."

"They also mentioned one landmark," Zeke said. "The Bank of the State."

"We can assume that is an important location then," Alexina said. "Perhaps we should head there first and see what we can find."

"On it," Zeke said.

"So four goals – Save Trecheon's arms, get to the Bank of the State, take out Ackerson…" Jaden folded his hands and closed his eyes. "…And survive."

353

They rode in silence. Jaden tried to get some sleep, but it proved impossible with the pre-battle jitters. He had to survive. But this very much could be the battle that killed him. And his team.

He couldn't let that happen.

The sun had vanished behind the horizon, setting the sky on fire, when Zeke said, "About to enter DC airspace."

Jaden sat up. "And you haven't been hailed?"

"I... think there's a reason for it."

An explosion rocked the air, stinging Jaden's ears. Leah gave a little yelp, Alexina winced, and Embrik gripped the seat. Jaden peered out the window.

The world was pure chaos.

Fires and smoke rose up from the ground, and anti-aircraft artillery lit up the sky. Skyscrapers crumbled around them, bathed in flaming pillars. The dying sunlight caught a few planes flying haphazardly through the air before vanishing into the smoke. Explosions rocked their plane, even this far from the heart of the battle.

Then the plane stopped in place. Jaden flattened his ears. "Zeke?"

"That's a death trap," Zeke said. "Especially in a Raven with no way to fight back. I don't... I don't know what to do. We--"

"Attention Raven-247!" a voice sounded on the comms. *"Do not enter DC airspace, I repeat, do NOT enter DC airspace--"*

Zeke sputtered, his eyes wide. "No, no, *no!"*

Alexina twitched her tail. "Who is that?"

"That's my mom!" Zeke said. He frantically tapped at the communication console. "Raven-247 to Estelle Brightclaw, do you read?" Nothing. "Mom, answer the comm, do you read?" Still nothing. Zeke banged his hand against the yoke. "Damn it, why are they here? They were supposed to stay away!"

"We need to get in there, *now,"* Leah said.

"No," Zeke said. He lowered the plane over a flat spot of dirt just outside the city limits. "I'm not putting you all at risk for my moms. That's my job." He opened the doors. "Everyone *out."*

Jaden gritted his teeth. "Zeke, you can't be *serious.* This is literally why we're all *here.* We're going to help!"

"I'm not going to lose both my families, damnit," Zeke said. "I can't do that. You have to stay here. You can't be in this plane. You'll *die."*

"So it's acceptable for *you* to die?" Jaden said.

Zeke hunched down.

"You told me you reenlisted so you could die in battle like your moms," Jaden said. He threw off his belt and stood. Alexina and Embrik followed his example. "But you said you had gotten past that, Zeke. You have something to live for. Don't do this to yourself. Don't go out there alone."

Zeke frowned. He unbuckled from his seat, took several steps forward, and wrapped Jaden and Alexina in his arms. "You all have given me a reason to give up that heroic suicide nonsense." He pulled back and looked into their eyes. "But it's also given me a reason to risk everything to save those I love. I have to do this alone."

"No, you don't," Leah said. Zeke turned. She stared at him, fists held tight. "You have a partner, Zeke." She met Jaden's eyes. "And you protect your partner at all costs." Her features softened. "I understand wanting to protect us. And maybe you don't feel like you can take all of us. But you are not going alone. I started this with you. I'll end it if I have to. That's what partners do."

Jaden felt the truth of it like a kick to the gut.

Zeke frowned. "Okay. You're right." He turned back to Jaden. "But I won't endanger all of you."

"You've got your own dangers anyway," the Cloak said. He held a hand outside the door and Rashard and Kjorn manifested in a flurry of ice and fire,

355

the scent of sulfur mixing with the scent of winter and snow. The Cloak turned to the group. "Come with me to the Bank of the State."

Jaden flicked his ears back. "Why?"

"You laid out four goals," the Cloak said. "At least two of them lie that way." He held out a hand. "Come with me."

Jaden stared at the Cloak, then turned to Zeke.

Zeke shrugged. "We apparently make it that far. 'Dynamic duo' and all that."

Jaden closed his eyes a moment. Everything screamed at him to hold on to Zeke. His son. But a quiet voice calmed him.

Part of being a healer means knowing when to let go.

Part of healing meant knowing when to let go, too. He glanced at Zeke, eyes watery. "Okay. We'll meet at the Bank. But you better be there, understand?"

Zeke nodded.

Jaden held him tight again. It might be the final time. Better make it count.

Then he let go.

Alexina threw her arms around Zeke and held him close, weeping openly. "Please... come back to us."

Zeke held her too. "I'll do everything I can to make sure I do."

"Take Kyrie," Alexina said, waving a hand. Kyrie appeared on the co-pilot's seat. "She will protect you."

Zeke nodded, then turned to Embrik.

Embrik embraced him. "You really are like your father," he said. "For better and worse. But I think you have inherited some of his better qualities."

Zeke smiled and hugged him back. "Yeah, I think so too."

"Running out of time," the Cloak said. "Everyone saddle up."

Leah ran up and gave all three of them hugs as well. But she held Jaden for the longest. "Thank you."

Jaden didn't know how to respond to that, so he just gave her a squeeze.

"See you soon," Leah said. She and Zeke took their seats. Jaden, Alexina, and Embrik walked out of the plane.

The Cloak turned to Zeke. "Just a word of caution. Watch the wind, bird whisperer."

Zeke gave him a funny look, but didn't question it.

The Cloak walked out and Zeke closed the doors. In a second, the plane lifted into the air and headed into the thick of battle.

Jaden's throat closed up watching them. "Draso protect them…"

The Cloak laid a hand on Jaden's shoulder. His grip was surprisingly warm. "Ready?"

Jaden stared into the Cloak's vibrant green eyes. He breathed deeply, then reached into his shirt and pulled out his pendant, letting it rest on his chest. Time to be the Guardian again.

"Now I am."

Then he and his team got on Rashard and Kjorn's backs and dove into battle.

AWAKENING THE GUARDIAN

Jaden clung to Rashard's feathers, Alexina at his back, anxiety running through his bones, making everything buzz.

No matter how many battles he had faced, it never got easier. The smell of artillery, the taste of smoke, the hot, hot air, the screams, the shrieks of victims as they ran... or died. Adrenaline kept his heart pumping in his ears, spreading a constant ringing over all the other sounds. Instinctively, he shielded his team, but he knew it'd do no good against most of the weapons being fired in their direction.

"We have one task!" the Cloak shouted over the cacophony. He and Embrik rode Kjorn. "Get to Trecheon Omnir!"

Jaden's quills stood on end. "What? Why?"

"Leah was right," the Cloak said. "We need to save him. I can do that. But I can't get there on my own. I need the Guardian. With me?"

Jaden ran a finger over his pendant. "I'm with you."

"And we're with you," Embrik said. Alexina nodded as well.

They banked around a large, burning apartment building and landed. Rubble littered the ground all around them, spewing fire and smoke into the air. Jaden coughed.

The Cloak slid off Kjorn's back, so Jaden and the others followed his example. The Cloak pressed his forehead to Kjorn's and muttered something in a familiar language, though Jaden couldn't quite make it out.

Alexina gripped his shoulder. "Old Athánatos," she said. "I do not fully understand it myself, but he is asking for their help."

The two gryfons nodded. Rashard waved his wings and stood on his back legs, keening. The sound and wind from his wing flaps forced Jaden to turn away. Kjorn followed his example and the two of them took to the sky again, leaving only the Black Cloak behind.

The Black Cloak nodded to the team, his eyes and mask shaded in the fading light. "We're less likely to be targets on the ground and the gryfons are needed elsewhere. But without Rashard and Kjorn, I'm vulnerable." He lowered his head. "I need your protection, Guardian."

Jaden stood tall, drawing on all his training. "You have it." He waved a hand. "Protective circle around the Cloak. Divide our attentions, keep alert." He stood in front of the Cloak, Embrik stood to his left, and Alexina to his right. Jaden nodded to his team. "Let's go!" He ran into the rubble.

"On your left, Jaden!" Embrik shouted. Jaden turned and shielded as a piece of rubble fell, then he blasted ice spikes at the falling debris, destroying it.

"Watch that building there!" Alexina called. Embrik blasted fire at a falling parapet and shattered it. Alexina blew away the gravel with wind.

"Alexina, eyes up!" Jaden shouted. A massive piece of what must have been a fighter plane flew toward them, but Alexina called a wall of stone up from the ground and deflected it.

The group worked like a well-oiled machine, fighting, deflecting, and protecting each other in the battlefield. It brought Jaden back to his missions as a Guardian – Vanguard in particular stood out in his mind, fighting his way through smugglers with Dyne at his side.

Civilians all around them ran past, screaming, crying, covered in ash and dust. Jaden protected them when he could, but there was so little they could do. He didn't know where to send them, how to protect them.

The Cloak seemed to know though, and he pointed them in various directions as they ran.

They ran for what felt like hours. Every war game, every battle, every war Jaden had lived through repeated their lessons over and over in his mind as he worked to keep himself and his team alive. The sun sank behind the horizon, and the smoke hid the moon, leaving only the fires of war and a few scattered streetlights to light the path.

The Black Cloak stayed in the middle of their group, looking to each one of them for protection. Sometimes it seemed like he could anticipate the dangers. Jaden kept an eye on where he looked. But they stopped every threat, stray bullet, and falling debris.

"That's the Guardian I know," the Cloak told Jaden. The pendant bounced against Jaden's chest in affirmation.

Most of their way was flat, but as exhaustion started beating at Jaden's lungs, they came across a hill of burning grass and building debris. Jaden was trying to figure out how to get around it, when the Cloak started climbing. Jaden flicked his ears back, nodded to his companions, and followed, shielding them all. They slowed, and by the time they reached the top, Jaden's legs felt like jelly, and his magic was nearly spent.

"How much further?" Embrik asked, panting. He could only conjure a handful of embers at this point.

The Cloak stood at the top of the hill, oddly stoic. "We're here."

Jaden looked over the hill.

The ground below them might as well have been the surface of the moon – flat, dusty, full of craters, no signs of life. Fires raged all around them, except for a massive clearing that had once been a park. At the far side of the clearing nearly two miles away, unscathed and glowing in the dark, towered the Bank of the State. From their vantage point, it had to be at least two miles away, though it was hard to judge in the darkness. Jaden frowned. "And Trecheon's there."

"No," the Cloak said. "He's there." He pointed.

At the bottom of the hill, a good half-mile away from where they were perched, stood three tiny figures. A flickering streetlight lit them well enough that Jaden recognized that unmistakable red immediately.

Despite the war all around him, his mind instantly flashed back to Sol, watching red quilar run after its citizens, viciously tearing them down, leaving nothing but blood and death. He saw Kyo, facing Jaden in the wide hallway of the Sanctum while Jaden tried to save the Sol Gems. Then flashes of Matt, Izzy, and Charlotte running in, screaming for help. Kyo smashing Jaden's Gem, sending him tumbling into the void, far away from his kits, leaving them to die.

His heart hurt.

But he could adjust that vision now. He had to. His children hadn't died like he had thought. Jaden's efforts hadn't been in vain.

And after all, Trecheon was his son's friend. It was Jaden's job to protect him. "Let's get down there."

The Cloak held out a hand and stopped him.

Jaden frowned. "Aren't we going to save him?"

"We are." The Cloak shook his head. "Well, I am."

Jaden flicked his ears back. "I don't understand."

The Cloak took a deep breath. "As a time traveler, I've had to learn a lot about letting go. I've moved from event to event with knowledge of what's going to happen – who lives, who dies, who is left with permanent scars as a result of their pain. And I want nothing more than to stop it all. End the suffering. But I can't. Because every one of these events is a domino in a much larger cycle, and stopping one breaks everything."

Jaden furrowed his brow. "You knew Leah was going to get shot going after that basilisk."

"I did," the Cloak said.

Jaden lowered his gaze. He formed a fist. "And you didn't stop it."

"No," the Cloak said. "I couldn't do anything to prevent it. I couldn't even hint that I already knew what was going to happen."

Jaden snarled. "You--"

"If I had," the Cloak continued, cutting Jaden off. "Zeke wouldn't have felt compelled to bind to his Ei-Ei jewels, or fix his relationship with Leah. We wouldn't have gone after Hunt. We wouldn't have traveled across the country. You and Zeke would never have reconciled." His shoulders drooped. "…Ari wouldn't have died, which sets off a whole different set of dominos. And if she hadn't died, you wouldn't have become the Guardian again. I wouldn't have been able to get to Trecheon, to save him, because I needed that Guardian. Trecheon's path from here on out sets off dominos in a dozen directions." The Cloak dropped his hand. "It's all connected. So I've had to learn to let go. Like Leah and Zeke." He turned to Jaden. "Like you."

Jaden met the Cloak's eyes and gasped.

The Cloak's eyes were no longer green. They were icy blue.

"In a lot of ways," the Cloak continued. "It's a lot harder to let go when I know the outcome, even if the end goal is eventually happy. But it has to be done." He reached over and gripped Jaden's shoulder.

362

The air cracked with the sound of a high-powered rifle, followed by an agonized scream from down the hill. Both Alexina and Embrik's jaws dropped. Jaden's fur and quills stood on end and a buzz ran through his skin.

Alexina drew her hand to her face. "Leah said that Trecheon gets his arms shot off by a sniper."

Good *Draso*. No wonder Leah wanted to save him.

The Cloak smiled at Jaden with his eyes. "Get to the Bank of the State. Go around the clearing."

Another shot rang out, but no scream followed that one.

"Zeke is going to have to learn this lesson," the Cloak said. "And he should have all his parents there while he learns it."

Jaden flicked his ears back. "You were never going to help us change the past."

Someone down the hill shouted, screaming about a Gem working. Pistol shots peppered the air.

"I don't change the past," the Cloak said. "I guide it. Someday you'll know why."

"We have to go," a feminine voice said. Jaden turned. A second cloaked person, with deep purple eyes and a less ornate bronze mask stood by them.

The Cloak faced her and nodded, then turned to Jaden. "We'll see each other soon – facing the Desert Wall. Take care of yourself and your team. They'll need you." He and the other cloaked figure turned and ran down the hill toward Outlander.

Alexina and Embrik walked up to Jaden. He reached for their hands and held them tight as they watched the Cloak descend on Trecheon. He couldn't make out much. One of the figures lay on the ground next to them. The third kneeled by Trecheon, speaking frantically while the Cloak's companion leaned over him. There was a bright red glow, then the companion stepped back. The third figure gripped his head and pressed his forehead to Trecheon's chest. Jaden couldn't make out many features, but he appeared to be a quilar, caked with blood and dirt. Drowning in sorrow.

Carter, Jaden realized.

And Trecheon lay there, without arms.

It was like watching himself, when he had lost his family on Sol. But Trecheon's story didn't end here. It continued on.

So would Jaden's.

Jaden squeezed Embrik and Alexina's hands. "Let's get to the Bank of the State. Zeke and Leah need us." They turned and ran.

THE DAY THE WIND REBELLED

Zeke pressed forward on the yoke and headed deeper into DC airspace, his heart pumping. This was foolish at best and suicidal at worst. What could they possibly do to save his parents? Absolutely *nothing,* it was why he had tried calling them instead. Damn it all, why couldn't they just listen to him and stay in the UK? He just—

"Zeke," Leah said. "Do you trust me?"

Zeke frowned. He turned. "What?"

"Do you trust me?"

Zeke's ear flattened. "Well, yeah, but--"

"We're headed into certain death if I don't do something," Leah said. "So I'm going to try and shield the Raven. But I can't do it alone."

Zeke frowned. "So what are you going to do?"

"Borrow power from you."

Zeke's eyes widened. "Leah, that's exactly why Jaden didn't want us to have this bond. That's *dangerous.*"

"So's going into this battle with this plane," Leah said.

"Will it even protect us?"

Leah met Zeke's eyes. "I guess we'll find out."

Zeke stared at her.

An explosion rocked the plane – anti-aircraft artillery near them. "Alright, I see your point, just do it!"

Leah nodded. She held her hands out and closed her eyes. Something tugged at Zeke. It felt like it grasped at his very essence, like it was trying to pull him apart atom by atom. The skin around his Ei-Ei jewels tingled, and his reflection in the window showed that they glowed. It didn't hurt, but by Draso, it was like being stripped away.

And then it wasn't. The feeling vanished and instead he felt a warmth and comfort. Everything settled.

"Hold on." Leah squeezed her hands into fists. The air in front of the viewing window shimmered green, then purple, then vanished, but it still left a slight iridescent sheen in the air around them. She opened her eyes, sweat beading on her fur. "There."

"Good," Zeke said. He tried pulling up the comms again when the plane violently rocked to the left. "What the hell?"

"Were we hit?" Leah asked.

Zeke checked over the instruments. "I don't--" Another blast rocked them. "What the hell! I'm not showing any damage, but--"

Prínkipas! Archángeli said suddenly. *It is the wind! It is vicious and unnatural.*

Leah blinked. "Unnatural?"

Magical, Archángeli said. *Not haphazard, but focused… hunting.*

Malicious, Kyrie said, with a sense of cold against Zeke's neck. *Trying to take down the planes.*

Leah gasped. "Someone is trying to *deliberately* take down the planes?"

Zeke gritted his teeth. *Watch the wind, bird whisperer,* the Cloak had said. "But where's it coming from?"

I don't know, Archángeli said.

Zeke cursed. He glanced out the window, but he could only see one thing. In the distance, a towering building – the Bank of the State, labeled in bright letters.

"Raven-247, you were told to stay out of this airspace!" A voice shouted over the comms. *"What are you--"*

Zeke fumbled with the comm controls. "Mom, it's Zeke, it's Zeke!"

Estelle gasped over the comms. *"Zeke! What are you* doing *here?"*

"I could ask you the same thing!" Zeke said. "I told you to stay away!"

"We couldn't!" Estelle said.

Allanah came on now. *"We followed Ackerson here. He's--"*

"He's here, I know!" Zeke said. He got the tracking system searching for the source of the comm and a tiny green blip showed up his HUD. His moms, in a two-seater stealth fighter, headed for the Bank of the State at breakneck speed. *Archángeli, Kyrie, get to them, now!* The Phonar keened a response at him, though he knew there was no way they'd match the speed of his moms' fighter jet. "Mom, Mama, you have to get out of here *right now--"*

"Zeke, *watch out!"* Leah called.

A string of anti-aircraft artillery flew through the air. Zeke banked sharp right, barely evading them.

But then his moms screamed. Warnings buzzed and beeped through the comms. *"Wings damaged! Eject, eject!"* The rushing sound of wind and explosions blasted over the comms, threatening to break Zeke's ears. Leah pulled her ears down over her head.

"No!" Zeke banged on the yoke. "Archángeli, get them, *now!"*

Archángeli and Kyrie dashed past the Raven at speeds Zeke had never seen them pull before and vanished in the darkness, headed for the Bank of the

367

State. Zeke waited for several tense seconds, his heart pounding. "Archángeli?"

I've caught their parachutes, Archángeli said. *But—*

Something slammed into the side of the Raven, shaking it violently. Leah screamed. His nose burned with the scent of hot peppers. Warnings beeped across the instruments, flashing violent red. He stared, wide eyed.

They had lost both engines on the right side.

Leah, shield us! Zeke shouted into her mind, where she'd be more likely to hear it. *There's a red lever under your seat. Pull it on my signal!*

Leah grabbed the lever, shaking. A shimmer of purple and green washed over them both, then vanished. She panted with fear, her eyes wide.

"Now!" He pulled on the lever. Leah did the same, and they flew into the air. *Hold on!*

The Raven crashed to the ground in a slow-motion fireball, leaving a trail of smoke behind it. Then Zeke and Leah's parachutes deployed.

A gentle wind caught them, directing them slowly toward the Bank of the State. Zeke turned, expecting Archángeli, but finding Rashard and Kjorn instead. They keened at him. *Take heart, Prínkipas, and hold fast to your partner!* The pair of them vanished into the darkness again, just as Leah and Zeke touched down. Zeke landed hard, and his foot caught on the seat, cracking something and sending fire up his foot and leg. He winced, but held in a scream. Leah's seat tilted to the left and she grunted, but they seemed otherwise fine. Zeke quickly unbuckled himself, hobbled over as best he could, and got Leah free.

Leah shook herself and met his eyes. "The Bank of the State."

"Go!" Zeke said. They ran as fast as they could over the rubble. Zeke pushed the pain out of his mind. His moms were more important.

Zeke saw the parachutes before his moms. His heart pounded in his ears. "Mom? Mama?"

They're here. Off to the side, Archángeli stood in full zyfaunos form, a sharp breeze blasting from their person. Kyrie stood by their side, also in zyfaunos form, staring at the ground and hugging herself. They frowned at Zeke and Leah as they approached. *But they need help that I can't offer.*

Zeke glanced around, and saw only black. Only black... Then he got the faint image of the ejection seats, with nothing but black in them. "Oh my god, they've been *burned--*"

Leah pulled him back and turned him around. "Don't look. I'll save them. I'm going to need your power, okay?"

Zeke turned back to his moms. "But--"

"Don't look." Leah turned him around again and ran for his moms.

Zeke forced himself to stare at the ground and keep his focus there. Archángeli and Kyrie moved next to him, shielding him with open wings. He shut his eyes and gritted his teeth, as Leah took his power again, atom by atom.

Gentle smells entered his nose, which he took to be Leah trying to comfort him. He dove into it. Soft, fresh baked cookies, fried ice cream, a six-course family meal with turkey, gravy, mashed potatoes, and corn. Then the images floated in. His moms preparing a plate at Thanksgiving, his great aunt burning the turkey like she did every year until the day she died, playing in the backyard after dinner, the whole family enjoying his great aunt's famous pies just as the sun set.

Then, Andre, greeting him with the same morbid joke every morning, gripping his shoulders, laughing at everything, keeping the tone light, and being there for Zeke every time he wanted to give up. Being Zeke's literal anchor to this world.

Then... his new family. Jaden, Alexina, Embrik... Leah. Not so many happy memories there, but there was strength. Encouraging Zeke when he was down, binding him to his Ei-Ei jewels, teaching him magic, working through their own problems, and bonding in ways Zeke had dreamed of since high school.

He clung to every last image, letting himself drown in them.

Then, slowly, they faded. He opened his eyes, afraid to turn around.

Zeke, Leah said. *It's okay.*

Zeke slowly turned.

Estelle and Allanah stood there, wearing tattered flight suits, their faces covered in dirt and grime, looking at their hands like they couldn't believe what they saw. But they were healed. Healthy. Safe. Zeke let out a choked sound.

They both looked up.

Zeke ran forward and threw his arms around them. He tried to speak, tried to say anything to them, but all he could do was sob.

They held him back, crying as well. Estelle pressed her head against Zeke's. "Zeke... honey, we are so sorry..."

"W-we shouldn't have come here," Allanah said, burying her face in Zeke's shoulder.

He squeezed them tight. "It's okay... It's okay, you're here now, you're safe, you're alive." He sniffled loudly. "Oh Draso, you're *alive...*"

"Yeah, well," a voice said with a heavy Brooklyn accent. "Not for long."

ANGELS

Zeke immediately whipped about, blasting the air with elements, not caring who got in the way.

The magic didn't come out as strong as he expected though - he couldn't manage more than a few marbles of plasma. Leah had taken too much power. *Shit!*

A familiar rabbit stood in front of them, grinning. The rabbit who had attacked them in the café. Both Archángeli and Kyrie lay on the ground, knives in their throats and gurgling before vanishing in light motes. He flicked his finger at a marble of water. "For a mage, you're pretty pathetic," he said, his accent thick. He held out a pistol. "Now--"

A shield flashed in front of Zeke and his moms, and Leah dashed forward, staff in hand. She swung the staff around Zeke's lingering magic, gathering up marbles of ice, fire, and electricity, then charged the rabbit, slamming the elements into the rabbit's stomach. He coughed and gagged as Zeke's elements swirled all about him, sticking to his fur, setting it ablaze, soaking it, or freezing it, all while electricity shot through him. He doubled over and collapsed to the ground, shaking, trying to fight the lightning attacks back enough to smack the fire off his fur.

Leah stepped back and flipped her staff around, but then the rabbit vanished from view. Leah cursed. "It's that cloaker, Kitta."

"That means Wish Dusters." Zeke held his hands in front of his moms. "Stay close, and don't question what I'm about to say. The Wish Dusters will make it look like your worst fear has come true, but it's not real. Focus on me, and know that I'm safe."

"Good *god,*" Estelle breathed. Allanah closed her eyes tight.

Leah hunched down, staff in hand, glancing around with twitchy ears. *Got any more elemental magic in you?*

Zeke frowned, still protecting his parents. *You kind of drained me healing them.*

Then take some from me, Leah said. *The shield will hold, and we need firepower.*

Zeke chewed his lip, but he carefully reached out and "pulled."

Immediately he could feel his magic reserves ballooning.

Slowly! Leah shouted. *Slowly...* She wobbled slightly.

Zeke slowed down, but it didn't matter much anyway. He had the strength. He held his hands forward and called on the one power he hadn't really tried while training.

Wind.

He dragged up dirt, debris, and fire from the battle scene all around and whipped them into tornados, throwing them about. They responded beautifully, spinning gracefully around the area, searching.

Shrieks littered the air as Theophania and her Wishing Dust partner suddenly showed up from behind a piece of concrete and rebar, caught in one of Zeke's twisters, flickering in and out of view while Kitta tried keeping them

372

in her cloak. Zeke snarled and pushed, forcing the tornado as far away from them as he could, taking the Dusters with it. He smirked. No more magic fears.

But the tornados faded after that. He was spent. He leaned on his knees.

The cloaker, Kitta, shot out from behind another piece of rebar, heading straight for them.

Leah turned and swung the staff at the blue otter, but she ducked and kneed Leah in the stomach, knocking her down.

Zeke growled and dashed toward Kitta. She flipped over and charged, but Leah got back up and smashed her staff into Kitta's stomach, sending her flying. Kitta slid along the ground, and wouldn't get back up. Leah held her staff out. "Is that it? Did we get them all?"

A tiny drone appeared near Leah's head.

All the heat left Zeke's face. "Leah, drone, watch out!"

Leah shielded, but the drone exploded on her, sending her flying into Zeke, and then into his moms, knocking all of them down. Leah coughed.

Zeke sat up as best he could, trying to pull on his power, but he was totally drained between the tornados and Leah's syphoning. He glanced up.

The rabbit and the red wolf they had fought earlier, Caster, stood in front of them, both grinning. Caster held up his hand and half a dozen tiny drones hovered around him.

Zeke spread his arms in front of Leah and his moms. Leah tried to create a shield, but it fizzled and died. Zeke gritted his teeth.

Caster left the drones where they were and the two of them took a step back, a smirk on his face. "Sorry, just doing my duty. You understand."

Estelle pulled a sidearm out of her hip holster, but the weapon was black and smoldering and wouldn't fire. She winced and gripped Zeke and Allanah instead.

A wall of ice shot up in front of Zeke and the others, blocking the drones. An intense wind gathered the bombs up and threw them to the sky. They exploded harmlessly.

Zeke turned.

Jaden ran past, ice sword in hand. He rushed up and stabbed Caster in the gut. Caster drew in a sharp breath, eyes wide, blood dripping out of his mouth and soaking his shirt. "Don't touch my son," Jaden snarled. His ice sword vanished, leaving a gaping, bleeding wound, and Caster fell over, his eyes blank. Jaden turned on the rabbit. Embrik and Alexina walked in behind him, elements flying all about them.

The rabbit stepped back, panic in his eyes. "Who the hell are you people? I thought you were just Ackerson's play things."

"I am a *Guardian,*" Jaden said. "And we are the Defenders. Don't you forget it."

The rabbit's ears twitched, and he hesitated.

Then he vanished.

"Corbin, run!" Kitta called.

Zeke turned, but he couldn't see where Kitta was anymore. The otter had escaped too.

Jaden brought down his ice wall and ran to Zeke and his team. He pulled Zeke to his feet. "Are you okay?"

"Yeah... yeah." Zeke helped Leah up, then turned to help his moms. They looked bewildered, but Zeke didn't care. They were alive. He pulled them up and hugged them again.

Estelle broke the hug first. She eyed Jaden. "Someone want to explain what's going on? Why did you call Zeke your son?"

Jaden flicked his ears back, and opened his mouth, but didn't seem to have the words.

"It's... it's because he's my father, Mom," Zeke said.

Estelle and Allanah's jaws dropped.

Zeke pulled Jaden and Alexina forward. "These are my biological parents."

Allanah stared at them both, but then a slow smile crossed her face. "So I was right. They did find you. Didn't expect it to be this quick." She reached over and gripped Estelle's hand tightly.

Zeke tilted his head. "Wait, what?"

"It's…" Estelle glanced at Allanah. "I'm… not sure how to explain. Not sure if you'll even understand."

Leah flicked her ears back, and Embrik shifted uncomfortably.

Zeke lowered his gaze, frowning. "I might understand better than you think."

Estelle just smiled sadly and gripped Zeke's hand with her free one. Tears filled her eyes. "I think… maybe it'd be better to just tell you that we love you, and are so very proud of you." She turned to Jaden and Alexina. "Take care of him, okay?"

Jaden faltered. "I… I mean, of course, but--"

Both his moms held him close, though they wouldn't let each other go. Zeke's heart raced. He gripped them tight. Something was very, very wrong.

"We love you, honey," Estelle said. They broke the hug and stepped back.

Zeke reached for them.

A pistol fired twice, opening up two gaping wounds in his moms' foreheads. They fell with incredible speed into the dust.

Everything blurred. He vaguely noticed several sets of hands on his body, trying to hold him up. A faded, barely recognizable voice called his name, called his moms' names, called for anyone. The pinging sound of a shield forming zipped between his ears. The taste of dust and blood settled on his tongue, mingling so completely that he couldn't tell which was real. A sharp spice hit his nose, alarm, fear, anger, but he couldn't name the spice or recall where it came from. Somewhere in his head, a panic that wasn't his own fought for space, crying out, echoing against empty walls.

Then his atoms started pulling apart again, scrambling to whatever source stole his power. His knees grew weak, his face cold, his senses dull. Another voice called, masculine this time, begging, begging, begging.

Then he snapped into sharp focus. He was on the ground, sitting, held up by Embrik and Alexina. Alexina had her arms around him, holding him tight. Jaden kneeled near Leah, gripping her shoulders, while she sobbed loudly, tears streaming down her face. She huddled in on herself, heaving breaths while she cried.

Zeke couldn't make out the words she spoke, so he sought her mind.

I'm sorry, Leah said, over and over and over again. *I'm sorry, I'm sorry, I failed, I lost them, I couldn't save them, couldn't save ANYONE, I failed, I'm a terrible healer, a terrible Defender.*

You saved me, Zeke said without really thinking. Leah's crying slowed and she turned to Zeke. He tried to offer her a smile, but he didn't feel fully in control of his body. He passed the message telepathically. *You saved me. Over and over again.*

She blinked at him, tears still overflowing, mind blank. But he caught one phrase floating around her head, even if she didn't actively think it.

We saved each other.

Leah sniffled. "Zeke... I couldn't save them."

"It's okay," Jaden said, squeezing her again. "It's okay. Let them go."

"But I *failed.*"

Zeke glanced at his moms. Dead. Bullet wounds through the head, just like in their files. His chest and heart hurt, an old wound from when he had first learned about their deaths, aching like a phantom limb.

But there was also peace. A strange, unsettling peace, but peace nonetheless. He knew this would happen. And it almost seemed like they did

376

too, somehow. And he could be okay with that. In time. This… was okay. Not good, not right, but… acceptable, even if he couldn't articulate why.

But the files had been wrong. They had pinned Mage as his moms' killers. But they weren't.

So who was?

Zeke peered around, trying to focus, searching fallen pillars, broken glass, the burning sky.

Then the Bank of the State. He looked up.

Ackerson stood in a fourth-floor window, glaring down at them. Then he vanished into the building.

A red-hot rage built in Zeke's belly, incinerating all the other complex emotions. He leapt to his feet and ran for the entrance to the bank, pushing his injured foot out of his mind. He didn't care if the others followed.

Ackerson was *dead.*

He burst through the front door, shoved aside fallen desks, and ran for the emergency exit, then rushed up the stairs as fast as he could and landed on the spacious fourth floor. Ruined cubicles, broken computer equipment, and dust covered everything. He ran for the window, but didn't see anything. Leah came up behind him, and gripped his arm. Jaden and the others were right behind her.

"Someone *help!"* a desperate voice shouted. Zeke brushed it aside, but Leah's voice came screaming into his mind, along with the bright smell of food burning, declaring desperation. *We need to help them!* He growled, but followed the voice with Leah at his side. Shields popped up all around them. Zeke turned the corner.

A red quilar with deep blue eyes sat on the ground holding a silver fox in his hands, tears running down his face. The fox held a bloody jacket to her chest, eyes wide, gasping for air. The quilar glanced up at Zeke, panic gripping his face, then he held up a hand and a bolt of electricity flew at them. Zeke held his arms up, but it fizzled on the shield.

"Stop!" Leah said. "I can help, but not if you're shooting lightning at us."

"Sorry, sorry, *sorry,*" the quilar said, panic in his voice. "Help her, please, *please.*"

Leah kneeled down and began working on the wound.

The fox met Leah's eyes. "I'm sorry, I'm *sorry,* I tried to stop him, I really did--"

"Save your breath," Leah said, working her hands into the fox's wound.

"Carter!" The quilar pointed to Jaden.

Jaden held his hands up. "I'm not Carter."

The quilar blinked at him, then shook his head. "No... You... no..." He rocked back and forth.

"Stay still, please," Leah said.

The quilar stopped rocking, but his panicked breaths only got more frantic. "Are you Ackerson's?" he asked.

"Not anymore," Embrik said. He narrowed his eyes. "You are an Omnir, are you not?"

The quilar shrunk down. Jaden's ears flattened, but didn't say anything.

Leah perked her ears and she stared at the quilar. "Ryota."

The quilar stared at her. "H-how did...?"

"N-never mind," Leah said. She finished with the fox.

"Which way did Ackerson go?" Zeke asked.

The fox sat up, coughed, and glanced at Ryota. She turned to Zeke. "I don't know... I'm sorry..." she scrunched up her snout. "I truly am..."

Zeke flicked his ears back.

Jaden gripped Zeke's shoulder. "I think we lost him."

"*No,*" Zeke said. He dashed to the back of the room, toward another fire exit, but the door handle burned red. He kicked at the door instead, but it wouldn't budge. He turned back to the couple on the ground. "Where is he?"

The fox trembled. "I don't know... He ran and I don't know..."

Jaden walked up to him. "Zeke, the building is on the verge of collapse."

"*I don't care,*" Zeke said. "He killed my moms and he's going to pay for it!" He frantically searched the room. "There has to be another exit."

Jaden furrowed his brow. "Zeke."

"Don't start, Jaden!" Zeke said. "I lost them again. *I lost them, damnit, and someone's going to pay.*"

"Zeke..." Jaden walked slowly toward him. "Son... You... you sound like me."

Zeke paused and his breath hitched.

Jaden flicked his ears back. "Don't do that. Don't become the bitter person I did."

Zeke dropped his hands at his sides. He shut his eyes. Damn it. Damn it all...

Leah wrapped her arms around his torso and pressed her head to his chest. A small sob escaped him and he wrapped his arms around her. His throat burned. He had lost everything again.

"We should... we should bury your moms," Jaden said.

The fox let out a dark, choked sound.

Zeke stared at the ground, focusing on Leah's hug. Jaden walked up and wrapped an arm across Zeke's shoulder. Embrik gripped his other shoulder, and Alexina laid her head on his back.

Comfort. Comfort he didn't have when he had lost his moms the first time. Friends. Family.

He was wrong. He hadn't lost everything. "No... I don't think so."

Jaden raised an eyebrow. "Why not?"

379

"I…" Zeke shook his head. "I don't have the energy to explain." He rubbed his arms. Gotta… preserve the timeline. Or something. He couldn't articulate it. "I just want out of here."

Leah gave him a squeeze. "Trecheon mentioned something about a field hospital in DC. We should head there." She let Zeke go and turned to Ryota and the fox. "Come with us?"

The fox stared at her, slack jawed. "You said Trecheon."

Leah's ears flattened. "I did."

"He survives," the fox said.

Zeke's tail flicked. Survives. Not survived.

Leah chewed her lip. "Yes… he does."

She glanced at Ryota again, then back to Leah. "Tell him… tell him I'm sorry." She and Ryota stood. "We… can't come with you." She nodded to Leah. "Thank you. Take care."

"We need to go," Ryota said.

"Wait, Ryota," Leah said. He turned to her. She chewed her lip. Her thoughts ran through Zeke's mind. *Don't go with Theron. Don't let him use you. Seek Trecheon out, he'll take you back.* But she wouldn't say the words out loud.

Ryota narrowed his gaze. "Well?"

Leah slumped down, her tail drooping. "N-never mind."

Ryota flipped his ears back, stared at the fox for a moment, then took off. The fox apologized once more, then left with him.

Zeke watched them. Everything felt numb. He wandered to the window and got one more glimpse of his moms on the ground. They looked very much like the pictures from their files.

Leah gripped Zeke's hand. "Let's… let's go."

LETTING GO

Leah sat on a dirty mat in the field hospital. Large tents littered the broken ground, hastily erected. Injured civilians and soldiers lined up along the edges, waiting for treatment, or food, or water. The air smelled of antiseptic, mud, fire, and smoke, with a near unbearable stench of blood and burned flesh hovering over it all.

Leah had chosen a spot away from the main area, while the others searched for food and water. The medics ignored her as they rushed by. With all the burns, the broken bones, the crushed flesh, the amputations, and the screams, a small cat with a few bruises and a bloodied forehead wasn't a priority.

But her heart had been torn into a thousand pieces.

She had failed. She hadn't saved Zeke's parents, despite her promise. In her haste to save them, she had also lost Trecheon, Carter, and Neil. Trecheon was in here, somewhere, with no arms. Neil, buried in a tent, while he fought off PTSD so extreme, he'd try to kill himself. And Carter... who knew where Carter was. He had gone MIA. For all she knew, he was already dead.

She pulled her knees up to her face. She wasn't the Defender she pretended she was. She wasn't Guardian material like Jaden thought.

She was a failure.

Another vicious scream echoed through the hospital, from one of the tents a few meters away, followed by a yowl that was distinctively puma-like. Neil. Tears ran down her face. One of the medics, a white wolf with ice-blue eyes, walked out of the tent, shaking his head.

A quilar in dirty fatigues ran up to the medic, his white and blue quills barely recognizable under the layers of dirt and blood. A long ponytail ran down his back.

Leah perked her ears and lifted her head, staring.

Carter.

Carter talked quietly with the medic for a moment, then entered the tent that housed Neil.

Leah stared. Carter. He had made it to the field hospital. He was still alive. Despite the dirt and grime, he actually looked fine.

The Thought Factory ran at full speed. Leah hadn't been able to save all of Outlander but... maybe she could save one. She kept her gaze on the tent, resolving to talk to Carter the moment he came out.

Sloshing footsteps beat in the sloppy mud. Leah turned to see Zeke walking up to her. He sat next to her on the mat and pulled her into a sideways hug. She leaned on him, breathing deeply. "You have three broken toes."

"Thought I might," Zeke said.

Leah held out a hand. "May I?"

"Always."

Leah held his foot and healed the toes, then leaned back against him again. "...I'm sorry."

"Please don't be," Zeke said. "You did all you could. It was enough."

Leah's throat burned and tears filled her eyes again. She sniffled.

Zeke wrapped his other arm around her and held her tight. "Thank you. For giving me one more moment with them."

"But I still lost them."

"No, you didn't," Zeke said. "Ackerson took them." He breathed deeply. His presence smelled like strawberries for some reason. "And… I think I'm okay with that."

Leah glanced up at him.

"When I lost my parents the first time, I lost everything," Zeke said. "And I was alone to stew in guilt, and shame, and grief. But I've already mourned them. Yeah, we didn't know if we would succeed, so it hurts that we failed. But I have you now, and Jaden and Alexina and Embrik. People I can lean on." He paused. "And the more I think about it, the more I think I wouldn't have had that without them dying in the first place."

"What do you mean?" Leah asked.

"I reenlisted because of their deaths," Zeke said. "If I hadn't, I wouldn't have continued through flight school, or met Andre, or found some slim purpose to cling to." He shifted. "And if I hadn't had that… I wouldn't have met you. Or Embrik or Alexina, or… Jaden." He stared at the ground. "I hate to say it but I think it's okay my moms died. It's definitely not *good* but… it's okay. For what it's worth. I don't know what my life would have been like if they had lived but I'm at peace with what it's become."

Leah twitched an ear. "Like… everything happens for a reason?"

Zeke paused. "No, I don't think that's the right answer. There's plenty of terrible things that happen for no reason. More like… good things can still come from tragedies." He sighed. "I love my moms, and I'll never forget their chapter in my life. But I'm able to turn to a new chapter now." He squeezed Leah. "And it looks bright, even if it's bleak now. I just needed to let them go." He rubbed Leah's shoulder. "I know you said you were going to save my parents no matter what. In some way, I think you did. Just not the parents you thought you were saving."

Leah watched him a moment, then leaned into him and relaxed when Jaden walked up to them, ears pinned back.

"Alexina and Embrik are in the food line." Jaden nodded to Zeke. "How are you holding up?"

"Better than I thought I'd be," Zeke said.

Jaden scrunched his snout. "I am so sorry we couldn't save your moms. I know Alexina and I can't replace them, but if you need anything, we're here for you."

Zeke watched him a moment, then stood and drew Jaden into a big hug. Jaden hugged him back. They held each other for several moments, wordless, but sniffling. A deep, calming peace ran through Leah's mind from Zeke.

"Thank you," Zeke said. "I mean that."

"Anything for my... son," Jaden said.

Zeke pulled back, smiling, though crying. Jaden patted his shoulder then turned to Leah, arms out. "Leah--"

She didn't hesitate. She threw herself into Jaden's arms. His little wounds and poor energy resonated through her body, but all that was overshadowed by his warmth. He held her tight, then let go and gripped both their hands. "I'm sorry for how I treated you both. Neither of you deserved it. I let my grief get to me. I couldn't let go of my past. But I'm ready to let go now and see the family I have. I hope you'll both be a part of that."

Leah squeezed his hand and smiled. "I'd like that." Zeke nodded, grinning now. Jaden hugged them both.

As Leah wrapped an arm around Jaden's back, Neil's tent flap opened. The wolf medic walked out with Carter in tow. Urgency clawed at Leah's chest. She had to talk to him, had to stop him going MIA.

384

But she paused. *Sometimes good things come from tragedies.*

But only if you let go, a little voice in the Thought Factory said. She breathed deeply. She didn't know what would become of Carter but... maybe that was okay. It was okay to finally let go. After all, maybe Carter's disappearance was the link Trecheon needed to find Matt. And Trecheon had told her he came out okay. Tragedy didn't always mean the end of life. Sometimes it meant turning to a new chapter, for better or worse.

Carter nodded to the medic, then vanished into the crowd. And Leah let him go.

"Pardon me," a voice said.

Leah broke the hug and turned.

A dark-skinned human with thick black hair, a well-trimmed beard, and a crisp uniform decorated with officer bars stood before them, a serious look on their face.

Jaden eyed them. "Can I help you?"

"I hope so," the human said. "Commander Asher Reddy, head of black ops. They/them pronouns, please." They lowered their gaze. "I'm sure you're loathe to hear this but I know you're a part of Bob Ackerson's teams."

"Not by choice," Jaden said, raising his hands.

"I know," Commander Reddy said. "Not our choice either. However, I'd like to actually give you a choice now."

Zeke narrowed his gaze. "Where are you going with this?"

Commander Reddy smirked. "How'd you like to finally end this war?"

PROPOSAL

Jaden and his team followed a young private, a white wolf with ice-blue eyes, down a long, dimly lit hallway. The kind of hallway they lead war prisoners down to intimidate them before interrogation. Jaden ran a finger down his Defender pendant. If that's what Commander Reddy had planned for them, they had another thing coming.

It had been one week since the Commander picked them up in the DC field hospital. They'd been clothed, fed, and housed, with the freedom to leave at any point. Jaden had to admit – it was tempting to leave. But when the Commander mentioned the Desert Wall, the Cloak's words floated back through Jaden's mind. *We'll see each other soon, facing the Desert Wall.*

So Jaden stayed. And so did his team. The rest was nice, though he could sense the collective anxiety from his team as the meet-up date approached.

But not now. The anxiety had faded in favor of confidence, Jaden decided. He glanced back.

Embrik and Alexina walked to his left, and Leah and Zeke on his right. Heads held high. Faces stoic. Magic at the ready, buzzing in the air, eager to let loose at a moment's notice.

They were ready.

"In here, please," the wolf private said, and he opened the doors to a dark briefing room with short bleachers.

And they weren't alone.

"Ethos!" Leah exclaimed. "Draso's horns, you're all here!"

The three doe looked up in surprise. Pathos immediately stood and ran down the bleachers, throwing herself at Leah, hugging her tight. Leah hugged her back. Pathos stepped back. "Thank Draso you survived DC. We saw the whole thing on the news and…" she choked.

"It's fine, we're okay," Leah said.

Angus stood now, his wingtips hitting the edges of the bleachers. "Zeke, were you able to save your moms?"

Zeke flicked his ears back. "No."

Ethos' hunched down. "I'm sorry."

"It's… I'm okay," Zeke said, rubbing the back of his head. "At least I got to say a proper goodbye this time."

Logos smiled sadly. "It's the best you can hope for."

"Defenders save us," someone said, breathless. "Do I spy a Golden Guardian?"

Jaden turned. A black jaguar and a white stoat with faint purple in their fur stood on the far end of the bleachers, staring at Jaden, jaws slack.

Both wore tarnished Defender pendants around their necks.

Jaden faced them, studying their pendants. "Wha… who are you?"

Both of them swept their fists across their chests in a traditional Defender salute. "Chadwick Moonbeam, and Jordan Quicktail at your service, Guardian," the leopard said. "I'm Chadwick, this is Jordan." He stared at Jaden

387

like he was watching a ghost. "Forgive me but… we never thought we'd see a Defender again, let alone a Guardian."

Jaden raised an eyebrow. "Explain."

"We're colony survivors," the stoat said. He twitched his tail. "Well, 'refugees' is the better term we've learned, and we're many, many generations removed but…"

Leah stared. "Are you saying you're descendants from the *original* refugees? Like, from the Great Colonization?"

"We are," Chadwick said. "It's a long story, but our family were engineers on one of the refugee ships and didn't live in cryo like the others. We got to keep our Gems because of that. And our traditions."

"Good Draso," Jaden said. "How many generations have you been passing on Gems?"

"Countless," Jordan said. He frowned. "We've been holding on to a hope that we'd see a Zyearthling again for that long too. And maybe finally get home."

Jaden scrunched his snout. He glanced at Leah. She smiled encouragingly at him and nodded. He paused a moment, then turned to Chadwick and Jordan. "I'm happy to get you home, as soon as I'm able."

"Greetings, soldiers," Commander Reddy said, walking into the room. The Black Cloak walked in with them. Jaden tensed up. The Cloak had green eyes again. He winked at Jaden, then took a seat on the bleachers.

Commander Reddy stacked a handful of papers on a podium. "If everyone can take a seat, we can finally discuss what's been going on. Some of this is bound to be confusing, so please feel free to ask questions as we go along. We all need to be on the same page." Everyone sat. The Commander cleared their throat. "First, I'd like to extend my sincerest apologies for what you all got stuck with working for Ackerson."

Jaden raised an eyebrow. "Apologies, Commander?"

"Yes," the Commander said. "Ackerson acted outside his station. He hurt and killed not only friends of the US, but his own charges, because he fell to corruption and greed." They shook their head. "Like a lot people in this military unfortunately. There's very little we can do to offer compensation for the damage he inflicted on his teams. He purposefully recruited people who had little to no connections. Easier to manipulate."

"If I may ask, Commander," Chadwick said. "What's being done about Ackerson? Will he face justice? My squad is all either dead or went traitor and we want retribution."

"That remains to be seen, unfortunately," the Commander said. "But we're doing everything in our power to make sure he pays for his actions." They tapped the podium. "However, with corruption running rampant, I can't promise anything, other than we will try."

"A promise to try is a good start," Embrik said.

The Commander nodded. "Despite Ackerson's unconventional means of recruiting, he knew how to pick them. Which is why we've gathered all we could for this mission." They sighed. "You represent all the surviving members of his teams. Mage is the only team fully intact. Half of Outlander's members are either MIA or KIA and the others are too injured to fight. Chaos... well, all of them are currently MIA, but we believe many are working for Ackerson willingly and in secret." They pointed to Chadwick and Jordan. "Chadwick and Jordan represent the surviving members of Guardian." Then they pointed to the doe and Angus. "And Hunt is nearly intact, except for Ari... and Ronan."

Angus growled under his breath.

The Commander flipped a page. "We think it's significant that Ronan is missing. Because we believe he's connected to the Desert Wall."

Angus perked an eyebrow. "My *brother?* How?"

389

"You all likely know that the Desert Wall is the one thing keeping us from engaging our enemies in the east and recovering the hydrogen scientists needed to end this energy crisis," the Commander said. "Saudi's government is still uncooperative, and what little intel we can gather, their citizens are paying a deep price for that at the hands of their own military. The Desert Wall stalled our efforts to end this war. It came out of nowhere, and while both China's and North Korea's governments claim responsibility for it, everything we know about them suggests this is impossible. No known technology anywhere on Earth can create such a powerful, consistent force field." They lifted their chin. "So we explored unconventional means." They pressed their lips together. "Magic."

Jaden crossed his arms. "You can't expect me to believe that a world superpower decided *magic* was the problem they were facing the whole time. Half your government doesn't even believe in proven science."

The Commander sighed. "I'll admit, I'm with you there. Which is why we haven't brought it to the higherups. It stops with me. In a way, it's a good thing Ackerson kept his files under wraps, or it might have been found out by a skeptic and dismissed and we'd be back at square one."

"I don't see how this has to do with Ronan," Angus said. "Even with his magic, he doesn't have that kind of power."

"No one does," Jaden said. "You'd have to have several platoons of high-level mages rotating round the clock for that kind of shield, and it'd never be perfect. You'd be left with holes."

"I'm not talking about 'conventional' magic," Commander Reddy said. "In whatever way magic can be 'conventional.' From what I gathered from Ackerson's files, he believed the Desert Wall was the work of a creature called a 'summon.'"

The whole room grew silent. Jaden turned to Leah.

Leah flicked her ears back. "I did a five-year research study on summons, and I don't know of any in our history with that kind of power."

Alexina shifted. "I do."

Jaden turned to her.

Alexina lowered her head. "But the Four Sisters sealed her, according to the Book of Summons."

Leah's eyes grew wide. "You can't mean..."

The Cloak folded his arms. "Three of the Sisters have cracked," he said. "The Seal is nothing but dust."

Embrik's ears twitched. "Oh, Draso…" Alexina brought her hands to her snout.

Zeke scrunched his face. "Is this the universe-destroying summon you told me was exaggerated?"

"It is," the Cloak said. "Still exaggerated, but honestly not by much."

Zeke narrowed his gaze. "You're not filling me with hope here."

"So what is this universe-destroying summon?" Jaden asked.

"Not what," Embrik said. "Who. He speaks of Judgement, the first Basilea of the Athánatos. And the creator of the original Shadow Cast. She turned herself into a summon when the Four Sisters and the Phonar fought her. It was her only way to overpower them. At least, that is what we have gathered from the holes in the Book of Summons."

A hush fell over the room.

"So let me get this straight," Angus said. "You think my pathetic brother has somehow picked up the most powerful summon this universe has ever known and is using it to block your way into the east to take down your enemies."

Commander Reddy shrugged. "That's the gist of it."

"And you have all of us here," Angus said. "Because we're all mages, and your idea is fight fire with fire."

"Unless you have a better idea," the Commander said. "But at this point, we've run out of options."

Ethos snorted. "And you think that because we're mages, we have any hope of beating this monster."

"We do," Alexina said. She waved her hand and Kyrie appeared overhead. "The Order of Phonar were created to fight Judgement and subdue her should she escape again." Her tail twitched. "But there are eight Phonar, and we have only two. I do not know how effective they will be alone."

"We have more than two," the Cloak said. He held out his hands and four more Phonar appeared – Excelsis, Deo, Lumen, and Sémini. Excelsis spread his wings, sending purple embers into the air, and Deo followed suit, mixing her white flames with his purple ones. Lumen, the kori bustard, rustled his feathers, throwing tiny stones into the air, and Sémini, the falcon, wiggled her flight feathers and spun rivers around them all.

Jaden stared in awe.

"Natassa and Melaina's summons," the Cloak said. "Borrowed with permission, using my privilege as the Cloak." He shifted. "Ouranos is not currently in a state where he can willingly lend me Jústi and Pax. We'll have to make do with what we have."

Alexina held a hand out to the summons. Excelsis butt his head against her palm. She sniffled. "Sisters alive... It is almost like being with my family again."

"Well then," Commander Reddy said. "Can I assume I have at least one volunteer?"

"I volunteer," Leah said, standing.

"Where Leah goes, I go," Zeke said, also standing. He called Archángeli, who joined the other Phonar.

Ethos, Pathos, and Logos followed next. "For our lost sister," Ethos said.

"For Ari," Angus said, standing. "And to get at Ronan, the bastard."

392

"For the Defenders," Chadwick said. Jordan nodded and stood too.

"For Athánatos," Embrik said.

"And to rid the world of Judgement, once and for all," Alexina added. The two stood as one.

Jaden stood last, giving a sweeping Defender salute. "Guardian Azure at your service, Commander."

Commander Reddy smiled. "Excellent." They tapped the stack of papers. "I'm sure none of you want to continue using Ackerson's code names, so I'll give you the option to pick something new for communication purposes."

"I vote Defender," Zeke said.

Jaden turned to him. Zeke smiled. Jaden gripped his shoulder. "I second this."

"I third it," Angus said with a grin.

"It's a good name," Chadwick said.

"Defender it is," Commander Reddy said. They stacked up their papers. "Let's go take down the Wall."

INVICTUS

Jaden and his squad stood on the deck of a massive battleship, the *USS Invictus,* awaiting orders. They led a squadron of ships over the open seas and were nearly to their destination – the invisible, magical Desert Wall, which stalled the end of the war.

A wall Jaden's team was expected to take down. A tall order. Jaden wasn't sure they could do it, even with all their magic at hand. But they had to try something. They were Defenders. It was their job.

At their backs, a battalion of Marines stood ready to fight on the ground once the Wall came down. It was Jaden's job to make sure they could do their jobs as safely as possible.

He was once again, a full Guardian. His Defender pendant gleaned with pride. And, in some ways, Dyne's pride. He chanced a glance at Leah to his right. She stood proud and tall, a huge change from the feline she was when he first met her. His chest swelled. He was looking forward to training her more formally. She'd respond beautifully.

"Officer on deck!" someone shouted. Jaden's squad whipped about face and as one, everyone gave a sharp salute.

Commander Reddy walked out, having traded their crisp dress uniform for desert battle fatigues. "At ease, Marines. I'm Commander Reddy. I use they/them pronouns. The first one of you to misgender me or make fun of my pronouns will be tossed overboard, and I am *not* joking. Don't test me." They walked in front of Jaden, then turned and faced the Marines. "As I'm sure you're all aware, we're headed to the Desert Wall. I've heard people say this is a suicide mission. After all, we haven't been able to scratch it since this damn war started. But we have a secret weapon this time." They waved to Jaden's squad. "These soldiers have weapons beyond your wildest imaginations. And you lucky sons of bitches get to witness that firsthand."

The Marines glanced at each other, muttering quietly.

Commander Reddy continued. "We intend to use these soldiers and their weapons to attack at the best location possible to infiltrate enemy territory. And draw out the enemy creating the wall in the first place." The Commander rested their hands behind their back. "I'm going to emphasize what your briefings said. What you witness here, what you see these soldiers doing, is absolutely top secret. If there is even the slightest belief that you've shared this confidential information, there will be no due process. You will disappear. Full stop. That's how deep this goes. Do I make myself clear, Marines?"

"Yes, Commander!" the Marines echoed.

Except one up front. He crossed his arms and narrowed his gaze at Jaden.

"Problem, Goodwin?" Commander Reddy asked.

"I'm counting, Commander," he said.

"Wow, the man can *count,*" a soldier said next to him. "Guess you did pass second grade after all." Several Marines chuckled.

Commander Reddy snorted. "Mendoza, drop and give me fifteen for disrespecting your fellow solider."

395

"Worth it," Mendoza said, and he dropped to the deck.

"Can you tell me *what* you're counting, Goodwin?" the Commander asked.

"Your miracle squad," Goodwin said. "There's only twelve soldiers here."

"There a problem with that?"

"With all due respect, Commander," Goodwin said. "We've been throwing everything short of nukes at the Desert Wall. What makes you think twelve fuzzies are going to be able to do what the entire Navy has failed at?"

The Commander glared. "You will not use slurs in my presence. Show these soldiers some respect, or you can spend the rest of this trip in the brig."

"Respect has to be *earned,* Commander," Goodwin said, glaring at Jaden and his team. "And no fuzzy's ever going to earn that from me."

The Commander lowered their gaze and took a step forward.

Jaden walked up next to them. "Commander, permission to hit this man with a snowball should he disrespect my team again."

The Commander turned. They smiled. "Permission granted."

Goodwin's whole platoon laughed now. "A *snowball?* Where the hell you gonna get a snowball on the open seas in July, fuzzy?"

The Commander shrugged. "Open fire, Guardian Azure."

Goodwin laughed even louder. And then a snowball smacked him in the face. He stumbled back and wiped his face, bewildered.

Jaden tossed a snowball up and down. "Want another?"

Goodwin growled. "How the hell did you do that?"

Jaden formed two more snowballs and juggled them. "Come here and find out."

Goodwin gritted his teeth and rushed Jaden.

Jaden slammed a foot to the ground and sharp ice spikes formed in front of him. Goodwin stopped short and fell over. Jaden formed an icicle that ran right up between Goodwin's eyes, millimeters from his skin. Jaden kneeled beside him. "Call me fuzzy again."

Goodwin held his hands up. "I-I'm good. I apologize."

"That's what I thought."

Goodwin scrambled to his feet and ran back to his platoon. No one laughed anymore. Mendoza let out a low whistle.

Jaden took a step back.

The Commander nodded to Jaden's team. "Defenders, care to demonstrate?"

One by one, the team showed off their magic. Embrik with fireballs all around, Zeke and Alexina with elemental spheres orbiting their heads, Leah with her staff ablaze with Zeke's magic, Angus, hovering in place with telekinesis, and the doe each showing off their item-based magic with massive swords and firearms. In a burst of color and smells, the summons came next – the six Phonar, flying about, elements fluttering off their long tails. The two gryfons, Rashard and Kjorn, shaking the air with lion roars and magic. Magna, letting out a dark whinny, and Lysander, silent, but threatening with those energy orbs.

And in a final display of power, they all vanished – courtesy of Chadwick and Jordan, both cloakers. The battalion let out a collective gasp, then Chadwick and Jordan brought them all back. Several Marines whooped and hollered, throwing their fists in the air, and more than one whistled.

"Marines," Commander Reddy said. "You see before you, a circle of mages. They have power we can only dream of. And if any of you speak a word of this to *anyone,* the US military will personally erase your family from history. This is too delicate to get out. Am I clear?"

"Yes, Commander!" the Marines shouted.

"We have reason to believe that the Desert Wall isn't the result of some unknown technology, but of magic like these soldiers have," Commander

397

Ready said. "The best way to fight magic is with magic of our own." The Commander stood tall. "These are the Defenders. They will take out the wall, lure in the source of its power, and engage it. Our job is to infiltrate enemy territory when they succeed. You have your assignments. Our signal will be a dragon made of fire in the sky to give the all clear. Then you'll move to your transports. Raven hovercrafts and Salamander assault ships are ready and waiting." They grinned. "So for now, sit tight and enjoy the fireworks." They turned to Jaden. "Guardian Azure, you have the floor."

Jaden nodded. "Defenders, mount up!"

Rashard walked over the Jaden and pressed his forehead against him. Jaden stroked his feathers, then he, Embrik, and Alexina climbed on his back. The rest of the group followed suit. The three doe climbed on Kjorn's back and Angus mounted Magna. The six Phonar grew in size, large enough for one passenger each. Chadwick and Jordan careful got on Lumen and Sémini's backs. Zeke turned to Archángeli, who nodded, then climbed on their back. Leah climbed on Kyrie's.

The Black Cloak stepped forward and held his hands out to Excelsis and Deo. The pair flew into the air, trailing their fire, then smashed into the Cloak's chest, exploding feathers into the air. The feathers swirled around the Cloak's back, forming two wings, one black and one white. Feathers formed around the Cloak's eyes, sticking out of the holes in his mask. He turned to Jaden and nodded.

The Commander's communicator crackled. *"Desert Wall spotted, Commander."* In the distance, several rows of opposing battleships all waving the Saudi Arabia flag lined the shallow waters along the undisturbed Yeman shore. Behind them, the air shimmered with strange reflections. The Desert Wall.

"I can feel her," Zeke said quietly.

398

Jaden's heart pumped adrenaline through his veins, his body and mind reverting to old combat training. He gripped the feathers on Rashard's neck.

"I feel her too," Alexina said. "That is definitely Judgement. And she knows we are here."

"Alexina," Zeke said. "I saw an image of an angry Athánatos with four women behind her when you bound me. Was that Judgement?"

Alexina nodded. "It was, which is probably why you feel her now."

Jaden pressed his lips together. "Hopefully we have enough strength to take her down."

Alexina didn't respond.

The Commander nodded. "Commence Operation Purgatory."

"Rise up, Defenders!" Jaden called. Chadwick and Jordan cloaked the team and they took to the sky as high as they could go.

The *Invictus* fired a volley of missiles at the encroaching enemy ships, while several Apache helicopters took to the sky. The enemy responded with anti-aircraft artillery, peppering the sky with smoke and fire.

Jaden clung to Rashard's feathers, feeling Alexina and Embrik behind them. For the magic to truly be effective, Chadwick and Jordan would have to drop the cloak. Which meant they got one shot. One chance to take down the Wall and fly past the battleships before the inevitable attack from anti-aircraft artillery.

Better make it count.

They flew over the intense sounds of the battle, weaving around pockets of smoke and debris, staying as high as they could. When they were about fifty meters from the Wall, Jaden called out.

"Magic at the ready!" he shouted. "Chadwick, Jordan, drop the cloak! Fire at will!"

The cloak dropped just as a barrage of magic flew through the air and slammed into the Wall. Every element imaginable – streams of fire, bolts of lightning, ice and water swirling together, massive boulders, swaths of earth, and massive tornados pulling it all together. It was power like Jaden had never seen, even as a Golden Guardian.

It'd be enough. It *had* to be. Their lives depended on it. Thousands of lives did.

The Wall shimmered and shook, wobbling like ripples on water, but it stubbornly stayed firm.

Jaden snarled. He held out his hands and swirled ice around the entire mass of magic. "Zeke, Alexina, help me direct it!" Zeke held out his hands and ribbons of magic flew from them, mixing with the magic tornados. Alexina skillfully twirled her hands about, concentrating the elements.

Then the Wall cracked and shattered, littering pieces all over the shore, like a massive shield from a Lexi Gem.

But when it shattered, it no longer showed peaceful white beaches, rocky shores, and seaside towns, but smoldering sand and pillars of smoke. The remains of a town sent small plumes of fire and ash into the air. The shore was dotted with bodies, both human and zyfaunos.

Nothing moved.

Leah gasped.

Alexina gripped Jaden. "Sisters save us… what happened?"

"Yemen resisted," Jaden said. "And their people paid the price."

"And Judgement concealed the damage," Embrik said. "Or caused it in the first place."

"I feel her more strongly than ever now," Alexina said. "Judgement is here." She pressed her forehead to Jaden's back. "And her summoner."

Kjorn keened into the air, and dove down to a crater alongside the beach. The other summons responded to his call and followed suit. Their target, Jaden assumed. As they neared the ground, Jaden spotted a figure standing in the middle of the crater.

But it wasn't Judgement.

It was Ronan.

CHAPTER 50

JUDGEMENT

A hot anger built in Zeke's belly seeing Ronan. The bat stood there, arms crossed, almost looking bored, in the middle of a dusty crater. One Judgement created no doubt. He didn't even react when the group landed.

Angus landed first and slid off Magna's back. He marched up to his brother. "Ronan, what the hell are you doing?"

Ronan lifted his chin. "Avenging Vanguard. And Mom and Dad. Like you should be doing."

Zeke held tight to Archángeli, trying to keep his anger under control.

Jaden gripped Rashard's feathers. "I'm sorry we couldn't save them Ronan, but I promise you, we did all you could."

"Don't give me that wind and vapor," Ronan said. "You save people who could be *used*. People who could be manipulated to work dead-end jobs as slave labor for you, wasting the potential they had on their home planets, believing the Defenders were Zepher-sent saviors. My brother praises you because he's a damn sheep."

Jaden twitched an ear. "Ronan, that's--"

"And then what?" Ronan continued. "You have one incident with a literal stone-age tribe on an underdeveloped planet and you just shut down. Disappear from the collective. Vanish without a trace, refusing to even *pretend* to help anymore. You freak out and give up because you lost *two damn soldiers.* You're the most powerful army in the known universe, and that stopped you. You have the resources to make sure no one ever started a war again. You could prevent *all* wars. That's your *job*. Your moral obligation!"

Zeke frowned, his tail flicking back and forth, and he turned to Jaden.

Jaden furrowed his brow. "Alright, I agree with you. The Defenders choosing to isolate and run after the Sol Genocide was wrong."

"So you *admit it*--"

"However," Jaden said, gripping Rashard's feathers even tighter. "You're wrong about our moral obligation. You can't prevent all wars without controlling all people. That's tyranny. Being powerful means we have an obligation to *not* get involved in every war across the universe. We have the potential to be used, or cause more damage. Our job is to mitigate the damage wars leave behind and rescue war victims, regardless of what side they're on, because death and injury doesn't know sides. We're *Defenders,* Ronan. We *defend."*

Ronan snarled, fire in his eyes. "Defend against this."

Jaden held his hands out. "Shields up!" He, Leah, Chadwick, and Jordan shielded their teams in a wave of green and purple. Zeke held his arms up, but kept his eye on Ronan.

Ronan blasted the air with a sonic boom, but the shields held.

"Defenders, summons, fan out and fire at will!" Jaden shouted. He spread his arms and called a wave of snow and ice to his fingertips and shoved it toward Ronan. Embrik matched his strength with a wave of fire, and Alexina fired volley after volley of elements, bathing Ronan in a swirl of elemental plasma. The summons roared, whinnied, and squawked, matching the strength of their riders, setting the air ablaze with power.

Zeke drew on as much energy as he could and threw it forward. No ineffective marbles of magic this time. Streams of elements flowed from his body, mixing with his teammate's elements, enveloping Ronan. The magic fought for space, colliding in the air in hisses of steam, explosions of light and color, and crashing stone and earth, making everything taste metallic and hot, singeing Zeke's nose.

This had to get him. End it quick, stop him before he ever called on Judgement, just--

Another sonic boom echoed through the air and a shockwave blasted the magic back at them, cracking their shields. The wave slammed into Archángeli, knocking them clean out of the sky. Zeke crashed to the ground, kicking up dust, sending waves of fire and pain through his body. Leah crashed near him, her pain ripping through his mind and nose in a vicious scent of cayenne and peppers.

Jaden, Alexina, and Embrik flew clean off Rashard, vanishing into the lingering magic. Ethos, Pathos, and Logos managed to hold on just long enough for Kjorn to land, but they got faces full of magic and dust. Chadwick and Jordan landed relatively safely, and ran for the respective teams.

Angus took the brunt of the hit though. The very air rippled as the wave hit him. He shrieked and flew off Magna, crashing along the ground until he smashed into a rock and stopped moving. Ethos, Pathos, and Logos ran for him, screaming his name.

Ronan turned to the main group, flaring his wings in anger. His left wing had been fully healed, but glitched even more out of time than it had before. His fur and skin had a dozen injuries though, likely from the magic barrage. He hovered a few inches off the ground, no doubt from his telekinetic power. A faint white glow surrounded him. "You won't *win.*"

The Cloak landed near Zeke, the only one unscathed. "Rashard, Kjorn, no hesitation this time. Go!"

Rashard and Kjorn both roared and dashed for Ronan, elements flying. Ronan raised both hands now and discharged another shockwave, louder than before. Zeke winced and Leah pulled her ears down over her head. The gryfons took Ronan's attack head on and flew back, helpless. They crashed to the dirt and vanished in a spray of colorful motes.

The Cloak cursed.

Zeke shook with adrenaline, his mind a muddied mess of fear and Leah's racing thoughts, moving so fast he couldn't pin one down.

Ronan lifted his head. "We're done here. She can finish you off." He held out a hand. A dank smell of spilled ink and rotting flesh filled the air, as motes of light formed behind the bat and manifested into a solid figure. Behind him stood a massive Athánatos summon – Judgement.

The same Athánatos queen Zeke had seen in his head when he had been bound to his jewels.

She stood three times his size, easily five meters or more, with jet black fur, burnt orange- and cream-colored streaks above her brows, angry yellow eyes, and massive, black wings, dripping inky blobs down the wing shapes. The ink reminded Zeke strongly of the faint images of Shadow Cast he had seen in his head. She and Ronan crossed their arms at the same time, almost like they were one being.

Zeke cursed. Like Ronan was getting power from Judgement. No wonder he was so strong.

Jaden immerged from the fading magic and settling dust and blasted ice at Ronan.

Ronan stepped back and Judgement's massive form moved in front of him, blocking the attack. Jaden's splat of ice decorated her shin, then absorbed into her body. He faltered, ears pinned back. She held out her hands and waved her wings. Thick blobs of black rained down on them, carrying her deep, genderless voice with them.

Judgement is at hand.

Jaden snarled. "Alexina!"

Alexina strode forward, held out her hands, and spoke in the Athánatos language. Archángeli translated in Zeke's head.

"I call on the Order of the Phonar!"

The Cloak released Excelsis and Deo and together with Kyrie, Archángeli, Sémini and Lumen, the six Phonar stood in formation in front of Judgement, plumes of their magic flying around them. The magic dissipated, showing the Phonar standing tall in their zyfaunos forms. Excelsis and Deo took point, spewing purple and white fire into the air. Embers scattered in the air.

We meet again, Judgement, Excelsis said.

Judgement raised an eyebrow. *You still have the Phonar!* she said, dripping black from her wings. *I would have thought your Basileus would have killed one of you by now and broken the vow.* She shook her head. *A shame you have only six of the nine needed.*

Alexina raised an eyebrow. "Nine?"

You wish to fight, Judgement said, ignoring Alexina. *Then we shall fight.* She manifested a large knife in her hand and thrust it toward the ground.

"Shields up!" Jaden shouted. "Get back, *now!*"

Zeke pulled Leah away and dove left just as the massive knife pierced the earth. Leah shielded them both, then threw another shield over the doe and Angus. Jaden managed to shield his team and Chadwick and Jordan.

Then everyone vanished. Chadwick and Jordan had cloaked them.

All except the Phonar. They spread their wings and took to the air. Purple streams of fire twisted with white, ice and water wrapped around each other in dancing lights from the overhead sun, and massive boulders littered the air, all caught up in invisible, swirling tornados, before crashing into Judgement.

She batted at them like annoying flies. The magic didn't seem to do much damage, but she was at least distracted.

Zeke waved his hands around. *Leah?*

Here. Leah gripped his hand and they ran to Magna. Zeke could hear Leah drop to the ground near her. The alicorn summon sniffed the ground apparently trying to find Angus. Leah's disembodied voice hit Zeke's ears. "Angus? Can you hear me? Are you okay?"

Angus groaned.

Someone gripped Zeke's shoulder. "It's Jordan. I'm the one cloaking you all, but I assume Leah needs to see to heal Angus."

"Please," Leah said.

"Then the rest of you will have to protect Leah while she heals him," Jordan said. "I'll admit, it'll be hard to hide you while you're running around. I can still shield though."

"Then don't bother shielding us," Zeke said. "We need to see each other to coordinate anyway. Concentrate a shield on Leah and Angus." He glanced around. Cloaking must be useful at times, but it definitely wasn't now. "Ethos? Pathos? Logos? You around?"

"We are," Ethos said, her voice shaking. "We're ready to help."

Jordan nodded. "Let's do this." He dropped the cloak.

Zeke winced. Angus looked terrible. Both wings ripped, his leg twisted badly, and blood soaking the fur on his head. But he was breathing.

Leah got to work. *Gonna need you to buy me some time, Zeke!*

On it! Zeke called. He stood. "Jaden, Alexina, Embrik, keep Judgement occupied!"

Jaden answered with a blast of ice to the massive summon. She brushed it off, but turned her attention to him. But that wouldn't hold for long. All this magic use was going to catch up to them. Zeke already felt drained, and he couldn't take anything from Leah. She needed every ounce for Angus.

"Zeke," Pathos said. "We may have a plan to destroy the summon's knife, but we need to get it out of the ground. Help Jaden and the others distract her."

"I'll do what I can." He called on his elements and aimed them at Judgement's midsection, but he couldn't get much more than a few elemental marbles again. Shit!

Judgement stomped the ground near Jaden. Alexina screamed.

Zeke's heart pumped. *No.* Not another parent. "Hey!" he waved a hand at Judgement. She turned away from Jaden and the others. Zeke pulled at every atom of magic he could muster.

You are stronger with the proper motivation.

"Don't you dare hurt my family!" He manifested a large boulder and threw it at Judgement. It slammed into her stomach, making her double over.

Zeke scanned the air for his summon. *Archángeli!*

Here, Prínkipas!

Judgement stood straight and shook herself. She pulled her knife out of the ground, glaring. *Who is this fly to attack me?* she called.

"Look closely!" Zeke snarled. "I'm a Prínkipas of Athánatos, you murderous bitch, and I am sick and tired of you hurting my family." He spread his arms. "Come at me!"

Judgement tilted her head, curious, judging. *A Prínkipas? With white in the quills? Have the Athánatos embraced the sins of the outside world and bred with mainlanders?* She snorted. *The royalty have fallen below their station.*

Zeke snarled. Elements flew off his person in his rage. "My parents, all of them, have sacrificed everything for me. Don't you dare talk about them like that."

408

Jaden caught the corner of Zeke's eye. He held Alexina, safe. Embrik stood by his side. Then the three of them vanished. Chadwick cloaking them no doubt.

Little rat, Judgement said. *I will show you the Judgement of Athánatos royalty!* She brought her blade down.

Zeke stood his ground. This was their chance. *Archángeli!*

Archángeli swooped in and snatched Zeke out from under the blade. Magna whinnied and slammed her hooves on the ground, bringing up several massive slabs of rock, pinning the knife between them just before it hit the ground. Judgement roared and tried pulling it free, but Magna snorted and charged, horn out. She pierced Judgement's hand, forcing the summon to let go of the knife. Judgement cried out in pain, throwing Magna to the side, though the alicorn caught herself in midair and flew safely to the ground.

The three does rushed forward now. "Zeke, I need your help!" Pathos called.

Archángeli flew Zeke near the doe. "What are you doing?"

"My wish says I can only degrade items I can lift," Pathos said. "But the wish doesn't say I can't have help lifting it."

Zeke smirked. "Brilliant." They ran for the knife's handle, and with all of them pushing as one, they "lifted" it. Pathos shouted, her eye glowing with magic.

Then the knife shrank to the size of her hand. She passed it to Logos, who stared wide eyed at it. "This is brimming with magic."

"Then let's use it!" Ethos said. She grabbed Logos' hand and ran for Judgement. Zeke and Pathos followed behind. Ethos ripped the knife from Logos' hand, held it over her head, and thrust it toward Judgement's shin, her magic shining. The knife exploded into a massive sword and pierced through the summon's fur and skin, spilling purple motes and black blood, sending shocks of violet magic up Judgement's leg. Judgement wailed and kicked.

Logos and Pathos got out of the way, and Archángeli snatched Zeke up again, but Ethos took the full brunt of it, sending her flying.

Zeke cried out. "Ethos!"

Lysander appeared and snatched Ethos out of the air, holding her to his chest and rolling to protect them both from the impact. Zeke turned.

Angus stood next to Leah, fully healed, an angry scowl on his face.

Judgement roared, shaking the air around her. *You flies will not end me!* She shook her wings, dropping dozens of little blobs to the ground. Zeke stared in disgust, but then the blobs started... glowing. Three little blue lights on each one. Then they moved – each one bulged out, and broke apart, almost in a grin. They kind of look liked--

"Shadow Cast!" Alexina shouted, still hidden behind a cloak. "Everyone back, they cannot be killed!"

But Leah snarled and pulled out her staff. *Zeke, give me a blast of lightning, and hit them with all the fire you've got!*

Zeke growled. "Get me to her, Archángeli!" The summon flew him low to the ground and he threw lightning on Leah's staff. She charged one Shadow Cast and pinned it down with electricity. The lightning rushed through the Cast's body and blew it apart, spraying ink all over Leah's outfit.

Zeke pumped the air. "Hell yeah!" He blasted a wave of fire over the other Cast. The fire spread over the creatures and in a flurry of ash and wailing, the flames engulfed them and swallowed them whole.

Alexina walked toward the doe now, with Jaden, Embrik, and Chadwick, fully visible. "But how?"

"They aren't true Shadow Cast," Leah called. "Fire and electricity are the most effective. Take them down!"

Zeke nodded and threw two more batches at Leah's staff. She eliminated two more Cast in quick succession. He sent a series of shocks into another mess of Cast. Jaden followed suit, freezing the Cast in place while Alexina

410

exploded the frozen creatures with electricity. Embrik skillfully ran fire over their inky bodies, ripping them apart.

But even as the team started dwindling down the Cast, Judgement shook her wings and made more. Hundreds more.

Magna whinnied and stopped, shooting stone spikes through the Cast. It ripped them to shreds, but they immediately reformed and went on the attack. Several dozen engulfed Magna, pulling her to the ground.

Lysander roared and charged, shooting energy orbs at the Shadow Cast, but he was quickly overwhelmed too. The Cast enveloped both of them and compressed. The two summons vanished in black and white motes.

"Damn it!" Zeke snarled. He turned. *Archángeli, we need to end this before it gets out of control!*

We are trying! Archángeli said. *But without all the Phonar, we are limited in what we can do!*

"Shit." Zeke ran up to Leah. "We can't keep this up. How do we stop her?"

"I don't know!" Leah said. She bashed in another Cast. "The Book of Summons mentioned her briefly, but anything about how to defeat her was purged."

"Zeke, Leah, watch out!" Jaden shouted. Zeke turned.

A massive amount of Cast had combined together in one gargantuan Cast, towering over them, their blinking eyes glaring down.

Zeke gasped and blasted the tower of Cast with fire, but they brushed it off and continued toward them. Leah pulled at his arm. "Run, go!" They turned, but another Cast tower blocked their way. They stood back to back, elements flying, but they couldn't keep the Cast back. Zeke gripped Leah's hand, her fear manifesting as a thousand smells at once. Zeke closed his eyes.

Then the Cast started wailing. Zeke glanced up.

Ice crystals ran up both Cast towers, freezing them in place. The Cast tried escaping the oncoming ice, but they simply weren't fast enough, and the ice engulfed them in seconds.

Jaden ran up, blasting both towers with his magic, shouting. "You're not going to take my family away from me again!"

Alexina ran up behind him, her hands alight with electricity. She shot one tower with lightning, breaking the Cast apart. Embrik blasted the other tower with a wave of fire, destroying it. Tiny black pebbles rained down on them, then vanished.

Zeke sighed relief. "Thank you."

"Don't thank me yet," Jaden said. He pointed. "We have a lot more."

"This is not working," Embrik said. "We need to end this now before we all run out of magic."

"Yeah, but what can we do?" Alexina said. "How do you defeat an all-powerful summon?"

Then Leah's eyes grew wide. "A summon. She *is* a summon."

Zeke raised an eyebrow. "Well, yeah."

"But a summon," Leah said. "Requires a *summoner.*"

Zeke perked his ears. He turned, looking for Ronan.

The black and orange bat stood far off from the battle, holding his hands over his body. A green, pulsating magic surrounded his hand while he worked on injuries on his body. Healing himself. They had hurt him after all.

Which meant he wasn't invincible.

Leah held up her staff. "Defeat the summoner…"

"Defeat the summon," Zeke said. "Jaden, Alexina, Embrik, you and the others need to keep the Cast and Judgement busy. We'll go after Ronan."

Jaden flicked his ears back. "Are you sure?"

"I owe him for what he did to Ari."

"We both do," Leah said.

Jaden took a deep breath. "Okay." He gripped both their shoulders. "Stay safe. You better come back to us, you understand?"

Zeke nodded. "We will."

Alexina hugged Zeke tight. "Come home to us." He squeezed her back.

Jaden waved to her and Embrik and they ran off, blasting Judgement with their magic.

Chadwick ran up to the pair of them, his black tail shaking as he ran. "I'll cloak you as long as I can, but I've been running low trying to protect your team."

"We'll use what we can," Zeke said. He nodded to Leah, lit her staff ablaze, then formed a dozen fireballs in the air around him. "Like Embrik's training." She nodded back. Chadwick cloaked them both and they ran for Ronan.

The bat didn't seem focused on the battle. His gaze was entirely focused on himself, healing burns and cuts, but so, so slowly. Time based healing must be a lot slower of a process.

Ronan winced as his body glitched like a broken video game, distorting space and time around it. It was as if he wasn't on the same time plane as them. He bounced around the arena a moment before resettling. "Damn it all, this time distortion is gonna be hell to fix," he muttered to himself.

One shot. Zeke threw his fireballs forward.

But then the cloak dropped, and Ronan noticed them instantly. He threw a hand forward, shooting them with a telekinetic blast. Leah shielded them and absorbed most of the blast, but they still tumbled back, rolling along the dusty floor. Zeke's muscles ached and he groaned.

Chadwick lay off to the side, unmoving.

Ronan turned to them. "Stay out of this. You don't know what the Defenders did to me."

413

"They didn't do *anything* to you," Leah said, standing up. "You have the wrong idea!"

"You're a Defender," Ronan said. "You're on their side."

Zeke snarled. "Ronan, I don't know who gave you the idea that the Defenders are at fault for what happened to your planet, but you're smarter than that. You don't--"

"We're *done.*" Ronan blasted them back again.

This time Zeke let himself slide back, thrusting his hands forward and bombarding Ronan with fireballs. Ronan gasped and managed to knock most of them away, but several hit his fur and set him ablaze. Leah gathered the other fireballs that he threw back and charged Ronan, stabbing him hard in the stomach with her staff. He doubled over, gasping for air. Once again, his body glitched in space and time, struggling to keep up. Fire plumed up over his fur, catching on the leather of his wings and burning down to his skin while he wailed.

And Judgement wailed too, flickering in and out of view.

Ronan stumbled toward Leah, but Zeke stopped him, bombarding him with more fire. The flames engulfed him.

Leah flicked her ears back. "Zeke, *stop!*"

"After what he did to Ari?"

She gripped his arm. "This isn't *right.* Stop right now, we've killed *enough!*"

Zeke frowned. He gritted his teeth. She was right. He pushed the fire aside and shot water instead, drowning the flames. It was probably too late anyway.

The water killed the flames in a cloud of steam, leaving Ronan lying on the ground. His fur lay in ash on the ground, his wings smoldered, and his skin bubbled and popped, black as coal. Leah's tail drooped.

Then Judgement disappeared.

414

The Phonar stopped flying about, each one hovering in place, looking confused. Jaden peered about, darting his gaze this way and that, as if expecting another attack. The does moved close to the rest of their team, also frantically looking about.

Zeke glanced around, thinking she'd appear somewhere else, but… she didn't. He felt to his knees. "Good Draso… it's over."

"Wait," Leah whispered.

Zeke turned. To his surprise, Ronan twitched and lifted his head, shaking. Fur fell off in embers and ashes, and his bubbling skin popped and oozed. The leather of his wings had burned away completely, giving him a rotting skeleton look. Zeke felt sick. He had taken it too far.

Ronan glared weakly at them and gritted his teeth. "I-if the Defenders have any m-merit," he said, his voice harsh and broken. "Y-you will end this m-misery…"

Jaden walked up, frowning. He called ice to his hands. "I can freeze your brain. It's painless."

Ronan coughed and fell over. "P-please."

Jaden took a step forward.

Then Judgement's hand formed out the ground and caged Ronan under her palm. Ronan screamed.

I think not. Judgement pulled, dragging Ronan away, before vanishing in a flash of light.

Zeke shot forward, elements clinging to his hands. "No, *wait!*" But she was gone. Damn it, they got away! He punched the ground, shooting magic marbles into the air.

Leah was at his side in an instant, that gentle smell of coffee hitting his nose. It did nothing to calm him though.

The doe walked up with Angus, Chadwick, and Jordan behind them. Embrik and Alexina gripped Jaden's hands. Angus flattened his ears and his wings drooped. "Is it over?"

A war plane flew overhead now. Zeke traced it through the sky.

And then the plane exploded. Anti-aircraft artillery.

"Time to leave," the Cloak said, coming up behind them. The six Phonar followed, each in their feral forms. "Wall is down, summon is gone. The calvary's on its way."

Angus held his hands out. "I can't summon Magna!"

"I know," the Cloak said. "We're short three flying summons, so double up on the Phonar. Ethos, with me." He climbed on Excelsis' back.

Zeke glared. "You didn't even *try* to help us."

"There's no *time,*" the Cloak said. "Get on the summons now!"

Another six planes went sailing overhead. Two exploded before their eyes.

"Let's go!" the Cloak shouted.

Zeke climbed on Archángeli's back, Leah behind him. She wrapped her arms around his waist. Zeke turned to the Cloak. "What if we get separated?"

"The Phonar will know what to do," the Cloak said. He patted Excelsis' neck. "Time to go, old friend." Excelsis spread his wings and took to the sky. The others followed, each carrying a load. They headed back toward the ships.

Then the artillery started in.

"Shield, *shield!*" Zeke called, though he knew it'd be useless. If one of them got hit by it, they'd all be dead.

Jaden and Alexina flew close to Zeke on Kyrie, dodging bullets. Zeke turned to them. Jaden frowned. "Zeke, if we don't make it--"

"We'll make it."

"If we *don't*," Jaden said. "I want you both to know that I'm proud of you." He smiled sadly. "Thanks for pulling me out of the hole I had dug for myself. I needed that."

Zeke smiled. "Feeling's mutual."

An explosion rocked the air, forcing the birds apart. Jaden called out to them as they flew to the side, vanishing in a cloud of smoke.

Leah gasped. "No, *Jaden!*"

"They're fine," the Cloak said. He came up behind Archángeli, though he was alone.

Zeke flicked his ears back. "Where's Ethos?"

"She's safe," the Cloak said. "Now--"

"Your eyes are *blue,*" Leah said.

Zeke stared. She was right. They weren't green anymore – they were icy blue. "What--"

"There isn't time," the Cloak said. "Do you two remember where you said you would meet Jaden if you got separated?"

Zeke frowned. "Yeah, the Casino Beach pier, but--"

"Then get there," the Cloak said. He held out a glowing hand.

Leah gripped tighter to Zeke. "Are you sending us home?"

"I get one shot," the Cloak said. "This is that shot, and we're wasting it."

"Wait!" Zeke said. "Do they others make it?"

The Cloak eyed him with those icy blue eyes. "Get to the pier." He touched the tip of Archángeli's wing with his glowing hand.

Then everything went white.

LAST WORDS

When the light faded, Leah crashed onto a hard concrete floor in total darkness. Zeke tumbled over her and rolled a few centimeters away. He groaned. "Good Draso, where are we?"

Leah let her eyes adjust. A half-moon bathed the area in soft light. Tall garages with large doors surrounded them. a set of tables and chairs sat around them, with small potted plants. Leah looked up. A big sign across the top of the building read "Suzy's." Leah frowned. "We're back at the café."

"And it's *night?*" Zeke said. "God, how many hours have we lost?"

"More like weeks," Leah said, rubbing her arms. "It's chilly. Definitely wasn't when we left. It might even be months."

"Come on," Zeke said, pulling Leah to her feet. "We need to get to the Casino Beach pier."

They wandered the warehouses until they found a bus stop with a night bus waiting. The driver, a white wolf with icy blue eyes, gave them strange looks, but Leah could hardly blame him. They were in full military battle fatigues, covered in blood, dust, and black spots from the Cast. But he let them on and they headed on the way to Casino Beach.

Leah found a newspaper on one of the benches and picked it up. She glanced at the date. "Uh... Zeke. What day did you say you had your last flight? Before we time traveled?"

"In May," Zeke said. He glanced over her shoulder. "What month is it now? How much time have we lost?"

Leah handed him the paper. "We're in November. I don't know your months all that well but..."

Zeke cursed. "Damn, that's a lot of time. We--" He paused.

Leah frowned. "What?"

"This says 2041."

Leah twitched an ear. "Something wrong with that?"

"We left in 2039."

Leah's eyes grew wide. "Oh *Draso.*" Would Matt and the other Defenders still even be here? Was she stuck here like Jaden? No, she wouldn't be. She'd be able to get to Athánatos and contact Matt. He wouldn't leave Ouranos alone. Heck, if she couldn't do that, she could get to--

"Casino Beach," the driver said, and he opened the doors. Zeke thanked him and rushed out, with Leah following close behind.

Leah ran across the tarmac, between the rotting buildings, and hitting the sand as fast as she could go. Soon the pier was in sight.

But no Jaden.

Zeke stopped and leaned on his knees. "The Cloak said to be here," he said, panting. "But I don't see anyone."

Leah pulled up her pendant. "Let's see what I can find." She activated the homing device and searched for Defender pendant signals.

419

And found one in the pier. She tilted her head. Wait. *In* the pier? "I'm picking up something in the pier. The fourth pillar from the shore."

Zeke raised an eyebrow. "*In* it?"

"That's what it shows."

Zeke shrugged. "Let's see what we can find." They walked slowly to the pier.

Draso's mercy, everything ached. The adrenaline from battle had worn off by now, and pain shot through Leah like random needles sewing through her skin. She leaned against Zeke for support and frowned. He had dozens of little injuries. "You need healing."

He wrapped an arm around her. "I know, but this first."

They got to the pillar, but still didn't see anyone. Leah glanced at her scanner again. "It looks like the pendant is inside this pillar."

Zeke gave her a dark look. "Not a good sign."

"Look for a hidey hole or something," Leah said. She poked around the wood.

Zeke found it first – a burnt out knot in the wood that pulled loose if Zeke yanked hard enough. Inside was a plastic bag holding Jaden's Golden Guardian pendant.

Leah's heart ached. "Oh Draso…"

Zeke pulled the pendant out of the bag and held it up. It was dull and dented with age and use. "How do you make it work?"

"Press your thumb against the back of it," Leah said. "Though I don't know what'll happen, since it's Jaden's pendant, not yours. They typically only work for their users."

Zeke pressed his thumb against it. A hologram appeared and a tiny voice spoke. *"DNA print confirmed. Playing last message."*

Leah's whiskers drooped. Last message?

Jaden's upper half appeared in the hologram now, his face tired and worn. *"Greetings,"* he said. *"I've set this to pendant to play with either my DNA or any DNA similar to mine. If you're seeing this, then you're family. I don't know if I'm speaking to Matt or Zeke, but whoever it is… you might want to sit down for this."*

Zeke exchanged a glance with Leah she squeezed his hand and nodded and the two of them sat down in the sand.

"This was recorded on July 22nd, 2038 by the Earth calendar," Jaden continued. *"We had tried so hard to hold out until after Matt and Trecheon first met, but time ran out and we had no choice. I hope Matt doesn't find this too early and mess with the timeline, but this is a risk we have to take."*

Leah clenched Zeke's hand.

"After the Battle of the Desert Wall, we escaped and were honorably discharged by Commander Leigh as a way to protect us while they prosecuted Ackerson." His face grew dark. *"Zeke, Leah, I'm sure you know how that went. Not ideal. We ended up going into hiding as his trial was quite public and his teams became targets for his sympathizers. We suspect Matron Fawn may have had some hand in that, but there's no way to prove it. Unfortunately, our friends weren't successful in taking her out. Someone else did later though, so she got her comeuppance.*

"Things quieted down for a little while after the trials, but we soon found that we had shadows. Didn't take long to realize it was Angel hunting us down."

Leah gasped. "Oh *no.*"

"We did our best to warn the other teams – Ackerson was covering his tracks again. But we couldn't risk talking to Trecheon or Neil from Outlander. We got the message to Chadwick though. Hopefully he and Jordan were able to contact Trecheon. Jordan has a plan to hide us all. Hopefully it works.

"I'm leaving this here to let you know that as of right now, we're safe. All of us… Zeke included. This is probably the absolute worst time for this, but Alexina is six months pregnant right now."

Zeke bit his lip, flicking his ears back.

"I dare not leave our exact location on this pendant, just in case, but I left information that will hopefully help. Information that only a Defender should be able to access. You'll need an A.I. to crack it. Wasn't easy to get the lock on there, but I think I was pretty successful."

Leah frowned. An *A.I.?* She could only hope Matt hadn't left yet. There were no Defender A.I.'s on Earth that she knew of.

"I hope that this message finds you well," Jaden continued. *"And I hope that you'll find us well too. We'll hold out as long as we can. But… if the worst should happen… know that I'm proud of you. All of you. Leah, Zeke… and Matt, Izzy, and Charlotte. Take care. Find us soon. This military might fear the Angel, but the Angel never met the Defender."* He gave a slight smirk. *"Guardian Azure out."* The hologram faded.

Zeke stood there, his shock coming through Leah's nose like a sharp, tangy scent of peppers. "After all that and they still didn't make it."

"You don't know that," Leah said.

"Leah, it's been three *years* since this recording," Zeke said. "There's no way Jaden and the others held out that long."

Leah stood, her bones aching. She brushed the sand off her pants. That couldn't be true. They had to be alive. They *had* to be. Jaden had to see Matt and Charlotte and Izzy again. Heck, she had to see them again. Zeke did.

It couldn't end this way.

A gentle smell of hot chocolate wafted through her nose. It was supposed to be comfort, she knew. But she waved it away.

Zeke wrinkled his snout. "You smell like a raging fire."

"This isn't over," Leah said. "We're not done, and neither are they." She held out her hand to Zeke. "Do you trust me?"

Zeke took her hand. "To the ends of the universe."

Leah pulled him to his feet, surprised at her own strength. He gripped her hand warmly. She gripped it back. "Then we have someone we need to see."

Zeke flicked an ear back. "Who?"

"Trecheon Omnir."

The End

About the Author

R. A. Meenan was born in London during the golden age of science fiction, but somehow time traveled to the Modern Era (some say a mad man with a blue box was involved). She was dropped on the doorstep of a house owned by anthropomorphic cats and though they were disappointed she didn't have furry ears and a tail, they took her in to teach her the ways of elemental magic. After setting fire to her furry cat friends' tails one too many times (final score – fire: 2612, cat's tails: 0) they called an exterminator and sent her out on her way.

Others would call this "going to college" and "getting a job" but she disagrees.

Now an adult (physically, not mentally), she ride-hops intergalactic military spacecraft, combing the outer reaches of space and time, writing science fiction and urban fantasy stories based on her experiences. She's also hoping to find the perfect cup of coffee and a better way to grow dinosaurs. Humans kind of look at her funny, but she's managed to make herself an honorary ambassador for furry and anthropomorphic aliens and space dragons.

She carefully feeds and brushes her wonderful husband Joe and the pair have four furry children (which are really cats, but don't tell them that) and a human child named after a video game character. She also spends her spare time teaching essay-writing haters, molding them into people resembling Actual Students and Lovers of English.

She may not win the hearts of stiff military men or students who want good grades for no effort, but she certainly captures the spirit and imagination of time travelers, magic users, nerds, Students-In-Training, and fantasy lovers. Welcome to her nonsensical world. We hope you like it here.

You can email R. A. Meenan at r.a.meenan@zyearth.com. Check out more of her works at www.zyearth.com. You can also follow her on Facebook at https://www.facebook.com/zyearthchronicles or on Twitter at @sammieauburn or on Instagram @zyearthdefender, where she posts snippets and artwork from the Zyearth chronicles.

If you enjoyed this book, consider reviewing it at the retailer where you purchased it!

Enter the World of Zyearth

Liked this book? FREE short stories for buying this book! Scan the codes below to get your free short stories at Zyearth.com

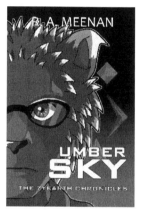

Zeke Brightclaw is an elite test pilot, but he knows he's little more than just an insurance claim waiting to happen. But when he gets a chance to prove himself to the head of the Air Corps Academy, he needs to decide if it's worth the risk.

Read about Zeke's battle for his life and career for FREE for buying this book!

Leah Nealia is a rare healer-S – a healer who can see your ailments just by touching you. She struggles to find her place in the world while setting boundaries with her mom and fighting a bully determined to make her life hell.

Read about Leah's struggle as a healer for FREE for buying this book!

Glossary

Learn more about the World of Zyearth at Zyearth.com!

Zyfaunos: Zyfaunos are anthropomorphic animal-like bipeds. All zyfaunos have similar characteristics -- plantigrade or near plantigrade legs, human stance structure in the spine, humanlike eyes and sometimes lips, generally short snouts, and have humanlike, five fingered hands, usually with tiny, somewhat sharp retractable claws instead of fingernails. Zyfaunos tend to have the same height range as humans, with a few extreme examples of very short or very tall species. All zyfaunos can interbreed regardless of the individual's species. Unlike most faunos, zyfaunos are not always "traditionally" colored, and often have unnatural colors in their fur, such as red, blue, green, purple, and others. Though relationships are rare, humans and zyfaunos can produce children. Zyfaunos are named as such because the DNA strain originated from the planet Zyearth and Zyearth has the purest forms of this species.

Quilar: Quilar are perhaps the most unusual of all zyfaunos, as it is unclear what animal they evolved from. They have several key characteristics

-- catlike ears and snout, slightly humanlike lips, though usually black or dark pink, humanlike feet and hands, tails, and quills of various lengths on their head in place of hair. Quilar quills are hard, though not usually sharp like a porcupine or hedgehog. Instead of fingernails, quilar have tiny retractable claws on each hand. These claws are not very sharp and are mainly used for scratching. Quilar can be divided by color and physical characteristics into three different categories.

Zyearth Quilar: Zyearth quilar have very short, very soft fur and generally longer, thicker quills on their heads. Their snouts are short and flat and many even have human-like lips. They tend to have catlike ears and human-like eyes. Quilar are the most human-like of all faunos. Human-faunos relationships usually involve a quilar. Zyearth quilar tend to have browns, whites, blacks, and grays for their colors. Jason, pictured on the previous page, is wearing the Defender Elemental uniform colors, indicating his status as an elemental user.

Jason is modeling a Zyearth quilar. Jason's fur is soft golden brown.

Earth Quilar: Earth quilar are physically very similar to Zyearth quilar, though their colors tend to be more vibrant. They also generally have streaks of color in their fur and quills while Zyearth quilars tend to be one solid color.

Trecheon is, reluctantly, modeling an Earth quilar.

Athánatos Quilar: Athánatos quilar are typically taller than their Zyearth and Earth kin. They have ears that bend backwards and more animal-like tails and feet. Their snouts are short and flat and like other quilar, they can have human-like lips.

Ouranos is modeling an Athánatos quilar here.

Focus Jewels: Focus jewels are found on many different planets throughout the universe. The term refers to any jewel that can be bound to a user's skin, soul, or lifeforce that grants supernatural powers. Sometimes focus jewel power only grants simple powers, such as long life, but others exhibit more extravagant powers.

Lexi Gems: Lexi Gems are focus jewels bound to the user's soul and grants users several powers. Average Gem users are granted long life, up to four hundred Zyearth years, and slow aging. Advanced users develop "Gem

Specialties" through the Gem "breaking" usually after a stressful, dramatic, or difficult event in the user's life. Military personnel are the most likely to have broken Gems and most Gems break in training.

There are a variety of specialties that users can develop. The most common specialty is healing, followed by elemental fabricators and manipulators, and a select few specialize in cloaking and shielding. Users are usually granted only one specialty, though a rare few have two. In the case of a duel specialist, both specialties are significantly weaker than those in a single specialist.

Lexi Gems are usually about the size of a user's fist. Gems often take on the colors of their users in one of several forms, but they lose their color if the user doesn't touch their Gem for extended periods of time or if the user dies, which also results in the Gem's bond breaking with their user. Gems can be used again by another user after a previous user has died.

Ei-Ei Jewels: Ei-Ei Jewels, like Lexi Gems, are focus jewels and are the source of magic and power for a member of the Athánatos tribe. Ei-Ei jewels are small and they are fused to the skin of the user just around the edge of their eyes. Ei-Ei jewels also come in pairs. Each eye has one set of the pairs. There are three jewels, but all of them work together to properly function.

The first jewel, the Mind Jewel, is yellow, representing the sophia flower, a symbol of wisdom. This jewel set keeps the user's mind fresh and free of deterioration. They even protect against mind aging issues like Alzheimer's and dementia.

The second set, the Body Jewel, is red, representing the purity of blood and flesh. This jewel set keeps the body from deterioration. Athánatos tribe members are immortal because of this jewel, but they are not invincible.

The final set, the Soul Jewel, is the color of the users eyes, representing the user's soul. This jewel set keeps the soul pinned to the body. Together the three sets make the user immortal.

Wishing Dust: Wishing Dust is created from ground up focus jewels and is used by applying the dust to the eye while making a "wish." Wishes are very specific, detailed spells that do one thing really well, but with a cost. Wishing Dust users are called Wish Dusters.

Wishing Dust is very volatile and a majority of attempted users wish too large for the wish to compensate. If the wish cannot properly compensate, the user will go insane and physically rip themselves apart trying to remove the dust. If a wish goes wrong, the user will always die. There is no saving them. Because the dust is so powerful and so deadly, most major civilizations in the universe have banned it. As a result, Wishing Dust is mostly found in black markets and smuggler's groups.

Wishing Dust comes in a variety of colors and will add a light, very subtle dusting of that color to the user's eye. It's difficult to identify a Wish Duster until they've used their magic. Common wishes include magic tracking, object manifestation or enhancement, body morphing, and various magical defenses.

Continuum Stones: Continuum Stones are a pair of magical stones that manipulate time and space. They're almost exclusively used by the zyfaunos bat species of Vanguard from the Tribus continent. Users wear the stones attached to the skin in the inner parts of their ears.

Most Continuum Stone users live beyond their biological lifespans, but how long that is depends on their time powers. Powers are granted randomly as the user grows.

Time powers include healing, which reverses time on the user's body, scrying, and very temporary time freezes, with limited range. Each one has their own down sides. Too much healing can put a user outside of time, which takes time and effort to fix. Scrying is very imprecise as a whole. Time freezing robs the user of time off their lifespan – one hour for every second of frozen time.

Space powers include telekinesis, or the ability to lift things with the mind. Telekinesis users can only lift objects that they would otherwise be able to lift with their own strength. Teleportation, or space jumping, which allows users to jump 50 or 60 feet from where they stand. This is very energy intensive and needs a long recovery time between jumps. Finally, gravity manipulation, which allows a user to increase or decrease gravity on an object or in a small radius for a very short period of time. This is also energy intensive and cannot completely negate natural gravity, which means a user cannot eliminate gravity completely and send someone into space.

Jewel Shards: Jewel Shards are a relatively new focus jewel discovered on the Paleofaunos-inhabited planet Erdoglyan. Jewel Shards are pointed cone-shaped jewels and bound physical to a user, usually grafted onto bone or teeth and held in place with ornate metal holders. As they are a permanent fixture, they're often on the face or snout and positioned to face forward like a unicorn horn.

Jewel Shards manifest a single elemental magic, one of the main seven elements. The inhabitants who own jewels call themselves the Forged and name themselves off the element they have. For example,

"Fireforged" or "Lightningforged." The element it manifests will also determine its user's remaining lifespan. Some shorten the lifespan, such as lightning, which only grants 30 to 50 years of life after binding. Others lengthen it, such as stone, which can grant up to 350 years of additional life after binding. Some claim the element manifested is a reflection of the user's personality, though this has yet to be proven.

Jewel Shards are powered by UV rays. If they are left uncharged for too long, it causes psychosis in the user.

Blood Crystals: Unlike other jewels, Blood Crystals are shaped to look like things, typically something that their users find solace in. Blood Crystals are unique in the sense that they need two or more users to work properly. When bound, users will borrow magic or energy from their partner (called the Bleeder) and use it to create massive, destructive spells. Blood Partners can kill each other if they're not careful with how they pull magic.

Blood Crystals are highly regulated by Galactic InterPol because they were once used to bring people back to life, though very temporarily. The process is all but forgotten now, except for the knowledge that in order to use a Blood Crystal to revive someone, someone else had to be sacrificed.

Defender: The Defenders are a military group run by a small country called Zedric on the continent of Yelar on the plant Zyearth.

Guardian: Guardians are an essential part of the Defender military. Guardians are high ranking, highly trained individuals that perform tasks that average Defenders aren't trained for. There are two important types of Guardians.

Master Guardian: The role of Master Guardian is usually held by two people at the same time, often a former Golden Guardian pair. Master Guardians have a duel task – they are both the head of the Defender army and the leaders of the country of Zedric. Master Guardians must be smart, strong, courageous, and influential. Master Guardians are usually in office for life, though there are checks and balances that can remove a Master Guardian if the governing Assembly or the people of Zedric feels like they are not properly performing duties, and some Master Guardians choose to retire. Master Guardians are generally considered by most Defenders to be the most powerful zyfaunos of their time.

Golden Guardian: Golden Guardians are a team of two Defenders specially trained to handle delicate situations and complete covert and difficult missions that need small strike teams. Golden Guardians are selected by the Master Guardian of their era, and are given an extra five years of special training beyond typical Defender training. Usually the team has one healer and one elemental user.

Defender Pendant: Defender pendants are worn by all Defenders, regardless of their position in the army or Academy. They carry holographic identification cards and are the most common means of communication among Defenders. The pendant also carries several symbols. On Zyearth, a legless dragon is a sign of peace, so the Defenders made the legless dragon the center of their pendant. The dragon's neck is tucked under, a classic move that prevents strangulation in battle. This represents defense. The outstretched wings are a sign of openness and welcome. Finally, the Gem at the dragon's side represents the world of Zyearth, since nearly all native Zyearthlings are bound to Gems.

Made in the USA
Columbia, SC
16 February 2024

31699800R00259